1940 -

# LONESOME RANGERS

Also by John Leonard


*When the Kissing had to Stop*

*Smoke and Mirrors:*
*Violence, Television, and Other American Cultures*

*The Last Innocent White Man in America*

*Private Lives in the Imperial City*

*This Pen for Hire*

*Black Conceit*

*Crybaby of the Western World*

*Wyke Regis*

*The Naked Martini*

# LONESOME RANGERS

*Homeless Minds, Promised Lands,*
*Fugitive Cultures*

JOHN LEONARD

PUBLISHED IN THE UNITED STATES BY THE NEW PRESS, NEW YORK, 2002
DISTRIBUTED BY W. W. NORTON & COMPANY, INC., NEW YORK

Versions of these essays appeared in earlier and shorter forms elsewhere, mostly in the *Nation*
but also in the *New York Review of Books*, the *New York Times Book Review*, *Newsday*, *Tikkun*,
and Salon.com. The last chapter, "How the Caged Bird Learns to Sing," was originally published in *The Business of Books*, edited by William Serrin (The New Press, 2000).

LIBRARY OF CONGRESS CATALOGING-IN-PUBLICATION DATA

Leonard, John.
    Lonesome rangers : homeless minds, promised lands, fugitive cultures /
John Leonard.
      p.  cm.
    Essays originally published between 1997 and 2001.
    ISBN 1-56584-694-X (hc.)
    I.  Title.

PS3562.E56 L6 2002
814'.54—dc21     2001030962

The New Press was established in 1990 as a not-for-profit alternative to the large, commercial
publishing houses currently dominating the book publishing industry. The New Press oper-
ates in the public interest rather than for private gain, and is committed to publishing, in
innovative ways, works of educational, cultural, and community value that are often deemed
insufficiently profitable.

The New Press, 450 West 41st Street, 6th floor, New York, NY 10036
www.thenewpress.com

PRINTED IN THE UNITED STATES OF AMERICA

2   4   6   8   10   9   7   5   3   1

This book is for
Tiana and Eli, the grandest of children.

# CONTENTS

# ELSEWHERE:
## AN INTRODUCTION

S O PICTURE ME, the day before Christmas 2000, in a Victorian gazebo on the back lawn of the family compound of an American diplomat in Rangoon—reading the stories of John Cheever, spied on by Burmese military intelligence, honked at by indignant geese. Why Cheever? Because I've been asked to talk about him in a library. Why spooks? Because the security organs of this subtropical police state, where fax machines and modems are illegal, like to keep a minatory eye and ear on anyone who thinks in public. Why geese? Because they scare away the snakes.

The diplomat and his wife are old friends. I first met them a quarter of a century ago, on a USIA–sponsored tour of America's client states in Southeast Asia. I had been opinionizing for a couple of weeks in Imelda's Manila and Kuomintang Taipei before I got to sordid Seoul in curfewed Korea, where the universities were full of furious students and the *makkolli* houses full of Peace Corps dropouts and the upper-crust salons full of serial collaborators who had nimble-footed from Japanese to American patrons. Then I went south by train to Taegu, to explain *Gravity's Rainbow* and *Nashville* to clusters of the curious in canteens and pup tents, sicken myself on milky-white rice wine, and collapse of culture shock at the home of a Foreign Service officer, Ron Post, whose dynamite Korean wife, Gi Won, popped corn to munch while we watched the Marx Brothers in *A Night at the Opera* on their living-room wall. The next morning, before practicing her tai chi, Gi Won fed me a medicinal orange.

That afternoon, having pickled me with kimchi, she drove two hours up into the foggy mountains to show me the Haein Temple and the *Tripitaka*—the sutras of Buddhism, on 81,258 wooden printing blocks, in both Sanskrit and Chinese characters—and to proselytize for metempsychosis. That night, in my stretch socks on her rug, surrounded by poets and professors, I was asked what single thing of surpassing beauty or perfect thought, among the many I had seen on my travels, I'd like to take back to New York from the East. As if possessed by the white tigers of Korean art, I replied: "Gi Won."

Instead of an international incident, this caused a lifelong friendship. Wherever Ron and Gi Won have since been posted, I try to follow, like the circus. It's a different sort of travel, with different pairs of spectacles and sneakers—voluntary of course, but not tourism nor a vacation, and somewhat punitive. If the State Department pays your way, by coach on an American carrier, it also works you like a mule, serving up strangers for breakfast, lunch, tea, and dinner, who are better acquainted with your literature than you are with theirs, have done time in penal colonies and psychiatric wards for their criminal opinions, and have urgent meanings to communicate in morose code. For his semi-novel *Headbirths*, Günter Grass invented a "Sisyphus Travel Agency" that specialized in "destitution as a course of study," booking guilty German liberals into squalid slums from Bombay to Bangkok. This must be the agency the State Department uses for types like me. If I am willing to go somewhere forlorn, like Abidjan or Bucharest, they cheerfully oblige. If I want to go to Tuscany, it's my dime.

I want to go anywhere, and to feel ambivalent about it. To get out of their heads, Aztecs ate *teonanacatl*, a sacred mushroom. Zaparos drank *ayahuasca*, a hex potion. Mixtecs munched *gi-i-wa* puffballs and the Yurimagua of Peru were partial to an alkaloid exudate of tree fungus very much like belladonna. I dislocate myself, either by reading my way abroad or by leaving town to wallow in it. After too much keyboard time in a home office like a monastic cell, sorting the signals of an overheated publicity culture, manufacturing opinions

instead of widgets, I need some discrepancy and abrasion, a sandpa-
pering of nerve endings, the exasperations and romance of Elsewhere. Even so, to gondoliers or shoguns, to Toltec stelae, Veils of
Maya and puddles of cathedral light, I bring my white skin, male
chromosomes, U.S. passport, and gold credit cards. This is a lot of
privilege. I wish I had done more with it than compose dream songs
of second-guessing in centrifugal time. Certainly the writers I care
about in these pages have tried to do more with their witness. They
are less likely to be pilgrims than pariahs, runaways and getaways,
not on furlough but in flight. Even on those rare occasions—three,
if you're counting—when I have done something with my privilege
that was helpful or useful, their example shames me.

But I am who I am, an American bookie, who is paid more to
opinionize about visual arts like movies and television. On a vacation, Americans like to baste, golf, and slalom. On a tour, we seek a
culture fix, as if the past were a boutique into which we wandered
with a shopping list—Greek light, Russian soul, German sausage,
French sauce, Spanish bull. On a quest, much more problematically,
we like to rub our fuzzy heads against the strange and see if something kindles—Zen koans, hearts of darkness, blood of lambs. Or, if
we can't leave home, we bolt like Alice down an inky rabbit hole. So
what if, crossing borders and changing funny money, we lose a few
idioms? We collect a lot of frequent-flyer miles. There is an artist in
Michael Ondaatje's novel about Sri Lanka, *Anil's Ghost*, who specializes in painting the eyes of a brand-new Buddha after the rest of
the statue has been sculpted. He must do so backward, looking over
his shoulder into a mirror, averting his direct gaze from the calm
regard of the god to be. This is how I would like to believe we see
another culture, through high craft and hard work, with mirrors. Yet
mirrors themselves are odd, reversing left and right, but not up and
down. In *Upside Down: A Primer for the Looking-Glass World*, the
Uruguayan Groucho Marxist Eduardo Galeano has reminded us
that perspectives differ according to whose boot is on our face:
"From the point of view of the Indians of the Caribbean islands,
Christopher Columbus, with his plumed cap and red velvet cape,

was the biggest parrot they had ever seen." Galeano also quotes Archbishop Oscar Romero, who was assassinated in San Salvador in 1980: "Justice is like a snake: it only bites the barefooted."

In Burma, you must go barefoot to visit the Buddhist shrines—not just the Shwedagon Pagoda in Rangoon, in whose adoration halls and at whose planetary posts we would pray for our children on Christmas morning, but everywhere else in the country, too, including the thousands of temples and stupas on the ancient plain of Bagan, from which the government has removed the indigenous population to make more room for tourists. And not just shoeless—no *socks*, either, which means bleeding feet for the soft Westerner seeking the highest terrace for the best view of the sun setting on the Ayeyarwady, which may have been the wicked idea of Burmese monks in the first place, to torment their British colonial masters. In Thailand, even at the Temple of Dawn in Bangkok, socks are allowed. In Cambodia, even at Angkor Wat, you can keep your shoes on.

In Kyoto once, after a trudge on the Path of Philosophers, we hung a left at a cherry tree, toward Honen-in. Honen himself pushed a subversive egalitarian variety of Buddhism. The dominant but threatened Tendai sectarians accused him of advocating sexual relations between noble ladies and lowly proles. He fasted himself to death in 1211, at age seventy-nine. Near his temple is the tomb of the novelist Junichiro Tanizaki. Anyone who has read *The Key* or *Diary of a Mad Old Man* knows that Tanizaki fetishized the female foot. When we finally found his tomb, even though they didn't have to, the women in our party unstrapped their sandals. They stood barefoot on his oblong shade. I'd like to think that he was tickled.

So much information, so little wisdom, like the World Wide Web: Penguins are dying in the Falklands, and nobody knows why. The novelist Gabriel García Márquez shows up in the *Brenda Starr* comic strip. During the Gulf War there was a sign posted in a Manhattan bookshop: PLEASE DON'T THROW BOOKS BY EDWARD SAID ON THE FLOOR. In 1964 in Copenhagen, someone decapitated the statue of Hans Christian Andersen's Little Mermaid; her severed head was never found. The fact that nobody in eighteenth-century France ever took a bath caused a revolution; the nobility went to the guillotine smelling like oranges, lemons, jasmine, lavender, acacia, ambergris, cinnamon, rosewood, vetiver, and ylang-ylang. A Vonnegut novel once imagined a world in which gravity was variable and we had to worry about inhaling microscopic Chinese Communists. About the German Jewish refugees from Hitler, Bernard Malamud told us: "Articulate as they were, the great loss was the loss of language—that they could not say what was in them to say. You have some subtle thought and it comes out like a piece of broken bottle."

> One can foresee a revolution or a war, but it is impossible to foresee the consequences of an autumn shooting-trip for wild ducks. (Leon Trotsky, *My Life*)

In her Bill Blass suit among the twelfth-century icons in the Tretyakov Gallery in headcheese Moscow, Nancy Reagan complained to the running dogs of the media: "I don't know how you can neglect the religious elements. I mean, they're there for everyone to see." This was before the fall of the Evil Empire, but she had a point. From personal experience, I can tell you that to look at the Tretyakov icons is to see an odd God indeed, the size of the medieval mind and haunted by fires and bears and church bells melted down for cannon balls and golden hordes of Scythians in cloaks of sewn-together scalps. Out of such a mind rode Ivan the Terrible's Oprichniki, and secret police on black horses with severed heads tethered to their saddlebows. Out of it rode the dwarfs of the Empress Anna, and Pugachev in an iron cage, and the goat-smelling Rasputin.

And even for a medieval mind, it was malnourished. When Christianity came to Russia, it spoke neither Latin nor Greek, only Church Slavonic. It brought no news of antique or classical culture, no pagan or secular Byzantine literature, no humanism, science, philosophy. It toadied to whichever prince had the most clout. In return for court favors, it canonized promiscuously, counterfeiting saints from Gleb to Nevsky. About the serfs, those "dead souls," it was silent.

No wonder crazy Gogol was afraid of caterpillars. And beat up on lizards with a cane. And strangled cats. Russia is at least as complicated as one of its wooden *matryoshka* dolls, those nests of little mothers. Inside the Russian Orthodox Church is the nineteenth-century novel, and inside the nineteenth-century novel is the alienated intelligentsia, full of vodka, dominoes, smoked fish, sable skins, onion domes, six-winged seraphs, a snuff box, and the knout. According to the critic Belinsky, who got Dostoyevsky into so much trouble, "It's a well-known fact that when lightning does not strike, the peasant does not cross himself, he has no lord . . . whereas the holy mother La Guillotine is a good thing." This helps explain both Peter the Great and Josef Stalin.

From the 1970s I remember Moscow: a nasal passage of green skies, blue snow, dark red basalt, the great clock above the Spassky Gate chiming "The Internationale" at midnight, and, at Lenin's Tomb, goose steps. And Leningrad in the arctic-angled light: canary yellow, sky blue, Venetian red, pistachio green, Baskin-Robbins orange. I was traveling with people who blamed everything they didn't like, from the traffic and the toilet paper to the unreadable Cyrillics and the unspeakable weather, on Bolshevism. It was as if they expected Graceland. Palace-hopping in the vicinity of Catherine's summer residence, between Gorky and Pushkin, they demanded a look at the last digs of those blue-bleeders, Nicholas and Alexandra. "This is not yet history!" cried the Intourist guide, at whose plaintiveness the tour group hooted. But none of it was history *yet*, not the "deconsecrated" churches, nor the Peter and Paul Fortress, nor the brassbound coffin of Ivan the Terrible, nor any of these palaces—these Oriental agate pleasure domes, these opium dreams made of malachite and paved with jasper. Russia, seething with rage at her past, nevertheless employed an army of artisans to restore every gold leaf, marble pilaster, and porcelain plotz of it. The very icons that Nancy so admired can only be seen in all their flat-earth filigree because *Soviet* artisans cleaned them up. The church fathers had always insisted that icons were *supposed* to be dirty, under their shellac, from centuries of candle soot. And you, too, can become ambivalent by looking up Nancy's Blessed Virgin in a twelfth-century manuscript called *Visitation by the Mother of God*, a sort of pan-Slavic *Divine Comedy*, in which the Virgin descends into hell to forgive those damned for everything from gossip to lechery to cannibalism. The only sufferers she refuses to forgive are Jews.

"I could not simplify myself," said Nezhdanov in Turgenev's *Fathers and Sons*. I will now briefly mention one of the times when I did something besides just read about the wounded world. You must imagine the Hotel Rossyia in Moscow: instant drab, Stalinoid tacky, spy-flecked with a watchful troll on every floor. I am being visited, after the opera, by an old college friend who is now *Newsweek*'s Moscow bureau chief, and a colleague of his from *Le Monde*. We assume that they have been followed and my room is bugged, and so communicate on a child's Magic Slate. Questions are asked by scribble, answered in scrawl, and disappeared. I gather I am being asked to smuggle something out of Mother Russia, and I agree to do so. Later, at the GUM department store, there is a furtive exchange. And then I will fly away, on Aeroflot no less, with a box of something in my shaving kit and sheets of whatever in my raincoat lining.

Back in New York, these mysterious tiles, enigmatic musings, abstract photographs, and dumbfounding musical scores don't add up to any espionage I can recognize, even with the help of Russian-speaking friends. Before the drop, we insist on explanations. And they are forthcoming from the owner of a Manhattan gallery, Ronald Feldman. What I had smuggled out weren't police-state secrets, nor suppressed footnotes to Solzhenitsyn's *Gulag Archipelago*, not even a poem by Pasternak, but the jokey underground art of a couple of conceptual black humorists, Komar and Melamid, who would subsequently emigrate to New Jersey and publish a book called *Painting by Numbers*. It hurts when I laugh.

Things are worse in Burma now than they were in the Soviet Union in the seventies. And Burma has a recorded history going back a lot longer than Russia's, at least to the fifth century B.C., when Buddha himself spent a week there preaching, which you can read about in a palm-leaf manuscript called *Sappadanapakarana*. But since the end of the Cold War, a little thing like slave labor doesn't count against a member in good standing of the World Trade Organization.

*We want to open men's eyes, not tear them out.* (Herzen to Bakunin)

For some reason, *The Wapshot Chronicle* has just been translated into Burmese and they want me to tell them why. This is another of those weird requests you get when you travel on the State Department's dime. The night before I left the Philippines, there was a banquet for visiting pooh-bahs. Seated on one side of me at this banquet was the novelist Mario Vargas Llosa, on his way to a PEN Congress in Australia. Seated on the other side was Vilgot Sjöman, the director of *I Am Curious* (Yellow), in town for a Swedish film festival. When I explained I was off next to Taipei, where I had been asked to discuss Sinclair Lewis and *Main Street*, they actually became excited. A Peruvian novelist, a Swedish filmmaker, and a New York book reviewer spent the rest of the night in Manila talking about a midwestern American novel all three had relished reading when we were kids who longed to escape our own small towns for a glittering metropolis and a radiant future, and mourning a dead writer whose brave heart we had devoured like young cannibals.

In Taipei, it would turn out that a professor very much emeritus had been translating *Main Street* into Mandarin ever since Chiang Kai-shek made the big jump from the mainland in 1949. The professor's habit was to quiz every visiting American on the recondite meanings of twenties slang. From me, he needed to know: "What does it mean, *bees' knees*?"

According to a Tao master, "The mind of the perfect man is like a mirror. It grasps nothing but repulses nothing. It receives but does not sustain." This sounds to me like a Magic Slate. But for "bees' knees," at least I had an answer. The same could not be said for what happened a decade later in Japan, at a conference on cultural relations in Hakone, where I was told by a remarkable young woman that she sculpted fog. Fog? Yes, fog. Why? Because. In the valleys are villages that have festivals. Everybody dresses up, and puts on masks, for a parade. They would like some fog for the parade, but all the fog is in the mountains. So Fujiko Nakaya brings fog to the valley, using agricultural nozzles. She sculpts air itself, dreamy weathers. And why would a valley want fog belonging to the mountains? To see unseens, she says; to make visible what is not. Such as? Well, for instance, wind. How can you see wind without fog?

After which I had dinner, on the floor, in translation, with the novelist Kobo Abe. And that went okay while we chatted about Tanizaki, who should have won the Nobel Prize, and Kawabata, who maybe shouldn't have, plus Allen Ginsberg and Günter Grass, until I made the big mistake of asking, through his English-speaking wife, the obvious, innocent question: What is his new book about? And all of a sudden you could have cut the gloom with a *kodachi*. Kobo Abe wasn't working; he had stopped dead on a novel about the world after nuclear war; he hadn't written a single word since . . . well, *One Hundred Years of Solitude* had just been translated into Japanese, and Gabriel García Márquez was not only *exactly* Kobo Abe's age, but so much the superior novelist that Abe would never write again.

The next day, on my way by bullet train to Kyoto for some temple-hopping, I would read in the English-language Tokyo daily that García Márquez had won the Nobel Prize, and I was crazed. I knew what Japanese writers do when they're depressed. They take gas, like Kawabata. They fall on swords, like Mishima. From Kyoto, between rock gardens, I called the *New York Times* Tokyo bureau and was patched through to Hakone. Mrs. Kobo Abe answered the phone. I asked about her husband's state of mind. She said it was dandy: He makes great progress on his book! But how can this be, I said, I do not understand. You do not understand, she agreed. Gabriel García Márquez has joined the company of the immortals. Abe is no longer in competition with him.

This, it seemed to me, was Un-American.

But I was going to tell you something else about the Philippines. In Manila, never mind how, I secured the names of many political prisoners held incommunicado by the Marcos dictatorship. Among them, because theater is such a popular medium of protest in a country with hundreds of languages, were a surprising number of playwrights, including Ben Cervantes. I would publish these names in a "Literary Letter from the Philippines," in the *New York Times Book Review*, after the Foreign Desk turned me down. A week later the *Times* ran a letter from the Philippines Ambassador to the U.N., expressing resentment and perplexity. During my visit to Manila, hadn't I received a private audience with Immaculate Imelda, who had promised to look into this regrettable misunderstanding? And hadn't she already done so, as a result of which Ben Cervantes and the others had been immediately released from prison, where they shouldn't have been in the first place? So what was my problem and where was my gratitude?

I think I'd recall meeting Imelda, at least her shoes. Real life is less thrilling. But I have to say that getting a playwright out of jail is a lot more satisfying than getting a joke out of Russia.

> *He thought of pain and suffering as a principality, lying somewhere beyond the legitimate borders of western Europe.* (John Cheever, *Bullet Park*)

So I am rereading John Cheever in a gazebo, surrounded by geese. If his collected stories are a grand occasion in English literature, *The Wapshot Chronicle* is not. Still, it conveys a powerful idea of one America: New England, where the first Anglo-Saxons landed early in the seventeenth century; our original aristocracy of captains, clergymen, schoolmasters, and merchants; that sea coast from which the clipper ships sailed off to triangle trade in rum and whales and slaves; the ghostly stomping grounds of Nathaniel Hawthorne and Herman Melville. And what Cheever saw in *The Wapshot Chronicle* was a long decline to a leaky boat, turned into a gift shop.

Other elegiac notes are sounded in the novel. When a cloud crosses the valley, the Wapshots feel "a deep and momentary uneasiness, as if they apprehended how darkness can fall over the continents of the mind." Later, unnoticed by her own family as she walks past a window, Honora stops, leaning on her cane, "engrossed in an emotion so violent and so nameless that she wonders if this feeling of loneliness and bewilderment is not the mysteriousness of life." Why should she feel "so miserable and abraded" in a world "where she was meant to be"? Moses Wapshot knows "the blues of uprootedness," "impermanence," and "imposture." Coverly Wapshot contemplates the "parochialism" of certain kinds of misery, fears that he's been condemned to "some strange place where the hazards of grace and beauty were outlawed," and worries at the power of anxiety "to light the world with lovely morbid colors."

This melancholia is clearer still in Cheever's stories. He always claimed to be looking for such "constants" as "a love of light and a determination to trace some moral chain of being." But in suburban Shady Hill and Bullet Park, otherwise perfectly wholesome middle-class Americans run out of charm, luck, and money; get drunk and break all the dishes and dream about hydrogen bombs. Ping-Pong tables wash over the side of ocean liners on Atlantic crossings. Old lady music teachers are murdered by motorcycle hoodlets. Small children vanish from lawns and streets, or eat ant poison thinking it is candy. Backyard barbecues explode, pigs drown in wells, kittens are ground up in kitchen blenders. There is lighter fluid instead of vinegar in the mixed green salad, a wife shoots her husband dead as he hurdles their living-room furniture, a man is devoured by his own attack dogs, and the neck of a little girl is broken on a ski tow. Even when hillsides shine in glancing light like bolts of velvet, even while fathers and daughters are playing checkers, even on nights "where kings in golden suits ride elephants over the mountains," even so, something is missing, something misplaced, something broken, like a shoelace or a heart.

So much "bitterness, irresolution, and cowardice": Why do these people feel so displaced, like strangers in their own land? Why this homesickness for what Cheever has elsewhere called "that sense of sanctuary that is the essence of love"? Sanctuary! It's not an idea, or even a word, I'd have associated with American literature half a century ago. Our writers were forever on the move running away from boring jobs, bossy schoolmarms, fathers and *Main Street*, civilization and its discontents—into the woods; the wild; fangs, foam, and a furry embrace; tropics of cancer and bare ruined choirs; loose women and easy money. The last thing they ever seemed to want to do was to stick around, stick it out, see what happened to the kids or crop. They certainly never worried whether they belonged at the spot they chanced to land on, after so much rambunctious velocity, such a frantic greediness. Home was where they chose to stop, their personal squatting space, with Coca-Cola, blue jeans, pop music, and gangster movies to prove it.

"Mickey Mouse will see you dead!" shouted Holliwell, the North American anthropologist, at a lecture audience in Central America, in Robert Stone's *A Flag for Sunrise*. But we are not so sure anymore that this is so. In John Updike's African novel, *The Coup*, Hakim Felix Ellellou told us: "I perceived that a man, in America, is a failed boy." In Romania in December Saul Bellow's Dean discovered the "inappropriate American—in all circumstances inappropriate, incapable of learning the lessons of the twentieth century; spared or scorned by the forces of history or fate or whatever a European might want to call them." Americans used to go abroad, says Don DeLillo in *The Names*, "to write and paint and study, to find deeper textures. Now we do business": bank loans, arms credits, technology. Unless, that is, like James Axton in *The Names*, like Holliwell in *Sunrise*, like almost everybody in a Joan Didion novel, we work for the CIA. In which case, Stone suggests, "we've located ourselves beyond coincidence."

And if we stay put, how lonely we are, not only in DeLillo and Didion but from Philip Roth to Richard Powers. Updike's Rabbit, "a fearsome bulk with eyes that see and hands that grab and teeth that bite, a body eating enough at one meal to feed three Ethiopians for a day, a shameless consumer of gasoline, electricity, newspapers, hydrocarbons, carbohydrates," is *dead*. From too much consumption of junk food, cheap sensations and disposable ideas, his heart exploded.

It is as if—while all those writers on our own margins, Other Americans like Toni Morrison, Maxine Hong Kingston, John Edgar Wideman, and Fae Myenne Ng, rose up to meet and greet the rush from Elsewhere of the Latin American Magical Realists, the Eastern European Aesopian Fabulists, and those postcolonials still innocent enough of postmodern theories on "liminality" as to persist in writing epics of emancipation, on singing songs that aren't just whistling in the dark—our Old Boy Lit retreated into arctic solitude and an unbearable whiteness of being.

So this is what I say to the Burmese in the library. When you worry out loud about your own country, your audience is encouraged to worry about theirs. They ask polite questions with just enough ellipses for me to duck and dodge and wing my way into gray zones where we flirt with what they really want to say. Thus, in talking about Henry David Thoreau, Martin Luther King, Joan Baez, and civil disobedience, I open the door to Aung San Suu Kyi, who is still under house arrest. Thus, in talking about monopolistic media conglomerates in the United States, I open the door to their own newspapers—those Rangoon dailies so craven as to lie even about yesterday's weather when hailstones fell on the generals while they dedicated the new bell on the Shwedagon Pagoda. Thus, in discussing our sui generis First Amendment and why it's so unpopular, I open the door to a Burmese censorship as harrowing and as protracted as a skyscraper elevator shaft where the writers must stop on every floor on their way down to jail or hell. Thus, even in talking about John Cheever in the closet, I open the door to a Burmese AIDS epidemic the existence of which the government denies, although you can rent a car in Mandalay, drive to the jade mines, and see the miners lined up like dairy cows for heroin injections, eight hundred to a single dirty needle. But, of course, the government is as much into narcotrafficking as it is into every other business as usual in "Myanmar."

None of this is said in the library. It is said instead on the streets outside, or circling the Buddhas at Shwedagon, or in tea houses where the doctors and lawyers who write stories and the students who write poems will slip you weak carbon copies on pages thinner than razor cuts, as careless, reckless, and voluble in their own domains of sociability as they are wary and reticent on the American campus. Where else but in tea houses are teachers and students to gather when their university has been shut down and removed from the insurrectionary capital to the safer sticks? Horror stories, yes. Everybody has one and needs to tell it in spite of surveillance and informers, in spite of the fact that from our hotel breakfast table we can all see the louts from military intelligence lolling across the lobby in their camouflage uniforms, over gratis cups of cappuccino and stinkweed cigarillos. These louts *want* to be seen. They swell with self-important menace. All the cars in which they trail you are the same model, on purpose, like the black Ford Falcons that came for the *desaparecidos* in Argentina.

> *Fear tastes like a rusty knife and do not let her into your house. Courage tastes of blood. Stand up straight. Admire the world.* (John Cheever, *The Wapshot Chronicles*)

After twelve days in Burma, we flew to Cambodia. We thought we were going to Cambodia for the ruins. And, indeed, we would walk on the Elephant Terrace at Angkor Thom, and climb to the top of Angkor Wat. I've decided not to contribute to whatever it is about these sixty square miles of collapsing temples in the jungle, this sandstone model of the Hindu universe, with its corncob towers, golden Buddhas, rainbow bridges and naga serpents, its pyramids and cat's eyes, that has inspired so much melancholy introspection, savage ideologizing, and literary vapors. As beautiful as Angkor certainly is, it was made possible by the same command economy of slaves that created the Khmer irrigation system that made possible the cash surplus to raise and pay a Khmer army to terrorize the neighbors. Nor was I tempted, like André Malraux, to steal a loose *apsara*—one of those ornamental nymphs the poet Claudel accused of smiling an "Ethiopian smile" and of "dancing a kind of sinister can-can over the ruins." I am not a European.

But we had come to Cambodia as if ordained to see something else by accident. We were led in Phnom Penh first to a school for torture and then, by jeep, to another sort of pagoda, the opposite in meaning from Shwedagon, consisting entirely of skulls and teeth dug up from the killing fields. Say hello to Pol Pot, who so loved the poetry of Verlaine, and who tried to kill every Cambodian who had gone to school, spoke a foreign language, or wore glasses. And those he failed to finish off must daily negotiate our seeding of their earth with land mines.

I have only occasionally been exactly where I wanted to be and when: In Prague for instance, the summer after the Velvet Revolution. In Dubrovnik, the summer before civil war and genocide in Yugoslavia. In Johannesburg, between the release of Mandela and the first free elections, just in time for the memorial service for Oliver Tambo in a Soweto soccer stadium. And in Stockholm when they gave the Nobel Prize to Toni Morrison. More often, like most other tourists, I am late. In China, India, Egypt, and Greece, history already happened. In Israel it never stops. Cambodia is the only place I have ever been to that made me come and insisted on my looking, against my will, at a wound beyond words. And so, naturally, having lost myself, I would rush back to words—to my writers and witnesses, in exodus and exile, in diaspora and displacement.

There is one last story. The year is 1959, a month and a half after the Cuban Revolution, a month before my twentieth birthday. I am in Havana, at the direction of William F. Buckley Jr., my editor at *National Review*. I have brought with me my very first passport and my high-school Spanish, to research a story on a friend of Buckley's from his CIA days in Mexico. Ernesto de la Fe was a conservative newspaperman who had resigned from one of Batista's cabinets to protest a rigged election, gone into exile in Mexico City, where he wrote a column for one of the dailies, and then flew back after the Revolution—only to be immediately clapped into La Cabaña prison and sentenced to death, for reasons known only to Raul Castro, Fidel's brother.

It was, of course, my first revolution, and I wasn't up to it. The iconography may have been thrilling. And in the bars along Malé-con Drive you could buy packets of Batista atrocity snapshots from teenaged *barbudos* who waved around their submachine guns while drinking rum and Coke. But I was followed wherever I went by the only man in Havana who wore a Stetson. And they were *shooting* people in the sports stadium. And everyone I talked to in the morning was arrested that afternoon, and so, when I called back the following day to doublecheck on something, I understood myself to be a blue-eyed Kiss of Death.

I am sorry to say that when they came to my hotel and arrested a German photographer, I panicked. I mean, I had a first novel still in the typewriter and a fiancée finishing her senior year at Radcliffe. I packed up my notebook, passport, shaving kit, and pesos, and lit out for the vulgar Hilton. They'll never get me at the Hilton, I told myself as I bought rounds of drinks at the foam rubber bar while waiting for a limo to the airport and a flight to Free Miami. And they didn't. Lucky for the Bolsheviks in St. Petersburg that they weren't waiting around for me in October 1917. At the Finland Station, I would have been heading away from the action.

But my article was a *National Review* cover story. And rather to Buckley's dismay, the only powerful people who took an interest in it were the maverick Republican senator Wayne Morse, who put it into the *Congressional Record*, and the liberal Democratic senator Hubert Humphrey, who brought it to the attention of the Eisenhower State Department, which made representations to a Cuban government with whom we still had diplomatic relations. And a month later, Ernesto de la Fe's sentence was reduced from death to twenty years in prison, every minute of which he served. This got him out of La Cabaña in late January 1979. When he reached Miami, he wrote to Buckley, who forwarded my address to him. And so, from Ernesto de la Fe, I got a thank-you note for saving his life.

This is the only demonstrable good I've ever done in more than forty years of writing for a living, and I did it when I was nineteen, not knowing any better or the worst. Is it any wonder that when I go

to the movies with my Magic Slate, I am lost? That I wait to be found
by the braver men and women you will meet in the pages that follow, who have dreamed of making a difference in these elsewheres
and elsewhens, who have joined the company of the immortals, and
who scare away the spooks and snakes?

*Part One*

# DOWN AMONG
# THE INTELLECTUALS

# PRIMO LEVI
# READS FRANZ KAFKA

E JUMPED, OF COURSE. But also he was pushed. And when Primo Levi, on "a sudden violent impulse," threw himself down four flights of stairwell in the Art Nouveau apartment house on the Corso Re Umberto in Turin—where, except for twenty months during World War II as "a dead man on vacation," he had lived his entire life—he killed something else besides a sixty-seven-year-old chemist, writer, and witness (Auschwitz #174517). For lack of a better way to characterize our complicated investment in everything he stood for, let's just say that on April 11, 1987, he killed our wishful thinking.

I am about to blame Franz Kafka. This is spurious, even hysterical. But why let the Nazis have the last word? From Myriam Anissimov's anguishing biography, *Primo Levi: Tragedy of an Optimist*, and a quarter-century of remarkable interviews assembled by Marco Belpoliti and Robert Gordon in *The Voice of Memory*, I want to cobble up some options.

We could blame instead a Corso Re Umberto family atmosphere that Anissimov describes as "both protective and repressive," with Levi, "the prisoner of Turin," trapped in servitude to a ninety-one-year-old mother ("paralyzed, tyrannical, and senile") and a ninety-five-year-old mother-in-law (blind, requiring round-the-clock care). Besides which, he had stopped taking antidepressants because of prostate surgery, he was so immobilized by fear of memory loss that he spent whole days playing chess with his computer, and his adult children, the botanist Lisa and the physicist Renzo, "turned pale and burst into tears" whenever he tried to talk about the death camps, wouldn't even admit to reading his books, and had always wanted a "normal" father.

We could blame as well the Holocaust deniers, who had made a well-publicized comeback in the mid-eighties. Or Ronald Reagan, who had recently gone to Bitburg to honor the SS dead. Or *Commentary* magazine, which had published, in October 1985, a shameful essay accusing Levi not only of "denatured pseudo-scientific prose" and "a tin ear for religion," but also opportunism. Or Jean Améry, the Austrian philosopher who had likewise survived Auschwitz, also wrote about it, and, before killing himself, called Levi "the forgiver." Or even Italo Calvino, who on that fateful April Saturday was already two years dead, which meant that instead of telephoning his old friend for help, Levi phoned instead the Chief Rabbi of Rome, who neglected to tell anyone until ten years later. What the writer said to the rabbi was: "I don't know how to go on, I can't stand this life any longer. My mother has cancer, and each time I look at her face I remember the faces of the men lying dead on the planks of the bunks in Auschwitz."

Anyway, he lost his balance. And balance was what we needed from him, along with what H. Stuart Hughes called his "equanimity" and Irving Howe his "moral poise." Against the odds and the century, we relied on his integrity and even his charm—the Pan-like "exuberance" Philip Roth mentions in his interview in *The Voice of Memory*, like "some little quicksilver woodland creature empowered by the forest's most astute intelligence." Every word he ever wrote, in a prose as purely Mediterranean as the best Greek poets, opposed the Nazi "world of shame," as if the bankrupt moral economy they left behind demanded all our goods and services to square the account, a humanity "commensurate" to the horror. "Commensurate" was a favorite word of his. So was "counter-weight." And so was "proportion." He was troubled in *The Drowned and the Saved* (1986) by the idea that his testimony "could by itself gain me the privilege of surviving. . . . I cannot see any proportion between the privilege and the outcome."

Elsewhere in those final essays, through which we scuttle for clues to his secession, the sociologist, anthropologist, linguist, and camera-eye of the Holocaust worried that "reason, art and poetry are no help in deciphering a place where they are banned." He quoted Jean Améry, his accuser, to agree with him: "Anyone who has been tortured, remains tortured. . . . Anyone who has suffered torture never again will be able to be at ease in the world." But he refused the label of "forgiver": "I demand justice, but I am not able, personally, to trade punches or return blows." He sought redress in law: "I know how badly these mechanisms function, but I am the way I was made." (As he had already explained in *The Periodic Table*: "I am not the Count of Monte Cristo.") And he disdained all "confusions, small-change Freudianism, morbidities, or indulgences. The oppressor remains what he is, and so does his victim. They are not interchangeable. The former is to be punished and execrated (but, if possible, understood), the latter is to be pitied and helped; but both, faced by the indecency of the irrevocable act, need refuge and protection, and instinctively search for them. Not all, but most—and often for their entire lives."

And he thought about suicide—"an act of man and not of the animal," "a mediated, non-instinctive, unnatural choice." While the "enslaved animals" in the Lager might have sometimes *let* themselves die, they did not *choose* to: "Svevo's remark in *The Confessions of Zeno* . . . has the rawness of truth: 'When one is dying, one is much too busy to think about death. All one's organism is devoted to breathing.' " Suicide, he said, "is born from a feeling of guilt that no punishment has attenuated." But in the camps "the harshness of imprisonment was perceived as punishment, and the feeling of guilt (if there is punishment, there must have been guilt) was relegated to the background, only to reemerge after the liberation." *What* guilt? That "we had not done anything, or not enough. . . . And this is a judgment that the survivor believes he sees in the eyes of those (especially the young) who listen to his stories and judge with facile hindsight, or who perhaps feel cruelly repelled." Leading to the worst of introspections:

I might be alive in the place of another, at the expense of another; I might have usurped, that is, in fact, killed. The "saved" of the Lager were not the best, those predestined to do good, the bearers of a message: what I had seen and lived through proved the exact contrary. Preferably the worst survived, the selfish, the violent, the insensitive, the collaborators of the "gray zone," the spies. It was not a certain rule (there were none, nor are there certain rules in human matters), but it was nevertheless a rule. I felt innocent, yes, but enrolled among the saved and therefore in permanent search of a justification in my own eyes and those of others. The worst survived, that is, the fittest; the best all died.

Which brings us back, like a black boomerang, to Kafka.

*Someone must have been telling lies about Joseph K . . .* (Kafka, *The Trial*)

*It's a pathogenic book. Like an onion, one layer after another. Each of us could be tried and condemned and executed, without ever knowing why. It was as if it predicted the time when it was a crime to be a Jew.* (Primo Levi to Germaine Greer)

In the summer of 1982, a publisher asked Levi to translate *The Trial*, as Italo Calvino and Natalia Ginzburg had been asked to translate *Lord Jim* and *Madame Bovary*. For his bedridden mother, he needed the money. While he would have preferred Joseph Conrad or Thomas Mann, he sounded at the time almost cheerful about the project:

I like and admire Kafka because he writes in a manner that is totally foreign to me. In my writings, for better or worse, knowingly or unknowingly, I have always made an effort to move from dark to clear, like a filtration pump that sucks in cloudy water and expels it clarified, if not sterile. Kafka takes an opposite path; he pours out an endless stream of the hallucinations dredged up from levels unbelievably deep, and never filters them. The reader feels them swarming with seeds and spores: they are burning with meaning, but he is never helped to tear down or bypass the veil, so as to see things in the place where they are hidden. Kafka never touches ground, he never deigns to offer you the clue to the maze.

His tune would soon change. In a 1983 interview, this dutiful child of the Enlightenment conceded that Kafka had a gift "that went beyond everyday reason . . . an almost animalesque sensitivity, like snakes that know when earthquakes are coming." But Levi also wondered "if it is a good idea to give a book like this to a fifteen-year-old. . . . Now this ending is so cruel, so unexpectedly cruel, that if I had a young child I would spare him. I fear it would disturb him, make him suffer, although of course it is the truth. We will die, each of us will die, more or less like that." This is odd enough from a writer whose feelings had been hurt when his own children declined to discuss his books. But, he confessed, "the undertaking disturbed me badly. I went into a deep, deep depression." And: "I felt assaulted by this book." Disappearing into Joseph K., "I accused myself, as he did."

Levi was well known for his impatience with long-winded, solipsistic, or obscurantist prose. (About Beckett: "It is the duty of every human being to communicate." About Ezra Pound: "writing in Chinese simply showed a disrespect for the reader." Borges he found "alien and distant," Proust "boring," and Dostoyevsky "rebarbative" and "portentous.") But this was different. Kafka got to him so much that he resolved never to read him again: "I feel a repulsion that is clearly of a psychoanalytic nature."

How so? Let's look at that strange unfinished novel, written shortly after Franz broke off his engagement to Felice, under the influence of Søren Kierkegaard and the "rebarbative" author of *Crime and Punishment*, with its attic offices and courts of impeachment, its brittle beards and colored badges, its "ostensible acquittals" and "indefinite postponements," its hopelessness, sinfulness, and sinister-enigmatic tropes: "It did not follow that the case was lost, by no means, at least there was no decisive evidence for such an assumption; you simply knew nothing more about the case and would never know anything more about it."

Imagine a Primo Levi meditating on, for instance, this creepy middle passage:

> One must lie low, no matter how much it went against the grain, and try to understand that this great organization remained, so to speak, in a state of delicate balance, and that if someone took it upon himself to alter the disposition of things around him, he ran the risk of losing his footing and falling to destruction, while the organization would simply right itself by

some compensating reaction in another part of its machinery—since everything is interlocked—and remain unchanged, unless, indeed, which was very probable, it became still more rigid, more vigilant, severer, and more ruthless.

Or, at the very end of the novel, such an impasse:

Were there arguments in his favor that had been overlooked? Of course there must be. Logic is doubtless unshakable, but it cannot withstand a man who wants to go on living. Where was the Judge whom he had never seen? Where was the High Court, to which he had never penetrated? He raised his hands and spread out all his fingers.

Easy enough to say that the survivor read himself into such paranoid cloud shapes, where guilt was nameless, justice faceless, space liquid, time centrifugal, God absent, and Law a myth—because everybody does. We all feel something ominous and devouring about corporations and bureaucracies, about banking and religion, even about Prague, that baroque estrangement. But a sentence like this one had to seem personal: "Only our concept of time makes it possible for us to speak of the Day of Judgment by that name; in reality it is a summary court in perpetual session." And still more chilling: "The hunting dogs are playing in the courtyard, but the hare will not escape them, no matter how fast it may be flying already through the woods."

Moreover, Franz K.'s Joseph K. is devoured as well by sexuality—by Elsa, the cabaret waitress, who receives visitors in bed; by Leni, the lawyer's servant, who only sleeps with men who have been accused; by Fräulein Bürstner and the usher's wife; by the half-naked mothers nursing babies in the Lower Court, the prostitute maids and prostitute custodians, and the little girls who molest him in the painter Titorelli's garret, behind the red door—never even mind the mother he hasn't seen for three years. Maybe that butcher's knife wasn't intended, after all, for his self-interrogating heart.

Well, Kafka: He was all about failure. Everything was incomprehensible, nothing could be known, and there were no happy endings. (His three sisters all died in the camps.) Kafka told us: "Balzac carried a cane on which was carved the legend: I smash every obstacle; my legend reads: Every obstacle smashes me." And about this Kafka, Primo Levi, "a puritan introvert," was crystal clear: "I fear him, like a great machine that crashes in on you, like the prophet who tells you the day you will die."

*If there is an Auschwitz, then there cannot be a God.* (Primo Levi)

For the most part, the Primo we meet in *The Voice of Memory* is the man in his books: "I'm Italian, but I'm also Jewish. It's like having a spare wheel, or an extra gear." He is also an "amphibian, a centaur," split in two—on the one hand, the chemist and technician; on the other, the writer who gives interviews. That he survived, unlike 647 of the 650 Italians who accompanied him to Poland, he attributes again to "sheer luck," "sound instinct," "unsuspected stamina," "knowing German," and "professional background." (Believing in God, which he didn't, and bearing witness, as he would, were irrelevant. He had happened to be a chemist in a concentration camp that was also an I.G. Farben synthetic rubber factory.) That he should have passed through the dark of *Survival at Auschwitz* to the light of *The Reawakening*, fifteen years later, seems miraculous. That he should have married, fathered, worked in a paint shop, made radio programs, won literary prizes ("Paradoxically, my baggage of atrocious memories became a wealth, a seed; it seemed to me that, by writing, I was growing like a plant"), and lectured school children in the same "calm and reasonable tone" is practically a benediction.

In the Roth interview, we see him in his study, in the room where he was born, with the flowered sofa, easy chair, word processor, color-coded notebooks, a big wire butterfly, a little wire bug, and an owl. In the pages that follow, as if from Dr. Gottlieb in *The Reawakening*, "Intelligence and cunning emanated from him like energy from radium, with the same silent and penetrating continuity." Or so we want to believe. He repeats, rethinks, amends, clarifies. We hear again about the spoons and shoes; the "healing" in his first book, the "joy" of his second. About socialism and *Sophie's Choice*. About Villon, Rabelais, Swift, Dante, and Ariosto. About solidarity in the camps (none) and resistance (futile). About James Joyce (whom he likes) and Bruno Bettelheim (whom he doesn't). He describes his chemical work ("at war with the obtuse and malign inertia of matter"), his responsibilities as a writer ("All we can ask of those who create is that they should be neither servile nor false"), and what he reads in his spare time ("I prefer to stick to the tried and tested, to make a hole and then nibble away at it, perhaps for an entire lifetime, like woodworms when they find a piece of wood to their taste").

This is who we want him to be. It argues that maybe something of the best of us, skeptical, ironic and aware, could outlive the worst. Like a Nobel Prize acceptance speech, it answers our secular humanist need for a secular humanist grace, a darting and undaunted intelligence capable of suggesting, in 1980, that "Auschwitz may be the punishment of barbarian Germany, of the barbarian Nazis, against Jewish civilization—that is to say, the punishment for daring, just as the shipwreck of Ulysses is the punishment of a barbarian god for human daring. I was thinking of that vein of German anti-Semitism that struck chiefly at the intellectual daring of the Jews, such as Freud, Marx, and all the innovators, in every field. It was that daring that irked a certain German philistinism *much more* than the fact of blood or race."

So if, in *The Reawakening*, he asked us to look at a Chagall-like scene in Zhmerinka ("The walls of one of the station latrines were plastered with German banknotes, meticulously stuck there with excrement"), we also saw the Russians dancing, the gypsy orchestra at Slutsk and the train with a piano car. And if, in *The Periodic Table*, he recalled "the vilification of the prayer shawl," turned into underwear for Lager Jews, he also explained the political chemistry of Jewishness: "In order for the wheel to turn, for life to be lived, impurities are needed . . . in the soil, too, as is known, if it is to be fertile. Dissension, diversity, the grain of salt and mustard are needed. . . . I am the impurity that makes the zinc react, I am the grain of salt or mustard." And if, in *The Monkey's Wrench*, he had to tell us about the German engineer who went to the Towers of Silence in Bombay and informed the Parsees "how German technicians had designed a grille to be placed at the bottom of the towers: a grille of electric resistors that would burn the dead body without flames, without smell, and without contaminating anything," he also told us, wonderfully, what it tastes like to drink a glacier's melting snow: "I couldn't explain it to you, because you know how hard it is to explain taste and smells, except with examples, like if you say the smell of garlic or the taste of salami. But I would actually say that water tasted like sky, and, in fact, it came straight down from the sky."

But by the time he got to *The Drowned and the Saved*, the year before he died, it was as if the dogs ate the hare. It tore him apart to consider the pathos, ambiguities, and collaborations of the "gray zone" in the camps, the "filtered memories" of the victims and the survival strategies of even the bravest: "I come first, second, and third. Then nothing, then again I; and then all the others." This calm man was suddenly furious: "We survivors are not only an exiguous but also an anomalous minority: we are those who by their prevarications or abilities or good luck did not touch bottom. Those who did so, those who saw the Gorgon, have not returned to tell about it or have returned mute, but they are the 'muslims,' the submerged, the complete witnesses, the ones whose deposition would have a general significance. They are the rule, we are the exception." He seemed almost to relish the sleazy story of Chaim Rumkowski, "King of the Jews" of Lodz, who collaborated himself all the way to the gas house:

> Like Rumkowksi, we too are so dazzled by power and prestige as to forget our essential fragility, forgetting that we are all in the ghetto, that the ghetto is walled in, that outside the ghetto reign the lords of death, and that close by the train is waiting.

Of this change of heart or perhaps a buried shadow, there are passing hints in *The Voice of Memory*: "My defect is lack of courage,

fear for myself and others." And: "I'm not very balanced at all. I go
through long periods of imbalance . . . I find it hard to cope with
problems. This side of myself I've never written about"—although
it might show up in his angry, oblique poems, "suffused with auras
and shadows." But: "I am incapable of analyzing myself. My work is
nocturnal, often carried out unconsciously." Was it possible, he was
asked, to destroy the humanity in man? His abrupt answer: "Yes, I'm
afraid so."

In Anissimov's biography, however, the shadows hound us from
the start. She's done all the busy work; read the report cards; buried
the engineer father in 1942; tracked down the real Alberto; explained, on the one wing, Cesare Pavese, Benedetto Croce, and An-
tonio Gramsci, and, on the other, the sinister clowns of Italian
Futurism and Italian fascism; looked at the racial laws, the Chemical
Institute, and the asbestos mine; gone into the beast's belly with all
the rage that Levi suppressed (the vertical stripes and brass bands,
the Jewish women in the camp orchestra wearing blue hats with
polka dots while they play Viennese waltzes, the children burned
alive in order to economize on hydrogen cyanide, the tobacco
pouches made from tanned scrotums); the engagement to Lucia
Morpurgo ("Levi was infinitely grateful to Lucia for having con-
sented to love him—an ex-deportee, a shy and repressed young
man"); the suicide of Pavese, after all his friends left town for the
summer, and *Moby-Dick* was not enough; the cigarettes (mentho-
lated); the literary life (smarmy); the Red Brigades (appalling); Israel (get out of Lebanon, get rid of Sharon); Saul Bellow's famous-
making praise for *The Periodic Table*; mother, witness, mother,
witness, mother—

But all along—from a childhood fear of spiders dating back to his
first glimpse of Doré's sketch of Arachne in Canto XII of Dante's
*Purgatorio*, to a pubescent belief in what he was told by his Christian
classmates about circumcision and castration, to his peculiar detes-
tation of rabbits ("like certain human beings, they had nothing in
their heads but food and sex") that somehow extended to the girls
around him, none of whom he could bring himself to touch, to the

tormenting "dream within a dream" that came to him even after he was married ("I am alone in the center of a grey and turbid nothing, and now, I *know* what this thing means, and I also know that I have always known it; I am in the Lager once more, and nothing is true outside the Lager. All the rest was a brief pause, a deception of the senses, a dream; my family, nature in flower, my home."), to the obscene absurdity of receiving in the mail an autographed copy of the Spandau diaries of Albert Speer, who claimed to be reading Levi, which may account for a renewed fever of the poetry-writing he called an "illness" ("dark and morbid themes," "violent feelings of rage," chimneys, shadows) and another downward spiral into depression, which is where he met Joseph K.—all along, it seems, he may have been as buggy and neurotic as Kafka himself, with more reason and less crawl-space.

In his last letter to Ruth Feldman, the American translator of his poetry, two months before he died, he said that "the period he was living through was worse than Auschwitz, because he was no longer young and no longer had the ability to react and take a grip on himself." His last essay, published two weeks after the stairwell, was called "A Fear of Spiders":

> Their hairiness is supposed to have a sexual significance, and the repulsion we feel supposedly reveals our unconscious rejection of sex: this is how we express it and at the same time this is how we try to free ourselves of it. . . . The spider is the enemy-mother who envelops and encompasses, who wants to make us re-enter the womb from which we have issued, bind us tightly to take us back to the impotence of infancy, subject us again to her power. . . .

Like a great machine that crashes down on you . . .

*I would have reformulated Adorno's remark like this: After Auschwitz, there can be no more poetry, except about Auschwitz.* (Primo Levi)

*It is not necessary to accept everything as true, one must only accept it as necessary.* (Kafka, *The Trial*)

Cynthia Ozick reviewed *The Drowned and the Saved* as if it were a suicide note. He had at last let loose his rage. She was proud of him for finally giving in to hate. So what if it cost him his life? She only wished that all his books "had been as vehement." And there's the ugly rub. In order to approve of his farewell testament, she needed somehow to trash everything else he had written. Ladling on such inverted-comma words and phrases as "curious peacefulness," "famous 'detachment,'" "so transparent, so untainted," "pure spirit," "vessel of clear water," "well-mannered cicerone of hell," "Darwin of the death camps," and—worst of all—purveyor of "uplift," she actually seemed to sneer.

At the time I thought Ozick's essay impudent and maybe even ulterior. Imagine blaming a writer for his blurbs and a witness for his reasonableness. Why not come right out and complain that he was a Sephardic Jew instead of an Ashkenazi, an assimilated Italian instead of a lacerated Pole, a socialist instead of a Zionist, a nonbeliever going into the camps and a nonbeliever coming out, pro-Diaspora and anti-Eretz Israel, who didn't even speak Yiddish?

I'm older now, and ulterior on my own time. And while it still seems to me that anyone unmoved to tears and scruple by a brilliant book like *The Reawakening* has been sadly coarsened and gone tone-deaf, I am also aware of our desperate need to cling to whatever purchase we think we have on the sudden edge and the bloody sleeve and the fiery sign. Reading mirrors, we are horrified by what we see. We abduct and torment our heroes of consciousness as if we were Giacomettis torturing metals and ideas.

"We hate in ourselves our masters' insane dream of greatness, and their contempt for God and men, and for ourselves, as men," wrote Levi. And: "It is naive, absurd, and historically false to believe that an infernal system such as National Socialism was, sanctifies its victims; on the contrary, it degrades them, it makes them similar to itself, and this all the more when they are available, blank, and lack a political or moral armature." Where to find such armature? To this bonfire, he can't be said to have brought a sword: "We must be democrats first, Jews or Italians, or anything else, second." But that is who he was, and it killed him. "I tell you they are just like other people," he said of the *Sonderkommandos*, "only a lot more unhappy."

He had never wanted to be a writer, or an intellectual, or a victim, or a witness. He had troubles of his own, ordinary spiders, before he met Kafka in the gray zone. And now that we know all about those troubles, there still remains the mystery of his transcendence. For awhile, only for awhile, but all the more astonishing—water tasted like the sky.

# RIMBAUD AND ORWELL:
# RADICAL ICONS

THEY LAUGHED WHEN I SAT DOWN with these two writers—and never mind that both books arrived in the same box. The bad gay boy and the Cold War saint! The apostle of derangement and the lexicographer of Newspeak! The red cape and the tweed jacket, the rotting knee and the lousy lung, the drunken boat and the memory hole! "I came to find my mind's disorder sacred," said the poet on a camel. "Good prose is like a window pane," said the novelist who shot elephants.

But both Arthur Rimbaud and George Orwell did go down-and-out in Paris and London. (Arthur actually preferred London, for the yellow fog. George needed someplace he could fish.) Both their fathers were mostly absent, doing time as globocops in third-world tropics of the French and British empires. (On a sand dune, Captain Rimbaud taught himself Bedouin ways, the better to repress them. Orwell's dad was a deputy opium agent, making sure the poppy juice got from India to the Chinese addicts.) Both their mothers loved cards more than kids. Both sons, hating school, gifted at languages, hostile to religion, intrigued by popular culture, would follow their fathers to the colonies, enlist in foreign wars, lose not only their tempers but also amazing amounts of manuscript, and die younger than they should have, after dreaming up and acting out alternative identities. (Take a hike, Eric Blair: "I is somebody else.")

Both live on as cautionary tales, litmus tests, celebrity role models, and undead icons. In *Rimbaud*, his wickedly entertaining revised version of the delinquent poet, Graham Robb points to his posthu-

mous career "as Symbolist, Surrealist, Beat poet, student revolutionary, rock lyricist, gay pioneer and inspired drug-user," as well as "an
emergency exit from the house of convention" for avant-gardes everywhere. Well-thumbed editions of *A Season in Hell* and *The Illuminations* are to be found in the portmanteaus of Picasso, Breton,
Cocteau, and Malraux, and in the backpacks of Allen Ginsberg, Bob
Dylan, Bruce Chatwin, and Kurt Cobain. Jim Morrison, that swing-
ing Door, is even rumored "to have faked his death in Paris and
followed Rimbaud to Ethiopia"—just the right splash of mythic
Tabasco.

Whereas Orwell's name is mentioned every time we are looked
down upon by surveillance cameras, lied to by governments, read
about journalists who have been "disappeared," or hear about dissidents in mental hospitals. Big Brother is a member of our extended
family, the pigs go on drinking all the milk and eating all the apples,
and the SLORC word for Burma in Newspeak is "Myanmar." In
*Democracy*, her 1984 (!) novel of skulduggery on the Pacific Rim,
Joan Didion would notice that "all reporters had paperback copies of
*Homage to Catalonia*, and kept them in the same place where they
kept the matches and the candle and the notebook, for when the
hotel was bombed." So postmodern is Curious George that he has
even been abducted by such aliens as Norman Podhoretz.

And both for a season or so professed revolutionary socialism.
Even if the moment passed like measles, Rimbaud was there for the
Paris Commune, and Orwell was there for the Spanish Republic,
and these, of course, are two of the biggest Super Bowl games in the
Left's long losing streak, and it makes you want to weep.

Robb reminds us that the massacre of the Communards in 1871
"was the single bloodiest week in French history: a savage humiliation of the proletariat. Thousands were shot, inexpertly tortured or
shipped to the penal colonies without a proper trial. Women carrying bottles in the street were bayoneted by soldiers who had heard of
the mythical, bomb-throwing '*petroleuses*.'" More people died during *la Semaine Sanglante* than during the Reign of Terror or the
Franco-Prussian War. While the Rimbaud article in my *Britannica*

omits any mention of the Commune, the young poet yo-yo'd in and
out of all of it, and Robb suggests that he may have been raped by a
gang of jeering soldiers while trying to slip through the lines a
couple of weeks before the slaughter, after which he wrote his famous *Lettres du voyant*—announcing the poet as Romantic Lucifer
and Promethean Satan, whose job was to rescue man from God.

On the open wound of the Spanish Republic, Jeffrey Meyers in
*Orwell: Wintry Conscience of a Generation* quotes Albert Camus: "It
was in Spain that men learned that one can be right and yet be
beaten, that force can vanquish spirit, that there are times when
courage is not its own recompense. It is this, doubtless, which explains why so many men, the world over, regard the Spanish drama
as a personal tragedy." Certainly it was personal for George. On his
first stop in Barcelona, he found a socialist community "where no
one was on the make, where there was a shortage of everything but
no privilege and no bootlicking," and the dining rooms in the luxury
hotels had been turned into canteens for the militias. But his second
time around he saw fat men eating quails while children begged for
bread, and commissars were hunting down his Anarchist friends like
deer. And then he took a bullet in the throat.

Anyway, both of them were lonely guys: vagabonds and vanishing acts. And they somehow hang together, coincidental and corre-
sponding, in a rainbow arc from the Cult of the Artist to the Writer
on the Barricades to Joe DiMaggio for Mr. Coffee and Bob Dole for
Viagra. In *Democracy*, Joan Didion also quotes Kierkegaard: "Life
can only be understood backwards, but it must be lived forwards."

*It can only be the end of the world, ahead of time.* (Rimbaud, *Illuminations*)

"The first poet of a civilization not yet born," as René Char later
called him, showed up on October 20, 1854, in Charleville in French
Flanders, three years after Napoleon III's coup d'état. At age four,
already precocious, he tried to trade his baby sister for some colored
prints in a bookseller's window. At age six, his father shipped off for
Algeria and never came back, leaving Arthur at the mercy of a

mother devoted to church, shopping, and whist, with a "phenom-
enal capacity for not showing affection." At age seven, he entered
the "corpse-yellow" rooms of the local lycée as if preparing "for a
life in prison." By age fourteen, he had inhaled all of French poetry,
won every academic prize, and developed acute self-consciousness:

> I have the bluish-white eyes of my ancestors the Gauls, their small brains,
> their clumsiness in battle. I find my dress as barbaric as theirs. But I do not
> butter my hair.

Picture him in the summer of 1870, reading Paul Verlaine for the
first time, chatting up navvies, quarrymen, and vagrants, and stow-
ing away under a seat on the train to Paris, where he will be arrested
on suspicion of republicanism and/or spying for Bismarck, and
spend maybe a week in prison, during which not even Robb can say
for sure what happens to him, except lice. There followed as if on an
elastic string that kept snapping him back to "the Mouth of Darkness," as he called his disapproving mother, an itchy six-month period of itinerant journalism, café polemics, Bohemian sonnets, and a
shopping spree for surrogate fathers, during which he swore like a
prisoner, ate like a pig, refused to pass the salt, and came to believe
that "the mind could be shaped by an act of will," that morality "is
a weakness of the brain," and that Society "will fall to the axe, the
pick and the steamroller."

> In the cities, the mud suddenly appeared to me red and black, like a mirror
> when the lamp moves about in the next room, like a treasure in the forest!
> Good luck, I cried, and saw a sea of flames and smoke in the sky, and, to left
> and to right, all riches blazing like a billion thunders.

This is a kid ready for a Commune. He sells his watch for a third-
class ticket to Paris in February 1871, and for two weeks walks the
streets "feasting on theatre bills, advertisements, pamphlets and
shop signs," sleeping on coal barges, competing with dogs for scraps
of food—a "vagrant poet with a fish in his pants." Six days after he
has hoofed it home, the workers rise, generals are lynched, and he
has to go right back again: "Paris had fallen to poets who worked
with laws and human beings instead of words." A new police chief

removes "Saint" from every street-name and issues a warrant for God's arrest. Maybe words actually do have "a direct, controllable influence on reality."

"Order is vanquished!" declares the sixteen-year-old poet, and writes his own revolutionary constitution: A permanent state of referendum! Abolition of families and their "slave-holding" of children! Intelligent communication with animals, plants, and extra-terrestrials! He returns in late April, at the delirious height of the Commune, to enlist as a Left Bank guerrilla: "To whom shall I hire myself? What beast should I worship? What holy image are we attacking? Which hearts shall I break? What lie must I keep?—In what blood shall I walk?" When government troops bomb their own capital, he slips away, suffers what he suffers, and enters the gaudy tent of his own legend: "I owe my superiority to the fact that I have no heart."

In fact, says Robb, he has decided "to seize control of the means of intellectual production. . . . In terms that were unavailable to him in 1871, he was considering the possibility of detaching the censorious superego from the endlessly imaginative id." And the "superego incarnate" is Mme. Rimbaud, from whom he is always hiding out in attics, cellars, or latrines, and to whom he always returns, until Africa. You are saying this is reductive. But every once in a while, praxis so improves on theory that we get a penguin.

That summer of 1871 he posts a batch of poems to Verlaine so full of kinky innuendo that The Nasty Fellows will raise a subscription to bring the prodigy to the capital and subsidize his genius. Rimbaud arrives with "a strange nostalgia for the future," one of the most remarkable poems in any language, "The Drunken Boat," and a plan to fold, bend, spindle, and mutilate his own personality. Almost immediately, he will trash hotel rooms like a rock star and leave turds behind on pillows. Verlaine, of course, will fall in love with him, when he isn't rotting his brain with absinthe or setting his wife's hair on fire. Verlaine, who would eventually shoot Rimbaud in the wrist before experiencing a convenient religious conversion, is easy to make fun of only if you have never been smitten by somebody bad for you, or until you are reminded that Pol Pot was one of his greatest admirers.

We are now in familiar territory, with the familiar contradictions. Rimbaud the vandal, hooligan, sadist, and "murderous" prankster is also the Rimbaud who writes a lovely article about "human alarm-clocks" who for a small fee rush around in the early hours in the poorer sections of the city waking up factory workers. The "vile, vicious, disgusting, smutty little schoolboy" is also the author of the marvelous "Voyelles," a poem in which each vowel has its own color (noir, blanc, rouge, vert, bleu)—inspired by Ernest Cabaner, a composer who plays piano in a seedy bar and believes that each note of the octave corresponds to a particular color and a particular vowel. According to Robb:

> This is the ambiguity that lies at the heart of Rimbaud's work: the ardent search for powerful systems of thought that could be used like magic spells, conducted by an acutely ironic intelligence—a combination that rarely survives adolescence.

He loses a notebook, the Belgian poems, and the manuscript of *Spiritual Hunt*. Since he believes "every being . . . to be entitled to several *other* lives," why not go to England, live with Paul in SoHo, grub sixpence from writing business letters and teaching French, ogle the little boys in tight-fitting suits waiting outside the public urinals, and read Shakespeare, Longfellow, Poe, and Swinburne? Certainly, like all ex-Communards in jittery Europe, they are spied upon and hassled. So should they be. They hobnob with the inter-national socialist underground. They *see* Karl Marx. Robb even sug-gests that several of *The Illuminations* can be construed as glosses on *Das Kapital*—on "the alienated consumers of the modern metropo-lis, the disinherited masses, the resurrectionary mythology of the Commune and the magic wand of global capitalism."

Not so his astonishing *A Season in Hell*, in which modernism rears its contrary head; in which experiments with language are investi-gations into the unstable self; in which, "like a particle accelerator," repellent forms of thought collide—Job and Goethe, fairy tales and

Taine, *Fleurs du Mal* and "the Mouth of Darkness": "Rimbaud, at
the age of eighteen, had invented a linguistic world that can be happily explored for years like the scrapyard of a civilization." After
which, confoundingly, he would abandon literature, France, fame,
and his mother.

Well, now: Brussels, Stuttgart, Milan, Siena. Enlisting in the Car-
list rebel army, then absconding with the cash bonus. Enlisting in
the Dutch Colonial Army, then deserting the minute he gets to Java.
Trying to enlist in the U.S. Navy, then having instead to run off to
Scandinavia with a circus. Going over the Alps on foot, setting sail
for Alexandria, learning Russian, Arabic, and Hindi. Discovering at
last that while no tree grows in Aden, there is a nearby Forbidden
City unseen by Europeans since Richard Burton and money to be
made trading coffee, tobacco, incense, ivory, spices, spears, swords,
ostrich eggs, animal skins, and guns. He will wear a turban, keep a
woman, chew khat, catch syphilis, ride camels, write home to mom,
lose another manuscript (on Abyssinia) and then his right leg (to
bone cancer). At the end, he refuses opium for fear of what he might
say in his delirium to his sister.

Disregard previous rumors, even in Enid Starkie. He neither converted to Islam nor traded in slaves, although you could not do business in his part of Africa without cutting the warlords in on the deal.
What he did do, by selling guns to King Menelik of Ethiopia, was to
help an African army defeat a European nation—well, at least
Italy—for the first time. Disregard as well the Tragic Aura. He
didn't die bitter and broke. He actually made a lot of money, which
he hid from his mother in bank accounts all over the Middle East.
Some people are still looking for it.

Some people are also still looking for the poet. Rimbaud killed
him off when he stopped living with other people, after he realized
that the world couldn't be changed by verbal innovation. Literature,
Robb explains, hadn't worked:

> For Rimbaud, poetry had always been the means to an end: winning es-
> teem, causing irritation, changing the nature of reality. Each redefinition

of the goal had rendered the old technology obsolete. The prose Rimbaud had shown no more nostalgia for verse than most mathematicians showed for their slide-rules after the invention of the personal computer.

It's hard to read this as anything other than hard cheese for bohemia.

*My starting point is always a feeling of partisanship, a sense of injustice.*
(George Orwell, "Why I Write")

Orwell lasted ten years longer, but all of it was much less thrilling. And so, compared to Graham Robb, is Jeffrey Meyers. Whether, after two volumes by William Abrahams and Peter Stansky, one full-length biography by Bernard Crick and another by Michael Shelden, a short and elegant "Literary Life" by the editor of the twenty-volume "Complete Works," Peter Davison, and a brilliant black valentine by Raymond Williams in the "Modern Masters" series, we even need another account is open to question. " 'Father Knew George Orwell' is a cracked old song," wrote Williams almost three decades ago. But the centennial of his birth will be suddenly upon us in 2003, so batten down your aspidistra.

According to Meyers he felt guilty about everything: "his colonial heritage, his bourgeois background, his inverted snobbery and his elite education," not to mention his behavior as a policeman in Burma, his inability to get himself arrested while he was collecting material for *Down and Out,* and maybe even the uncircumcised penis that so mortified him at Eton among such contemporaries as Anthony Powell, Henry Green, and Harold Acton. And so his whole life was a kind of penance, never taking care of himself, doing it all the hard way, always off to another dangerous front, ending up on an island off the coast of Scotland as far away from medical attention as an Englishman with tuberculosis could get. "All these risky moves were prompted by the inner need to sabotage his chance of a happy life," Meyers the schoolmarm tells us.

We've heard this before, from everybody else, and it still doesn't explain anything. How many boys went to Eton and not to Spain?

How many writers went to Spain, like Hemingway, and failed to notice anything peculiar? How come Lawrence Durrell and Anthony Burgess never felt guilty about *their* colonial service or imperial privilege? Who else (who didn't have to) went down the Wigan mines, or into the casual wards of a public hospital to find out how the poor died, or saw a man hanged and decided on the spot, "When a murderer is hanged, there is only one person at the ceremony who is not guilty of murder"?

From Meyers, we also get a surprising amount of sex, all of it depressing. Orwell was nervous about women, apparently not much good in bed with them, and would complain in his "Last Literary Notebook" about "their incorrigible dirtiness & untidiness" and "their terrible, devouring sexuality":

> Within any marriage or regular love affair, he suspected that it was always the woman who was the sexually insistent partner. In his experience women were quite insatiable, & never seemed fatigued by no matter how much love-making. . . . In any marriage of more than a year or two's standing, intercourse was thought of as a duty, a service owed by the man to the woman. And he suspected that in every marriage the struggle was always the same — the man trying to escape from sexual intercourse, to do it only when he felt like it (or with other women), the woman demanding it more & more, & more & more consciously despising her husband for his lack of virility.

How does this square with his adventures in Rangoon brothels or among Parisian trollops and Berber girls in Marrakech? Was the former colonial cop and declassed intellectual only capable of getting it up with the lower orders? Raymond Williams was much exercised by this class angle in Orwell—an unconscious condescension, a double standard, his writing off of the brute masses because he had come to feel all politics "was a mode of adjustment to one's own wishes and fantasies." Hadn't he, in *1984*, projected his *own* apathy on the oppressed proles by willfully insisting that, "Under the spreading chestnut tree / I sold you and you sold me"?

But these are difficult thoughts, getting into what Williams called Orwell's "submerged despairs"—the "radical pessimism" and "accommodation to capitalism" of this self-described "shock-absorber of the bourgeoisie." Meyers will no more entertain them than he will explore the kinds of craft questions that bring out the best in Peter Davison—on, for instance, the origins of *Animal Farm* in his childhood enthusiasm for Beatrix Potter's *Pigling Bland,* or how those magnificent essays about elephants, toads, and Dickens got written, or the precise debt of *1984* to Zamyatin's *We,* Jack London's *Iron Heel,* and Katherine Burdekin's *Swastika Night.* No mention in Meyers, either, of how the 1955 film version of *Animal Farm* omitted the last-scene melding of men and pigs, which might have opened up questions about cultural expropriation, body snatching and even Doublethink, all for the greater good of the Cold War cause. Not a single sentence in Meyers's many pages stops us in mid-platitude to say anything half as intellectually arresting as these several in Raymond Williams, on Orwell's recurring patterns:

> This experience of awareness, rejection, and flight is repeatedly enacted. Yet it would be truer to say that most of Orwell's important writing is about someone who tries to get away but fails. That failure, that reabsorption, happens, in the end, in all the novels mentioned, though of course the experience of awareness, rejection, and flight has made its important mark.

Instead, we get the same old stories: St. Cyprian's, with Cyril Connolly and Cecil Beaton; Eton and his unrequited crush on a younger boy; Burma, where he briefly imagined that "the greatest joy in the world would be to drive a bayonet into a Buddhist priest's guts"; Paris, where he wrote and destroyed two novels; teaching boys, selling books, being rejected by T. S. Eliot, marrying Eileen; Spain, Morocco, and the Blitz; the BBC, the adopted child, and the dead Eileen; P. G. Wodehouse, Edmund Wilson, and *Animal Farm*; the peculiar disinclination to visit museums, art galleries, concerts, opera, ballet, Italy, or Greece; the black tobacco and the long audition of widows-in-waiting, which would lead to the egregious Sonia, that sexual trapeze artist whom all the biographers love so much to hate, who seems to have let go of Lucian Freud only to dangle from Maurice

Merleau-Ponty until she got a better grip on George—and who is reported here to have spat in disgust whenever she passed a nun on the street, although it isn't clear whether this was before or after she showed up in an Angus Wilson novel (*Anglo-Saxon Attitudes*).

In case you are wondering, the thirty-five lefties Orwell warned the Labour government against asking to write propaganda for the Foreign Office in 1948 included Charlie Chaplin, Michael Redgrave, Orson Welles, Paul Robeson, Nancy Cunard, Louis Untermeyer, and John Steinbeck. (John Steinbeck?!?) He also believed that "the best writers of our time have been reactionary," e.g., Wyndham Lewis, Ezra Pound, and T. S. Eliot. His was a pessimism so radical as to end up in "My Country Right or Left" endorsing a "spiritual need for patriotism and military values" for which "the boiled rabbits of the Left can find no substitute."

And along with the famous decency, the equally famous abusiveness: W. H. Auden was "a sort of gutless Kipling." William Morris, Bernard Shaw, Henri Barbusse, and Upton Sinclair were "dull, empty windbags." Off with the heads of "the creepy eunuchs in pansy-left circles" and "all that dreary tribe of high-minded women and sandal-wearing and bearded fruit-juice drinkers who come flocking towards the smell of 'progress' like bluebottles to a dead cat." Wouldn't it be loverly "if only the sandals and the pistachio-colored shirts could be put in a pile and burnt and every vegetarian, teetotaler and creeping Jesus sent home to Welwyn Garden City to do his yoga exercises quietly!"

Wilfrid Sheed once said that Orwell wrote best about the things he hated. So maybe we're just lucky that some of the things he hated were more important than sandals and vegetarianism.

> *But for now, it's the night before. Let us receive all the influxes of vigor and real tenderness. And at dawn, armed with ardent patience, we shall enter into the splendid cities.* (Rimbaud)

I am reminded of Simone Weil, who also negated herself, who willed her body out of this world. At her funeral, the priest arrived too late, because of a stalled train. At Rimbaud's funeral, nobody came, because his mother kept it secret. Orwell is remembered on the one hand, by Malcolm Muggeridge, as having "loved the past, hated the present and dreaded the future," and on the other, by H. G. Wells, as "a Trotskyist with big feet." George himself told us that "saints should always be judged guilty until they are proved innocent."

So Rimbaud gave up poetry when it failed to change the world. Orwell at the end must have had his doubts about language, too, or he wouldn't have dreamed up Newspeak. Neither is remembered for why they happened to be on hand in the first place for historical convulsions like the Paris Commune and the Spanish Civil War, or for their hard work at identity-making, or for their several minds about most of the events that shaped or shattered those identities. Instead, Rimbaud's name is worn by freaks, geeks, and videodrones as if it were a logo on a T-shirt or a jet-propelled sneaker, but anyway sufficient unto our buzzy day as a style accessory, no poems necessary. And never mind the bad news Orwell brought back about social injustice at home and abroad; he is propped up on a Cold War horse like the dead El Cid, to frighten the Moorish hordes.

I have been rereading *1984*. It is, if not quite a sacred text, at least an illuminated manuscript in the monastic cells of the American neocons. Whether or not its lugubrious author would have delighted in their company any more than he enjoyed the acquaintance of the "pansy-left," they nevertheless get what they need from this Big Brother how-to manual, which is a totalitarianism so absolute as to authorize a Holy War against it. But *1984* is not a book, and they are not a crowd, with anything of fundamental importance to say to anyone made of better stuff than Winston Smith. If everyone who tries to get away is preordained to fail, where does that leave the reader, not to mention citizens, serfs, and slaves?

Fortunately, the world is full of people better than Winston Smith. For vivid example, there are those who strung along with Gandhi on his Salt March to decolonize the Indian mind in 1930. And the Dutch doctors who refused, during the Nazi occupation, to screen for genetic "defects." And the Danes who declined to build German ships, feed the German army, or honor the Nazi racial laws, while whisking away their Jewish fellow citizens to Sweden. And the students at Fisk University who desegregated Nashville's downtown lunch counters in 1960 and thereby launched a second American revolution. And the Polish workers in Solidarity who occupied a shipyard in 1980, and, by insisting on their right to strike, began, without firing a single shot, the dismantling of the nonprofit police states of Eastern Europe. And the disenfranchised citizens of martial-law South Africa whose economic boycott spread from the black townships to the conscience-stricken West, paralyzed the apartheid state, and led eventually to free elections. And those Chileans who ended Pinochet's dictatorship with street festivals, protest songs, a union movement, vigils by the mothers of the "disappeared," and a surprise plebiscite. Plus the women of Manila who shamed the tanks of Marcos with a fusillade of yellow flowers, the Chinese students in Tiananmen Square, and Aung San Suu Kyi under Rangoon house arrest.

Everywhere it is written—in bulletholes and amputations, in shellshock and mushroom clouds, in brainwash and shrinkwrap—that political science is a clenched fist, that power flows from the mouths of guns, that bloodlust and servitude are coded in our genome, and that obedience or death is the inevitable trajectory of narrative. But there is another way to read this atrocious century, the view from Gandhi's spinning wheel, in which, against tyranny and exploitation, occupation and oppression, popular movements of tens of thousands withhold their consent. They refuse, secede, mobilize, challenge, humiliate, disrupt, and disobey. And their principled civil disobedience—tactical, strategic, improvisatory, sometimes even whimsical—creates the very wherewithal of a civil society. When Václav Havel and his friends wrote a new social contract in 1989 in the Magic Lantern Theatre in Prague, on a stage set for Dürrenmatt's *Minotaurus*, they weren't reading Orwell. Nor were the students from Charles University, calling themselves the Committee for a More Joyful Present and dressed comically as Young Pioneers in red kerchiefs, white blouses, and pigtails, who joined these jail-bird intellectuals when they were depressed and weary: "We have come," the students said, "to cheer you up—and make sure you don't turn into another politboro." And so the students gave to the members of Havel's plenum little circular mirrors to examine them-selves as they wrote the future of the Republic to the music of the Beatles—to be on the lookout for revanchist pigginess.

# ARTHUR KOESTLER,
# HOMELESS MIND

TO HER BIOGRAPHER, Simone de Beauvoir confided a less than rhapsodic one-night stand, in 1946, with the Hungarian malcontent Arthur Koestler: "One night I got so drunk I let him come home with me. We slept together. It wasn't any good. It didn't mean anything. He was too drunk, so was I. Only that night was real, the rest is how I loathed him." Beauvoir was rather kinder in *Force of Circumstance*, the third volume of her memoirs, recalling K.'s curiosity and generosity as well as his self-importance: "Touchy, tormented, greedy for human warmth, but cut off from others by his personal obsessions." And rather more ambivalent in that plum-pudding roman à clef *The Mandarins*, where her alterego Anne will notice, almost immediately after succumbing to the "Slavic charm" of the Koestler-like Scriassine, "a lot of hate" in those "fiery eyes," and the delusion that "loneliness can be cured by force."

They got around like a virus or the clap, these European intellectuals. Nor did they fail to ideologize their sadness in the sack. (Kronstadt! Slansky!) So delirious, in fact, were the bistro behaviors of The Second Sex and Darkness at Noon, not to mention The Myth of Sisyphus, Nausea and Man's Fate, that we are tempted to linger and to wallow. Imagine Jean-Paul Words so drunk over onion soup in Les Halles that he fills up paper napkins with pepper and salt and hides them in his pockets. Or Darkness and Sisyphus getting into a fist fight, not because Camus was having it off with Koestler's main squeeze, Mamaine "The Mermaid" Paget, but because Caligula accused Scum of the Earth of cheating to win their wager on who could scuttle the fastest across the Place St. Michel on all fours. Or Being and Nothingness calling off their friendship because Invisible Writing insisted on remaining buddies with Voices of Silence, which oracular Silence, André Malraux, had been pressuring Gallimard to cease publication of No Exit's favorite magazine, *Les Temps modernes*. And maybe "Mermaid" Paget needs a biography of her own. While The God That Failed was knocking her about—before and after The Stranger ran away with her—Jean-Paul Saint Genet also made a clumsy pass, and so did that Dead Sea Scroll at the Finland Station, Edmund Wilson, while he was still married to The Group.

But if we are to believe David Cesarani's weird book *Arthur Koestler: The Homeless Mind*, Beauvoir was luckier than many of K.'s bedmates. What might just as easily have happened is Koestler's inviting himself into her flat, bullying her into batching up an omelette, helping her to towel the plates, grabbing her by her hair or throat, pulling her down to the linoleum, banging her head a couple of times, and then raping her, after which explaining: "I thought you had a bit of a yen for me." This is what he did to Jill Craigie, the filmmaker wife of Labor M.P. Michael Foot. (Craigie died shortly before Christmas 1999, but not before the details of her interview with Cesarani made headlines in the British tabloids.) And probably what he did to a fair number of other young women in his long career of sexual conquest. It certainly bears a striking resemblance to the "seduction" of Odette by Slavek in his Lisbon novel, *Arrival and Departure*. More than a user, Koestler was an abuser—of women, alcohol, automobiles, and ideas.

This abusiveness—and the evidence is overwhelming that he was an "intemperate, obsessive, egomaniacal, bullying, petty, selfish, arrogant, lecherous, duplicitous and self-deluding" "serial rapist" addicted late in life to "happy pills" (Dexedrine)—is one of two main accusations in a relentless bill of indictment. The other is "the negativity of his Jewishness," by which Cesarani, a professor of Modern Jewish History at Southampton University, means more than ambivalence, but a denial verging on self-hatred: "At odds with his origins, uneasy with himself and unable to settle because with no clear identity it was not clear where he belonged, he was condemned to a nomadic life-style. Homelessness became his domicile, and his politics were the politics of location and dislocation."

Cesarani can't quite bring himself to *link* these impeachments— to suggest that Koestler was depraved because he was deracinated; that not only couldn't he stay put geographically or ideologically, but also drank too much, cracked up cars, punched up cops and raped women, all because he was running away from his Jewishness. This would require actually thinking about other homeless Jewish minds in an era that specialized in forcible evictions and what K. himself once called "stepfatherlands." Einstein? Marcuse? Jacques Derrida and Algeria? Elias Canetti and his mother? It's worth recalling that when Freud finally got permission to leave Vienna in 1938, the Gestapo obliged him to sign a certificate saying that he had been well-treated by the authorities. He added a sentence of his own: "I can heartily recommend the Gestapo to anyone."

Still, Jewish self-hatred is an odd charge to level against the ex-Zionist, ex-Communist and original Cold Warrior, perhaps our pre-eminent parajournalist of totalitarianism and surely the ultimate waffle on the twentieth-century grid—with score marks on his thick hide to prove it from Hitler, Franco, and Stalin—who made no secret of his origins in four autobiographies. Who worked part time for the Jewish National Fund and joined a Jewish dueling fraternity at the University of Vienna. Who accompanied the Zionist firebrand Vladimir Jabotinsky on a speaking tour of Austria and Czechoslovakia in 1924 and then to the World Zionist Congress in 1925. Who dropped out of college and shipped off to Palestine in 1926, where for the next three years he flunked kibbutzing, sought in Tel Aviv to start a cabaret, settled in Jerusalem to string for publications in Budapest and Cairo, concocted the first Hebrew crossword puzzle, and covered the Middle East for the Ullstein newspaper chain until they promoted him to Paris. Who returned in 1944 after writing one novel, *Arrival and Departure* (1942), even Cesarani admits is "almost the only work of fiction published in Britain during the war, or even *after* the war, to register the catastrophe" of the Holocaust, in order to research another, *Thieves in the Night* (1946), that endorsed Stern Gang terrorism. And who made one last 1948 trip to the fledgling State of Israel, where like so many Revisionists he seemed to hate almost everything about Ben-Gurion's "totalitarian Lilliput," including the fact that his jeep was commandeered at gunpoint by Moshe Dayan's 89th Battalion, after which he published an account, *Promise and Fulfillment* (1949), that called quits to his love affair with the Promised Land—although he would have gone back in 1967, at Teddy Kollek's personal request, if not for the Six-Day War. According to Cesarani:

> Once Koestler had decisively rejected the realisation of his Jewish identity through Zionism he deliberately cultivated a cosmopolitan, de-Judaised image in his autobiographical writing. The break with Jewishness and Zionism, which is flagged at the end of *Promise and Fulfillment,* began a process of repression that inflected all his subsequent activities.

Which repression would explain why, for instance, he was so ulterior as to fail to mention he was Jewish in a 1961 speech to the Royal Society of Literature—about a trip to India and Japan! But not, perhaps, his motivation in taking time off from his chats with Kingsley Amis about ESP to write *The Thirteenth Tribe* (1976). This eccentric foray into Jewish history argued—from scrappy texts of the tenth-century Arab geographer Muqaddasi and the Byzantine historian Constantine Porphyrogenitus; from dialogues in *Al Kuzari*, a dreamy theological tract by the Jewish poet/philosopher of Moorish Spain, Judah Halevi; from conflicting reports by sundry Hebrew, Persian, Syrian, and Armenian sources; and from meditations on such fragments by modern scholars like Toynbee, Bury, Dunlop, and the perplexed Hungarian Marxist Dr. Antal Bartha— that the Jews of Eastern Europe were actually Khazars, descended from a Caucasian tribe of Turkish stock that thrived more than a thousand years ago between the Black Sea and the Caspian; whose king, court, and military caste inexplicably converted to Judaism in 740 A.D. and then, two hundred years and a Russian invasion later, vanished into the mists. Those mists, insisted Koestler, were Hungary, Poland, Lithuania, the Crimea, and the Ukraine. Thus, the Holocaust's primary victims weren't really Jewish, at least genetically. So much for a Chosen People.

Some of us took *The Thirteenth Tribe* to be on a par with Koestler's other enthusiasms of the raffish 1970s—like levitation, psychokinesis, catastrophism, Tories, and canines. But Cesarani sees a more sinister subtext, "a deep, personal reason for this bizarre exercise":

> He was prepared to go extraordinary lengths to prove that he was not a Jew, or at least a Jew of the "seed of Abraham." Koestler could not simply renounce Juadism: he was not a believing Jew and, in any case, saw Jewishness as more than a creed—it was a national identity. Indeed, it was even more than that: it was a package of acquired characteristics, a racial type. Given his geneticist convictions the only way he could emancipate himself from the "seed of Abraham" was by tracing his lineage to the loins of the Khazar tribesmen.

Well, maybe. On the other hand, maybe not. "There is nothing more easily falsified than the unconscious," Italo Calvino has explained. Cesarani only got into the private papers at the Edinburgh Library by promising to write a book about "Koestler's Jewish identity and themes in his life and work." So he has to blow this bagpipe every other chapter, or look like a magpie. But imagine his surprise at all that best-selling date-rape stuff—and the commensurate dismay of Michael Scammell, whose authorized biography, as yet unfinished, is now preempted. Likewise preempted, one supposes, are the revelations about Koestler's activities as a Comintern agent in Berlin, Paris, and Spain, as faithfully recorded in the suddenly leaky archives of the KGB. Of another famous renegade, the Rilke-reading translator of *Bambi* Whittaker Chambers, Koestler himself would remark: "Such peculiar birds are found only in the tree of the revolution."

Except for his self-help encyclopedias on sex, which Cesarani says weren't bad for their nervous times, I've read all of Arthur Koestler's books. When I was fifteen years old, *The Invisible Writing* was as thrilling as *Look Homeward, Angel, Catcher in the Rye*, and Thomas Merton's *The Seven-Storey Mountain*. Do I like him less, now that I know so much more from Cesarani about his piggy personal behavior? Of course. But looking back, it seems to me it was never the man I admired, anyway. It was the career and the way he wrote about it, in the saddle as it were, like Isaac Babel in *Red Cavalry*, or as if, like Trotsky and the millworkers in Petersburg in 1917, we ducked under the bellies of the horses at a friendly Cossack wink. In this extreme Western, I wanted to be a cowboy too, one of Hobsbawm's "social bandits," a cangaceiro or a haiduk—if not Robin Hood, MacHeath, or Pancho Villa, then Schinderhannes or the Opportune Rain Sung Chiang.

His great gift, in fact, was to remember the excitement of ideas in action, and to refresh that memory with language, never cheating on the original exaltation no matter how many times he rewrote the events of his life as a yogi, lotus, robot, commissar, call-girl, or the ghost in his own machine—and Cesarani has counted them all, every revised word, in search of "stupendous act[s] of deception." In these pages, we are reacquainted with exactly what it felt like to read Karl May and Jules Verne, listen to Lehár operettas, and wait for the football scores as a child in Budapest; to discover Rilke, Heine, Hölderlin, Strindberg, Ibsen, and Hamsun as a precocious adolescent, as well as Darwin and Kepler; to experience both a revolution (Béla Kun) and a counterrevolutionary terror (Admiral Horthy) at age thirteen; to fall in love, as a student in Vienna, with Einstein, Bohr, Heisenberg, Adler, and Jung; to look for a cause in Palestine, a brothel in Paris, a job in Berlin, the future in Bokhara, Samarkand, and Tashkent (with a laidback Langston Hughes as his companion), and the North Pole from a graf zeppelin; to consort with Wilhelm Reich, Karl Radek, André Malraux, Alfred Döblin, Ignazio Silone, George Orwell, Thomas Mann, Dylan Thomas, Café Flor phenomenologists, Left Book Club social democrats, Congress for Cultural Freedom-Fighting Partisan Reviewers, and even Timothy Leary, who tripped him out on acid; to fear death in a Franco prison (while reading John Stuart Mill in Spanish) and then again in a French DP camp (where Walter Benjamin would slip him morphine); and to be unbelieved when he told everybody about the Final Solution and the Gulag.

To be sure, the novels were *romans à thèse*, too anal in their schematizing. But they were also true to the mythomaniacs who inhabited them. Whether, for instance, the Old Bolshevik Rubashov in *Darkness at Noon* was based on Bukharin or not, or even whether Bukharin really confessed at his own show trial, the case for revolution has seldom been better made, by a writer who had come to revile that revolution. Peter, in *Arrival and Departure*, leaves Portugal for almost certain death, in spite of a Jungian psychoanalysis by Sonia that not only persuades the reader of the childhood origins of his unconscious guilt, but persuades Peter, too. (And even the Nazi who goes on about the mineral veins of Europe as a sort of central nervous system is allowed to be more eloquent than any other Nazi I'm aware of in any other antifascist novel.) Like Koestler on his first trip to Palestine, Joseph in *Thieves in the Night* may have his doubts about a collective run on a woozy amalgam of the principles of Tolstoy and Marx, but we see him as well through the eyes of the communards, in all his vanity, impatience, and disdain for manual labor. *The Age of Longing* (1951), alas, was worse than ugly, it was smug— "To imitate the past and to abolish the past are equal sins against life," says Monsieur Anatole; "Therefore all reactionaries suffer from constipation and all revolutionaries from diarrhea"—but at least he got to do to Beauvoir what she had done to him. By the time he dialed up *The Call Girls* two decades later, he had lost this passionate knack and was reduced to ventriloquism, even if the dummies included W. H. Auden and Konrad Lorenz. Still, it had been a long run for a novelist of rambunctious ideas.

And over all this hectic activity, this compulsive curiosity and headlong rush to covenant, peril, repentance, and the raptures of the deep, these big ideas slapped on like adhesive plasters to the wounds of self, and the bigger discrepancies for which no poultice ever proved medicinal, he would spritz promiscuous metaphors and Homeric myth. It was as if, by literary fiat, in chapters of escapade with such neon headings as "From the Mount of Olives to Montparnasse," "Liberal Götterdämmerung," and "The Return of Ahor," he could aggrandize his only childhood, his "emotional measles" and traumatic tonsillectomy, his father's selling of radioactive soap and his mother's ever-so-convenient migraines, his "bridge-burning," vagabondage, and violent divestitures, unto a "language of destiny," an "invisible writing," and an "oceanic feeling," a "third order" and a parallel universe of "wonder rabbis," helpful shamans and wax-winged effigies of Icarus—into which Blue he shot his Arrow. This was thrilling, too, like grand opera, or Post-Impressionism, or Catherine Deneuve.

It's possible to forgive Cesarani his lax misspellings of Nicola Chiaromonte as "Nicolas," of James Fenimore Cooper with an extra *n*, and of the philosopher Zeno as "Xeno" (twice: a Greek paradox?); his risible description of Henry and Clare Boothe Luce as "pillars of the American liberal establishment"; and even his tricking up of a shaky thesis with pomoblab about "marginality," "contingency," "intertextuality," and "deterritorialised identities"—but not his tin ear for the work itself while he purses prim lips at erotic adventurism; not when he's tone-deaf in the middle of so much symphonic noise. Koestler may have come to distrust "the great nineteenth-century narratives of progress," but every bassoon note of that century's Romantic afflatus resounded in his prose and in his head. And for all his disenchantment, he would nevertheless maintain:

> In the 1930s conversion to the Communist faith was not a fashion or a craze—it was a sincere and spontaneous expression of an optimism born of despair: an abortive revolution of the spirit, a misfired Renaissance, a false dawn of history. To be attracted to the new faith was, I still believe, an honorable error. We were wrong for the right reasons.

I seem alone among my peer group to have kept on reading him through what K. called his "pilgrim's regress" into astronomy, ethnology, brain theory, parapsychology, and mysticism—*The Sleepwalkers, The Act of Creation, The Ghost in the Machine, Drinkers of Infinity, The Case of the Midwife Toad,* and *The Roots of Coinci-*

*dence.* The Kepler material was terrific, and *Creation* at least contained jokes. But the more he disappeared into subatomic particles and "supragalactic spaces," the less persuasive he became, arguing science by random analogy, citing anecdotes as proofs, picking and choosing among half-grasped experiments on a frantic bias, buying into neo-Lamarckian fantasies of inherited memory and J. B. Rhine's spoon-bending down at paranormal Duke, infatuated with prime numbers and flatworms, going almost Zen on us with "holons" and "hierarchies," prematurely sociobiologizing: instead of Communism, "cosmic consciousness"; instead of fraternity, "collective mind" and "disincarnate mental energy"; instead of dialectical materialism, "bisociation" (a mating of "matrices" along "integrative gradients"); instead of revolution, self-transcendence and a death wish and better living through modern chemistry and super enzymes (a pill to pacify the limbic "crocodile" in our old reptilian brains).

To his credit, Cesarani slogs through all this, when you know he'd really rather talk some more about the many abortions Koestler foisted on his "masochistic" wives and groupies, the daughter he refused to see, his "pathological need to wander," his "pathological promiscuity" and his "feeble" attempts at suicide—before, of course, fed up with Parkinson's and lympathic leukemia, he finally succeeded in finishing himself off, taking his much younger last wife and his much-loved old dog with him. But I'm inclined to agree with the Nobel Prize–winning biologist Peter Medawar—no fan of pseudoscience—who refused to discuss astrology at cocktail parties because "I prefer to let sleeping unicorns lie."

Well, then, homelessness: Where's the mystery? He had been raised to expect a secular culture capable not only of assimilating but of embracing and promoting someone with his manifold talents. It should have been possible, in Wittgenstein's Vienna, to listen to Mozart or Schoenberg, read von Hoffmansthal or Herzel, go to a play by Schnitzler, look at Secessionists, consult Freud, and consume a Sacher torte. It should have been possible, in Weimar Berlin, to listen to Weill and Hindemith, read Kafka and Rilke, look at Grosz and Dix, go to plays by Brecht and Piscator, and lollygag with Gropius in a Bauhaus. But they kept closing the borders, burning the books, banning the music, and killing the thinkers, until there were no more homes, only camps. In this respect Koestler was every bit as "representative" of his generation as he wanted us to think, no matter how much Cesarani needs him to be some singular subspecies. Like most of the Left in this century, he didn't believe in God, and who can blame him? He tried Israel and didn't like it: also hardly unique. He settled in England, where he was at last as safe as Spinoza had been in Amsterdam. Isaiah Berlin once quoted Kant at him: "Out of the crooked timber of humanity no straight thing was ever made"—not even by super enzymes. I'm sorry this "Casanova of Causes" was personally such a swine, the way I'm sorry John left Paul for Yoko. But I prefer to remember Koestler as the Pest from Buda, the refugee stormbird, who, almost singlehandedly, got capital punishment abolished in his very last stepfatherland.

# MARY McCARTHYISM

A T B A R D , Mary McCarthy gave a Russian Novel party. Students were asked to come dressed up as their favorite characters. Mary, of course, was Anna Karenina. I mean, who else? Father Zossima? "Our Diana," poemed Robert Lowell, "rash to awkwardness. . . . Whose well-shot arrows sing cleaner through the pelt?" He also called her a Dark Age luminary and an Irish hothead. Of the hundreds of people who talked to Frances Kiernan for her delicious new biography, *Seeing Mary Plain*—posting, as it were, on a M.M. website—more than one recalls her as "a black-haired Grace Kelly." That she identified with Catiline in a Latin Club play at the Annie Wright Seminary is easy to imagine. That she was the Virgin in a nativity pageant later on at Vassar is a bit harder. But when an angry nun in parochial school told her, "You're just like Lord Byron, brilliant but unsound," she was positively thrilled.

Not that there weren't dissenting opinions. From Rosalind Baker Wilson, for instance, the angry stepdaughter: "She was Anna Karenina without the warmth, and if there was a Vronsky, he was not a handsome officer but a complicated Jewish intellectual." For Delmore Schwartz, she was always "the whore," which didn't prevent him from making a pass, as did Paul Tillich, Arthur Koestler, John Berryman, and Igor Stravinsky. Saul Bellow, who hasn't a nice thing to say about anyone in these many pages, thought that she was beautiful but "in a sort of enameled way. I mean, she had a perfect exterior finish. It was a little unnatural." To Alfred Kazin, she was "too clever and talkative. And then there was that Irish jaw." And although Randall Jarrell had praised her stories to butter up her important husband, he turned on her in *Pictures from an Institution:* "Torn animals were removed at sunset from that smile."

But the bullyboys at *Partisan Review* were used to dishing it out, not taking it. And Mary usually gave better than she got. Very early on, for instance, in "The Man in the Brooks Brothers Suit"—about a one-night stand in a Pullman sleeper that could have been the inspiration for the car-wash episode of *Ally McBeal*—she summed up her experience so far with the opposite sex:

> And if she had felt safe with the different men who had been in love with her it was because—she saw it now—in one way or another they were all of them lame ducks. The handsome ones, like her fiancé, were good-for-nothings, the reliable ones, like her husband, were peculiar-looking, the well-to-do ones were short and wore lifts in their shoes or fat with glasses, the clever ones were alcoholic or slightly homosexual, the serious ones were foreigners or else wore beards and black shirts or were desperately poor and had no table manners. Somehow each of them was handicapped for American life and therefore humble in love. And was she too disqualified, did she really belong to their fraternity of cripples, or was she not a sound and normal woman who had been spending her life in self-imposed exile, a princess among trolls?

Note the dying fall and saving qualm, the characteristic turning of the scissors on herself for the briefest of bloody snips. She had been theatrical—Hotspur! Trotsky! Cinderella!—even before she started saying terrible things about Tennessee Williams, Eugene O'Neill, and Arthur Miller in her *PR* "Theatre Chronicle." But she had also been masochistic, turning her satirical eye on her posturing self: "an ardent literary little girl in an Episcopal boarding school on the West Coast, getting up at four in the morning to write a seventeen-page medieval romance before breakfast, smoking on the fire-escape and thinking of suicide, meeting a crippled boy in the woods by the cindery athletic field, composing a novelette in study hall about the life of a middle-aged prostitute." If she became notorious, at age twenty-three, for shooting the wounded in a *Nation* survey of the state of American book-reviewing, she would be no less merciless reviewing herself: "Laughter is the great antidote for self-pity, maybe a specific for the malady. Yet probably it does tend to dry one's feelings out a little, as if by exposing them to a vigorous wind. . . . There is no dampness in my emotions, and some moisture, I think, is needed to produce the deeper, the tragic notes." Besides: "Something happens in my writing—I don't mean it to—a sort of distortion, a sort of writing on the bias, seeing things with a sort of swerve and swoop."

Well, I'm writing on a bias too. Beware of swerves and swoops. "Before I met her," Mary Gordon tells us, "I often had a big fantasy . . . I knew she had a son, so I thought what I would try to do was marry her son and she could be my mother-in-law." My own fantasy—since high school, when *A Charmed Life* (1955) sent me immediately back to *Cast a Cold Eye*, *Groves of Academe*, *The Oasis* and (oh my) *The Company She Keeps*—was hairier. Ideas had genitals! My adolescent conviction that everything would've been better for both of us if only I'd been born twenty-five years earlier, or she had waited to appear for another generation, was confirmed my freshman year of college, by *Memories of a Catholic Girlhood*. Like her, hadn't I grown up word-drunk and moon-maddened on the wrong ocean, gone off to an Ivy League finishing school where everybody had more money, and secretly feared disgracing myself in New York, among the high-browsing categorical imperatives, the Gogols, Babels, and Kafkas? But if this brainy woman, this "female Stendhal," this wild Irish orphan with the abusive Papist uncle and the secret Jewish grandmother, could go to bed with trolls like Philip Rahv and Edmund Wilson, surely there was hope for all of us. Remember the nerdiest!

By the time I finally did meet her, in the seventies, she was between her ferocious books on Vietnam and Watergate, settled into her fourth marriage, to the diplomat James West, and full of gray-eyed matronly advice, to be followed up with little blue aerograms from Paris, gently reproving. But the woman I saw was still Meg Sargent, and I still wanted to run away with her to Venice, where we would read Sylvia Townsend Warner's novel on the Revolution of 1848 and translate Simone Weil's essay on the *Iliad* into fierce

English. How it must gall the *PR* boys, in whatever circle of Dante's Inferno they were shipped to, on money laundered by the Congress for Cultural Freedom, to watch "the witch of Endor" get her fourth biography, to find that they are once more merely footnotes to her friendship with Hannah Arendt, and to see that we still care. No wonder Edmund Wilson hit her with a chair.

I have a theory—actually, a prejudice cross-dressing, as if for a Russian Novel party. Perhaps you remember Jim Barnett in "Portrait of the Intellectual as a Yale Man." He was the "regular young guy, anywhere in America" who came down in 1932 to New York from New Haven, where he could have been Bones but wasn't, to start writing about class war for liberal magazines as if it were a regular American thing to do. The Old Left loved him:

> Most men had come to socialism by some all-too-human compulsion— they were out of work or lonely or sexually unsatisfied or foreign-born or queer in one of a hundred bitter, irremediable ways. They resembled the original twelve apostles in the New Testament; there was no real merit in their adherence, and no hope, either. But Jim was like the Roman centurion or Saint Paul; he came to socialism freely, from the happy center of things, by a pure act of perception which could only have been brought about by grace; and his conversion might be interpreted as a prelude to the conversion of the world.

McCarthy appears to have modeled Jim on John Chamberlain, whose rightward passage from these bright beginnings took him first to the *New York Times* (where, in fact, he gamely reviewed *The Company She Keeps*: "its satire is administered as gently and as murderously as a cat administers death to a mouse"), then to Henry Luce, and finally to Bill Buckley's *National Review.* Which passage has an ironic echo: So, in a kind of antistrophe, must the ex-Communist ex-sinners at *National Review,* the James Burnhams and Frank Meyers, have rejoiced when Garry Wills showed up from the heartland in the late fifties—a prelude to the conversion of the world!—before civil rights and Vietnam caused him to apostasize.

But while these grizzled backroom Lefties, many of them European, most of them Jewish, all of them hard-drinking males, looked

out their windows on Washington Square for young men from the
Regular America to rally to their cause, blowing through the front
door, in high heels, came Mary McCarthy from Seattle and Jean
Stafford from Montana and Elizabeth Hardwick from Kentucky—
American beauty roses every one of them. ("Among Stalinist
males," Mary recalled, "the Trotskyists were believed to have a mo-
nopoly on 'all the beautiful girls.'") And the young women went not
only to their parties and barricades but also to their beds. What did
this signify? A reward for virtue? A miracle of faith? Perhaps even
*entitlement*? Who knew that the beautiful girls were taking notes,
and would publish stories, novels, and memoirs about *them*? At least,
later on, their guilty secrets were safe with the CIA.

She must have looked like a Permanent Revolution.

> *My sympathies rained equally on Communists, Socialists, Anarchists, and
> the brave Catholic Basques. My heart was tense and swollen with popular-
> front solidarity. I applauded the Lincoln Battalion, protested non-
> intervention, hurried into Wanamaker's to look for cotton-lace stockings: I
> was boycotting silk on account of Japan in China. I was careful to smoke only
> union-made cigarettes.* (Mary McCarthy, "My Confession")

For the politics, Carol Brightman's *Writing Dangerously* (1992) is a
better biography. From Brightman, we get a livelier sense of exactly
what happened to the anti-Communist Left in the Cold War—"the
sweetheart deal that American intellectuals enjoyed with the dark
angel of American government for nearly two decades." And what
Brightman sketched in broad scan has just received the close-up
treatment in Frances Stonor Saunders's new book, *The Cultural
Cold War: The CIA and the World of Arts and Letters*, full of what
McCarthy herself once called "the prurient details of moral deflo-
ration." Indulge this brief digression:

During the first two decades of the Cold War, the CIA, like its very
good friend the Ford Foundation, was "a large body of money com-
pletely surrounded by people who want some." The descriptive
phrase is Dwight Macdonald's, from an article on Ford in the *New
Yorker*. But Macdonald himself took money from the Agency, as an

associate editor for *Encounter* magazine in 1957. And so did so many other leading American intellectuals—professors, poets, novelists, critics, *Partisan Review* editors, even Action painters on the East Hampton barricades—that I'd stamp my foot in indignation if the subsequent shameless self-marketing of tenured greedheads in our own low time hadn't left me without a leg to stand on.

Fortunately, Saunders is indignant enough for both of us. With the help of the Freedom of Information Act, the cooperation of the embittered widow of a longtime apparatchik at the Congress for Cultural Freedom, excerpts from letters, memoirs, and minutes of the giddy period, and interviews with any number of breast-beaters, rationalizers, hairshirts, and tattletales, she has compiled an impeachment of the clerks that reads like a gossip column in *Lingua Franca*. She names so many compromised names that the reader, like W. C. Fields, must fight his way "through a wall of human flesh, dragging my goat and my canoe behind me." Jackson Pollock! George Orwell! Isaiah Berlin! Robert Lowell! Arthur Schlesinger Jr.!

Return with her to those thrilling days of yesteryear, when an elite Bruderbund of Ivy League Whiffenpoofs, a Skull and Bones patrician class of covert derring-doers, graduated from clandestine wartime service with "Wild Bill" Donovan and the OSS to clandestine peacetime geopoliticking with the CIA—and mounted a propaganda counteroffensive against Communism. That these Whiffenpoofs should have sought to co-opt "the Non-Communist Left" is no surprise. Nor is it a surprise that they did so by establishing highbrow magazines that towed the Anglo-American line and by subsidizing book publishers, museum programs, art exhibits, youth festivals, and what Arthur Koestler (who had turned a trick or two himself) would later mock as the "international academic call-girl circuit" of lofty symposia in agreeable spas like Bellagio.

Better in fact that they should have been spending their slush fund, mostly "counterpart" monies left over from the Marshall Plan, on the occasional bloodless *Kulturkampf* than on such other Agency activities as breaking up strikes by dockworkers in Marseilles, rigging the Italian elections, overthrowing Mossadegh in Iran in 1953 and Arbenz in Guatemala in 1954, plotting to assassinate dozens of foreign leaders, spying on tens of thousands of American citizens, the Bay of Pigs in 1961, the Phoenix program in Vietnam, and lying to Congress like a Persian carpet. Paying for one group of American intellectuals (Mary McCarthy among them) to shout "Softies!" at another group of American intellectuals (among them Lillian Hellman) at a conference on world peace at the Waldorf Astoria Hotel in New York City in 1949, while banging the floor with their umbrellas and chaining themselves to their chairs, even sounds like college beer-blast fun.

But what does surprise is how easy it was. While CIA case officers like Frank Wisner and Tom Braden worried constantly about being exposed in the unbought media, the intellectuals they suborned went on eagerly, cluelessly scribbling. Despite rumors about *Encounter* that reached such remote precincts as my own California high school by the mid-fifties, nobody in London ever seemed to notice either Malcolm Muggeridge or those thick brown envelopes of cash he brought to the magazine's offices at regular intervals. (Through lapdog foundation fronts that funded the Congress for Cultural Freedom, the CIA paid most of *Encounter*'s expenses, including salaries for Irving Kristol and Melvin Lasky. But MI6 was responsible for the co-editor, Stephen Spender, and his secretary.) After *Ramparts* blew the lid off of all this scamming in 1967, a lot of embarrassed people insisted that no one had ever told them what to say. But, of course, a higher power had determined who would edit the magazine, inviting whom to contribute on what subjects, which subjects didn't include, for instance, red-baiting on the domestic front or such adventurisms abroad as Vietnam. And for a long time nobody cared where the money came from, so long as it ended up their way. They had been out in the cold so long, kvetching, that this warm official embrace seemed no more than their overdue.

*Encounter*, then, in London. In Paris, *Preuves*. In Berlin, *Der Monat*. In Vienna, *Forum*. In Italy, *Tempo Presente*. In Australia, *Quadrant*. In India, *Quest*. In Japan, *Jiyu*. Not to mention *Transition* (Uganda), *Hiwar* (in Arabic), *Cuadernos* (in Spanish), or *Science and*

*Freedom* and *Soviet Survey*. Nor does Saunders neglect the Agency's assistance to the *Partisan, Kenyon, Hudson,* and *Sewanee Reviews,* plus *Daedalus* and the *New Leader,* through grants and subscriptions and tax-exempt fronts and IRS loopholes. Besides enabling Frederick Praeger to publish more than twenty books, the CIA subsidized at least another thousand, from Lasky's very own *La Révolution Hongroise* to new editions of Machiavelli's *The Prince* to a Russian translation of T. S. Eliot's *Four Quartets* air-dropped on the evil empire from helium balloons.

Publishers like Cass Canfield and Hamish Hamilton were on the take, and almost all of John Crowe Ransom's "boys" at the *Kenyon Review,* not to mention Aaron Copland, James T. Farrell, Robert Motherwell, Allen Tate, Virgil Thomson, Robert Penn Warren, and Tennessee Williams. And, oh my, the foundations that funneled the funds from one pocket to the next, with seldom a smirk—Wright Patman's 1964 Congressional investigation only scratched an old-boy network surface that included Ford, Rockefeller, Carnegie, Chase Manhattan, and Welch's Grape Juice. Among many other beneficiaries of such spook largesse, we find the American Council of Learned Societies, the Modern Language Association, the Boston Symphony Orchestra, the New York City Ballet, Derek Walcott, Lionel Trilling, and PEN.

Sidney Hook, Carson McCullers, W. H. Auden, Clement Greenberg, A. J. Ayer, Mark Rothko, Reinhold Niebuhr, and the Alsop brothers! Did you know that, once upon a time, James Michener, Peter Matthiessen, and William Sloane Coffin worked for the CIA? That Peter Falk was turned down because he had belonged to a left-wing union? That Julia Child had been up to something surreptitious in Chungking? That Eugene Fodor was more than willing to let his travel guides be used as mobile fronts? That after Robert Lowell went crazy behind the Tortilla Curtain, in Buenos Aires, the Agency deemed it safer to rely on Robert Penn Warren and Norman Podhoretz to sabotage the hopes of Pablo Neruda for a Nobel Prize in Literature, even as the FBI was busy sabotaging the hopes of William Carlos Williams to become Poetry Consultant to the Library of

Congress? That Henry Luce told *Time* reporters to provide Agency cover, and that William Paley insisted that CBS correspodents were briefed each year at tête-à-têtes with Allen Dulles in his George-town home or at his private club, The Alibi? Could I make any of this up? Aren't you pleased as pink to know that Leslie Fiedler's famous essay in *Encounter*, rooting on the execution of the Rosenbergs, was paid for by American intelligence?

In the postmodern era where almost every professional wisehead is a paid-for corporate Pinocchio, a sardine in a think-tank, or a fu-turist spook; where they stampede over one another on their free-market way to an Op-Ed parking space or a yakshow cable-TV camera; where they sell, lease, or leverage their skepticism, their intellectual property rights, their first-born children, and their double helix to the highest bidder straight out of progressive preschool—all this must seem quaint. But perhaps it explains why so much of the rest of the world tends to assume that our journalists, novelists, scientists, labor leaders, and even our exchange students are secret agents of the imperium of Mickey Mouse.

But while Mary McCarthy went to some of these Whiffenpoof parties, Carol Brightman makes it clear in *Writing Dangerously* that she could never keep either her eyes or her mouth shut. The orphan from the West, the poor girl at rich Vassar, the woman among men, the panther among porcupines, had a moral compass that pointed away from doctrinaire politics, toward magnetic poles like the anarchism of Carlo Tresca and the passive resistance of Gandhi. Of Gandhi, she wrote in 1948: "Was [he] murdered, as his assassin claimed, because of what he stood for on the Indian question, or rather because what he stood for in his life—simplicity, good humor, steadfastness—affronted his assassin's sense of human prob-ability?" This, says Brightman, is the same question she asked about the assassination of Tresca, and even of Trotsky, with much the same answer: "to the murderer, the serenity of the victim comes as a last straw." She would go on to find a similar "goodness" in figures as different as Ho Chi Minh and, during the Watergate hearings, Sena-tor Sam Ervin. It was also the light—of Virgil and Dante in a sphere of hell—in which she examined the bomb on Hiroshima, "a kind of hole in human history."

From Frances Kiernan, on the other hand, we get the psychodrama, minute by minute, house by house, and it's scrumptious reading, with choral commentary at the end of each soap-operatic episode by everyone who remembers differently, wants to set the record straight, has old scores to settle, or just loves to dish—from Isaiah Berlin, Jason Epstein, and Elizabeth Hardwick to Arthur Schlesinger Jr., Gore Vidal, and Helen Wolff. *Seeing Mary Plain* is a sort of Wagnerian Rinse Cycle of the higher gossip. If, as applied to Mary, "bitch" was a noun, applied to the rest of her toothy circle it was a verb so active as to amount to a vocation. William Phillips, for instance, recalling from his more practical perch her gloomy scruples about atom bombs:

> My main criticism is that she substituted morality for politics. She was always moralizing. She was always taking the high road. It could be annoying.

Or Alison Lurie, who obviously learned a lot from Mary about social satire, and has this to say about her marriage to Edmund Wilson:

> Going with a stronger older man was then and still is now a way of getting ahead in the world. It is a way of instantly skipping ten or twenty years socially and professionally. There's a downside to this that comes later when you realize that you're only Mrs. So-and-So. It's a trade-off. But if you go into it with your eyes open, it does have its advantages. It can work out if you're fast on your feet, like Mary was.

Or Susan Sontag, who was next in line after her as the obligatory, one-at-a-time Dark Lady of American Letters, the box seat for which Camille Paglia has been auditioning for about a decade now, an endowed Cher:

> The one thing that follows from her being so pretty, which I've seen in my own knowledge of women and men, is that extremely beautiful people don't care about good looks in their partners. The great beauties often

have homely mates. The Greta Garbos, as it were. They don't care. They've got enough beauty for two.

And so again, the Dickensian childhood and the Vassar literary magazine (with Muriel Rukeyser and Elizabeth Bishop: why didn't *they* make it into *The Group?*); the affair with Rahv and the marriage to the alcoholic minotaur; failed psychoanalysis, savage stories, gourmet cooking, and Dwight Macdonald's *politics*; Nicola Chiaromonte and Hannah Arendt; Bernard Berenson, James Jones, Max Ascoli, and Pham Van Dong; Dick Cavett, egging her on, and Lillian Hellman, the wrath of God in Blackgama mink; Mary in Florence, Paris, Castine, and Hanoi, while, of course, Eichmann was in Jerusalem. Writing to Hannah, whose *Eichmann* had been attacked as savagely as *The Group*, McCarthy was still enough of a stylist to turn a nifty phrase:

> It occurs to me that a desire to make a sensation has taken precedence in New York over everything else. . . . If I am upset, I can imagine what you must be. And combining being upset for you and upset for myself has made my head spin. In this revolving door one is caught without an exit, and in this multiple vision—like a Picasso image—there is no cheek left to turn.

Nor does anybody turn one in the multiple vision and Moscow Trial of *Seeing Mary Plain*, which ends up as fish-eyed as Picasso. Did you know that William Shawn once asked her to do for Jerusalem what she'd done to Venice and Florence, and aren't you sorry that she declined? That when Mary turned him down, Arthur Koestler promptly pounced on Elizabeth Hardwick? That Hardwick and Philip Rahv both complained to amused third parties about each other's performance in bed? That Hardwick, Eugene McCarthy, and Renata Adler all show up as characters in *Cannibals and Missionaries*? That before he became a professor of D. H. Lawrence and W. B. Yeats, F. W. Dupee slummed as a labor organizer on the New York City waterfront? That the *New York Review* rejected Pauline Kael's review of *The Group* in favor of Norman Mailer's vial of bile? That Saul Bellow thinks that Edmund Wilson looked like Mister Magoo?

That Isaiah Berlin hated Hannah Arendt? That Allen Tate and Caroline Gordon deserved each other, giving the rest of us a break? So what if Mary reviewed *A Streetcar Named Desire* without even mentioning Marlon Brando? The lesson of Philoctetes, as one of her husbands taught us himself, is that if you want the artist, you have to take her wounds and all.

Because she made fun of herself, the tendency has been to think of McCarthy's politics as lacking the higher seriousness of, say, a Trilling or a Hook. (Never mind that she behaved with more principle during the Joe McCarthy rampage, and opposed, in print, our war on Vietnam as early as 1964, and was no more satisfied by verdicts in the My Lai trials of Calley and Medina than she would be by Nixon White House cover stories on the Plumbers. So the books she wrote on these grave matters weren't as good as the books that Frances FitzGerald, Michael Herr, David Halberstam, or Woodward and Bernstein wrote. But where were the books by Rahv or Phillips, by Lionel Abel or William Barrett?) Because she slept with, by her count, perhaps a hundred men, and married four of them—"I have seldom been capable of living without love, not for more than a month"—the tendency has been to write her off as a slyboots bimbo. (Never mind that Mailer, Bellow, Wilson, and even Rahv seem never to have slept alone.) Because she disdained sixties feminism, the tendency has been to forget that the movement had many mothers and she was not the least of them, breaking the double standard even among eggheads, refusing to be victimized. (Kiernan is especially interesting on her inspirational value to Monique Wittig, Mary Gordon, Diane Johnson, and Renata Adler.) Because she went on at such length about clothes, furniture, food, and pessaries, the tendency has been to Tom Wolfe or Judith Krantz her. (But she was a nineteenth-century novelist, wanting always to know how things worked, where the money came from, who did what to whom—"What I do is take real plums and put them in an imaginary cake"—and at least she wrote and wrote and wrote, instead of drinking and raving.) Because *The Group* was a bad book, and *Birds of America* even worse, the tendency has been to ignore the excel-lence of *The Company She Keeps, Memories of a Catholic Girlhood, The Writing on the Wall,* and *Venice Observed.* (So she couldn't be bothered to read Pynchon or Roth or Walker Percy. Just look what happened when she read Nabokov or Burroughs, not to mention Orwell, Salinger, and Dr. Kinsey.)

She believed in loyalty, friendship, honor, love, reason, and the Enlightenment. She stood up for things, says Inge Morath, who knew her in Paris: "She was a true artist in that she didn't have a small mind. She was like a young chevalier with his sword. You know gallant soldiers don't always defend the right side." I still imagine her skinnydipping like Lord Byron in Connecticut, among ungrateful trolls. What she really needed, besides me, was another Troy to burn.

# ELIZABETH HARDWICK
# MEETS HERMAN MELVILLE

ELIZABETH HARDWICK and the whale: although it is very dark inside the whiteness, she will read her way by oil lamp to Melville, "the most bookish of writers, a tireless midnight student." Thigh-high in ambergris and spermaceti, she makes herself as much at home as on the prison ship, or the cannibal islands, or the Berkshire farm where Herman wrote in twelve-hour shifts, or inside the Manhattan townhouse down whose stairs he may have tossed his wife. Wherever and whatever—novels, letters, and biographies; marriage and derangement; carnival or crypt—Hardwick always moves in with her subject. And before she entertains, she will have picked the locks, ransacked the closets, let the madwomen out of the attic, brought up bodies from the basement, and bounced on the double bed like Goldilocks or Freud.

About this brilliant domesticity, there is also a jujitsu. "How certain human beings are able to create works of art is a mystery," she wrote in an essay on Katherine Anne Porter, "and why they should wish to do so, at a great cost to themselves usually, is another mystery." This seems amiable enough. Likewise, in a discussion of Nadine Gordimer, she might be describing her own critical method: "Note the way the author opens the plot, arranges the magical correspondences, finds the fixed points, and sets them in a broad open space where many drifting, always to the point, things can wander." We are so comfortable in such company that we lean on her, as if she were a brother or a broom. And then all of a sudden, by rag doll twinkletoes and sleight-of-hand, we are head over heels. We have been thrown by our own weight, tumbled into deeper meanings, rueful reflections, and surprise perspectives. (Is Holly Golightly in *Breakfast at Tiffany's* a plagiarism of Sally Bowles in *Goodbye to Berlin*? In which ways did Gertrude Stein anticipate Philip Glass? And how dare Peter Conrad ever publish another book after her roadkill review of *Imagining America*?) If great literature is where we go alone to complicate ourselves, a criticism worthy of it has to be equally nuanced—not bullying, not preemptive, not reductive, and certainly not French, but subversive of lazy or reflex opinion. Once we have read William James, Margaret Fuller, Eugene O'Neill, Sylvia Plath, Robert Frost, Nathaniel Hawthorne, and Thomas Mann through Hardwick's all-seeing eye, they are more interesting and so are we.

And Melville, our first modern! She has been after him for decades. He shows up in her pages almost as often as Tolstoy (*The Kreutzer Sonata*) and Dreiser (*Sister Carrie*). There was, of course, the famous essay that gave her the title for her collection, *Bartleby in Manhattan*, in which Melville's story—"of austere minimalism, of philosophical quietism, of radical literary shape, of consummate despair, and withal beautiful in the perfection of the telling"—sounded in her radar reading of it as if it had been written by Samuel Beckett, of whose *Endgame* she has said elsewhere that it is "complete, merciless," with "a sort of therapeutic beauty and truth, like the sight of an open grave . . . overpowering in the purity of its deathly summations." But Herman is also mentioned when she is saying all those negative things about Simone de Beauvoir, and again in the middle of all those positive things about Joan Didion. *Pierre* appears in her exquisite exploration of the ambiguities of John Cheever, and *Billy Budd* in her cross-burning of a twiggy Billy Graham. And she probably heard more than she needed to about *Benito Cereno* in the early 1960s, when Robert Lowell was turning it into a play; he liked to read his stuff aloud a lot.

Naturally, she'd be fascinated by the prehistory of a well-born family reduced to shabby gentility by its "genetic disposition to bankruptcy." (One of Herman's grandfathers dumped tea into Boston Harbor, and the other torched villages and massacred Mohawks during the Revolutionary War.) As she would be in the psychodynamics of the lost father (dead when Herman was twelve), the difficult mother (who loved his older brother best), the dreamy little boy (slow to talk and slower to read), and the long, odd marriage of this self-described "isolato"; his hard drinking, manic depression, and unrequited love affair with Hawthorne; the cabin boy, merchant marine, castaway, and mutineer, who read everything from Rabelais and Dante to Kant and Carlyle, from Spinoza and Burke to Heine and Schopenhauer, from the *Travels of Marco Polo* to the *Confessions* of Rousseau, plus Thomas Maurice's seven-volume *History of Hindostan*; who published ten astonishing books in eleven years, and yet ended up owing his publishers money; who spent his last nineteen years as a clerk in the Customs House, six days a week for four dollars a day, "living with cannibals in woolen suits and ties and yet tattooed with ignorance and greed," stuffing the pockets of his blue inspector's jacket with little squares of yellow paper on which he jotted notes for the epic poem about the Holy Land— 18,000 lines divided into 150 cantos—that he was writing secretly at night ("an act of defiance," says Hardwick, "a scream for the scaffold"), not to mention *Billy Budd*, which they discovered in a tin breadbox and only published in 1924, three decades after his death; who despised industrialism and capitalism, colonialism and imperialism, Indian-killing and slavery, missionaries and God.

On the one hand, as Father Mapple warned us in his *Moby-Dick* sermon on Jonah: "But Faith, like a jackal, feeds among the tombs, and even from these dead doubts she gathers her most vital hope." On the other, according to *Pierre*: "By vast pains we mine into the pyramid; by horrible gropings we come to the central room; with joy we espy the sarcophagus; but we lift the lid—and nobody is there!—appallingly vacant as vast is the soul of man!" Reviewing *The House of the Seven Gables*, Melville must have been thinking more about himself than Hawthorne: "He says NO! in thunder; but the Devil himself cannot make him say *yes*. For all men who say *yes*, lie; and all men who say *no*,—why they are in the happy condition of judicious, unencumbered travellers in Europe; they cross the frontiers into Eternity with nothing but a carpet-bag,—that is to say, the Ego." In his personal copy of the poems of Wordsworth, he underscored these lines: "The marble index of a mind forever / Voyaging through strange seas of Thought, alone."

Besides which, there was his sex life. Hardwick explains:

> Obsession and a compulsive need for *confession;* homoerotic intrusions came into his writing again and again with an unknown intention; subliminal matter, unconscious or boldly aware? Perhaps he is as blind as his readers, unacquainted with the naming of irregular impulses. Love scenes on the beach of his fiction lay undisturbed like any other specimen of conchology. Later readers picked up the bright shells with the avidity of collectors and would find that the crinkles and striations once held a secret, troubled heart.

It is this Melville—"Natural husband and father or one swimming in oceanic homoerotic yearnings?"—that Hardwick chooses to emphasize. It is well-plowed ground, from a cheeky Leslie A. Fiedler in *Love and Death in the American Novel* to the troubled but scrupulous Laurie Robertson-Lorant in her deeply affecting 1996 biography, *Melville,* from which Hardwick and I both borrow. But Melville-and-sexuality seems to be what everyone is interested in, except James Wood in *The Broken Estate,* who prefers Melville-and-Calvinism.

Thus, once more into the breach, which is what whales do when they leap out of the water. Or into the breech, which pertains more to male-bonding behavior among nineteenth-century sailors as theorized in contemporary scholarship on closet writing and gay reading. There is plenty of material to work with: in *Typee,* the Kory-Kory who seems at least as desirable as the bathing beauty Fayaway. In *Redburn,* the homosexual hustler Harry Bolton, the oil paintings of fellatio on the walls in a male brothel, and our narrator's feelings about Carlo, the Italian boy who plays a hand organ. In *Moby-Dick,* Ishmael and Queequeg's bedding down at the Spouter-Inn, and the notorious sperm-squeezing scene on the *Pequod.* In *Pierre,* the subplot about incest, which could be coded. In the epic poem *Clarel,* a

Mother Goddess, bisexual dreams, and the pilgrim's confusion of erotic attachments among beautiful Ruth, deformed Celio, and the young man from Lyona with a "rich, tumbled, chestnut hood of curls" as pretty as "a Polynesian girl's." And in *Billy Budd*, the Handsome Sailor himself, "all but feminine in purity of natural complexion," for whom, we are told, the malign Master-at-Arms feels an unspoken "touch of soft yearning, as if Claggart could even have loved Billy but for fate and ban." Even Starry Vere, says Hardwick, "is half in love with the Angel of God."

To which we must add Hawthorne, to whom *Moby-Dick* was dedicated, of whom unfriendly things would be said in *Clarel*. They were neighbors in the Berkshires, until Hawthorne defected to Concord. Melville, so desperate for any kind of intellectual kinship, seems to have inflated a few kind words into what Hardwick calls an "apostolic union," gushing in a letter: "Whence come you Hawthorne? By what right do you drink from my flagon of life? And when I put it to my lips—lo, they are yours, not mine. I feel that the Godhead is broken up like the bread at the Supper, and that we are the pieces." Still, Hawthorne never wrote a phrase of praise for *Moby-Dick*, which had been published to savage reviews and public indifference one year after the best-selling *Scarlet Letter*. The most he'd ever do for Melville's reputation was leave behind, for scholars to worry, a journal note on Herman's visit to his consular post in Liverpool in 1856: "Melville, as he always does, began to reason of Providence and futurity, and of everything that lies beyond human ken, and informed me that he had 'pretty much made up his mind to be annihilated'; but still he does not seem to rest in that anticipation; and, I think, will never rest until he gets hold of a definite belief."

The trouble was, Nathaniel already had the devoted Sophia. And he was later busy writing a campaign biography for Franklin Pierce. (As William Dean Howells would write a campaign biography for Abe Lincoln. How else had we imagined these nineteenth-century writers got themselves appointed as diplomats to Liverpool and Venice?) "It would seem the chagrin lies in personal inequality of affection," says Hardwick, to which she gives her usual mordant spin: "a

condition more often found in sentimental fiction than in life."
Robertson-Lorant informs us, besides, that Hawthorne had been on
his guard against physically demonstrative men ever since as a child
he'd been required, until age fifteen, to sleep with his uncle. Sophia
herself let us know that her husband "hates to be touched more than
anyone I ever knew." And from Hardwick's own magnificent essay
on Margaret Fuller, whom Hawthorne cruelly ridiculed in more
venues than *The Blithedale Romance*, even after her death by
drowning, we have reason to doubt not only his generosity, but his
decency. "Her culture was greater than his," says Hardwick, "and
greater than he needed."

Come to think it of it, wasn't Fuller's urgent need of Emerson's
approval pretty much the same as Melville's of Hawthorne's, and
equally unreciprocated? Aren't we really talking about needy ge-
niuses with father problems? But I have never found Melville's
sexuality, the truth of which we'll never know, as compelling as his
politics, about which the evidence is so abundant, even thrilling.
"The renegade," says Hardwick, with "the scars of knowing, choosing, the bleak underside of life." For all his obsessing about colonialism and slavery—cannibalism was his metaphor for economic and
social injustice; "white civilized man [is] the most ferocious animal
on the face of the earth"—he should certainly have been included
in Toni Morrison's *Playing in the Dark*. In *Mardi*, John C. Calhoun
himself is caricatured, arguing that slaves are soulless. Try to imagine the shock of meeting, in the 1850s in *Benito Cereno*, a black man
like Babo: "The head, that hive of subtlety, fixed on a pole, met,
unabashed, the gaze of the whites." Never mind that Hawthorne,
Emerson, Thoreau, Poe, Henry Ward Beecher, and Horace Greeley
all show up in *The Confidence-Man*; observe its chapter on "The
Metaphysics of Indian-Hating." When Irving Howe belatedly discovered *Redburn*, what he got out of it wasn't homoeroticism but an
exhilarating sense of American fraternity; of a young Melville "as
the tenderfoot only a step or two away from the greenhorn." Hardwick quotes Herman, among the poor, the diseased, and beggarly,
the Chartist soap box orators and the mixed-race romantics, in

dreary Liverpool: "You cannot spill a drop of American blood without spilling the blood of the whole world. . . . Our blood is as the
flood of the Amazon, made up of a thousand currents all pouring into
one. We are not a nation, so much as a world." The *Pequod* chasing
after the white whale, with Queequeg, Tashtego, Daggoo, and Pip,
is a dreamboat of multiculturalism as much as a ship of fools.
(Robertson-Lorant makes a good case for *Moby-Dick*'s debt to Native American folklore and myth—the vision quest, the sweat
lodge, the Ghost Dance—in addition to the usual biblical, Homeric,
Promethean, Shakespearean, and Faustian suspects.) And whether
or not *White-Jacket* was decisive in persuading Congress to abolish
flogging in the American navy, it obviously helped.

So "spectral Herman" went away in his own head after he could
no longer play with boats. Maybe he should never have married—
"His appalling 'celestial' labor and her earth-bound servitude,"
Hardwick tells us, "reduced them both to strange, well-born peons
landing in the cane fields"; they lost one son to suicide and another
to tuberculosis—even if his late-life "Rose Poems," written after he
had stopped drinking, suggest a return to marital fervor. I like to
think of his letting his granddaughters use his library books as building blocks; maybe he recalled the younger self who had been, after
jumping ship, a pinboy in a bowling alley in Honolulu. Anyway, this
sort of difficult marriage, which lasted forty-four years, is Elizabeth
Hardwick's specialty, from "George Eliot's Husband" to "Seduction
and Betrayal" to "Wives and Mistresses." She has earned the last
word:

> The marriage was more prudent for Melville than for his wife. He might
> have longed for male friendship, even for love, but marriage changed him
> from an unanchored wanderer into an obsessive writer, almost as if there,
> in a house, in a neighborhood, there was nothing else for this man to do
> except to use the capital he had found in himself.

But *his* words are what she cares most about, from the "wild, sunlit flow of adjective; an active, sonorous explosion of sheer sensation"
to "an azure, steel-blue streak of pity and loss" to the "loveliness of

whiteness in natural objects: marbles, japonicas, and pearls; royalty
mounted on white elephants or chargers; the innocence of brides;
the white ermine of judges; sacramental vestments"; after which we
must "yet consider the white bear of the poles and the white shark of
the tropics," not so innocent. Hardwick has always had the shaman's
gift of disappearing into writers she loves, speaking in their voices,
seeing through their eyes. Almost alone among our serious critics of
literature, she makes us *need* to read the books she has chosen to care
about. *Herman Melville* is quite short, but it will send us directly to
a lot of very long Melvilles. She has put on his "white savage" mask
like—well, like the foreskin of the sperm whale in *Moby-Dick*,
"stretched and dried by the ship's 'mincer,' [to become] large enough
for him to wear it as a 'canonical' cloak." "A wild impertinence" she
calls this ribald passage about foreskins turned into vestments. But
one reason we read both Melville and Hardwick is for such moments, when the great flood gates of the wonder-world swing open
and radical conceits sway us to their purpose.

"Oh, M.," she wrote in her novel *Sleepless Nights* (1979), by which
"M." she may or may not have meant Mary McCarthy, "when I
think of the people I have buried, North and South. Yet, why is it
that we cannot keep the note of irony, the jangle of carelessness at a
distance? Sentences in which I have tried for a certain light tone—
many of these have to do with events, upheavals, destructions that
caused me to weep like a child." Then, after a short poem and a
briefer reference to "a lifetime with its mound of men climbing on
and off," she appends: "The torment of personal relations. Nothing
new there except in the disguise, and in the escape on the wings of
adjectives. Sweet to be pierced by daggers at the end of paragraphs."
    Elizabeth Hardwick is eighty-three years and nine books old. She
has been putting on shaman skins, practicing jujitsu, picking locks,
and piercing paragraphs with daggers ever since the giddy days of
*Partisan Review*. (In her introduction to Mary McCarthy's *Intellectual Memoirs*, she gave us perhaps the best and certainly the most
succinct description of that "ring of bullies": "In that circle, the So-

viet Union, the Civil War in Spain, Hitler, and Mussolini were what you might call real life, but not in the magazine's pages more real, more apposite, than T. S. Eliot, Henry James, Kafka, and Dosto-evsky.") Quietly, with a serpent's tooth, a cat's paw, and a built-in shit-detector, with a deep focus and a zoom lens, with gravity and grace, she has put together a body of work as radiant and satisfying as a Mozart horn concerto.

Only by impudent inference is it possible to read portions of that work as autobiographical. She chose not, in *Sleepless Nights*, to write a rebuttal to *The Dolphin*. If, in Ian Hamilton's *Robert Lowell*, she was mostly an aggrieved spear-carrier in the grandly operatic psy-chodrama of the mad poet, that spear was heavy enough to caution us against the piling on of more dead weight. In *Partisans: Marriage, Politics, and Betrayal Among the New York Intellectuals*, David Laskin's tendentious put-down of Hardwick, McCarthy, and Jean Stafford for their messy private lives and their failure to be sixties feminists, he reads this paragraph from Hardwick's essay on Zelda Fitzgerald as personal, some sort of bean-spilling, and maybe so:

> Sick persons create guilt of a mysterious kind, whether by their own wish or merely by the peculiarities of their often luminous fixity. The will to blame, to hold them to account, soon appears futile to those closest. In-stead the mad entwine their relations in an unresolved, lingering, chafing connection, where guilt, exasperation and grief for the mysteries of life continue to choke. Perhaps the nearest feeling is the immensely suffering and baffling connection between those living and those slowly dying.

But it's also more eloquent and loving than anything in *Partisans*, whose generalizations about the "willed blindness" of "male-identified" career women are vulgar and cartoonish. Not only are marriage, madness, life, and literature more complicated than Laskin imagines, but even breakfast is more complicated. Of course, Hardwick has always been interested in literary couples, writers bent on self-destruction, and writers with terrible family secrets; in abandonment and nihilism and sex and betrayal. But she has also always been interested in writers who are women, writers who are lonely, writers who are American, English, French, and Russian,

writers who can really write, and all the books people keep on writing about these writers. And this is to scant her interest in murder,
from her second novel, *The Simple Truth* (1955), to her meditation
on Caryl Chessman in the gas chamber (1960), to her articles for the
*New York Review* on the trials of those pretty-boy voids, the Menen-
dez brothers, and, of course, O. J. and Nicole. And to ignore her in-
creasing suspicion that the body is a poor vehicle for transcendence.
Besides which, she actually went to and reported on a civil rights
march in Selma in 1965 and the funeral of Dr. Martin Luther King
Jr. in Atlanta in 1968. And she has also gone to and reviewed movies
and the theater.

Here's what's important about Hardwick, just skimming off the
top: her essays on David Riesman, Sylvia Plath, *The Scarlet Letter*,
Billy Graham, Simone Weil, Edith Wharton, Thomas Mann, John
Reed, Margaret Fuller, Gertrude Stein, John Cheever, Joan Didion,
Elizabeth Bishop, Truman Capote, *Bartleby the Scrivener*, Boston
and Brazil.

And here's what's wonderful about her, the shadow and the light:

On Dylan Thomas: "There was a certain amount of poison in our
good will."

On David Riesman: "But if you make yourself honey the flies will
eat you."

On Eugene O'Neill: "A certain humility is necessary about the
lowly, badly hammered nails if the poor house, completed, moves
you to tears. . . . Sometimes literature is not made with words."

On Henry David Thoreau: "It was [his] genius to carry landscape
and weather as far as they could go."

On Gertrude Stein: "Sturdy as a turnip."

On John Updike: "A bit of a parson, too, something icy inside the
melting flesh of concupiscence."

On Philip Roth: "Indeed the novels are prickled like a sea urchin
with the spines and fuzz of many indecencies."

On Katherine Anne Porter: "Research finds that in Germany,
Katherine Anne Porter did not always conduct herself with generosity or moral refinement."

On Truman Capote (and his "unique crocodilian celebrity"): "Capote never showed an interest in political or moral debate and perhaps this was prudent since ideas, to some degree, may define one's social life and could just be excess baggage he didn't need to bring aboard; and, worse, boring, like the ruins and works of art he declined to get off the yacht to see."

Or there is this unsurpassed passage in her great essay on "Seduction and Betrayal":

> The betrayed heroine, unlike the merely betrayed woman, is never under the illusion that love or sex confers rights upon human beings. She may, of course, begin with the hope, and romance would scarcely be possible otherwise; however, the truth hits her sharply, like vision or revelation when the time comes. Affections are not *things* and persons never can become possessions, matters of ownership. The desolate soul knows this immediately, and only the trivial pretend that it can be otherwise. When love goes wrong the survival of the spirit appears to stand upon endurance, independence, tolerance, solitary grief. These are tremendously moving qualities, and when they are called upon it is usual for the heroine to overshadow the man who is the origin of her torment. She is under the command of necessity, consequence, natural order, and a bending to these commands is the mark of a superior being. Or so it seems in the novel, a form not entirely commensurate with the heedlessness and rages of life.

So superior are these sentences to the churlishness that passes for criticism elswhere in our culture—the exorcism, the vampire bite, the vanity production, the body-snatching and the sperm-sucking—so generous and wise, that they seem to belong to an entirely different realm of discourse, where the liberal arts meet something like transubstantiation. There will be no dagger at the end of this paragraph. She sends up kites; she catches lightning.

# NORMAN PODHORETZ,
## ALONE AT LAST

IN *A PARTISAN VIEW*, one of the many memoirs in which score-settling refugees from the glory days of the anti-Stalinist, pro-Modernist quarterly pick each other's scabs, William Phillips remembers his co-editor, Philip Rahv, like so:

> He could not throw or catch a ball, ride a bike, play any game, or swim. He did not even seem to know that you can drown if you go in over your head. One summer when we had a house in Peekskill, Rahv came to visit and we went to swim at a nearby pool. Rahv flopped in, came up, gurgled, and went down again. He would have drowned if I had not jumped in and pulled him out. Fortunately, I had worked my way through school as a swimming counsellor and lifeguard.

You'll recognize in this passage at least four of the seven types of ambiguity identified by William Empson and embraced as theological dogma by the editors of the *Kenyon Review*, which was *Partisan Review*'s principal highbrow competition after the war. I love it. It reminds me of *Unspeakable Practices, Unnatural Acts,* when Donald Barthelme saved Robert Kennedy from drowning. One imagines Lionel Trilling, unable to make up his mind if Rahv deserves saving—or if getting wet is either authentic or sincere. And Mary McCarthy on a diving board, in her birthday suit because she's still boycotting silk since Japan invaded Manchuria, deciding that she'd really rather dog-paddle with Bunny Wilson instead. And Lionel Abel and Harold Rosenberg at the other end of the Olympic swimming hole, pushing Hannah Arendt's head underwater. And Irving Howe and Dwight Macdonald starting their own alternative

aquariums—one socialist, the other anarchist. While Meyer Scha-
piro explains to R. P. Blackmur, "Mr. Blackmur, when you use your
water wings, you don't use them *up!*" Meanwhile, in the cabana,
over and over like Punch and Judy, the axe comes down again on
Trotsky.

To this party, because he wrote a couple of books accusing these
people of sand-eating dune-buggery, Norman Podhoretz hasn't been
invited. So he will piss in their pool.

Not that Norman hasn't had his share of parties. In *Ex-Friends:
Falling Out with Allen Ginsberg, Lionel and Diana Trilling, Lillian
Hellman, Hannah Arendt, and Norman Mailer,* we learn that at Lillian Hellman's on Martha's Vineyard he met Leonard Bernstein and
William Styron. That at Truman Capote's Masked Ball at the Plaza
Hotel, hunkered down with Lillian and McGeorge Bundy, he had
had to dissuade Norman Mailer from duking it out with LBJ's national security adviser. That this same Mailer, who would subsequently stab Podhoretz in the back as he stabbed his wife, Adele, in
the upper abdomen, sought on several occasions to unlimber P. at
orgies. ("But I was simply not up to it," P. tells us.) That, in fact, the
editor of *Commentary* had been at that famous stabbing party, although he left early because Allen Ginsberg yelled at him.

On the other hand, Podhoretz invited Styron instead of Mailer to
have dinner with Jackie Kennedy, which is one reason why Mailer
panned *Making It* in *Partisan Review*—another reason being that,
fearful of losing his new-found late-sixties popularity, like "an old
Bolshevik fearful of being denounced as a traitor by his own Stalinist
comrades," Mailer "had been cowed into submission" by the reg-
nant "terror" of a Pod-hating "radical culture"; he was "not perhaps
as brave as he thought he was." Hadn't Norman M., after all, told the
Pod in private that he admired his book, before attacking it in public? Unlike the way Podhoretz praised Hellman's memoirs to her
face, because she was so "mischievous, bitchy, earthy, and always
up for a laugh"—while secretly despising "the political ideas and
attitudes in whose service she corrupted her work and brought . . .
lasting dishonor upon her name"—without ever, of course, saying

anything nice in *print*, which would have meant "corrupting my own writing or betraying those standards that were everything to me as a literary critic."

On the third hand, Lillian Hellman alone stood up for him when the rest of the world hated *Making It*. Even Jackie K. jumped off that poop deck.

Nor have I even mentioned the best Pod party of them all, in the fall of 1962, at a soirée sponsored by *Show* magazine on Paradise Island, a wholly owned subsidiary of Huntington Hartford off the Caribbean coast of Nassau:

> *This* was what Success looked like . . . and the look of it made me drunker than all the gallons of rum I consumed that week. This was what it meant to be rich: to sleep in a huge bright room with a terrace overlooking an incredibly translucent green sea, to stretch one's arms out idly by the side of a swimming pool and have two white-coated servants vie for the privilege of depositing a Bloody Mary into one's hands. . . . All around me, too, was the evidence of what it meant to be famous (for the North American delegation was mostly composed of people whose fame far outweighed my own meager measure of it): it meant that a serene self-assurance had been injected into the spirit to combat the uncertainties and anxieties which, to be sure, remained, but no longer had the field to themselves.

Paradise Island was for the author of *Making It* what that famous blaze of "indescribably white light" had been for Bill Wilson of Alcoholics Anonymous—either the sight of God or a "hot flash" of toxic psychosis, but definitely a conversion experience: "I loved everyone, and everyone loved me. I did not blame them; I even loved myself." Here, at last, he traded in the Cherokees S.A.C. red satin of his Brownsville tough-guy boyhood for a svelte suede jacket and an extension cord for his telephone. Norman no longer needed William Phillips, nor any other Elder of the *PR* Tribe. He had learned to swim with the sharks.

> *You may take sarza to open the liver; steel to open the spleen; flowers of sulphur for the lungs; castoreum for the brain; but no receipt openeth the heart but a true friend, to whom you may impart griefs, joys, fears, hopes, suspi-*

*cions, counsels and whatsoever lieth upon the heart to oppress it, in a kind of*
*civil shrift or confession.* (Francis Bacon)

*What men have given the name of friendship to is nothing but an alliance, a*
*reciprocal accommodation of interests, an exchange of good offices; in fact, it*
*is nothing but a system of traffic, in which self-love always proposes to itself*
*some advantage.* (La Rochefoucauld)

Except for Mailer, all of the ex-friends we meet in P.'s new book are
dead, than which no friend can be more emphatically ex. Whether
any were ever really friends is at least debatable, and he knows it.
Certainly not Ginsberg, a Columbia classmate and cohort Other.
(Bad Boy to Norman's Good.) The Trillings were *mentors*—placing
him at *Commentary*; seating him on the board of the American
Committee for Cultural Freedom. (Lionel, even now, is probably
looking down on him, like Laskell in *The Middle of the Journey:*
"He knew why they were angry at him. It was the anger of the
masked will at the appearance of an idea in modulation.") And Hellman seems merely to have been, as it were, a Party animal. (On one
page, P. allows that she was perhaps a life-long undercover Communist; on the next, he suggests that her commitment was more out of
loyalty to Dashiell Hammett than to the Soviet Union.) And Arendt,
who "certainly acted as though she liked me personally and thought
well of my work," had all along been secretly disparaging him in
letters to Mary McCarthy. (Maybe she was just buttering up Mary,
"our leading bitch intellectual," who never forgave P. for a negative
article he'd written about her in 1956.) Which leaves Mailer, on
whom he had conferred intellectual respectability; about whom in
*Making It* he was so shamelessly flattering; and whose new Jesus
novel he won't even read.

"Genuine friendship (or perhaps any kind of friendship at all) is
impossible with a writer whose work one does not admire," he rue-
fully concedes. For Podhoretz, who began his career by not admiring
Malamud's *The Natural* and Bellow's *Augie March*, and concludes it
by finding dishonor in everyone who didn't rejoice at *Making It* or
*Breaking Ranks*, this is a recipe for loneliness. And, indeed, *Ex-*

*Friends* hugs a latitude of loneliness—from the beginning ("there is hardly a one of my old friends left among the living with whom I am today so much as on speaking terms") to the end ("Conceivably, there are lively parties today to which I am not invited that are similar to the ones I used to go to and give. . . . But if similar parties are being held today, I think rumors of them would have reached me"). There is pathos here, among the bitters.

But we have also heard it all, twice before. These Norman Conquests, from Brownsville to Morningside Heights, from Columbia to Cambridge to *Commentary*, from *Partisan Review* to the Hudson Institute, were first rehearsed in *Making It* (1967), which also had shrewd things to say about the sticky tropics of highbrow, low-pay journalism. And were then repeated, word for word, with the same anecdotes and wisecracks, in *Breaking Ranks* (1979), to pad out a canned history of Holy Cold Warriorism. And are now trotted out yet again, between anathemas, with a best-selling eye on the more famous brand names. The not-quite-so-famous among his ex-friends, like Jason Epstein, are suddenly unmentionable.

Thrice-told, this Pilgrim's Progress from the mean streets where his father was a milk man to the dinner parties at the White House to the bunkers of the Olin and Bradley Foundations somehow coarsens. He was always a good boy, a teacher's pet, square, middle-class respectable, smarter than anybody else and never tempted by bohemia. Except for boot camp, he never even got his hands dirty. And except for the first five years of the sixties, when he imagined himself a radical because he published Paul Goodman, H. Stuart Hughes, and Staughton Lynd—although not, in 1962, an advance copy of the Port Huron Statement—he was also invariably right, while everybody else turned out to be either wrong or pusillanimous. No longer the Young Man from the Provinces, Julien Sorel, he is now an old man in a dry season, Gerontion, devoured by tigers. And after such knowledge, he is not about to forgive a mangy one of them.

What's been thrown overboard, of course, is what Alfred Kazin was referring to in the thirty-third anniversary issue of *Dissent:*

"When the great Reagan counterrevolution is over, what I shall remember most is the way accommodating intellectuals tried to bring to an end whatever was left among Jewish intellectuals of their old bond with the oppressed, the proscribed, the everlasting victims piled up now in every street."

Rereading *Making It*, one wants to calm P. down with a lollipop. It's okay, Norman, all of it—wanting money, status, power, fame. But what makes you think it's so *brave* to say so out loud? And why do you insist that everybody else wants these things just as much, all the time and forever, and if they pretend that they don't, they *must* be lying? Haven't you ever met *anyone* who had seconds thoughts on the subject? I know you don't get out much, but even in the library a little *Great Gatsby* is a purgative for too much Ayn Rand. A young fogy just as Oedipal about the old *Partisan Review* crowd as you are once informed a friend of mine, "You have a *job*; I have a *career*." Imagine that! The luminous thing! A motorscooter with a walkie-talkie! But haven't we all behaved, in our upwardly mobile whoosh, in various ways that would shame our mothers?

About this business of intellectuals suddenly getting paid to feel bad in the slicks, P. has a point worth pursuing. Besides Dwight Macdonald, Mary McCarthy, and Hannah Arendt all writing for the *New Yorker*—like Edmund Wilson, Alfred Kazin, and Lionel Trilling before them—as well as showing up to their own surprise in *Vogue, Life, Playboy*, and the *Saturday Evening Post*, had P. not been so preoccupied with his own cushy stint at Huntington Hartford's *Show*, he might have noticed Macdonald at *Fortune*, too, with John Kenneth Galbraith, and James Agee and Irving Howe at *Time*, which explains why they stopped writing for magazines like the *Nation*. While this might mean, as P. suggests, that they should no longer feel so alienated, it could also mean that they'd been bought, and risked confounding their self-interest with their employer's. This never happened to someone like, say, Bob Moses, whose career goals were less luminous than P.'s—who quit teaching at Horace Mann to spend the sixties enfranchising black sharecroppers in Mississippi, who spent the eighties and nineties bringing math literacy to inner-city schools with his Algebra Project, and who somehow never made it to Paradise Island.

Rereading *Breaking Ranks*, one becomes indignant. It's not just the grandiose framing device—a letter to his son John, as Whittaker Chambers in *Witness* petitioned *his* children—nor the monochroming of multicolored decades, the wholesale character assassination of entire categories of wrong-headed people and opinions (Panthers! Feminists! Gay Pride! Radical Chic! Ozone Layabouts!), or the contempt for pop culture (how dare Susan Sontag enjoy the Supremes, Richard Poirier the Beatles, or Leslie Fiedler comic books?), nor the promiscuous analogizing of bad reviews of Norman with Stalinism in the 1930s, nor the pernicious reiterations of "party line" and "terror" (always in quotes, like a condom) to explain why anybody ever disagreed with Norman.

No, one becomes indignant because almost everything he has to say about the sixties and the counterculture is at best innocent of nuance, and at worst meretricious. Having served my time at Pacifica Radio, at civil-rights protests, in the War on Poverty, among migrant workers and in the antiwar movement, before hopping onto the pogo stick of a New York career, I know for a *fact* that there were white liberals who felt some personal responsibility for the plight of black people even though the Pod insists that "I have rarely met a single one [*sic*] who really did experience a sense of guilt over the issue." I know for another fact that what torpedoed the War on Poverty was that all those young lawyers, VISTA volunteers, and organizers of communities and tenants' unions and welfare recipients began to threaten state and local buddy-system fiefdoms. I also know for a fact that the antiwar movement consisted of a whole lot more than Vietcong flags and "the scions of the First Families of American Stalinism." What's more, opposition to the war in Vietnam was created by the war itself, not by highbrows in whatever periodical or fishy think tank, who had less to do with changing public opinion than network television did.

For that matter, far from being what the Pod calls "very flimsy," the evidence that Adlai Stevenson in 1960 was "sympathetic to the cause of disarmament" was concrete and obvious to the rest of us—during the 1956 presidential campaign, Adlai had actually proposed a nuclear test–ban treaty, for which he was reviled by Richard Nixon.

And one is also indignant at the sort of homophobia that speaks of a "plague" that "rages" "among the kind of women who do not wish to be women and among those men who do not wish to be men. . . . There can be no more radical refusal of self-acceptance than the repudiation of one's own biological nature; and there can be no abdication of responsibility more fundamental than the refusal of a man to become, and to be, a father, or the refusal of a woman to become, and be, a mother." And there can be no more authoritarian an intellectual than the one who ordains that everybody else in the democratic motley must look and behave exactly like him.

Maybe it started at Columbia, where he resented "homosexuals with their supercilious disdain of my lower-class style of dress and my brash and impudent manner," and where he was "repelled" by Ginsberg's "sexual perversity." In *Ex-Friends*, Norman not only doubts that homosexuality is "inborn," but even suspects Ginsberg of "having become a homosexual not out of compulsion but by an act of will and as another way of expressing his contempt for normal life." This is almost as hilarious as the snit that seizes him when the Air Force Academy stages a 1986 conference to celebrate Joseph Heller's *Catch-22*, "a book viciously defaming the branch of the very service in which the academy was preparing its students to serve." P. is scrupulous enough to remind us that he praised *Catch-22* when he first reviewed it in *Show*. But that, of course, was before Joseph Heller savaged him in *Good as Gold*, which he neglects to mention.

But by the time we get to *Ex-Friends*, all this indignation has made us as tired as Lionel Trilling. I don't even want to talk about Hannah Arendt. I met her once myself, in the early seventies, at a dinner party for Nathalie Sarraute to which I had been invited not because of my personality or my prose style, but because I was the new editor of the *Times Book Review*. From where she sat, next to Mary McCarthy, she fixed on me a baleful eye, and what she said was this: "Young man, we are *watching* you." Well. This was a lot scarier than Trilling's wondering how anybody serious could even look at television, much less write about it, because at least I got Trilling to admit to an enthusiasm for *Kojak*. Ginsberg I met for the first time in North Beach in 1956, the summer of *Howl*, and again in 1968 at the Democratic convention, and he didn't care who any of us were: Om. *Everybody* went to Hellman's parties, so long as she thought they could do her some good. And I think Mailer was nicer to *Making It* than, in fact, such an advertisement for peculiar self deserved. And none of these luminaries, however condescending they may have been to the latest Young Man from the Provinces, had the least idea of a whole history of Left Coast progressivism picked up in the Wobbly redwoods or on the San Francisco docks, instead of Alcove 1 or Alcove 2 at the City College cafeteria.

Nevertheless, it seems to me that when Podhoretz goes on about the article Arendt wrote for *Commentary* in 1957 on school desegregation, an article whose rejection by *Commentary* caused him to quit his junior-editorial job there, an article subsequently published in Irving Howe's *Dissent*, he might have mentioned that what was most controversial about that article was its recommendation of miscegenation as the only solution to America's race-relations problem. Since P. does go on about how much trouble *he* got into later on with his essay "My Negro Problem—And Ours," which ended with the same recommendation, to omit to notice the resemblance is, shall we say, disingenuous. But after *Eichmann in Jerusalem*, P. decided that Hannah's "brilliance" was perverse, like Ginsberg's sexuality. And, in these pages, only Lillian Hellman is disingenuous. As for the rest of them, it's bad faith, false consciousness, failure of nerve, and cowardice. Not only does it never occur to Podhoretz that his ex-friends might have been right; it never even occurs to him that they might have been sincere. No wonder he's lonely.

*If I die, I forgive you; if I recover, we shall see.* (Spanish proverb)

It's an old story and even my own, so let's be brief. Once upon a time you were a *Wunderkind*, and now, oh so suddenly, you're an old fart.

And it turns out that a lot of people you thought were your friends really just wanted you to write something for them *or* publish something they had written *or* get them a foundation grant, and now they've gone to some party for Susan Sontag. This is unfair, but no excuse for a Lear-like rage, a howling on the blasted heath. Nor need you, in your failed hopes of a grander finish, have been so quick to junk the whole idea of a better world, of kinder people than the Partisan Reviewers, maybe organizing themselves as they please into co-ops, communes, collectives, or jazz bands, someplace where the free development of each is the condition for the free development of all—resolute solidarity and riotous individuality!—and where even the intellectuals know enough to think *against* their own surprising privilege, on behalf of the powerless and inarticulate, because who else will?

Marx said somewhere that when the locomotive of history turns a corner, all the thinkers fall off. The Partisan Reviewers, although they could stay up all night drinking Scotch and disputing whether John Dewey had been an agent of the Japanese Mikado or Jay Lovestone was really a Lovestoneite, were never as important as they thought they were. Nobody could be, and intellectuals never are—in a pillbox like a Waco, in Culture Wars of seething sects, full of grudge and doctrine, firing essays instead of bullets, throwing tantrums instead of bombs, killing reputations and also time. What they were, these elders of a vanished tribe (and this is the saddest sidebar to Norman's sob story), were patriarchs who didn't want any children.

# SAUL BELLOW (1):
# NOT DEAD YET

BOUT WOMEN, Moses Herzog told us: "They eat green salad and drink human blood." It is the same with biographers, who devour the brave hearts of the prey they stalk. Nor would the equally greedy readers of biographies want it any other way—a cannibal feast of family dysfunction, vile apprenticeship, open wounds, big scores, closet secrets, love gone wrong, grief and grudge. Like Henderson the Rain King, we require "large and real" emotions, plus every scrap of evidence before it's shredded. And on Saul Bellow, there's a lot. "If I had as many mouths as Siva has arms and kept them going all the time," his Dangling Man confided, "I still could not do myself justice." So good luck to James Atlas.

Bellow, moreover, seems bent on confounding even the most scrupulous of biographers. At age eighty-five, with his rakish Borsalino and Javanese walking stick, he won't get off the stage. Not only did he publish his best novel in years, *Ravelstein*, just this spring, but last December—in the eleventh year of his fifth marriage, after three different sons by three different wives—he fathered his first girl. Let the obit writers wait in line: "There are enough people with their thumbprint on my windpipe." He has apparently decided to stick around longer than Oedipus or Father Zossima. And, like Dr. Pep of Bughouse Square in one of his earliest stories, he will go down sermonizing:

> Yes, I feel the drum-dumps of the species in me. . . . I partake of everything in my own flesh; I strum on Venusberg and float in the swamp. I do

a one-leg schottische along Clark Street and buff the friendly public with my belly. I stroll in the zoo with my colleagues and ponder the throat-digging nails of the lynx and the pillars of the elephant; I sit in the New-berry and compassionate with the tender girls who have never felt anything warmer than a washcloth upon them. And I feel that I and all these creatures and persons are images of spirit, icons, symbols, versions and formations.

However confounded, a biographer more scrupulous than Atlas is hard to imagine. He has been on the case like a federal marshal for more than a decade. A hoary old reviewer's scam is to pretend you already knew all the inside stuff before you ever read the biography you're about to quibble with by poaching from. Let me be upfront: Almost everything I know about Bellow that I didn't guess from reading him, I got from the encyclopedic Atlas.

He has followed the spoor on its escape route—from Vilnius and the Pale of Settlement and the father fleeing the czar's police; to the working-class melting pot of immigrant alloys on the muddy out-skirts of Montreal, where the first New World Bellow was born in 1915; to rude Chicago, snobby New York, disappointing Paris, ambivalent-making Jerusalem, and enNobeling Stockholm—and then Looped back again. He has read every draft of every essay, story, speech, and novel (including theater chronicles for *Partisan Review* and movie reviews for *Horizon*); every letter dashed off by the touchy author (including heart-breakers to John Cheever and Cynthia Ozick); every previous stab at the St. Sebastian subject (Mark Harris, Ruth Miller, Daniel Fuchs, Harriet Wasserman); and more than fifty years of criticism (by erstwhile friends, abiding en-emies, and what Bellow has variously referred to as the "third-rate vaudevillians" of the daily press, "the reptiles of the literary estab-lishment," the "putty-headed academics," and the "Ivy League catamites").

If you know Bellow and aren't dead, Atlas will have talked to you. If you had an opinion but bought the farm, he's read your diaries, your FBI dossier, and maybe your genome. I wouldn't be surprised to learn that he'd done time in an orgone box, tried out an anthroposophical breathing exercise ("I Am It Thinks"), and even howled in the woods to find out what these whoop-de-doo's felt like. Anybody who reads a Jack Ludwig novel all the way through, just to get his side of the *Herzog* adultery story, will obviously stop at nothing to bag his unicorn.

Thus he has consulted the psychic yardgoods salesmen who worked the Chicago territory before Bellow, from Theodore Dreiser to James T. Farrell to Nelson Algren. He is intimate with the Great Books and 102 Great Ideas as enumerated by the "Great Bookie," Mortimer Adler, for whose *Syntopicon* young Saul swotted up Plato, Tacitus, and Hobbes. He has cozied in the memoirs of those back-biting ex-Bolsheviks at *Partisan Review* for whom the crisis of our culture boiled down to Kafka, Trotsky, and who got to sleep with Mary McCarthy. (Not Saul, says Atlas: he was "put off by [her] intellectual and sexual intensity," "needed more subservient women in order to serve his own shaky self-image," and "found women who challenged his dominance profoundly threatening.") He is voluble about the nineteenth-century masters (especially Stendhal) and the modernist illuminati (especially Joyce) with whom the mature Bellow saw himself in manly grapple. And he is knowledgeable about the whole literature of the Jewish experience in America from Abraham Cahan to, well, Nathan Zuckerman (though he might have said more about Mary Antin, Henry Roth, and Nathanael West)— which literature was delivered out of exile by Bellow's Augie and his Moses, and which deliverance was part assimilation, part synthesis, part transcendence and also ecstatic kabbala. "Orpheus, the son of Greenhorn," went a riff in *Humboldt's Gift:* "He brought Coney Island into the Aegean and united Buffalo Bill with Rasputin."

*Humboldt's Gift* is a key to this biography, as the overtly autobiographical *Herzog* was the "pivotal" novel in Bellow's career. Atlas is himself a child of Bellow's northwest side milieu, and so naturally the story of a "sensitive Jewish boy from Chicago" is "a theme dear to my heart." But he is also the author of a fine 1977 biography of Delmore Schwartz, and what the novelist did to the poet in *Humboldt* still rankles: "an act of revenge . . . in the guise of a tribute," he says, omitting "the deep sadness of [Delmore's] life—the talent wasted, the bright youthful ambition turned to ash." And while Atlas the critic is too sophisticated to confuse artful fiction with messy life—knowing that "genius assimilates and transforms whatever raw material comes to hand"—Atlas the biographer is suspicious of all those masks, sacred and profane, that the artist wears while digging up the buried bodies and playing with the bones.

So we get the best of several worlds—colored by a wary disapproval. The literary critic relates *Dangling Man* to Rilke's *Notebooks of Malte Laurids Brigge, The Victim* to Dostoyevsky's *The Eternal Husband,* and *Seize the Day* to Dreiser's *Jennie Gerhardt.* The scholar informs us that Bellow and Isaac Rosenfeld were known in high school as Zinoviev and Kamenev, the disaffected Bolsheviks; that Whittaker Chambers sabotaged Saul's chances of a job at *Time* magazine; that Augie March in an early draft went to work for Trotsky in Mexico; that an early draft of *Herzog* included a "homoerotic" bathtub scene; and that Jack Nicholson owns the film rights to *Henderson the Rain King.* The cultural historian relishes identifying Alf Steidler as Studs Terkel, Victor Wulpy as Harold Rosenberg, Zetland as Isaac Rosenfeld, Sewell as R. P. Blackmur, and Magnasco as Hilton Kramer, as well as the highbrow gossip, the mean-minded feuds and the caustic Bellovian wisecracks (about, for instance, a William Phillips essay on Susan Sontag: "One of the nice things about *Hamlet* is that Polonius gets stabbed"). And the Chicago-born biographer—even if he has decided that, as much as he admires the "moral depth and commanding vision" of the novelist, he doesn't especially care for the man—gets nevertheless to go home again, and dream Bellovian dreams of Julien Sorel, Frederic Moreau, Paul Morel, and Stephen Dedalus.

"Each man has his batch of poems," said Herzog, a self-mythology, almost a personal creation myth, like the Songlines and Dreamtime of Bruce Chatwin's Aboriginals. For Solomon Bellow, age eight, it was Ward H in the Chicago hospital to which he was committed for an emergency appendectomy and where he remained for six months, suffering from peritonitis and pneumonia, reading *Uncle Tom's Cabin* and the funny papers, rehearsing his subsequent abandonments. And sure enough, the mother who consumed novels and wore ostrich plumes died when Sol was seventeen, leaving him unprotected from the brutal Old World father (junk-dealing bootlegger) and the money-grubbing older brothers (coalyards, nursing homes, landfills) who were so contemptuous of his bookishness ("some schmuck with a pen," he would recall forty years after the fact). Already, he felt that "I was born to be a performing and interpretative creature, that I was meant to take part in a peculiar, exalted game." Already, he had that astonishing "singleness of purpose" that would sustain him while his contemporaries were cracking up ("They were all Stradivarius violins," wrote Leslie Fiedler, "and at any moment a string could snap"). And already, the world could never possibly love him enough.

It's this psychodynamic—depressed in the Depression; narcissistic and masochistic ever after; subverting determinism, denying dependency, leaving before he was left but always filling up pages with words—that Atlas emphasizes throughout, from Pushkin, the Pentateuch, and the Fourth International in high school; to those snatched semesters at the University of Chicago (too expensive), Northwestern (where the English Department's genteel anti-Semitism nudged him into anthropology), and Wisconsin (where he studied "savages" like himself and women like "a foreign tribe"); to the teaching of Flaubert and Joyce at Pestalozzi-Froebel Teacher's College and the collecting of his $24 weekly paycheck from the Federal Writers' Project; to his first story, in *Partisan Review*, and his first novel, *Dangling Man*—in which glum existential parenthesis Joseph wonderfully reminded us: "We are all drawn toward the same craters of the spirit—to know what we are and what we are for, to know our purpose, to seek grace."

Always, in the middle of writing a book, he was tearing up his life, trading in one wife for another a decade younger, complaining about child support, and punishing the castoffs in his next fiction. Atlas suggests that so long as Bellow "still experienced himself as the son," abandoned and betrayed by the mother who died without his permission, he was unable "to sustain relationships with women." Or with his oldest buddies: "He was ardently loyal to anyone who passed the rigorous test of friendship—as long as they served his needs." As well as colleagues and competitors: "Writers who posed a threat to his hegemony got the cold shoulder; writers who occupied a place safely below his own on the literary ladder were seen as comrades in the 'travail business.'" According to Atlas: "Divorces, estrangements from friends, abrupt departures from jobs, nonattendance at funerals—the defensive mechanism was the same. Leave before you're left."

Even the *PR* editors who did so much to boost his career were suspect: "Those dying beasts," he called them. "They want to cook their meals over Pater's hard gemlike flame and light their cigarettes at it." From Edmund Wilson and John Updike, he expected indifference, hostility, and "the whole WASP effort to suppress the Jewish novel." But from the New York intellectuals, he demanded unconditional, rhapsodic surrender: "It wasn't that they didn't love him; they didn't love him enough." And so he went into attack mode. And while holding a grudge against Norman Podhoretz— who had been designated by Clement Greenberg as *Commentary*'s "hit man" on *Augie*—may be the normal respiration of informed intelligence, attacking Lionel Trilling for things he never said, calling off a deal with his new publisher because it hired Ted Solotaroff (who had written a mixed review of *Herzog*), resigning from the Century Club because they voted in William Phillips and Richard Poirier, and never forgiving his old friend Alfred Kazin for his failure to adore *Mr. Sammler's Planet* are kindergarten tantrums.

Sammler! One is reminded of hitman Podhoretz, who, in *Ex-Friends*, accused almost everybody he'd ever known of bad faith, false consciousness, failure of nerve, and/or cowardice. Not only did it never occur to him that his ex-friends might have been right about anything; it never even occurred to him that they might have been sincere. This is how you end up at the *New York Post* or the Committee on Social Thought, wondering where the parties went. To be sure, the New York intellectuals needed Bellow to write the books that they couldn't. But if he was looking to these patriarchs for the approval he never got from his father, he looked in the wrong bound volume. Sons were the last thing they wanted.

So Saul Bellow has intimacy issues. We might have guessed. Philip Roth certainly did, in his *Ghost Writer* portrait of Felix Abravanel: "The charm was like a moat so oceanic that you could not even see the great turreted and buttressed thing it had been dug to protect." That he should also have what Atlas calls a "need to create obstacles and enemies" was obvious even to his creature Herzog, the last imploding Romantic: "The depressive character is narcissistic. It fears the disappearance of the beloved. Above all terrors it places the terror of abandonment and naked solitude. So with secret hate it cuts off the deserters."

Alas, the deeper into the biography, the harder it is to recall what we admired so much in the fiction. For the biographer, too, it all seems to turn as sour as Sammler. He is disinclined to rank Bellow among living writers or the noble dead, an odd reticence in such an ambitious book. (Though maybe a healthy one. Bellow himself wondered: "Why should writers wish to be rated—seeded—like tennis players? Handicapped like racehorses? What an epitaph for a novelist: 'He won all the polls'!") If Atlas doesn't shrug, he can at least be seen to wince at Bellow's blackballing of Amiri Baraka, Susan Sontag, and Edward Said as MacArthur Fellows, his general "misogyny" and particular animus for feminism ("All you're going to have to show for your movement ten years from now are *sagging breasts!*"), his "ill-concealed racism" and, till Allan Bloom came back to Chicago, his hectoring homophobia. Perhaps the stupidest thing he ever said—that reading Nadine Gordimer was "like gagging on Kotex"—is quoted by Atlas without comment, because there is nothing to add or subtract. He wants out, as if from Dewey Spangler's colostomy bag in *The Dean's December*.

And yet, and yet, despite, besides: In his wicked new biography of Arthur Rimbaud, Graham Robb reports on the young poet's moving into the Paris hotel room of a dissipated pianist who, in his spare time, "collected old shoes which he used for flower-pots." Isn't that nifty? Well, there are lots of old shoes in *Bellow* and some lovely flowers potted in them, too, such as the sight of Saul reading John Donne in a hammock. Or the words he wrote to Alice Adams, with whom he had a brief fling, when she was feeling low: "I am only urging you to utter the magic syllable 'Whoosh' in the face of psychological oppression. The nineteenth century drove writers into attics. The twentieth shuts them into nutshells. The only remedy is to declare yourself king, or queen, of infinite spaces." Or his imagining himself as "a novel written by the ghost of Jules Verne and raised by Tutankhamen and Wm. Faulkner—about a Prince of Egypt reincarnated in the twentieth century, fond of southern whiskey and doomed to jet about the earth." I'd rather imagine him talking to the dead like Herzog—or on the road somewhere between Kafka's Castle and the Leaning Tower of Isaac Babel, wearing Gogol's overcoat and Melville's whaling boots, with a wheelbarrow and a kite, fishing the sky for souls.

So, like Henderson, I want it all. Yeats believed in faeries, and Pound in funny money, and Doris Lessing in flying saucers. Let Bellow have his orgone box and his "peculiar metaphysics as flying creatures have their radar." Picasso was nasty, brutish, and short, but he changed the way we saw the world. It was the same for me in high school, when *The Adventures of Augie March* hit me as *Moby-Dick* hit Zetland, like a torpedo: "He thought he would drown. But he didn't drown; he floated." Shooting the rapids of his own verbal torrent, revving up to escape velocity, he not only took me into the eagle's "infinite spaces," but recharged the batteries of the ordinary all around. Words had colors, ideas had feelings, thinkers did push-ups in my bedroom, identity itself was up for grabs, and I was all of a sudden vouchsafed "the universal eligibility to be noble." Even to a lapsed Catholic on the blue-collar margins of a California beach town, it was as thrilling as modern art and teen sex.

Atlas must have felt the same before he began this long journey into knowing too much. I could no more stop reading his biography than I could stop reading Saul Bellow after he blew the blinds off the windows in my head. All over again in *Ravelstein*, with a flock of parrots eating red berries in the Chicago snow, he recovered his fast ball from his mean streak. It's the prose equivalent of break-dancing. Barbed, breezy, disheveled, and surreal; salt-savoring and brain-fevered; brilliant twitchy patter and Great Books patois; colloquial and mandarin, sentimental and neobaroque; Talmudic mutter and gangster slang; deep chords and stop-action; the long irony, the low laugh, the short fuse and a three-cushion bank shot into a side pocket where the anguish they speak may be Yiddish but we must all of us rise and fall and live and die without our mothers—such a style miracle-whips.

# BRUCE CHATWIN
# IN DREAMTIME

SHORTLY BEFORE HE DIED, Bruce Chatwin found God. This was on top of Mount Athos, after which he left for Katmandu. Looking down from the bees and grapes, he had seen an iron cross on a wet rock. "I had no idea," he told his wife Elizabeth. So he made time in his frenzied dying to hallucinate a Christos Pantokrator and convert to Greek Orthodoxy. The day after a memorial service for him in the Cathedral of St. Sophia in surprising Bayswater—where, as a matter of odd fact, a satanic Salman Rushdie first heard about the *fatwa* on his head—Elizabeth flew to Greece to bury her husband's ashes near the seaside town of Kardamili, next door to a ruined Byzantine chapel lapped at by olive trees, wild garlic, and wild geraniums.

One wishes the end of the "songline" had been more subversive. About almost everything else in a lifetime of running away from his country, his marriage, and his sexuality, Chatwin was unorthodox, with "the nomad's contempt for the pyramid." Once, on an undulating "leopard-spotted" savannah, he had declared an altogether different faith: "For whenever I went back to that Africa, and saw a camel caravan, a view of white tents, or a single blue turban far off in the heat haze, I knew that, no matter what the Persians said, Paradise was never a garden but a waste of white thorns."

Maybe he just liked smoky icons and singing monks. Maybe, with his legs paralyzed ("my little boys," he called them), there was nowhere else to run. Maybe a mind so far gone as to imagine that the filmmaker Werner Herzog had healing powers, and that the blood of a Nubian slave was a cure for AIDS, needed divine help. Or maybe God was the ultimate item to be purchased with a postdated check on his last crazy shopping spree, like the Bronze Age arm band, the Assyrian quartz duck, the Han tortoise inkwell, the wax *bozzetto* of Neptune, the portable twelfth-century altar from Lausanne and the Tibetan tiger rug. All of a sudden, the nomad wanted to possess everything, as if he were an Utz.

Aesthete, vagabond, crackpot, fabulist, fugitive: Nicholas Shakespeare's spellbinding biography allows us to hold all these Chatwins in kaleidoscopic focus simultaneously. In a Sotheby's uniform of silk tie, slip-on shoes, and a gray suit from Henry Poole on Savile Row, or a Lawrence of Arabia djellaba, or hiking shorts with kneesocks (to cover up his varicose veins), or the shawl he claimed was Freud's, babbling on about paleontology, John Donne, and the influence of Simonides of Ceos on the memory techniques of counter-Reformation Jesuits in China, he was a blue-eyed "compass without a needle," a masked harlequin, "arch improviser, zany trickster, master of the volteface . . . Mr. Chameleon himself"—the talking animal as performance artist.

Shakespeare, whose career as a novelist Chatwin encouraged, had access to the moleskin notebooks and the widow's good will. He spent almost a decade tracking the books across borders back to their author, from the black hills of Wales to the slave coast of Dahomey to the outback, the pampas, and Prague. He's chatted up everybody with a peppy opinion, from old friends, extant relatives, former lovers, testy scientists, and resentful natives to the luminary likes of Sybille Bedford, Robert Calasso, James Ivory, and Susan Sontag, plus of course Rushdie, who was amazed in Australia to find himself traveling with someone who talked more than he did. Like a shamus, he puzzles missing pieces, pounces on aggrandizement and evasion, plugs holes in cover stories and stops to marvel at mean-street seediness (for instance, the S/M bathhouse/leather bar/Mapplethorpe scene in seventies New York). Like an epicure, he luxuriates past the point of wallow in so much wanton artiness (an Etruscan bronze! an Ingres interior! a Ngoro lacquer snuffbox! an

Eastern Island canoe paddle!) Like a therapist, he empathizes and exorcizes. (Bruce was in denial the way Napoleon was itchy.) And like, of course, a novelist, he relishes every contradiction—hypochondrias and mythomanias; the longing to lose yourself in sand dunes but only after having gone horseback riding with Jacqueline Onassis in black-gold pyjama pants; the walkabouts and vanishing acts that circled round to home. (This "mother of all grasshoppers," who desired men more than women and wrote his books in other people's houses anywhere but England, ended up back with the wife who had never divorced him because she was Catholic.)

Much is also made of the famous Chatwin style and photographic memory, that transfer of graphic ideas into words with "the exact skill of a botanist or a sniper," seeking the prose equivalent of "the abstraction he admired in Sung dynasty painters, of flattened forms suspended in space with no suggestion of depth"—more like Daumier or the watercolors of Cézanne than Proust or Joyce; more Russian than English (Chekhov, Turgenev, Mandelstam, Babel, Bunin) and more French than Russian (Flaubert, Stendhal, Racine), with a dash of Hemingway's Cubism and a chilly pinch of Ernst Junger. Not for nothing, at his second-rate public school, did Bruce play the part of the Mayor in Gogol's *Government Inspector* and of Mrs. Candour in *School for Scandal*. Nor for nothing, when his father couldn't afford to send him to Oxford, did he apprentice at Sotheby's among Netsuke carvings, Syrian limestone antelope reliefs, and the usual Impressionists, before fleeing to Edinburgh, archaeology, and Sanskrit, somehow imagining that he'd turn himself into, if not Malraux or Indiana Jones, at least a Howard Carter (discovering Tut's tomb) or a Prosper Mérimée (inspecting monuments for the French admiralty). And certainly not for nothing did he serve a three-year stint as roving correspondent for the *Sunday Times Magazine*, where he learned to write with clarity, for an audience, to a deadline—and from which he fled again, this time famously to Patagonia.

According to Rushdie: "He was very scared. He was telling stories to keep the Jungle Beast away, the false sabre-tooth, whatever it is.

The Beast is the truth about himself. The great truth he's keeping away is who he is."

Yes, indeed. But I am trying to recall what it felt like to read his books without knowing who he was, to experience the exotic absence of an author from his own pages, to crack open the astonishing *In Patagonia* (1977) expecting yet another snotty English travelogue and discovering instead a "Wonder Voyage" that asked us to dream about not only penguins and gauchos but Caliban and Darwin, mobile gas ovens and a Lost City of the Caesars, giant sloths, slaughtered Indians, and a carapace of "enormous armadillo . . . each scale of its armour looking like a Japanese chrysanthemum." To venture next to *The Viceroy of Ouidah* (1980), expecting a slave-trade novel and getting instead a sadomasochistic fantasy of horned vipers, bloody goats, severed heads and Amazons, a voodoo brew of imperialist porn and *candomble* trance-dancing. To continue, chastened, to *On the Black Hill* (1982), alert to sinister subtexts but flummoxed by a lot of Thomas Hardy sheep, dissenting preachers, an Industrial Revolution, class war, Euripides and the Book of Revelation, as well as what John Updike decided must be "a homosexual marriage" of eighty-year-old twin brothers waiting for the arrival of a New Jerusalem. And none of this prepared me for *The Songlines* (1987), which is as close as he ever got to the geography in his own head— and even so, the man was missing.

In *The Songlines*, under a ghost-gum tree, attended by dingoes, bush devils, and black cockatoos, Chatwin reinvented Australia. Hadn't the Aboriginals specialized in his own sort of walkabout forever? Wasn't all their vast interior a labyrinth of invisible pathways, "Dreaming Tracks" or "Songlines"? Didn't their creation myths tell of legendary totemic beings who wandered the continent in Dreamtime, singing out the names of Fire, Spider, Wind, Grass, and Porcupine—and so summoning into existence the very world that would disappear if they didn't hit the road with their own sacred tunes? It seemed to Chatwin that Australia was one big musical score, "a spaghetti of Iliads and Odysseys." Not that he *saw* any of this on either visit. Rather, he *willed* it. According to Pam Bell, a poet who watched him in action: "He knew the mystery was there and he didn't understand it. In *The Songlines* he was desperately trying to go to the centre. It was the most important thing for him and he realized halfway through he wasn't going to be able to do it. He was excluded. You have to *earn* mystery. It's only lovers who get there." Where he arrived after a couple of hundred pages was back at his notes for a nomad book he'd abandoned before he ever left for Patagonia. These notes, tacked on and italicized, are *needy*.

He needed Ancient Greek and Hebrew, Old Norse, Old English, and all of classical mythology to be gigantic song maps too. He needed there to be a kinship between the songs of Aboriginals, the Gregorian chants of Catholic monks, the mantras of Tibetan lamas, and the drumbeats of African shamans. He needed our origins to have been nomadic and pacific, grounded in the "voluntary graces" of food-sharing, gift-giving, song-singing, and storytelling. He needed our development of weapons like fire to be defensive, after *Homo erectus* was menaced a million years ago on open grasslands by a giant predator, *dinofelis,* the beastly Prince of Darkness whose dragon shadow haunts our unconscious to this day. And—because the whole point of our Big Brain is to sing us through the wilderness, and our central nervous system has a built-in "migratory drive" that makes us want to walk all day, and only when we're "warped in conditions of settlement" do we seek "outlets in violence, greed, status-seeking or a mania for the new"—he needed agriculture to be a bad idea, and cities an even worse one. The Noble Savage was Chatwin's kind of guy.

Scientists who are really familiar with nomads tell us they'd just as soon stick around if only the animals let them, and actually like to hitch a ride. But even such wishful thinking—to be bickered about by competing ethnologists, paleontologists, and the rest of the blood-soaked and desert-crazed monomaniacs who dream up our past on an Ice Age toenail or a tooth—was still exhilarating to contemplate, and also a good reason to leave town.

Except for those of us who prefer to find and lose ourselves in cities—whose idea of a vibrant culture depends a lot on politics, newspapers, movie houses, street lights and street cars, labor unions and cobblestones, caffeine and maybe even cigarettes. For people like me, who never get out of Paris or St. Petersburg or Bombay or Istanbul, Noble Savagery is a good reason for *Bruce* to leave town, so we can read about it without having to stir. His last novel, *Utz* (1989), disappointed such urban types because it was too much about basilisks and unicorn cups and too little about Prague, which he first visited in a fateful 1968.

But he wasn't interested in politics. Other than Britain's bully behavior in the Falklands, which he deplored in a radio talk with Italo Calvino, he seems never to have expressed a political opinion in all his forty-eight years, not about Argentina, Afghanistan, the Situationists in Paris, Dubcek in Prague, or even the property claims and citizenship rights of modern-day Aboriginals. Nor did the rights of gays concern him. "Bruce said he had no time for gay politics, or the gay community," says a friend who lived with him in Rio; "and he abhorred the word 'gay.' 'I'd much rather be called a bugger,' and he roared with laughter."

*His ambivalence was his impetus. Sexually, Bruce was a polymorphous pervert. Think of the word "charming." Think of the word "seduction." Think of seduction as a driving force to conquer society . . . He's out to seduce everybody, it doesn't matter if you are male, female, an ocelot or a tea cosy.* (Miranda Rothschild)

*He slept with everyone, once: it goes with being a great beauty. His sexuality was like his possessions, a means of engaging and also of not engaging with the world. He was profoundly solitary and therefore conducted his sexual activity as a way of connecting with people. At such an industrial rate it meant not an exclusive or intensifying connection; it meant he had a connection. "I know this person because I've slept with him/her." It gave him the right to call someone the next time he was in town.* (Susan Sontag)

*I never felt he was nearly as much of a cruiser or sexually-obsessed person as most of my gang. But I think Bruce had a lot to hide. I think he liked danger. I always assumed he liked being violated in some way and preferably by brigands, gypsies, South American cowboys. It was part of his nomad pattern, to go off into the desert and get raped by Afghan brigands. It's*

*something Lady Hester Stanhope-ish. It wasn't so much the sex as the*
*sauce it came in, some Afghan chieftain draped in a cartridge belt.* (John
Richardson)

Once upon a time, Chatwin confided to a friend, "You'll never know
how *complicated* it is to be bisexual." And one of the reasons why
we'll never know is that he never told us. Another friend marvels,
"Of all the talented brilliant writers, Bruce wrote the shortest sentences I've ever read." Well, he left out a lot. "In the complete works
of Bruce Chatwin," says Salman Rushdie, "there is not a loving
fuck." But there's plenty of fancy footwork.

I am looking at his posthumously published collection of essays,
*What Am I Doing Here* (1989). See him, in the erstwhile Soviet
Union, going on about Constructivism. Or in Afghanistan, before it
was ruined by Russians and hippies. Or in India, looking for wolf-
boys, disliking Indira. Or in Nepal, stinking of rancid yak butter,
seeking the mythical yeti. Wherever, he meets interesting people,
famous or supremely odd. Besides Diana Vreeland, André Malraux,
and Werner Herzog, there is the Chinese geomancer hired to approve the "dragonlines" of a brand-new Hong Kong bank. And the
Englishman, investigating the activities of African Nazis in the late
1930s, who is so excited by the idea of "black men in black shirts
with red armbands and black swastikas." Stranger still are the
friends he makes, like Donald Evans, an American artist in Amsterdam who paints postage stamps for kingdoms of his own invention.
Or the South African composer Kevin Volans, who adapts Stock-
hausen, prehistoric insect sounds, Zulu guitar music, the chipping of
stones, and the shouts of children, for harpsichord and string quartet.
And always—whether down the Volga, remembering Turgenev; or
up an Everest, reading Dante; or on the pampas, reminded of Stone-
henge and the Temple of Heaven, St. Peter's and Red Square, Mecca
and Versailles—the same old fierce disdain of cities and the impos-
sibly romantic sympathy for icon-smashers and "anarchic peoples";
those "men of the fringe" who bedeviled Mesopotomania and ancient Egypt; Magyars and Mongols and wolf-masked Huns who rode
out of the steppes and into his heart.

From Shakespeare, we know that Bruce near the end of his life talked this same Kevin Volans into composing an opera based on Rimbaud's *Une Saison en enfer,* which he considered "a western Songline," and that he'd wanted himself to play and sing the poet's part. Had Bruce been gang-raped, like Rimbaud during the Paris Commune, like T. E. Lawrence by Turkish soldiers? He hinted so. Shakespeare isn't sure. Maybe he just liked musicals. He had loved *Hair* so much, for instance, that he wrote to Galt McDermott proposing something similar about Ikhnaton, in which the sun-worshipping Pharaoh would uproot his court from Thebes and relocate to, of course, the nomadic Iraqi desert.

When *Utz* was shortlisted for the Booker Prize, the satirical magazine *Private Eye* ran this playful description of what it called *Tutsi-Frutsi* by Bruce Hatpin:

> Wry, evocative, sensitive account of a Viennese ice-cream collector who fills his cavernous flat in Marxist Prague with hundreds of different flavoured ice-creams. One day he wakes up and finds that they have all melted. As the *Daily Telegraph* commented: *"Tutsi-Frutsi* is a wry, evocative novella in which ice-cream collecting is used as a paradigm for man's insatiable urge to eternalise the transient." Cheekwin is of course best known for his award-winning cult novel *Tramlines,* which shows how the ancient Incas invented trams. An insatiable nomad, he lives in Notting Hill like everybody else.

Pretty funny. But from Shakespeare we now know everything there is to know, plus what we can't, and more than enough to be sad. In addition to his weird fascination with such Nazi collaborators as Montherlant and Malaparte, and the fact that he once stole a young woman's paperback copy of D. H. Lawrence's *Kangaroo,* and those twenty-three years of marriage during which he never washed a single dish, and his lifelong partiality to a single work of art (a Peruvian wall hanging, probably for an Inca temple, of blue and yellow parrot feathers from a species of *papagayo* now extinct), we also know about his grandmother's cabinet, his father the sailor, the Mickey Mouse gas mask, the Viking grave, the royal python, the low sperm count ("He can't make babies so he eats them," it was said of

Ouidah's Viceroy) and the *Beziehungswahn,* not to mention the gold griffins, the throne of skulls, the tub of Crisco, the ecstasy pills, and the lithium—or Kaposi's sarcoma and black urine.

We wind up with something daunting, as if Nabokov had set out to net a butterfly that was itself a Nabokov, all gaudy wings: a life that was its own secret work of art, an art with that life omitted, a biography that makes both of them more compelling and fosters the queasy feeling that all of us, Chatwin, Shakespeare, and the reader too are equally voyeurs. It was obviously too much to expect that he would tell the truth about his dying when he hadn't told the truth about his living. To the dreadful end, he insisted on what García Márquez has called "the sacred right of the sick to die in peace along with the secret of their illness," dissembling to close friends and his own parents, even exoticizing what he suffered from: It was, he claimed, a bone-marrow-eating fungus peculiar to South Asian bamboo rats he'd picked up nibbling a slice of raw Cantonese whale or a black egg on the Thai border. Or maybe an Indian amoeba in the bat feces of a Javanese cave he'd stumbled into. Better yet, among Chinese peasants in Yunnan, while he was tracing the footsteps of botanist John Rock, whose book *The Kingdom of the Na-Khi* had been so much admired by Ezra Pound, perhaps . . . and so on, as if the deathbed were a proscenium arch.

OK, even if some overdue honesty might have helped dispel the hateful superstitions of the plague years, I am not so presumptuous as to instruct a stranger on how to die heroically. We didn't know about Rock Hudson in advance, so why should we have known about Bruce Chatwin? Who says writers have a higher obligation than actors? Or politicians? Or Han tortoise inkwells and Eastern Island canoe paddles? Tell it to your Christos Pantokrator.

# I SAY IT'S SPINACH

AS IF FROM ATLANTIS, Babylon, Brigadoon, the heart of darkness, or a progressive preschool food fight, refugees from William Shawn's *New Yorker* flee the catastrophe of Newhouse directly into lurid memoir. Because they have injured feelings and scores to settle, they tend to bite each other on their kneecaps and pineal glands. But they also lament an End of Days, when the old civil culture of good prose and good taste met a brand-new mediascape of unbearable lightness and free-fall spin; when static cling met buzz. The horror! The horror!

Mistah Shawn—he dead. And they bear his toasted pound cake with them into exile. Like St. Teresa's, his dismemberments are parceled out: eyes, feet, and collarbone; the heart in Alba, a cheek to Madrid, a jaw to Rome, and one ringed finger on Generalissimo Franco's bedside table. Like the original Adam, he awaits angelic reassembly. Meanwhile . . .

It is of course the *New Yorker*'s seventy-fifth birthday, celebrated by thousands of pages in half-a-dozen books. Already Ben Yagoda's equable, affectionate, and comprehensive history, *About Town: The New Yorker and the World It Made*, seems to have been swamped by a rising tide of blather about Renata Adler's *Gone: The Last Days of The New Yorker*, in which the novelist and critic sends out tiny toy sailboats of dreamy subjunctives, only to bring back weirdness and meanness. And these two are hard on the 1998 heels of memoirs by Lillian Ross (the embarrassing *Here But Not Here*) and Ved Mehta (the fulsome *Remembering Mr. Shawn's New Yorker*), both of which were nice to Adler, despite which she disdains them. (Beware of Renata when she calls you a friend; run for the hills when she says she loves you.)

Moreover, to bolster whatever generalizations we need to make about the magazine, there are also two anthologies hodgepodged together by the current editor, David Remnick—one of them, *Wonderful Town*, consisting of forty-four short fictions whose only excuse for cohabitation is that all are set in Manhattan; and the other, *Life Stories*, of twenty-five "profiles" reminding us that Shawn's oddest decision on succeeding Harold Ross as editor in 1952 was to shy away from articles "that criticized or mocked individuals"; his "ironclad rule," as conveyed to Mehta, "that we should never write about anyone who did not wish to be written about." So much, then, for the scathing attacks on Henry Luce, Frank Hague, Tom Dewey, Walter Winchell, and DeWitt Wallace in which a gleeful Ross delighted.

Finally, in his continuing campaign to rehabilitate Ross from posthumous caricature as a bumpkin who somehow achieved his remarkable magazine in spite of himself, Thomas Kunkel has followed up a biography, *Genius in Disguise*, with a thick volume of guided missives, *Letters from the Editor: The New Yorker's Harold Ross*. If Shawn, reluctant to leave a paper trail, seldom wrote letters and didn't keep carbons—"he is desperately afraid of being quoted," James Thurber complained to E. B. White—Ross couldn't help himself, firing off wheedles and jokes to everybody from J. Edgar Hoover to Noel Coward. But the editor who hired Dorothy Parker and Edmund Wilson to review books, Louise Bogan to review poetry, Lewis Mumford to review architecture, Ring Lardner to review radio, and Janet Flanner to review France, while overruling his own staff to publish Vladimir Nabokov's autobiography, needs no scholarly apology—unless you grudge his missing the point of the Holocaust till Nuremberg.

So you want the skinny on Si, Bob, Tina, Pauline, and maybe even Michael Kinsley, that prince of dither. Me, too. But an account of the peculiar institution is obligatory, before we get to the peculiar people. "For more than thirty years," says Adler, "The *New Yorker* was not only the finest magazine of its time but probably the finest English-language magazine of all time." Not, please note, the finest *weekly* with literary pretensions, nor the best one published on the best paper for the longest time, or the only serious one with half a million readers—not even, simply, the preferred periodical of an educated American middle-class that wanted regular reminding of its cozy status and an early radar warning against sneak attacks by the avant-garde. Almost at random, one thinks of *Dial*, or the *North American* and *Partisan Reviews*; of a *New Republic* that published Edmund Wilson's *To the Finland Station* twenty years before the *New Yorker* published *Patriotic Gore*; of *Scrutiny* with F. R. Leavis, Cyril Connolly's *Horizon*, the CIA's *Encounter*, the *Times Literary Supplement* in spite of Rupert Murdoch, *Commentary* before it went bananas, and Addison and Steele's *Spectator*.

But there is no sign in *Gone* that Adler has been to the library, nor any sign either that any of these memoirists ever noticed what the competition had got up to, except when reading the reviews of their own books in the reviled *Times*—no hint of interest in the ingenuities of Harold Hayes at *Esquire*, Willie Morris at *Harper's*, or Jann Wenner at *Rolling Stone*. Maybe it seemed beneath them, nesting already in Erewhon. Or perhaps they felt it would distract them from an office politics positively Pharaonic and an office culture, apparently designed to infantilize, that indulged so compulsively in what Freud has called "the narcissism of small differences." And yet the world is full of interesting magazines, and most of us read more than one.

That the *New Yorker* was a very good magazine for a very long time is sufficient for Ben Yagoda. If it "alternately reflected and justified bourgeois culture, denying by exclusion any inconvenient, unpleasant, or truly subversive facets of life," it was equally capable of contradicting itself with complexity and brilliance. Having grown up a passionate reader of its pages, Yagoda interviews some fifty writers, editors, and artists, burrows like a mad mole in 2,500 archival bins, and is blessed with a genius for apt quotation. (How nice to know, for instance, that Kenneth Tynan was not permitted to say "pissoir"—that his copy was changed to "a circular curbside construction." And that the very first sentence of John Updike's very first "Talk" piece read: "In Antarctica, everything turns left.") Ignore the silly survey of seven hundred longtime readers on their "relationship" with Eustace Tilley, and forgive as well the rush to meet a birthday deadline that reduces him to three pages on Bob Gottlieb's adagio, six on Tina Brown's go-down-Moses urban removal, and a couple of slapdashed graphs on nice-guy David Remnick. Everything else, Yagoda covers like a tarp.

He knows, for instance, where the money came from (yeast) and where it went (not to the writers). He can chat up the Algonquin Round Table without fawning; they were better drinkers and logrollers than writers or wits. He situates the rude fledging humor magazine in its jazz-age, mongrel-Manhattan, mass-culture, class-mobility context of advertising, movies, book clubs, sheet music, tabloids, and skyscrapers. He's worldly wise enough to notice that *Smart Set* had not only already published Dreiser and Willa Cather, but heavier weights like James Joyce, D. H. Lawrence, and Ford Madox Ford; that *Vanity Fair*, in a single issue in 1923, had T. S. Eliot, Ferenc Molnár, Gertrude Stein, Aldous Huxley, and Djuna Barnes. While he considers the decade before Pearl Harbor to be the magazine's Golden Age, he is alert to the philistinism of Clifton Fadiman nodding off over Faulkner and Robert Benchley flummoxed by Odets. He wishes they had said more about the Great Depression, or anything at all about Sacco and Vanzetti.

Still, for laughs, who beats S. J. Perelman, Woody Allen, and Veronica Geng? And where else could we count on seeing the art of Thurber, Saul Steinberg, George Price, Charles Addams, Ed Koren, and Roz Chast? Is there any poet they didn't publish, thanks to Howard Moss? If, till at least Jamaica Kincaid, the fiction was too well-bred and whitebread, weren't Irwin Shaw, Kay Boyle, Jean Stafford, and Eudora Welty around early, followed by the perennial Johns—O'Hara, Cheever, and Updike—plus J. D. Salinger, Donald Barthleme, and Ann Beattie, as well as I. B. Singer and Jorge Luis

Borges after the imbecilic policy against translations was abandoned in 1963?

Having been in the archives, though, Yagoda knows that "subversive graphic humorists" like Jules Feiffer, Edward Gorey, and Edward Sorel had to stand outside in the cold for decades of talking-animal cartoons. That Wallace Stevens and Robert Lowell were among the missing, and Auden's "September 1, 1939" got turned down. That Grace Paley had to publish two books of stories before she finally passed in 1978, and rejection slips of a flabbergasting condescension were issued to Saul Bellow, Stanley Elkin, William Gaddis, William Gass, Joe Heller, Bernard Malamud, Flannery O'Connor, Cynthia Ozick, Thomas Pynchon, William Styron, and Kurt Vonnegut, not to mention *Goodbye, Columbus*.

When, with A. J. Liebling's help, the *New Yorker*'s nonfiction came of age during World War II, so did Shawn, the last of a long line of managing editors and the first to be competent. While Katherine White was cultivating Elizabeth Bishop and V. S. Pritchett, Shawn, between hires of Harold Rosenberg, Kenneth Tynan, and Pauline Kael, initiated, annotated, sat on, and sometimes even hatched those long-form Fabergé eggs—*Hiroshima*, *Silent Spring*, *Eichmann in Jerusalem*, *In Cold Blood*, *The Fire Next Time*, *Gideon's Trumpet*, Dwight Macdonald on Michael Harrington's *The Other America*, Richard Harris on gun control, Richard Rovere on Joseph McCarthy, Mary McCarthy on Florence, Venice and her girlhood, and a dozen writers on Vietnam.

To be sure, as Yagoda observes, Shawn needed lots of copy to fill up all those fat issues of the ad-rich sixties and seventies. But this is a list of articles that will get any editor into heaven, even if it omits the usual suspects: the merry pranksters, redskinned wildboys, and punk subjectives; the Norman Mailers and Hunter Thompsons. (Although Joan Didion should have been a natural, wearing a bikini and a migraine to every convulsion of the postwar culture, her gnomic haikus had to wait for Gottlieb in the nineties.) But it is also this very same list that seems to infuriate Renata Adler, guilty as it is of association with "moral self-infatuation," "politically correct propaganda and heavy preaching," and a "tilt" "consistently, predictably, piously, and joylessly, to the Left."

Adler arrived at the *New Yorker* in 1963, by way of Bryn Mawr, Harvard, and the Sorbonne, and would maintain a drawing account and a cubicle there for more than thirty years, before, during and after her departures to ghost speeches for Peter Rodino and Elizabeth Arden, to write her eerie novels, to go to lunch with Felix Rohatyn, to law school at Yale, to the *Times* to review movies, and to *Vanity Fair* for the hell of it—entering the halls of Condé Nast, like so many of us, as the little children followed Stephen of Vendôme south to Marseilles in 1212, expecting the Club Med Red Sea to part and allow us to pass over to the Promised Land, being sold instead into slavery in Egypt. *Gone* is her elliptical essay on those years, with an emphasis on Late Shawn Decadence: "What had been at best a narrative out of *The Tempest* passed through the more deluded episodes of *A Midsummer Night's Dream* and ended in a parody of *King Lear.*"

We have come to the peculiar people. Not that everybody who works for the *New Yorker* is peculiar; only the ones who write memoirs. But as we read through conflicting accounts of the Tom Wolfe, Alastair Reid, Penelope Gilliatt, and Janet Malcolm scandals (whoops!), of the clean young men from Jonathan Schell to Charles McGrath who were so briefly anointed in the Wars of Succession (as if, says Adler, Shawn "had any intention of permitting the magazine to survive him"), of the hostile Newhouse takeover (did they really think they were immune from vulture capitalism?), of the Masada mentality that confronted Gottlieb (leading to only four indignant resignations, one of them by Shawn's paramour), and of the plunge into glitz and debt, the place itself, half homeless shelter, half hermetic cult, practically insisted on peculiarity.

Shawn, both a claustro- and an agoraphobe, fearful of heights, airplanes, elevators, cold, and blood, almost never turned down anything; he simply didn't publish it. And if indeed a piece was scheduled, you'd think the monks were illuminating a manuscript. ("Commas in the *New Yorker*," E. B. White told the *Paris Review*, "fall with the precision of knives in a circus act, outlining the victim.") Even then, after no matter how many edits and rewrites on fresh proofs, likely as not the piece was dropped overnight, in favor of something perverse, and you couldn't ask the editor why or when. Nor were you ever to inquire how much the editor intended to pay, which payment anyway was based on a sliding scale of one rate up to so many words, another rate after, depending on who you were, what you'd been promised in bonus points, or whether you threatened to sell it elsewhere, which meant you hurt the editor's passive-aggressive feelings. But so obstructed were the halls that you couldn't organize a betting pool, much less a rebellion, and so what you did was seethe.

It's hard to imagine a system better contrived to foster dependency, enable paranoia, and promote dysfunction. Oedipus! Peter Pan! Ved Mehta even speaks of "patricide." But then Ved also compares the whole *New Yorker* "extended family" to something out of Salinger. If, for Adler, Shawn toward the end was Lear, Ved is reminded of Alyosha in *The Brothers Karamazov* and Myshkin in *The Idiot*, whereas Harold Brodkey thought he combined "the best qualities of Napoleon and St. Francis of Assisi," and Janet Flanner believed him to be "beyond our human conception." Lillian Ross, contrarily, feels that Shawn martyred himself for the Mother Ship; he should have been writing his own stories instead of pacifying crybabies. And from his pillow talk to Lillian—"I am there but I am not there"; "Why am I more ghost than man?"; "Who has declared me null and void?"—he seems less like a character out of Shakespeare or Dostoyevsky than out of Beckett, having chewed his way to the end of his tether all the way down to squeak.

Does any of this matter? Adler says she loved him. She also says he loved her back. She says a lot of things, some of them so well (about editors, for instance, "who cannot leave a piece, or a line of a piece, intact—eating through a text, leaf and branch, like tent caterpillars, leaving everywhere their mark") that you want to click your heels. And then she says some more things, and you find that you believe maybe every other word of it. For instance:

Adler says that Shawn had created "a mystique and an ethic" of "silence," the feeling "that it was vulgar, perhaps morally wrong to write," which accounts for the Shane-like vanishing acts of Salinger, Joseph Mitchell, and Dwight Macdonald. But then how to explain John McPhee, Calvin Trillin, Janet Malcolm, Ren Weschler, John Updike, or Pauline Kael?

She says Shawn was so "honorable" that "the only way he could break his word . . . was to forget he had given it"—and that this habit "of saying, or promising, something and promptly forgetting it," "this duplicity, these lapses of memory" had become "an essential element of Mr. Shawn's way of running the magazine." Never mind that this is not precisely loving. It also suggests Renata should get out more. I've never known an editor anywhere, or any boss for that matter, who hasn't found it convenient to enunciate one historical imperative late at night, and then, snap, crackle, pop, make up a different absolute truth the following morning for breakfast.

She says that Lillian Ross is not to be trusted because she never quotes Shawn as saying "anything of even the slightest depth, wit, intelligence, or interest—on any subject." But then neither does Adler. Her Shawn is wholly furtive, evasive, self-deluding, if not in fact senile. Consciously or not (one of her favorite locutions), Adler is as hard on this man she says she loves as she is on the hapless Adam Gopnik.

And why Gopnik, a minor player, late to the stage? So what if he pedaled the tricycle of his career fast enough to lap three different editors? For this, does he really rate a raw scorn she only hints at for, say, Jonathan Schell and Roger Angell? The Gopnik pages are almost as ugly as her diary notation on life with her "friend" Bob Gottlieb: "the place has the air of a shabby boarding school—sans headmaster, sans faculty or curriculum. There is just the dormitory, run by prefects—complete with hazing, and a kind of undeclared, bullying homosexuality."

After awhile one wants to get out of these heads and closets, out of the hypnotherapy and the ecstatic Kabbala, back to the sunlit pages of Yagoda. So Cheever liked Salinger, but not Barthelme. So Barthelme and Brodkey couldn't stand each other. So Ved's feelings were hurt when Gottlieb bumped him for Doris Lessing. So Renata was shocked that Bob left his door open. So I now understand why, if I pan a book by Jonathan Schell, one set of *New Yorker* editors will embrace me, and if I pan a book by Janet Malcolm, an entirely different set will shine my shoes. A line from Barthelme's *Snow White* comes to queasy mind: "Do you feel that the creation of new modes of hysteria is a viable undertaking for the artist of today? Yes ( ) No ( )."

About the peculiar institution we all have a right to mourn. Who, exactly, ordained: Let them eat Hollywood and psychobabble? That all the *Talk* must be about *George*? Why should we shrug our shoulders at the glossy triumph of the kind of scratch-and-sniff journalism that, between pornographic ads for vodka and dot-coms, postures in front of experience instead of engaging it; that fidgets in its cynical opportunism for an angle, a spin or a take, instead of consulting compass points of principle; that strikes attitudes like matches, the better to admire its own wiseguy profile in the mirror of the slicks? Haven't *they* already shrugged off *us*? About the writers of memoirs, however, this caution: If you are infantilized, codependent, paranoid, blocked, or in any other way abused, stop complaining, get up from your sulk, get out of the dollhouse, slam the door behind you and take your sad songs on the road to some other honkytonk. Nora was a mensch.

Meanwhile, the old magazine gets better under its new editor every week. Of course, the last time I said something nice about the *New Yorker*, in these pages on the occasion of its fiftieth birthday, Pauline Kael accused me of angling for a job. She needed to get out more, too.

*Part Two*

THE POLITICS OF FICTION

# PHILIP ROTH (1):
# BEDTIME FOR BOLSHEVIKS

O N  H E A R I N G  T H A T  H I S  F I R S T  W I F E  "Josie" had
been killed in a car crash, Philip himself, not Tarnopol,
Kepesh, Portnoy, Zuckerman or any other counterfeit Roth,
told us in *The Facts:* "How could she be dead if I didn't do it?" And
he'd certainly tried to, in both *When She Was Good* and *My Life As
a Man.* So much for the alcoholic shiksa. Now it's Claire Bloom's
turn.

From a misleading excerpt in the *New Yorker,* there was reason to
expect that Roth's new novel, *I Married a Communist,* would explore blacklisting and a radical dream in ruins; that its announced
theme of "betrayal"—as in *Lear, Hamlet,* and *Othello,* or of Adam,
Esau, and Samson—had something to do with selling out a country
or a revolution or at least a sacred trust. We may even have hoped to
spend quality time with its high-school teacher, Murray Ringold,
who had made it his mission in postwar Newark to initiate young
Nathan Zuckerman into "masculine intensities," who had taught
him to *box* with books. After so many literary intellectuals choosing
up tetherball sides between Stalin and Trotsky in the thirties, after
so many Hollywood screenwriters wearing Spartacus hairshirts in
the 1950s, why not for once a homespun English teacher, a left-wing
*Centaur?*

Instead we get a rant. Half a century after Newark, Murray, age
ninety, and Nathan, age sixty-four, meet again in the Berkshires. For
six nights in a cabin to which Nathan has retreated like a Melville
*isolato,* they remember Murray's younger bigger ferocious brother

Ira—Ira, who used to descend on them from Manhattan like a hammer and sickle; Ira, who took a thrilled young Nathan to Progressive Party rallies where Paul Robeson sang; Ira, the very embodiment of stormbird virility, a Depression dropout with a murderous secret, a digger of ditches and a mucker of zinc mines who had been Bolshevized in World War II by the soldier/stevedore/steelworker Johnny O'Day. About this brother, Murray and Roth are both reductive:

> The pseudoscientific Marxist lexicon, the utopian cant that went with it—dish that stuff out to someone as unschooled and ill educated as Ira, indoctrinate an adult who is not too skilled in brainwork with the intellectual glamour of Big Sweeping Ideas, inculcate a man of limited intelligence, an excitable type who is as angry as Ira . . .

And what you get is "Iron Rinn," a workingstiff/ideologue whose flair for impersonating Abe Lincoln at union sing-alongs wins him a job on a network radio show, where he pretends to be Nathan Hale, Jack London, and Wild Bill Hickock; an outsized Comintern Mariner forever thumping strangers with the albatross of his "stump speech" on Negroes, Korea, and the Marshall Plan, whose worst mistake is to marry his leading lady, former silent-screen star Eve Frame. Evil Eve!—who used to be Chava Fromkin, a nice Jewish girl from Brooklyn, before she went Hollywood, cohabited with a gay actor who did icky things in the south of France, gave birth to an egregious girl-child (the harp-playing overeater Sylphid), and put on uppity English airs.

Come the Witch Hunt, and it's not *Red Channels*, Tailgunner Joe, Hearst and/or HUAC that do in Ira, nor even the Twentieth Party Congress. It's Eve, whose popular celebrity should have been his protective cocoon. But her thralldom to the jealous Sylphid causes her to abort a baby Ira longs for, and her fury at his infidelities with a vulgar Polish masseuse will lead her to publish a ghostwritten tell-all exposé, likewise called *I Married a Communist*, in which she fingers her own "Machiavellian" husband as the "ringleader of the underground Communist espionage unit committed to controlling

American radio." Iron Rinn, a blunt instrument, uses "the weapon of mass culture to tear down the American way of life."

So Ira loses his job, his marriage, his reputation, and his sanity. So his guilty-by-association brother Murray has to sell vacuum cleaners for six years, while the union appeals his blacklisting in Newark's public schools. So even Nathan, although he immediately abandons Howard Fast for Joseph Conrad at the University of Chicago, doesn't get a Fulbright he deserves. All this happens not before our eyes, but long ago, far away and mostly third-hand talked-about, a narrative of hearsay evidence. Such hearsay is, of course, Roth's specialty. Talking heads speak in tongues. In his bat cave, the sonar is always alert to Sneak Anxiety Attacks. On his crystal set, we pick up a spackle of vaudeville and harangue, a static of street-snitch and paranoid gibber, a Morse code asking if anybody's there, an SOS to all the Freudian slips at sea. Roth *raps*.

Between raps, he can be distracted. He is insatiably curious, and a village explainer. The best pages in *I Married a Communist*, not counting the two that parody a bodice busting historical novel about Abelard and Eloise, are devoted to zinc mining, harp music, taxidermy, Norman Corwin's radio plays, and a matched pair of funerals, one for a shoemaker's pet canary and the other for Richard Nixon. Johnny O'Day himself shows up briefly to disdain Nathan, with East Chicago in his narrowed eyes, and he's a fair Leninist copy of such Citizens of Virtue as Robespierre and St. Just, though nowhere near as scary as the Whittaker Chambers character, Gifford Maxim, in Lionel Trilling's otherwise complacent *The Middle of the Journey*. But we could have used a lot more curiosity about American radicalism in general, about the anti-Semitic component of the Red Scare in particular, and about the multiplicity of motives among stormbirds.

Here's the huge however. This time out Roth hasn't listened very hard. Or else decided that what he hears isn't worth his crafty body-English—that astral physics, those black holes and Doppler shifts, he customarily employs to mess with word-waves. At home or on the radio, what comes out of Ira's mouth is garbagy reptilian agitprop.

What comes out of Eve's is whiny and mendacious. What comes out of Murray's, unless he's talking about Shakespeare, is pissed-off-know-it-all. Even Nathan, when he isn't feeling lousy about his father or contemplating his very first artichoke, can barely rouse himself to sarcasm. He has headed to these hills to sulk: "I came here because I don't want a story any longer. I'd had my share." Only loathsome Sylphid has some bite, using her harp to slice and dice. Moreover, except for Leo Glucksman, the professor/esthete who summons Nathan to a higher literary calling (and who's also warm for his form), all the big yakkers in the novel sound too much alike, equally locker-room crude and tough-guy approximate, as if genuine manliness is suspicious of linguistic daintiness, of discriminations among ideas and feelings.

What's worse, we are bullied. Long before we've ever met Eve, we are *told* that her fake gentility had "hardened into a form like layers of wax" around a self-hating wick; that she was "steeped like a teabag in aristocratic pretensions." Long before we have ever met Sylphid, we already *know* that she's a "resentful, sullen, baleful" "time bomb" of a daughter, as well as fat. Not a page yet to themselves, but both have been trashed and baggied. Nor will either of these codependents subsequently surprise us—the mother "pathologically embarrassed" by her Jewish origins, and the daughter at ease in her own skin only when "hating her mother and playing the harp." If a crucial datum about Ira—his violent pre-Communist past—is withheld till late in the novel, its revelation simplifies rather than complicates him. Anyway, Murray has already *told* us what we're supposed to think about his politics and his marriage: "Why, emotionally, is a man of his type reciprocally connected to a woman of her type? The usual reason: Their flaws fit. Ira cannot leave that marriage any more than he can leave the Communist Party." As Murray will tell Nathan exactly what *he* was to Ira, just in case the reader missed it:

> You were the nurtured Newark boy given everything. You were the guy's
> Prince Hal. You were Johnny O'Day Ringold—that's what you were all

about. That was your job, whether you knew it or not. To help him shield himself against his nature, against all the force in that big body, all the murderous rage.

Nor has Murray any illusions about his own do-good self, calling down anathemas on the very idea of coherent politics and purposeful action. He stayed too long in Newark, until his was the last white family in the neighborhood. And so, of course, his wife was murdered by a mugger:

> When you loosen yourself, as I tried to, from all the obvious delusions — religion, ideology, Communism — you're still left with the myth of your own goodness. Which is the final delusion. And the one to which I sacrificed Doris.

In other words, there is no world-historical crisis. There are only talk-show issues.

This is not at all what Leo Glucksman called for in Chicago: "Your task is *not* to simplify. . . . Not to ease the contradiction, not to deny the contradiction, but to see where, within the contradiction, lies the tormented human being." But Roth is evening a score, as he has sought elsewhere to even scores with such critics as Irving Howe, Richard Gilman, Norman Podhoretz, and James Wolcott. Just like Eve Frame, Claire Bloom has published a tell-all exposé, in which she called her ex-husband Philip "Machiavellian." Like Eve, Claire has a musician-daughter (Anna) from a previous marriage (to Rod Steiger), who wanted to live with her mother. Like Eve, Claire is Jewish, though she seems to dislike herself for things she's done instead of who she is. Never mind that Bloom's *Leaving a Doll's House* wasn't much harder on Roth, after eighteen years of living with him, than he has been on himself and his facsimiles after six decades of the same. Nor that Anna was still a teen, not twenty-four, and singing at a piano instead of plucking on a harp, when her mother took up with Moishe Pipik. Nor that Claire never changed her name, and would seem — after several marriages, a long affair with Richard Burton, and brief flings with Lawrence Olivier, who didn't like her, Yul Brynner, who dumped her for Kim Novak, and Anthony Quinn, whom she despised—at least as sexually experienced as any Polish masseuse.

Never even mind that Bloom in print speaks a sort a therapized babytalk, explaining that Philip's problem was "a profound mistrust of the sexual power of women," whereas hers was that "fatherless women gravitate toward emotionally unavailable men." At least she likes his books, except for *Deception*, in which he *did* rub her nose in his hanky-pankies, real or imagined. Whereas Ira, Murray, and Nathan don't like anything about Eve. But you know how it is. When someone tells the whole world that you had to be hospitalized for depression because John Updike didn't like *Operation Shylock*, you tend to hold the kind of grudge that, if indulged, distorts a novel and trivializes an era.

Stop me before I transgress again. If not even Nathan is really Philip, Ira certainly can't be. Didn't he tell us in *The Facts* that what he's always done as a writer is "spontaneously set out to improve on actuality in the interest of being more interesting"? Naturally, he then submitted the manuscript of *The Facts* to Zuckerman, who advised him not to publish. In fact—or the preemptive fiction—there are so many counter-Roths whirling around us that they stick to the walls, staring at each other, in what seems less like a wilderness of mirrors than a centrifuge. For the purposes of *Shylock* he mitotically divided himself, like the two Oswalds, so one Roth could go to Jerusalem to write a book about a second Roth who promoted something called Diasporism, while both slept with the recovering anti-Semite Wanda Jane Possesski. In that novel, which was a lot better than Updike said it was, even Arab intellectuals like George Ziad (Edward Said?) got to be more interesting in four sentences— "What do an oppressed people's problems matter to a great comic artist like you? The show must go on. Say no more. You're a very amusing performer—and a moral idiot!"—than Ira is in a whole book. Just as, in *The Ghost Writer*, Anne Frank got to be sexier than Eve Frame. But then again, somebody or other told us in *Deception*: "I write fiction and I'm told it's autobiography, I write autobiography and I'm told it's fiction, so since I'm so dim and they're so smart, let *them* decide what it is or it isn't."

I've decided. On the other hand, I had hoped that after *Patrimony*, his splendid account of his custodianship of his dying father, none of this pettifogging would ever again be necessary. When his father died, at eighty-six, Philip at last seemed all grown up: "He wasn't just any father, he was *the* father, with everything there is to hate and everything there is to love." From a writer who has made this difficult stagecoach passage, who has advanced from dependency and rage to ambivalence and accommodation to changing the soiled underwear of the man who used to change his diapers, we expect more than Murray's myth of his own goodness.

In a review of *American Pastoral* in the *Nation*, Todd Gitlin lamented the "short list" of fiction, especially American fiction, "for a long history of radical politics." Short though it may be—and, on the sixties, Gitlin might also have mentioned Alice Walker's *Meridian* and Diane Johnson's *Lying Low* in addition to Sol Yurick, Marge Piercy, John Sayles, and Rosellen Brown—it's all we have to remind us that once upon a time there were men and women who failed to change the world, not because they were wrong to want to try, but because there weren't enough of them. Easy enough now to see that the Soviets themselves betrayed everybody else's Left. But way back when, it had to be at least as difficult to leave the Party as to jump out of wedlock with an alcoholic shiksa.

Daniel Aaron's *Writers on the Left* (1961) remains the best canvas of a half-century of bohemianism and rebellion, of show trials and apostasies, of waste and vituperation. He sends us back to John Dos Passos (on Sacco and Vanzetti and the two Americas) before he went to work for *National Review,* and Max Eastman (in whose novel *Venture* Big Bill Haywood makes an appearance) before he went to work for *Reader's Digest*; to Sherwood Anderson's *Marching Men,* Jack Conroy's *The Disinherited* and Joseph Freeman's *Never Call Retreat*; to Mike Gold's *Jews Without Money* and Granville Hicks's *Only One Storm*. Not all of this is zippy reading, but it's a better use of our time than trying to figure out why Tom Wolfe's new novel gets nominated for a National Book Award before it's even published while Toni Morrison's *Paradise* is chopped liver.

James T. Farrell, the Trotskyite deviationist who used to correct my every printed error in handwritten notes that were barely legible, gave us not only a trilogy about Studs Lonigan but a tetralogy about Danny O'Neill, who was radicalized at the University of Chicago before Nathan Zuckerman wasn't. Josephine Herbst wrote radical novels and went off to the Spanish Civil War with Dos Passos and sold a first edition of *Ulysses* to pay her way to Russia, before she was informed on to the FBI by Katherine Anne Porter. Mary Lee Settle gave us one novel in her Beulah Quintet, *The Scapegoat*, with Mother Jones as a character, and another, *Choices*, that went first to Harlan County, then to Spain, and finally to Mississippi on a freedom ride. Nelson Algren! Kay Boyle! Edward Dahlberg! Theodore Dreiser! Waldo Frank!

In *Going Away*, before Clancy Sigal got to Doris Lessing, he had to drive across country in the middle of the 1956 Hungarian Revolution, looking up every old radical from his left-wing union days, the sold-out and the burnt-out, the persevering and the purged, from A-bomb tests by dawn's early White Sands light over the ceaseless slots of Reno, to Walla Walla State Prison, to ever-Wobbly Coeur D'Alene, to the Mark Twain theme park of Hannibal, Mo., to his Chicago childhood antifascist stamping grounds, to a Houghton Mifflin literary fellowship in Boston. He managed in this fevered passage to acquaint us with aircraft workers, candy mixers, punch press operators, spot welders, geologists, and bookies, as well as a whole left-wing culture consisting of all those meetings Ira Ringold never seems to go to, plus a cassette in the head of Haymarket and Lawrence tapes, of Emma Goldman and Rosa Luxemburg, of Harry Bridges and Molly Maguire: "We are the residual legatees of struggle, of cultural involvement, of personal meaning, of the search for justice and honesty. Why is there no place for us in America?" And: "All my life I had tried to sink myself within some community, and all my life blood told. My racial memory was that of the borderer, the outlaw observer, the gangster Essene, the lustful Brook Valleyite, the Proudhonist with finger at side of nose, the irrevocably homeless revolutionary."

In *Standing Fast*, Harvey Swados followed a handful of American radicals from the Molotov Ribbentrop pact to the assassination of JFK—a college instructor, a labor organizer, a political cartoonist; one character who takes to journalism, another who takes to Israel, and a third who takes to drink; in lofts and libraries, on symposia and picket lines. "Work," says Vito. "That's all there is." "The trick," says Norm, "is to go on living even after you've found out what kind of world it really is." "One way or the other," says Sy, "we tried to keep an idea alive. There weren't enough of us, there never are. We were ridiculously wrong about a lot of things but who wasn't? And what idea did they keep alive, the others?"

In *The Book of Daniel*, E. L. Doctorow will end up at Disneyland, after Jones Beach and Paul Robeson, Hester Street and the Triangle fire, the Red Army Chorus singing "Meadowlands" and the Rosenbergs in the electric chair. He also spends time with the other Edgar (Allan Poe, "the scream from the smiling face of America"); with Abbie Hoffman ("Authority is momentum. Break the momentum. Legitimacy is illegitimate. Make it show its ass. Hit and run. You got forty seconds, man"); and with the Franny and Zooey of the Cold War. A red-diaper baby knows: "We understand St. Joan: You want to fuck her but if you do you miss the point." And: "To be a revolutionary you need only hold out your arms and dive. It is something like the sound barrier, there's a boom when you break through, a concussion of space, a compression of the content of space. An echo ricochets through the red pacific twilight all the way over the ocean." However:

> The Berlin Wall is not a wall. It is a seam. It is a seam that binds the world. The entire globe is encased in lead, riveted bolted stripped wired locked tight and sprocketed with spikes, like a giant mace. Inside is hollow. Occasionally this hot lead and steel casing expands or cracks in the heat of the sun, and along the seams, one of which is called the Berlin Wall, a space or crevice appears temporarily that is just big enough for a person to fall

through. In a world divided in two the radical is free to choose one side or
the other. That's the radical choice. The halves of the world are like the
two hemispheres of Mengleberg. My mother and father fell through an
open seam one day and then the hemispheres pressed shut.

I haven't the leisurely space to dilate on what Vivian Gornick and
Carl Bernstein had to say about their Communist parents. Nor the
confidence to guess out loud at what Norman Mailer might have
made of his *Barbary Shore* if he hadn't gone Hollywood, like Chava
Fromkin. But contemporary novelists like Chuck Wachtel, who left
the Lower East Side in *The Gates* for Managua and the revolution of
the Sandinistas, and Toni Cade Bambara, who spoke for the ghosts of
the murdered children of Atlanta in *Those Bones Are Not My Child,*
and Richard Powers, who abandoned genetics and computer science
long enough in *Operation Wandering Soul* to try to save the third
world orphans in a public hospital in Watts, belong to a long radical
lifeline from Margaret Fuller (who was wasted on Emerson) to
Tillie Olsen (who asked in *Tell Me a Riddle*: "Oh why do I have to
feel that it happens to me too? Why is it like this? And why do I have
to care?") to Grace Paley (who would enjoin us to "go forth, with
fear and courage and rage to save the world").

Roth, up there in the Berkshires less like Zapata than Dennis the
Menace, could do worse than consult Nathaniel Hawthorne, whose
poet in *The Blithesdale Romance* permitted himself this wistfulness:
"Whatever else I may repent of, therefore let it be reckoned neither
among my sins nor follies that I once had faith and force enough to
form generous hopes of the world's destiny."

# PHILIP ROTH (2):
## SKIN GAME

---

### 1.

Like Portnoy in the Holy Land, Zuckerman in the Berkshires can't get it up. The problem isn't the state of Israel. The problem is absence of a prostate. All that worry in *The Counterlife* about quintuple bypass heart surgery turns out to have been beside the point. Cancer is the point. Philip Roth's autumnal novels are riddled with it. As if the rioting cells were Mickey Sabbaths, anarchist-provocateurs, the body itself is besieged, plundered, ridiculed, and desecrated. At least since *American Pastoral* (1997), Zuckerman has been impotent. In *The Human Stain*, he is also incontinent, with cotton pads in his plastic underpants. Why should Roth spare us the prurient details of our dying—a morphine drip, an IV pole—any more than he has ever spared us the baroque graffiti of our unobstructed id, the priapic troll and *vagina dentata*?

Here I should say that I take this personally. Some of us have been taking Roth personally all our reading lives. If you happen to be an American male born six years after him, and allow for the usual cycle of his thinking up, writing down, and seeing published each of his twenty-four books, the books seem to arrive just in eerie time to be about exactly what you're going through. You are always following dreadful suit. When, say, *Goodbye, Columbus* shows up at the end of the fifties, in your junior year of college, you have already decided that you can't go home again, not without feeling like an anthropologist among the Moonies. On consulting *Letting Go*, you

find your doubts about grad school superscribed in fiery signs. Whatever its faults, *When She Was Good* is a Grimmly punitive fairy tale
about marrying too young, and the wrong person. If *Portnoy* is *sui
generis* (a "talking cure" for Salinger's Seymour), the rest of the
books somehow savagely correspond with your own discovery of
baseball and breasts; artistic vocation, erotic transgression, and political disgust; addictive behaviors, symbolic parricides, and pas-
tiched selves. Almost before you've felt bad, he crowds you with
second thought and hindsight, secret diaries and wiretap transcripts,
telephone calls from the governor at midnight and last-minute
DNA evidence. (This just in from the Witness Protection Program,
the Freedom of Information Act, and postmodernism: You are an
unreliable narrator of your own life.) At your window, his back is
turned: been there, done that, moved on, very spooky—like Anne
Frank in E. I. Lonoff's study, Angela Davis in Swede Levov's
kitchen, and the ghost of Mickey Sabbath's mother. Our feet are
stained with the gripes of Roth.

What's worse, we think like Roth, or at least the Zuckerman
we've known since he was a tadpole in short stories by Peter Tarnopol: "The disputatious stance, the aggressively marginal sensi-
bility, the disavowal of community ties, the taste for scrutinizing a
social event as though it were a dream or a work of art—to Zuckerman this was the very mark of the intellectual Jews . . . on whom
he was modeling his own style of thought." Roth is to us what Zuckerman is to Jimmy Ben-Joseph Lustig in *The Counterlife:* "You're a
real father to me, Nathan. And not only to me—to a whole generation of pathetic fuck-ups. We're all satirists *because* of you." We even
sound like him in our own skulls, as if we were stand-up comics or
late-night deejays or manic-depressive analysands picking up the
paranoia in the ether through the fillings in our speedfreak teeth,
the box scores and killing sprees, channeling Kafka, Céline, and
Lenny Bruce. Nor does it matter that we weren't born to it, under the
burning Spanish tile in a Southern California tract house, renegade
Catholics or lapsed Baptists. He *made* us. For children of the fifties
with literary ambitions, it was necessary to be horny, skeptical, sar-

castic, and Jewish—to Augie or to Nathan—just as it's obligatory for white kids in the punk suburbs these days to hip-hop.

And now, with the usual lag in Roth years, as if he were a pottery clock, a clam-bed fossil or a peat bog in reverse, he tells us that we've had it. That we are not safe in our ovaries or our colons or our aortas from "the stupendous decimation that is death sweeping us all away. . . . the ceaseless perishing." That we can't hold our water, get it up, figure it out, make amends. That we got everything wrong, and our children hate us: "Learn before you die," thinks Coleman Silk in *The Human Stain*, "to live beyond the jurisdiction of their enraged, loathsome, stupid blame." But our license has expired. "People come apart," Norman tells Mickey in *Sabbath's Theater*; "And aging doesn't help. I know a number of men our age, right here in Manhattan, clients, friends, who've been going through crises like this. Some shock just undoes them around sixty—the plates shift and the earth starts shaking and all the pictures fall off the wall."

Philip himself, in *Patrimony*, contemplates the tumor eating his father's brain, "the fingernail that had been aggrandizing the hollows of his skull for a decade, the material as obdurate and gristly as he was, that had cracked open the bone behind his nose and with a stubborn, unrelenting force just like his, had pushed tusklike through into the cavities of his face." Looking down at the grave these books dig for us, we feel like Nathan's brother Henry:

> My brother was a Zulu, or whoever the people are who wear bones in their noses, he was our Zulu, and ours were the heads he shrunk and stuck up on the post for everyone to gape at. The man was a cannibal. . . . a pure cannibal, murdering people, eating people, without ever quite having to pay the price. Then something putrid was stinging his nostrils and it was Henry who was leaning over and violently beginning to retch, Henry vomiting as though *he* had broken the primal taboo and eaten human flesh—Henry, like a cannibal who out of respect for his victim, to gain whatever history and power is there, eats the brain and learns that raw it tastes like poison.

Still, there's some jack left in the old box.

2.

*He explained that puppets were not for children; puppets did not say, "I am*
*innocent and good." They said the opposite. "I will play with you," they said,*
*"however I like." (Sabbath's Theater)*

There is this to be said for an impotent Zuckerman, hiding out in the
Berkshires: He has stopped playing with himself and jerking around
the rest of us. He's run out of his own multiple beings and sundry
counter-Zuckermans, those Moishe Pipiks and "Philip Roths." For
the moment, he seems even to have exhausted Israel as a subject,
although the last word on the Diaspora Blues will not be spoken
until both Roth and Cynthia Ozick are done with their career-long
cabalistic smackdown. He's more interested in other people, and all
of a sudden listening to them as though he were Studs Terkel or
Charles Kuralt. Thus, in *American Pastoral,* he will listen so hard to
Swede Levov, the athletic hero of his Newark youth, the manufac-
turer of fine gloves and monstrous daughters, that he has to write a
book about what he hasn't heard. Thus, in *I Married a Communist,*
he listens so hard to Murray Ringold, the high-school teacher who
initiated him into "masculine intensities," who taught him to box
with books, that he swallows and then spits back up at us a vulgar-
ized and reductive history of a lost American Left. And thus, in *The
Human Stain,* he listens so hard to Coleman Silk, a seventy-two-
year-old professor emeritus of classical literature at nearby Athena
College, that he actually intuits a resounding unspokenness.

Silk arrives on Zuckerman's doorstep in the summer of 1998 pur-
sued by furies. Three years before, this scholar who for decades at the
college taught "the wrath of Achilles, the rage of Philoctetes, the
fulminations of Medea, the nakedness of Ajax, the despair of Electra,
and the suffering of Prometheus," who for the next sixteen was
its first and only Jewish dean of faculty, had been hounded off campus, into seclusion, by accusations of racism. In a lecture hall he
had asked out loud about a couple of missing students—students
he had never seen in class, students he had no idea were African
Americans—"Does anyone know these people? Do they exist or are

they spooks?" Meaning, naturally, ghosts. (Hearing the word "spooks," you and I are likely to think of the CIA and *The X-Files*. This seems not to have occurred to anybody at Athena.) The ensuing abuse, much of it anti-Semitic, took a toll on Silk's equanimity and his wife's health. He stewed, she died, and now, to ratchet up a cycle of retaliation that's very Greek indeed, no sooner has Silk found a female willing to sleep with him—a thirty-four-year-old cleaning woman named Faunia Farley—than he starts getting poison-pen letters from the expat chairperson of the Department of Languages and Literature, Delphine Roux, and intimations of disgust from his Orthodox son, Mark, who likes to bloviate about what David did to Absalom and Isaac did to Esau. Silk wants Zuckerman to write a book on his persecution.

There is a lot to be said about Faunia—incest survior, apparent illiterate, abused wife, lethal mother, failed suicide, milker of cows, lover of crows, and one more example of the tendency of Roth's protagonists to find randy sexual partners among the lumpen, the declassed, or the Eastern European—who explains that "the human stain" is the trail we leave behind of "cruelty, abuse, error, excrement, semen." And as much to say about her stalker ex-husband, Les, an ice-fishing Vietnam vet so deranged by the feedback loop in his head of severed ears and rivers of blood that he's not to be trusted in a Chinese restaurant (Roth at his scary-Gogol best). And quite a bit to say, too, about Delphine Roux, who may look like Leslie Caron, and may have written a dissertation on "Self-Denial in Georges Bataille," but who has an inordinate amount of trouble composing a personals ad for the *New York Review*, in which the dreamboat she seeks seems most to resemble either Milan Kundera or Coleman Silk.

There are two brilliant dance scenes, one to Sinatra's recording of "Bewitched, Bothered, and Bewildered," the other to Gershwin's "The Man I Love," plus more of the Mahler we have come to expect in Roth; and pages on dairy farming that remind us of his love of know-how, those earlier inquiries into glove-making, zinc mining, and taxidermy; and a number of references to non-Greek literature, from Chaucer, Shakespeare, and Dickens to Balzac, Stendhal, and Mann to Hawthorne, Melville, and Thoreau to Kropotkin, Bakunin, and Kristeva. That all this happens in the Summer of Oval Orality and Monica Convergence allows Roth to hyperventilate, not at all persuasively, about the American propensity for "righteous grandstanding" and "ecstasies of sanctimony." In fact, most of us seem not to have cared what Bill Clinton put in his mouth so as he also put money in our pockets.

But the unspokenness is elsewhere. In several senses of the word, Coleman Silk himself will prove to be a "spook." At his funeral—there is an amazing amount of death in *The Human Stain*—his sister Ernestine tells Zuckerman: "As white a college as there was in New England, and that's where Coleman made his career. As white a subject as there was in the curriculum, and that's what Coleman chose to teach." And yet, as we begin to understand in an abrupt flashbacking on page 85, while we're still shaking our heads to get them started, Silk himself was born black, if light-skinned and green-eyed, on the wrong side of the psychic tracks in East Orange, New Jersey, not far from Zuckerman's own Weequahic. Ever since he got out of the Navy and moved to Greenwich Village in the Beat fifties, this Howard dropout has been passing as both white and *Jewish*. Not even his children have a clue.

Imagine Zuckerman's excitement at a "heretofore unknown amalgam of the most unalike of America's historic undesirables"— and his very own White Negro! He is permitted to picture Silk's desire, from earliest childhood, "to be free: not black, not white— just on his own and free"; his intoxication on "the elixir of the secret . . . like being fluent in another language"; his determination to forge "a distinct historical destiny," "to become a new being," to "bifurcate"; "the high drama of upping and leaving—and the energy and cruelty that rapturous drive demands"; plus, of course, his discovery of "the we that is inescapable: the present moment, the common lot, the current mood, the mind of one's country, the stranglehold of history." Playacting, imposture, ventriloquism, displacement, espionage, masquerades, counterlives, audacity, betray-

als, revenge, exile, hatred of decorum, "antipathies in collison,"
sexual terrorism, self-transformation, and the Dr. Presto Disappearing Act—aren't these the great Roth themes, strummed on as if
every novel of the last fifteen years were a harp like Sylphid's, in *I
Married a Communist?* Weren't we told in that novel, too, that "the
hardest thing in the world is to cut the knot of your life and leave"?

Moreover, Zuckerman is allowed to go back and look at New Jersey all over again through green eyes and black skin, to beat up Jewish kids in the boxing ring, visit West Point under false pretenses, be
refused a hot dog at Woolworth's in the nation's capital, get kicked
out of a whites-only cathouse in a southern port, and write poetry,
cultivate "singularity," and sleep like a spy with Steena, the blond
Icelandic Dane, in a who-cares bohemia, before marrying Iris, a left-
wing Jewish painter of abstractions whose "irreversible hair"—
"You could polish pots with it and no more alter its construction than
if it were harvested from the inky depths of the sea, some kind of
wiry reef-building organism, a dense living onyx hybrid of coral and
shrub"—will be the perfect camouflage for whatever their children
eventually look like. And finally, in a grueling scene that reminds us
of just how good Roth can be when he isn't telling us what to think
about his characters before we've even met them, Zuckerman's
imaginary Silk can "murder" his own mother, a dignified hospital
nurse, by ordaining her out of his life forever: "You don't have to
murder your father. The world will do that for you."

Nathan actually admires this brutal act: "It's like the savagery in
*The Iliad.*" On the other hand, and there's always another hand in
Roth, Silk's mother is more convincing: "You think like a prisoner.
You do, Coleman Brutus. You're white as snow and you think like a
slave."

It's an interesting try, more than merely perfunctory, which Roth
has made easier for himself by giving "Silky" Silk a family almost as
middle-class as Zuckerman's own—a father who is an optician instead of a chiropodist; a brother who becomes a teacher instead of
dentist. But about Coleman there is nothing so heartbreaking as
Swede Levov's belief that he has passed a citizenship exam, com-

pleted his assimilation, sealed "his unconscious oneness with America," by marrying Miss New Jersey, the daughter of an Irish Catholic plumber. Nor anything as soul-searing as the sight of Mickey Sabbath, with his dead brother's gun and his clarinet, wearing the Stars and Stripes like a poncho. Indeed, there are many pages in *American Pastoral* that seem more black-inflected than these— about discovering "Afro-Oriental rhythms" and "a belly-dancing beat" on the darker side of town; about, at length, the Newark riots of 1967. Nor does Silk get a King Lear rant of his own. (Far from deploring what John Updike calls the "blocks of *talk*" in Roth, "one babbled essay after another," I love him on his high hobbyhorses. Like Lippman on the West Bank of *The Counterlife*, he is a consummate "diatribalist." What a great word!) Nevertheless, the navel into which Nathan gazes turns out to be a wound in all of us. Look how far Roth has come from, arguably, his silliest novel, *The Breast*, to, certainly, one of his very best, *American Pastoral*.

From, so unsocialized:

> Why shouldn't I be rubbed and oiled and massaged and sucked and licked and fucked, too, if I want it! Why shouldn't I have anything and everything I can think of *every single minute of the day* if that can transport me from this miserable hell!

To, with a star-spangled flourish:

> . . . the angry, rebarbative spitting-out daughter with no interest whatever in being the next successful Levov, flushing him out of hiding as if he were a fugitive—initiating the Swede into the displacement of another America entirely, the daughter and the decade blasting to smithereens his particular form of utopian thinking, the plague America infiltrating the Swede's castle and there infecting everyone. The daughter who transports him out of the longed-for American pastoral and into everything that is its antithesis and its enemy, into the fury, the violence, and the desperation of the counterpastoral—into the indigenous American berserk.

At the end of *The Human Stain* Zuckerman knows that he will have to quit his cabin in the Berkshires if he hopes to save his own life. Where next for this "heretofore unknown amalgam" of Philoctetes and Woody Allen's Zelig, a counter-Forrest and anti-Gump? And on what mythic quest now that polymorphous perversity is out of the question? Jack and the Beanstalk? Puss in Boots? Blue Beard or Ferdinand the Bull? From too much consumption—of junk food and cheap sensations and disposable ideas—Updike's Rabbit exploded. But Nathan's "pathetic fuck-ups," the outlaw children of the Ike era of Freudian psychology, nuclear families, nuclear explosions, and modernist art, never wanted to sell cars or play golf. So?

### 3.

*What was astonishing to him was how people seemed to run out of their own being, run out of whatever the stuff was that made them into who they were and, drained of themselves, turn into the sort of people they would once have felt sorry for. (American Pastoral)*

I am guessing the idea of Coleman Silk was inspired by the case history of the late Anatole Broyard, the essayist and book critic and, once upon a time, a colleague of mine at the *New York Times*. I am told that he and Roth were almost neighbors in Connecticut. And certainly the broad outlines are similar—from the "charming and seductive boy" Roth describes, "a bit demonic even, a snub-nosed, goat-footed Pan," to the boxing, the military service, NYU, the Greenwich Village womanizing, and what a friend called Anatole's "dancing attitude toward life—he'd dance away from you," all the way to the thrilling conversation and the failure to tell the children the truth—although Anatole never pretended to be Jewish.

We had all heard rumors about Anatole, but were less interested in his passing than his sex life. Then Henry Louis Gates Jr. wrote an article on him for the *New Yorker*, later included in his 1997 book, *Thirteen Ways of Looking at a Black Man*. And it was necessary to think again. Being black in this country, Gates reminded us, isn't "elective or incidental." Every black child grows up shadowed by the fact that his or her actions will either "honor" or "betray" the race, even as the black body is eroticized, demonized, fantasized, merchandised, and lynched, in a bad-faith culture that would itself be unimaginable without the blues. Suppose Harry Belafonte never wanted to be "the first Negro matinee idol"? Suppose Colin Powell chose to refuse his role as a poster child for white liberals? Suppose O. J., on whom we ladle so much symbolic significance, is empty himself of any personal meaning, a ping-pong ball of "racialized" discourse? So when a Broyard won't tell his own grown children where he came from, who his parents were, or that he has a sister they have never even met, what are we to conclude, not only about passing or modernism's usual motley of fragmentation, alienation, and liminality, but also about the social construction of race from treaties, edicts, certificates of birth, cards of identity, and all the other barcoded tickets of admission to "authenticity"? "Authenticity," says Gates, "is one of the founding lies of the modern age."

Somewhere, Roth groans. In *The Facts*, he explained that what he does is "spontaneously set out to improve on actuality in the interest of being more interesting." And if we don't believe him, as, say, Claire Bloom obviously didn't on reading *Deception*, well, stuff it: "I write fiction and I'm told it's autobiography, I write autobiography and I'm told it's fiction, so if I'm so dim and they're so smart, let *them* decide what it is or it isn't." So Silk isn't Broyard, and Milton Appel wasn't Irving Howe, and E. I. Lonoff wasn't Bernard Malamud or I. B. Singer, and Felix Abravanel wasn't Saul Bellow, and Eve Frame in no way resembles Claire Bloom, and so far as Roth's concerned, Tarnopol, Kepesh, and Zuckerman are infielders for the Boston Red Sox, and I am the Shah of Iran. As Madeline tells Mickey in the fabulous madhouse scene in *Sabbath's Theater*: "The answer to every question is either Prozac or incest." And this is after she has already explained that "you can only be young once, but you can be immature forever."

I bring up Broyard so I can slip in Gates. Such questions as he raises—in passing, about passing—seem not to have occurred to Silk, Zuckerman, or Roth. Maybe they will come up when Nathan, as promised, goes to dinner at Ernestine's house. But blood-red Vietnam is a stronger presence in these pages than black-and-white America. Compared to the passing of little-boy Bliss to Senator Sunraider in Ralph Ellison's *Juneteenth*, or the underground scuttle in *The Shadow Man* of Mary Gordon's father from outcast Midwest Jewishness to the "iridescent ease" of Provence, Assisi, Languedoc, Toscana, and anti-Semitism, the treatment in *The Human Stain* of identity as a card trick, a stock option, or a designer-label accessory seems, well, slapdash. When Coleman Silk discovers what he should already have known from his Greeks—"how accidentally a fate is made . . . or how accidental it all may seem when it is inescapable"—he is really running into a brick wall of Philip Roth.

What follows is unfair but so is Roth, for whom all of nature is "terrifyingly provisional," the whole world is full of malice, and it is preposterous and maybe even evil that anyone should try to be, pretend to be, remember having been or believe in the marginal possibility of one day being, happy. Or even just getting away with it, whatever it is. (And sometimes we do get away with it.) Listen to what he tells us in *Stain*: "Of course nothing that befalls anyone is ever too senseless to have happened." And: "For all that the world is full of people who go around believing they've got you or your neighbor figured out, there is really no bottom to what is not known. The truth about us is endless. As are the lies."

Now listen to what Nathan said of Henry in *The Counterlife*: "He wants out of nowhere to have an elevated goal . . . Russian literature is replete with just such avid souls and their bizarre, heroic longings, probably more of them in Russian literature than in life." And about his general approach: "Wasn't everybody happier enraged? They were certainly more interesting. People are unjust to anger—it can be enlivening and a lot of fun." And what the stranger says about *him* at his imaginary funeral: "This insidious, unregenerate defiler, this irritant in the Jewish bloodstream, making people uncomfortable and angry by looking with a mirror up his own asshole." Or the great summing up: "The worm in the dream is always the past, that impediment to all renewal."

Meanwhile, in *Sabbath's Theater*, Mickey "liked to think that distrusting the sincerity of everyone armed him a little against betrayal by everything." And: "The puppet is *you*. The grotesque buffoon is *you. You're* Punch, schmuck, the puppet who toys with taboos." And: "Despite my many troubles I continue to know what matters in life: profound hatred." And: "King of the kingdom of the unillusioned, emperor of no expectations, crestfallen man-god of the double cross, Sabbath had *still* to learn that nothing but *nothing* will ever turn out—and this obtuseness was, in itself, a deep, deep shock." Finally: "Imagine, then, the history of the world. We are immoderate because grief is immoderate, all the hundreds and thousands of kinds of grief."

Whereas the Swede will learn, in *American Pastoral,* "the worst lesson that life can teach—that it makes no sense." Besides: "They were laughing at him. *Life* was laughing at him." And true manhood, according to *I Married a Communist,* is "when you're out there in this thing all alone." In addition to which: "Every soul is its own betrayal factory. For whatever reason: survival, excitement, advancement, idealism. For the sake of the damage that can be done, the pain that can be inflicted. For the cruelty of it."

Perhaps I've omitted some of your personal favorites. But compared to Roth, Nietzsche was Chuckles the Clown. It's all chaos theory, lacking even the pretty patterns of the fractals. Nowhere, of course, is it written that our great writers should cheer us up. Otherwise, the Shadow Warrior in Salman Rushdie's *Haroun and the Sea of Stories* would not have tried so hard to stutter out his "Gogogol" and his "Kafkafka." Still, with respect, I suggest that Maria had a point in *The Counterlife* when she wondered: "Why isn't it okay for us to be happy?" And so did Henry when he asked, "Is duty necessarily such a cheap idea, is the decent and the dutiful really shit?" (Where is common cause, or sanctuary?) Nor, really, did Roth answer his own questions at the end of *American Pastoral,* that dazzling return, as if from the dead, of a John Cheever novel: "And what is wrong with their life? What on earth is less reprehensible than the life of the Levovs?"

# SAUL BELLOW (2):
# BLOOM BURIED

*ok - how ?*

Y OU WILL RECALL that when Augie March went to Mexico, he hooked up with an eagle, which he called Caligula. (He also ran into Leon Trotsky, navigating "by the great stars." In this, Augie was luckier than his creator, Saul Bellow, who had an appointment in 1940 to see Trotsky on the very morning of his murder, and ended up in Coyoacan looking at a corpse: "A cone of bloody bandages was on his head. His cheeks, his nose, his beard, his throat, were streaked with blood and with dried iridescent trickles of iodine." But already I digress.) Suppose that instead of an eagle, Augie had grabbed a parrot, like a bag of Magical Realist feathers, and sneaked it back to Chicago. This might explain the marvel that knocks three times at the stained-glass window of *Ravelstein*.

(1) Abe Ravelstein, a political philosopher just out of intensive care and feeling shaky, is escorted by his friend Chick, a much-married older novelist, from the University of Chicago campus back to his apartment, stopping at every other corner to catch his breath. They happen, remarkably, on a flock of parrots in a clump of trees with red berries. Though not really interested in nature, Ravelstein needs to know: "What are we looking at?" Chick explains that the parrots, descendants of an escaped pair of caged birds, first built their long, sack-like nests in the lakefront park and later colonized the alleys; that "hundreds of green parrots" live in "bird tenements" hanging from utility poles; and that a new "garbage based ecology" involves raccoons and even possums, besides your usual rats and

squirrels. "You mean," says Ravelstein, "the urban jungle is no longer a metaphor."

(2) Thirty pages later, two years after Abe's death, Chick thinks back to "the morning of the day when he and I had come upon the parrot-filled holly bushes where the birds were feeding on red berries and scattering the snow." He re-experiences his friend's surprise: "You're just back from the dead, and you run into an entire tribe of green parrots, tropical animals surviving a midwestern winter." And this time a grinning Ravelstein is made to say: "They even have a Jew look to them."

(3) Finally, at the end of this lambent novel, this prayer for the dead, Chick seems to be channeling Ravelstein: "He loses himself in sublime music, a music in which ideas are dissolved, reflecting these ideas in the form of feeling. He carries them down to the street with him. There's an early snow on the tall shrubs, the same shrubs filled with a huge flock of parrots—the ones that escaped from cages and now build their long nest sacks in the back alleys. They are feeding on red berries. Ravelstein looks at me laughing with pleasure and astonishment, gesturing because he can't be heard in all this birdnoise."

By now, Bellow's got it down like a scroll painting or a haiku. Indeed, for all that *Ravelstein* is spiced with Western Civ's greatest hits—with long views from Athens and Jerusalem, as seen through the eyes of the noble dead (Plato, Rousseau, Nietzsche), the compulsive scribblers (Xenophon, Dr. Johnson, Joyce, Céline), the exemplary-prophetic (Job and Tolstoy) and the merely peculiar (Marie Antoinette and Whittaker Chambers), at whom, because "death does sharpen the comic sense," we are even encouraged to laugh "like Picasso's wounded horse in *Guernica*, rearing back"— there is something oddly Oriental about the novel, as if it were told by an odalisque with a folding fan. Or, to be even fancier, as if it were a series of tai chi exercises, a sequence of strenuous poses. Thus, for Ravelstein's many eccentricities—a white crane flashing its wings. For Chick's many marriages—a master strumming his lute. For the price exacted by world history and personal choice—a wild horse

shaking its mane. And, for a teller done with his tale, a hunter holding the tail of a bird. ("As birds went," Chick says of Abe, "he was an
eagle, while I was something like a flycatcher.")

I'm about to suggest that *Ravelstein* is the story of two deaths—of
the philosopher and the novelist—with only one Lazarus, who isn't
Socrates. I will argue that as much as Saul Bellow enjoyed the company of Allan Bloom, they had profound differences on how to live
and how to die, what happens afterward, and the way we best explain each other. These differences, as much as their friendship, are
what animate the novel. They are in fact what make it a novel and
not a tacky roman à clef, shellacked to fix its gaudy colors. But first
the tabloid tease.

*Humboldt wanted to drape the world in radiance, but he didn't have enough*
*material. (Humboldt's Gift)*

That Ravelstein is Bloom is obvious not only on the basis of internal
evidence—the gift for teaching; the best-selling book; the messy
eating habits; the expensive tastes and the sexual secrets; gossipy
friends in high places; contempt for relativism, feminism, black
power, gay pride, the social sciences, and rock-and-roll—but also on
the basis of Bellow's own remarks at a memorial service for Bloom in
1992, included in *It All Adds Up* (1994), which reappear here almost
word for word. (Mercedes will become BMV, and Michael Wu become Nikki, and Persian carpets, Chinese chests, Hermès porcelain,
and Ultimo cashmere coats will turn into Armani suits, Vuitton lug-
gage, Lalique crystal, and Cuban cigars, but the chain-smoking, the
Chicago Bulls, and Plato's *Symposium* remain the same.) That Chick
is Saul is equally obvious from the novels, the marriages, and the
gnarly grain of the prose, plus what we know from the news about
Bellow's near-death from food poisoning in 1994. Chick even para-
phrases a passage in an earlier Bellow novel, *More Die of Heart-*
*break*, on how he imagines death: "I said that the pictures would
stop." Of course, while everybody who ever met him at the University of Chicago knew Bloom to be a gay diva, there's no closet quite

like the Committee on Social Thought, and so at the memorial they chose to blame his death on liver failure instead of AIDS.

OK, Abe is Allan, Chick is Saul, and we are told in *Lingua Franca* that Rakhmiel Kogon is Edward Shils and Radu Grielescu is Mircea Eliade. I am already wise to Vela, the Rumanian-born "chaos" physicist who dumps Chick, because I met her before in *The Dean's December,* when she was a Rumanian-born astronomer named Minna. Thanks be, she will exit in time to make room for Chick's new wife, Rosamund, about whom there's reason to worry because if she really was a student of Bloom's, she should be feeling attentuated, if not invisible, since he is said to have looked right through even the brightest of his female students to likelier candidates for his coterie. This still leaves mysterious the secret identities of Battle, the Sanskrit-speaking ex-paratrooper who looks like "the Quaker on the oatmeal box," and of Morris Herbst, who's written a book on Goethe's *Elective Affinities* in spite of his weakness for dice and cards. One supposes we must wait for the James Atlas tell-all.

Or maybe not. While sometimes interesting, this piggish snuffling after factoid truffles is usually distracting, approximately as helpful as being told that García Márquez patterned the six chapters of *The Autumn of the Patriarch* on Bartók's six string quartets and Virginia Woolf's *The Waves,* and invariably reductive in the cranky manner of Ruth Miller's *Saul Bellow: A Biography of the Imagination* (1991), in which she insists that all the novels are autobiographical, cookie-cut to an identical pattern: A family that's a pain. (They may love him, but they don't understand him; he's a spiritual orphan.) Alter egos who are the same compulsively talkative, intellectually alienated, wisecracking, soul-stricken, and culture-freaked manic-depressive (Russian-Jewish Chicago street-smarties even when, like Henderson or Corde, they're not supposed to be). And women who do him wrong: "frumps" says Miller, "predators, trollops, cheats, mousies, doxies, harridans, emasculators, manipulators, betrayers, or rigid unyielding martinets, paranoids, dollies, or chumps." (Herzog wonders, "Will I ever understand what women want? . . . They eat green salad and drink human blood.")

But this is to read each novel as though it were a grudge—a settling of private scores on the reader's time. If you want to know who is or isn't Isaac Rosenfeld, Harold Rosenberg, Meyer Shapiro, Dwight Macdonald or John Berryman—if it matters to you that Joe Alsop is taken in vain in *The Dean's December*—then Miller's where to go. She even interviewed Owen Barfield on Anthroposophy. She will explain away *Henderson the Rain King* as a parodic acting out, in Africa, of the Reichian analysis Bellow submitted to in the mid-fifties, while keeping an orgone box like a humidifier in his Queens apartment. And explain away *Herzog* as the story of ex-wife Sondra and a perfidious Jack Ludwig. And explain away *Humboldt's Gift* as Saul's revenge on crazy Delmore Schwartz, who had accused him of selling out.

But all this says zilch about what Bellow *does* to everything he *notices*, the glad coatings he gives to the terrible world, his Jackson Pollock trickles, streaks and spatters, the ciphers he finds in straws and spiders, like Mr. Sammler, those magic acts of levitating language by which unhappy childhoods, scorched-earth marriages, erotic disasters, intellectual debacles and/or debauches, a plenitude of feeling, a hunger for transcendence, the death of a friend, the murder of a people, or the decline of the West are transmuted into agencies of sublime awareness. That style—snaky and hot, wrote Cynthia Ozick, "pumping street-smarts into literary blood-vessels," a "profane and holy comedy of dazzling, beating, multiform profusion"—would turn sitcoms into Chekhovs and lounge acts into Lear.

Moses Herzog will cry out against "the canned sauerkraut of Spengler's Prussian socialism, the commonplaces of the Wasteland outlook, the cheap mental stimulants of Alienation, the cant and rant of pipsqueaks about Inauthenticity and Forlornness" and "a merely aesthetic critique of modern history! After the wars and mass killings! You are too intelligent for this. You inherited rich blood. Your father peddled apples." And while we are told in *Humboldt's Gift* that "a heart can be fixed like a shoe. Resoled. Even new uppers," that's not what it feels like after we hear Sorella in *The Bellarosa Connection* explain "the slapstick side" of the death camps:

> Being a French teacher, she was familiar with Jarry and *Ubu Roi*, Pataphysics, Absurdism, Dada, Surrealism. Some camps were run in a burlesque style that forced you to make these connections. Prisoners were sent naked into a swamp and had to croak and hop like frogs. Children were hanged and starved, freezing slave laborers lined up on parade in front of the gallows and a prison band played Viennese light opera waltzes.

Some apples this father peddles.

> *Dear Doktor Professor Heidegger, I should like to know what you mean by the expression "The Fall into the Quotidian." When did this fall occur? Where were we standing when it happened?* (Herzog)

But so long as we think of Abe as Allan we are distracted. We are still fighting the Culture Wars, still reviewing *The Closing of the American Mind.* We can't forget that this is the man who accused Louis Armstrong of trashing Weimar, who compared Woodstock to Nuremberg, who fled Ithaca for Hyde Park in the parricidal sixties as if from Pompeii to Atlantis. Wolfpacks of Dread Relativism on dawn patrol! Student power! Student sex! We underline what Ravelstein says about Hayek, Bloomsbury, Islam, the Gulf War, the Grateful Dead, Mrs. Thatcher, the liberal arts, and the inner city— "the chaos the life of such people must be," he says after a chat with his cleaning lady; and, "Don't they give these people any training?" after a black nurse mentions in polite company that it's time for his AZT; but what do we expect from Chicago's dark South Side and its "noisy, pointless, nihilistic turmoil"?—as if we were writing articles of impeachment. Surely Saul Bellow, of all people, ought to prize diversity and inclusiveness. In the first twenty-seven pages of *Augie March* alone, mention was made of Heraclitus, *Tom Brown's Schooldays*, a coat factory, a laundry truck, *Anna Karenina*, and Nabisco wafers; popcorn and *Manon Lescaut;* football and Yiddish theater, pickled fish and *The Iliad.* Why, in Abe Ravelstein's Chicago, is it all right to love the Bulls but not the Beatles?

This is a mug's game. As male friendships in American literature go, Chick and Abe may not be in the same league with Ishmael and Queequeg, Huck and Jim, or Pynchon's Mason and Dixon, but they share a "sense of what was funny . . . A joyful noise—*immenso giubilo*—an outsize joint agreement picked us up together." You and I might have our doubts about a man who sends his neckties air express to be laundered by a silk specialist in Paris, who must sleep on Pratesi linens "under beautifully cured angora skins" and perk himself up in the morning with his very own espresso machine, while listening to eighteenth-century operas on compact disks through hi-fi speakers that cost $10,000 each, before venturing out to spend $4,500 on a Lanvin sports jacket the color of a Labrador retriever, on which he will sprinkle ashes from his incessant cigarettes while delivering "little anti-sermons in a wacko style" about "mass democracy and its characteristic—woeful—product" or maybe the Treaty of Versailles. You and I might prefer to pledge a vow of Trappist silence than talk so eagerly on our mobile phones to well-placed inside-dopesters—former students, war criminals with training wheels—at the State Department, on the staff of the National Security Adviser or columnizing for the *Washington Times*. But Bellow has always indulged his taste for the flamboyant. And better Abe, so full of big ideas that go all the way back, than . . . well, in *Augie*, there was Einhorn, and in *Seize the Day*, Tamkin, and in *Humboldt's Gift*, Cantabile. Bald Abe, with his milky white legs in a blue kimono "fit for a shogun," in the Crillon penthouse in Paris, among oil sheiks and Michael Jackson groupies, hating his father and scattering his food, is a distinct improvement on these charlatan gurus. At least, like his main man Socrates, he will die without self-pity.

Chick encouraged Abe to write his book, which is why Abe is now rich and no longer has to pawn his Jensen silver teapot and Quimper antique plates to his colleagues and admirers to pay for the Dunhill lighter or Mont Blanc pen that he suddenly can't live without. Abe laughs at Chick's jokes. (Example: "Maybe an unexamined life is not worth living. But a man's examined life can make him wish he was dead.") On the other hand, he seems to have an odd investment in Chick's guilelessness, especially about women. Whereas, while Chick likes to listen to Abe talk about anything—from Maimonides to Mel Brooks—he has his doubts about Abe's settled certainty on everything he talks about. ("Of course my needs were different from Ravelstein's. In my trade you have to make allowances, taking all sorts of ambiguities into account—to avoid hard-edged judgments. . . . In art, you become familiar with due process. You can't simply write off people or send them to hell.") Nor should you invite them to the country. Abe, for whom "nature and solitude are poison," is mystified by Chick's periodic idylls in the woods. ("He said, repeating the opinion of Socrates in the *Phaedrus*, that a tree, so beautiful to look at, never spoke a word and that conversation was possible only in the city, between men.")

Yet if we refuse to embrace the contradictions of our loved ones, we will be left loveless. Nobody wants to wind up like Norman Podhoretz, whose only remaining friend is America. So we are finally won over to these two old men, cranky and horny, discussing Greeks, Jews, death and sex, in their very own parrot-filled agora. "I was free," says Chick, "to confess to Ravelstein what I couldn't tell anyone else, to describe my weaknesses, my corrupt shameful secrets, and the cover-ups that drain your strength." And Ravelstein, though HIV-positive and dying of its complications and infections, nevertheless "insisted on telling me over and over again what love was— the neediness, the awareness of incompleteness, the longing for wholeness, and how the pains of Eros were joined to the most ecstatic pleasures":

> He was not one of those people for whom love has been debunked and punctured—for whom it is a historical, Romantic myth long in the dying but today finally dead. He thought—no, he *saw*—that every soul was looking for its peculiar other, longing for its complement. . . . there is a certain irreducible splendor about it without which we would not quite be human. Love is the highest function of our species—its vocation.

Thus, for Chick, even after flunking so many previous marriages, another gallant try with Rosamund. Thus, for Abe, even as the plague takes him, a devotion to Nikki which is reciprocated even after Nikki has stayed up till four in the morning watching kung fu movies from his native Singapore. But now we come to the distance between these strenuous poses.

For all that Chick tells us about Abe's disapproval "of queer antics and of what he called 'faggot behavior,'" about how "he couldn't bear the fluttering of effeminate men," about how "he despised campy homosexuality and took a very low view of 'gay pride,'" he also worries the subject like a sick tooth's socket. Sometimes this nervousness is high-minded:

> In matters of sex, I sometimes felt, Ravelstein saw me as a throwback, an anachronism. I was his close friend. But I was the child of a traditional European Jewish family, with a vocabulary for inversion going back two millennia or more. The ancestral Jewish terms for it were, first, *Tum-tum*, dating perhaps from the Babylon captivity. Sometimes the word was *andreygenes*, obviously of Alexandrian, Hellenistic origin—the two sexes merged into one erotic and perverse darkness.

At least as often, however, we are closer to wincing home. When Vera accuses Chick of having had corrupt sex with Ravelstein, "I laughed like anything. I told her I didn't even know how the act was done and that I wasn't ready to learn, at my age." He concedes that "you couldn't, as the intimate and friend of Ravelstein, avoid knowing a great deal more than you had an appetite for. But at a certain depth there were places in your psyche that still belonged to the Middle Ages. Or even to the age of the pyramids or Ur of the Chaldees."

Are we clear? Abe is "doomed to die for his irregular sexual ways," to be "destroyed by his reckless sex habits." Ravelstein's sinful "taste for sexy mischief," his relish for "*louche* encounters, the fishy and the equivocal," combined perhaps with his impatience for hygiene, his "biological patchiness," and his "faulty, darkened heart and lungs"—"When he coughed you heard the sump at the bottom of a mine shaft echoing"—add up to a shadowing of "risk, limit, death's blackout" on "every living moment." To be sure, "to prolong his life was not one of Ravelstein's aims," but it is certainly one of Chick's,

and has been ever since he chose, at age eight, not to die of peritonitis: "No one can give up on the pictures."

So the white crane flashing its wings faces off against the master
strumming his lute. Abe is an "atheist-materialist." Chick, for all his
passionate attachment to the faces of people and surfaces of things,
for all his sense of "privilege" at being "permitted to see—to see,
touch, hear" an "articulated reality" in "the interval of light between the darkness in which you awaited first birth and then the
darkness of the death that would receive you," nonetheless believes
that "the pictures can and will continue." *The dead aren't gone for
good.* Daily, he will talk to Ravelstein.

But only after he has gone there himself and then come back,
"blindly recovery-bent," with "the deep and special greed of the sick
when they have decided not to die." If the philosopher was teaching
us how to go, the novelist, with the heroic help of his wife, will
teach us how to stay. The last fifty extraordinary pages of *Ravelstein*
take us from Abe's memorial service . . . to a Caribbean vacation for
Chick and Rosamund . . . to a French restaurant, a toxic fish, food-
poisoning and nerve damage to a bewildered Chick . . . to an emergency airlift, actually an angelic skyjacking, prestidigitated by
resourceful Rosamund . . . to oxygen and Boston and a hospital
"end zone" . . . to a falling passage through circles of hellish
hallucination—nightmares of cannibalism, cryonics, bank vaults,
and Filene's basement—to the light again and the wife who saved
him. This may be the same light that Saul Bellow once saw in
Jerusalem, whose filtering of blood and thought allowed him to
imagine "the outer garment of God." But the wife is the novelist's
own, the mother-to-be of a brand-new child for an octogenarian
adept of due process. About this woman, our Lazarus will say: "Rosamund had studied love—Rousseauan romantic love and the Platonic Eros as well, with Ravelstein—*but she knew far more about it
than either her teacher or her husband.*" (Emphasis added.)

There's a punch line, like the grandest of ideas dissolved by music
into a form of feeling, like the opening of an American mind.

# RALPH ELLISON, SORT OF
# (PLUS HEMINGWAY
# AND SALINGER)

U PON HIS DEATH IN 1994, Ralph Ellison left behind
some two thousand pages of a never-finished second
novel—more than forty years of fine-tuning what his literary executor, John F. Callahan, calls a "mythic saga of race and
identity, language and kinship in the American experience" and
what the despairing rest of us, waiting for Ralph like Lefty or Godot,
came to think of as The Invisible Book. Two decades of stingy excerpts, from 1959 through 1977, were followed by two more of enigmatic silence. Of course, in 1967, between teases, a book-length
manuscript of "revisions" perished famously in the flames that consumed his Berkshires summer house. In the history of our literature,
this misfortune has assumed the symbolic heft of a Reichstag fire,
and maybe even the burning of the Library at Alexandria. Was it
also Ellison's alibi for failing to follow up on himself? Only Albert
Murray knows for sure.

While sitting on this second novel, he was otherwise not too ar-
duously engaged in writing about Duke Ellington, Mahalia Jackson,
Jimmy Rushing, Charlie Parker and the blues; lecturing on democ-
racy, morality, and the novel; reviewing Mark Twain, Stephen
Crane, Erskine Caldwell, and Gunnar Myrdal; rethinking the psy-
chic kinks in his relationship with William Faulkner and Richard
Wright; insisting, over and over again, that T. S. Eliot and André
Malraux had influenced his sense of vocation more decisively; show-

ing up at L. B. J.'s White House during the Vietnam war, speaking at a West Point commencement, getting himself interviewed. Almost everyone wanted, if not more *Invisibility*, then some other piece of him, some pound of black spokesperson. In the early sixties, there'd been an exchange of vituperations with Irving Howe, who thought he ought to be angrier. From the late sixties Willie Morris remembers, in *New York Days*, Ellison's being called an Uncle Tom at Grinnell College, in bloodthirsty Iowa. In the early seventies, I was an appalled witness at a literary cocktail party when Alfred Kazin told him he should spend less time at the Century Club and more at the typewriter, followed by a scuffle on the wet street, from which an equally appalled cabbie roared away without a fare, like the locomotive of history. And just last month, at a City University conference, a Rutgers professor who may have seen too many episodes of *The X-Files* actually suggested that Ellison, in his only novel, had said such terrible things about the "Brotherhood" of the Communist Party just to curry favor with a freaked public during the McCarthy shamefulness.

On the other hand, I also recall teaching *The Invisible Man* in paperback in the mid-sixties to a roomful of teenage girls in a belfry of an Episcopal church in Roxbury, Massachusetts. These quick-witted, slow-burning, high-flying Afro-Caribbean birds of paradise had been discarded by the racist Boston School Committee: bagged, tagged, and trashed. Yet they showed up two nights a week, a chapter at a time, to engage the selves they discovered in his pages, read aloud from their journals, write their own stories, and fall headlong into passionate disputation about metaphor and identity, politics and work, even incest—and tell me things I didn't want to know about their streets. Much later I'd receive invitations to several graduations from colleges like Spelman and Shaw. But this was long after yogurt-faced liberals like me had been told to get out of Roxbury—in the spring of 1967, pursuant to the secret resolutions of the Newark Black Power Conference, which resolutions had been written by precisely those militants who would call Ralph Ellison an Uncle Tom even as he was saving the lives of their sisters.

"Writers don't give prescriptions," said the poet Ikem in Chinua Achebe's *Anthills of the Savannah*; "They give headaches."

Anyway, here at last is a respectable chunk of what he withheld to the grave. Personally, I wish Random House had published all 2,000 pages, if not on a CD-ROM, then loose in a box for each reader to assemble on our own, according to our solitary need, like a customized mantra. Structure, about which he had been so finicky, be damned. Yes, from Ellison's notes and drafts Callahan has fashioned a shapely synecdoche that coheres—a duet between "Daddy" Hickman, the black Southern preacher who's come to Washington in 1955 to warn a man he raised as a boy of impending violence, and Sunraider, the white New England senator who was brought up black but turned savagely on the color of this kindness; a Lincoln-haunted and Oedipus-inflected dialogue of downhome homilies, grandiose dreams, and primal crime; a dialectic of masked pasts and screened memories; a call-and-response antiphony of flimflam riffs; a matched fall of twinned tricksters into shared mystery, lost history, and filmed illusions. As in Faulkner, the past keeps happening. But gripped at the throat, *Juneteenth* also seems to long for choral movement and symphonic orchestration; breathing space and digressive license; clarification, specificity, amplitude.

Nevertheless, there's still a lot of wow.

*Once there was a series consisting of a man and a boy and a boar hog, a cat and a big hairy spider—all shot in flight as they sought to escape, to run away from some unseen pursuer. And as I sat in the darkened hotel room watching the rushes, the day's takes, on a portable screen, the man seemed to change into the boy and the boy, changing his form as he ran, becoming swiftly boar and cat and tarantula, moving ever desperately away, until at the end he seemed, this boar-boy-spider-cat, to change into an old man riding serenely on a white mule as he puffed on a corncob pipe. I watched it several times and each time I broke into a sweat, shaking as with a fever. Why these images and what was their power? (Juneteenth)*

Imagine Bliss—a little white boy under a circus tent in a pine grove at a revival meeting of black Baptists, "a miniature man of God" inside a narrow box breathing through a tube. He is called Bliss "because they say that is what ignorance is." He is dressed to kill because he is presumed dead. The box he's in, with angels blowing long-belled trumpets and carved clouds floating in an egg-shaped space, is a coffin. When the singing stops, Bliss, his Bible, and his teddy bear will pop out "like God's own toast, to ask the Lord how come He has forsaken him":

> Hurry! They're moving slow, like an old boat drifting down the big river in the night and me inside looking up into the black sky, no moon nor stars and all the folks gone far beyond the levees. And I could feel the shivering creep up my legs now and squeezed Teddy's paw to force it down. Then the rising rhythm of the clapping hands was coming to me like storming waves heard from a distance; like waves that struck the boat and flew off into the black sky like silver sparks from the shaking of the shimmering tambourines, showering at the zenith like the tails of skyrockets. If only I could open my eyes. It hangs heavy-heavy over my lids. Please hurry! Restore my sight. The night is black and I am far . . . far . . . I thought of Easter Bunny, he came from the dark inside of a red-and-white striped egg.

Like rabbits popping out of a magic top hat, Bliss come back from the dead is a regularly scheduled trick in Daddy Hickman's circuit show. Never mind how this little white boy ended up with the black evangelicals, on the nomadic road during the Great Depression from Oklahoma to Alabama to Georgia, among so many surrogate parents who raised him to talk and to walk as if he were Yoruban. (A captivity narrative!) Never mind how Hickman got himself transformed from a juke-joint jazz man into Bliss's designated father and "God's own trombone," blowing his horn in the devil's outback. ("No mercy in my heart . . . Only the choking strangulation of some cord of kinship stronger and deeper than blood, hate or heartbreak.") Never even mind the mock Resurrection. Christ already rose for these Baptists. What they really seek is a Second Coming of Father Abraham—the emancipating Lincoln who, in freeing the slaves, freed himself, and so truly became "one of us." According to Hickman, "We just couldn't get around the hard fact that for a hope or an idea to become real it has to be embodied in a man, and men change and have wills and wear masks." And so: "We made a plan, or at least we dreamed a dream and worked for it but the world was simply too big for us and the dream got out of hand."

But look at it from Bliss's point of view, a "chicken in a casket." Being dead is hard work for which he wants to be paid, if not in sex, about which he's begun to wonder, then at least some ice cream. And what does he get instead? On Juneteenth—the anniversary of the summer's day in 1865 when Union troops landed in Galveston, Texas, and their commanding officer told the slaves only two and a half years late that they were free, for which 5,000 colored folks have gathered in an Alabama swamp to eat 500 pounds of catfish and snapper, 900 pounds of ribs, 85 hams, a cabbage patch of cole-slaw, and who knows how many frying chickens and butter beans, while listening as seven different preachers "shift to a higher gear," beyond the singing and the shouting into a territory of "pure un-blemished Word," the "Word that was both song and scream and whisper," beyond sense "but leaping like a tree of flittering birds with its *own* dictionary of light and meaning"—Bliss gets a white woman, a complete stranger, who says that she's his *mother*, who claims: "He's mine, MINE! . . . You gypsy niggers stole him, my baby."

So she isn't his mother. White people lie a lot. His *real* mother, as a matter of fact, caused the death and mutilation of Hickman's brother, after which baby Bliss was handed over as a sort of hostage to the jazz man, who accepted him "as I'd already accepted the blues, the clap, the loss of love, the fate of man." Why not? "Here was a chance to prove that there was something in this world stronger than all their ignorant superstition about blood and ghosts." Still, even to imagine such a mother, to conceive of an ice-creamy white birth-right, will lead Bliss to run away from Daddy Hickman; to deny and rage; to hide in "surprise, speed and camouflage"; to cut the string, scud high places, bruise himself and snag at times on treetops but keep on sailing into shadows—first to make movies and illusions, then to make a vengeful son, and finally, as Sunraider, to make hate-

ful politics. Ellison asks us to remember Greek legend, folk literature, and the entire Amerindian structuralist mythology of the
stolen child.

But the swamp scene alone is enough to remind us of his remarkable powers of sorcery. Though never a stranger to interior monologue, lyrical afflatus, or angry agit prop, Ellison may be the greatest
of jazz sermonizers and homiletic blues guitarists ever to write fiction. He probably picked up tips on how to do it from Melville in
*Moby-Dick* and Joyce in *Portrait of an Artist*, and passed them on for
Toni Morrison to improve on when Beloved's Baby Suggs took to her
sacred grove. As in the swamp, where on "this day of deliverance"
they look at "the figures writ on our bodies and on the living tablet
of our heart," so, too, at the Lincoln Memorial, with "the great image slumped in the huge stone chair" and then again on the floor of
Congress when Sunraider in mid-demagoggle is attacked by the
Great Seal of the United States—by E PLURIBUS UNUM itself, with the
olive branch, the sheaf of arrows, the sphinxlike eyes, a taloned
clutch, and a curved beak like a scimitar—he dazzles us into a surreal sentience.

For Ellison, that Great Seal is a hybrid, a mongrel, an alloy, a
scramble of stew meats and a weave of sinews, cultures, language,
genius, and love. This is the bass line. Admixed America is a Tin-
toretto:

> You can cut that cord and zoom off like a balloon and rise high—I mean
> that cord woven of love, of touching, ministering love, that's tied to a baby
> with its first swaddling clothes—but the cord don't shrivel and die like a
> navel cord beneath the first party dress or the first long suit of clothes. Oh,
> no, it parts with a cry like a rabbit torn by a hawk in the winter snows and
> it numbs quick and glazes like the eyes of a sledge-hammered ox and the
> blood don't show, it's like a wound that's cauterized. It snaps with the
> heart's denial back into the skull like a worm chased by a razor-beaked
> bird, and once inside it snarls, Bliss; it snarls up the mind. It won't die and
> there's no sun inside to set so it can stop its snakish wiggling. It bores
> reckless excursions between the brain and the heart and kills and kills
> again unkillable continuity. Bliss, when Eve deviled and Adam spawned
> we were all in the dark, and that's a fact.

The trouble with *Juneteenth* is that it's almost all sermons and jazzy dreaming. How did Bliss ever get into politics—in New England!—and become Sunraider? Surely there are pages, chapters, a whole other novel to explain his assassin, missing like the mothers. From *Invisible Man*, we knew what Tuskegee was like, Harlem, a paint factory, a cell meeting, and the sidewalk where Tod Clifton bled to death. *Juneteenth* asks us to intuit, from two men talking to each other and to ghosts, from nightmare passages and beseeching light, four hundred years of complicitous history that keeps Daddy Hickman from getting to the nation's capital in time to stop a fatal bullet. Charged by language alone to imagine the holy dove and winged bull, the Lion, the Lamb, and the Rock, what we see instead is "the devastation of the green wood! Ha! And in the blackened streets the entrails of men, women and baby grand pianos, their songs sunk to an empty twang struck by the aimless whirling of violent winds. Behold! the charred foundations of the House of God."

Maybe he couldn't finish because America, lacking in comfort and radiance, fresh out of Lincolns, wouldn't let him. We amounted to less than he needed and believed. Or maybe, more dreadfully, baby Bliss is Jesus after all. And Sunraider is the Christianity he grew up to be.

*Nothing ever stops; it divides and multiplies, and I guess sometimes it gets ground down to superfine, but it doesn't just blow away.* (*Juneteeth*)

Still, let's be grateful for what we have, and consider how much worse it could have been. It could have been, for dire instance, something like the posthumous Hemingway of *True at First Light*.

Between the Pulitzer Prize in 1953, for *The Old Man and the Sea*, and the Nobel Prize in 1954, which he didn't bother to collect in person, Ernest Hemingway left Cuba for Africa with his fourth wife, Mary, to shoot something for *Look* magazine—a leopard, a lion, or a gazelle; maybe even himself, at least symbolically. We know now from his biographers that the British colonial rulers of Kenya made him an honorary game warden, and set him up in a privately-stocked safari camp, to attract tourists who had been scared away by the Mau-Mau. That, overweight and manic-depressive, with bad eyes, bad knees, and a distended liver, he was so drunk most of the time that he couldn't shoot straight. That he would crack up two airplanes, rupturing a kidney, dislocating a shoulder, crushing several vertebrae, and collapsing an intestine. Nevertheless, in the bush, Papa shaved his head, dyed his shirts a tribal pink and orange, and carried a spear to go courting a local Wakamba girl, the "lovely and impudent" Debba. And never stopped writing for his life.

*True at First Light* is his "fictionalized memoir" of that African sojourn, published thirty-eight years after his suicide—a sad book and a bloated one, even though it was more than twice as long before his son Patrick shrunk it to this size. The Papa we meet in its pages is a Great White Hunter, a tribal chief, and a wiseguy medicine man. He drinks beer for breakfast; swigs gin from a Spanish double cartridge pouch after gunning down baboons; eats breaded cutlets of lion tenderloin; makes nasty remarks about John O'Hara, vegetarians, homosexual playwrights, and sherry-sodden and "syphilitic" Masai; satirizes religion by making up one of his own; masters the secret Kamba hand-grip; reads Simenon in French; remembers Paris and the Rockies, Orwell and D. H. Lawrence, Scott Fitzgerald and his old horse Kite; speaks babytalk to Mary and the natives, all of whom are infantilized, and bluster and blarney to his boozy white hunting buddies. He will get his leopard for *Look* magazine, as Mary will get her black-maned lion and marijuana tree for Christmas. But he will not, alas, because of local custom and propriety, ever get to sleep with Debba, his last chance for true "happiness."

No wonder he left this book in a drawer. I'm not saying that *True at First Light* is without grace notes. Although almost everybody talks as if translated from the Portuguese for a Dalton Trumbo screenplay about Spartacus or Geronimo, Hemingway did know how to *listen* to leopards and rhinos and the little boy he'd left behind. For instance:

There are always mystical countries that are a part of one's childhood. Those we remember and visit sometimes when we are asleep and dreaming. They are as lovely at night as they were when we were children. If you ever go back to see them they are not there. But they are as fine in the night as they ever were if you have the luck to dream of them.

Still, the prose of stories like "A Clean, Well-Lighted Place" and "Hills Like White Elephants" compares with the prose of *True at First Light* as early photos of a vital Hemingway compare with snapshots of late Papa, trapped in the blubber of his celebrityhood.

So he couldn't escape his own cultivated image. No more vanishing acts from a marriage or an impasse: to Wyoming; to Spain; to the bush; to the sea; to bag another beastliness or kill the big fish. No more blaming his mother. No more bull. Only the black bottle and electroshock at the Mayo Clinic, after which he bagged himself. Like his own father, Papa ate a gun.

Hanging out at the Century Club begins to seem a whole lot healthier, and *Juneteenth* a lot less shameless. Maybe we're better off not knowing what's in the drawers of writers who blinked off into radio silence. Maybe, for another instance, J. D. Salinger has the right idea.

Salinger, who is fifty years older than his third wife, may still be writing in a magic tower full of peppermints and pipe smoke somewhere in rustic New Hampshire with the curtains closed against the mountain view. But he hasn't published a story since 1966. According to his daughter Peggy, this is because he can't stand criticism. Among the many other things her father can't stand are country clubs, Ivy Leaguers, holidays, charity, white bread, soft butter, "primitive" art, "coarse" Negroes, "trashy" poets like Langston Hughes, "ignorant" languages like Spanish, as well as anything that's "second-rate," that isn't beautiful or perfect (including all marriage and most women), anyone who interrupts his work (including his wives and children), and all the "parasites" who sponge off him (*especially* his wives and children).

His daughter Peggy—Margaret A. Salinger—has written a memoir, *Dream Catcher*, that would break the heart even if her father weren't the reclusive author of *The Catcher in the Rye*. Perhaps there is a gene for splendid prose. She is a mother herself, an Episcopal chaplain, a graduate of Brandeis, Oxford, and Harvard Divinity School, a former garage mechanic and union organizer, a worker in a home for abused and abandoned children, and an occasional singer at Tanglewood in the Boston Symphony chorus. But, starting with childhood, she has also survived everything from bulimia to chronic fatigue syndrome, from hallucinations to dehydrations, from a scary abortion to postpartum panic attacks, from alcohol abuse to attempted suicide. Since that childhood, she has slept with one eye open, seeing UFOs and fairies. Now, she watches her own son, hoping like the Native American dream catcher hanging over his bed "to filter out the nightmares in its web and let the good dreams drip down the feather on his sleeping forehead."

But Peggy's father *is* the author of *Franny & Zooey*. And Peggy's mother *did* set fire to the house, cooking the gerbils. And the real-child Peggy could never be as perfect as the fictional Glass banana-fish. So we read *Dream Catcher* as we read the Ian Hamilton biography and the Joyce Maynard memoir, obsessively seeking clues to the writer who came back strange from World War II, having married and divorced a *Nazi*. Who insisted that one young woman after another abandon her family, her friends, and her possessions for him as if he were a cult. Who only sleeps in beds pointed true north, and has been a serial True Believer in Zen, Vedanta, L. Ron Hubbard's Dianetics, Wilhelm Reich's orgone box, Edgar Cayce, macrobiotics, and drinking urine.

"What are you doing," his daughter wonders, "that is so much more important than taking care of your kids and family?" The happiest she ever saw him was playing ring-toss with a dolphin. The only time he ever cried was when John Kennedy was shot. When she needed money for medical bills, he sent her a book by Mary Baker Eddy, a subscription to a Christian Science magazine about miracle healing, and a note saying she'd only get well when she stopped believing in the "illusion" of her sickness. Instead, she stopped believing in the illusion of her father.

Well, fathers—

It used to bother me that Ellison, in *Shadow and Act* and *Going to the Territory*, so seldom reviewed and never encouraged any of the other black American writers of his time, which was a long one. Ambivalence about Wright, who gave him his start, was one thing. Silence on the rest, so many of whom grew up nourished by his breakthrough novel, seemed downright hostile. And this is not to get into what isn't any of my business—the continuing argument about the responsibility of black artists to themselves versus their obligation to an aggrieved community; about primitivism, stereotypes, street cred, protest novels, the black aesthetic, and art for art's sake. I see no reason why Zora Neale Hurston, W. E. B. Du Bois, Richard Wright, Ralph Ellison, James Baldwin, Lorraine Hansberry, August Wilson, George C. Wolfe, Alvin Ailey, Bill T. Jones, Gwendolyn Brooks, Amiri Baraka, Alice Walker, Spike Lee, and Julie Dash shouldn't disagree as much about fundamentals as any other miscellaneous bunch of extravagant talents, any other pantheon. Baldwin, speaking to white America, was certainly right when he said, "If I am not who you say I am, then you are not who you think you are." And so was Toni Morrison, speaking to everybody: "The best art is unquestionably political and irrevocably beautiful at the same time." And maybe, anyway, the best model for any modern literature is the letter of transit, the message in a bottle from exile, displacement, and dispossession. Aren't all of us, even Ellison, homesick?

I'm talking less cosmically, about teachers, mentors, friends. He seems almost to have felt that encouraging the children who cherished his example, and struggled with his shadow, would cost him some body heat. So he hibernated for the long winter, and sucked like Ahab on the paws of his gloom.

But *Juneteenth*, so unlike and yet in surreal keeping with so much that's happened in the last half-century of African American writing, suggests those children got what they needed anyway. That Toni Morrison got sermons, jazz, the Civil War, the Reconstruction, magnanimity, and diaspora. That John Edgar Wideman got kinship, ancestry, basketball, deracination, Homewood, epiphany, Africa, and Caliban. That if Ellison neglected Martin Luther King Jr., Charles Johnson would have to dream about him. And that a phantasmal version of Ellison himself shows up on the last page of Wesley Brown's wonderful *Darktown Strutters*, in the person of the nineteenth-century minstrel Jim Crow, slyly ruining a photograph they're trying to take at P. T. Barnum's Southland theme park — a museum of the American distemper that includes a NIGRA WENCH, a HEATHEN CHINEE, a DUMB SWEDE, a DRUNKEN MICK, a SHYLOCKING JEW, a MURDEROUS PAISAN and a DEAD INDIAN. Jim Crow is supposed to be THE CONNIVING UNCLE TOM. But just as the powder goes flashpoof, Jim executes a brand-new fancy step: not there; long gone; you might even say invisible, but dancing somewhere on a coffin.

# TONI CADE BAMBARA
## IN ATLANTA,
## TOM WOLFE FULL OF IT

"PEOPLE," asks a bumpy-faced brother in seersucker overalls, "what are we pretending not to know today?"

Grand and grueling, exhaustive and exalted, *Those Bones Are Not My Child* is Toni Cade Bambara's long-promised and almost-given-up-on novel about the Atlanta child murders of the early nineteen-eighties. When Bambara died of cancer in 1995, she left behind, to be edited by her "sisterfriend" Toni Morrison, a manuscript twice as long as the splendid beast published here. Begun in the course of the terror, like that terror, it was never really finished. Endlessly revised during her late-life thralldom to filmmaking, it is as cinematic as Bely's *Petersburg* or Malraux's *Man's Fate*, but also layered, tactile, and encyclopedic; haunted by four hundred years of history and full of what Morrison calls "heartcling"; a bill of indictment of an entire political culture and a broadloom weave of lost children and child sacrifice—from Abraham and Isaac to Agamemnon and Iphigenia to Peter Pan, the Pied Piper, the Prodigal Son, and the "disappeared."

So the inevitable comparisons with Tom Wolfe's Atlanta novel, *A Man in Full*, are just as inevitably puerile: Dostoyevsky versus Ronald Firbank. Nobody knows better than Tom Wolfe the brand names and price tags of all our gee-whiz toys. We are what we own, eat, wear, drive, and shoot, after a heavy day of trading on the commodity-identity exchange. And Wolfe will tell us—in his

pump-up sneaker prose style, his ragtime/zydeco—that the furniture is Hepplewhite, the pram is British Silver Cross, the motor
yacht is Hatteras, and the private plane (a Gulfstream 5 with Sky-
Watch radar, on its way to a condominium in Vail) costs a way-cool
$40 million. And what Wolfe is *best* at is our fear of losing all of it, our
night-sweat panic that our charm and credit will run out, that the
banks and other savage tribes are out there just waiting for us to
under-develop or overextend or park our Lexus in the wrong hood.

But that's all Wolfe knows anything about or excels at, besides a
Dickensian penchant for funny names (Raymond Peepgass, Wismer
Strook, a Maws and Gullet Food Service Corporation, and law firms
with monikers like Tripp, Snayer & Billings, Fogg Nackers Render-
ing & Lean, and Wringer Fealsom & Tick). He is otherwise a right-
wing Andy Warhol, an Ayn Rand Mister Softee, thumbing his
ice-cream cone at modern art and modern architecture, at black hustlers and white kneejerks, at multiculturalists, radical feminists,
rock music ("Pus Casserole and the Child Abusers"), and gay pride
("lesbians wearing paratrooper boots"). On this last hot-button satirical target, *A Man in Full* is worse than *The Bonfire of the Vanities*,
featuring a nasty sendup of Robert Mapplethorpe as Wilson Lapeth
(photographs of gay sex on a chain-gang) and a series of contempt-
ible jokes about AIDS benefits ("Let's Rap for Clap," "Let's Riff for
Syph," "Let's Go Hug a Dyin' Bugger," "Let's Pay Our Dues to Pus-
tular Ooze," and "Glory Me—I Got da HIV.") That's as profound as
he gets on sexuality. On politics, he is even more succinct: It's all
about "seeing them jump."

Bambara, on the other hand, is tired of being made to jump. Yes,
in her Atlanta novel as in Wolfe's, there are white men on hold
"making the long-distance run on an exercise bike while making
the long-distance deal on the phone." But there are also solid citizens
like the Colored 400, filling box seats at the Civic Center, and the
Knights of Pythias. There are black lawyers, ministers, educators,
college students, upholsterers, carpenters, masons, secretaries, retired merchant seamen, short-order cooks, bricklayers, and even

journalists. And there are historical markers like the Blackstone Apartments on Peachtree and Fourth, Buttermilk Bottom, Margaret Mitchell Square, and the Romare Bearden Gallery. This is the Other Atlanta, the "Black Mecca of the South," and sometimes not a pretty picture:

> Job-starved and poverty-pinched, doily-fine and blue-veined privilege alike . . . Couples who'd pulled themselves up from day-old wares at Colonial Bakery and greens from the cemetery, fighting the mockingbirds for first licks on the purple-green leaves of the pokeberry bush. Called themselves middle-class so long as there were down-the-street neighbors still battling the birds and stopping the meat truck for fifty cents' worth of salt pork to cook up the poke salad with. Middle-class and up-and-coming. Bachelors who lived in their two-toned Sevilles, performing their A.M. toilette in bus-depot restrooms, their evening ablutions in bars, continually changing "address" two steps ahead of the collection agency. Teenage mothers on stoops rifling through *True Confessions* while their babies drank formula stretched with Kool-Aid.

Most of all, there are black children in danger and in limbo. From September 1979 to June 1981, more than forty of these children vanish from Atlanta's streets, parks, movies, schools, projects, buses, and bridges. If they are ever found at all, their bodies will have been bludgeoned, stabbed, lynched, drowned, and/or mutilated. More like the post–Civil War vampire New York of E. L. Doctorow's *The Waterworks* than "The City Too Busy to Hate" at which Wolfe quotes Epictetus, this nightmare Atlanta is under siege: a metropolis of denial, whose politicians worry about losing convention dollars to a serial-killer panic; a magnet for bounty hunters, soothsayers, crackpots, supercops, and paramilitary thugs; a war zone of helicopters, bullhorns, gun sales, and conspiracy theories—about the Nazis and the Klan; about diabolical scientists, organized child-molesters, snuff moviemakers, and psychopathic veterans back from Vietnam; about turf-poaching drug dealers killing off the competition's couriers, kidnappers looking for scared slave labor, alien abductors, and satanic cults.

While Bambara's wide-angle lens takes in the aggrieved community, the new black officialdoms of Mayor Maynard Jackson and Police Commissioner Lee Brown, the FBI, the ATF, the INS, and even the Securities and Exchange Commission, her close-up focus is on the estranged parents of one of the missing children, thirteen-year-old Sundiata. Sonny's mother Zala holds down jobs at a barbershop and the Arts Center, designs T-shirts and stained glass, sings in the church choir, goes to college at night, and eats dinner on her ironing board. His father Spence came back damaged from Vietnam, got bit by the easy-money Atlanta bug, ferries wealthy clients around town in a yellow limousine—to the Ritz Carlton for the opera collection, to Lenox Square for a Geoffrey Beane trunk show—and moonlights in depressed real estate.

Both, like so many characters in Bambara's short stories, were civil-rights activists in the sixties, shock troops of the sit-in. Indeed, African American history weeps like a watermark on every page, from the underground railroad to the sleeping car porters, from the Negro League to the Southern Tenants Association, from Garvey to Malcolm to SNCC and the Freedom Schools—even as events in Atlanta correspond by black magic to bad news the third world over, from the hostage-taking in Iran to torture in South Africa to Jonestown, death squads, and "disappearings" in Central and South America. Looking for their son ("a lost ball in the high grass"), Zala and Spence are also in search of their younger, braver, warrior selves. Once upon a time, they read Amilcar Cabral and C. L. R. James. Now, according to Spence, "His mind was mush from so many years of thinking he was thinking when he was not thinking." And Zala can "feel the dark streaming at her from four directions." Why not, in such a nation?

> The same programmed notions of invulnerability, progress, health, and superiority plagued the whole country, boasting of big bombs, good teeth, strong bones, a miracle science and an advanced technology—meanwhile spending half their income on pills, booze, doctors, psychiatrists, sex manuals, sleeping potions, and assorted witch doctors to help them un-mismanage their lives.

I won't tell you what becomes of Sonny in this masterly mix of multitude, solitude, trajectory, and vertigo, except that he and his younger brother and sister would have been safer living with their grandmother in an Alabama bee colony, or on the South Georgia Islands where ancestral graves are marked with seashells and coffee kettles, than trapped in this open-season, free-fire zone where the Defenders of the White Seed wear T-shirts proclaiming that GUN CONTROL IS HITTING YOUR TARGET. And happier, too, especially since their parents never get around to making pancakes or taking them to the planetarium or the zoo because they're too busy on neighborhood watch, or getting the runaround by the cops, or huddled over composite profiles and "killer maps" at the Community Committee of Inquiry, or tracking every blue Ford Galaxy or green station wagon that cruises by the grammar school, or exchanging hunches and sorting the mail at STOP (drawings by psychics go to the left, by children to the right), or being lied to by those guardians of the public order who insist that their missing children must be "runaways" (like Pinocchio! like the Gingerbread Boy!), or are just hustlers, prostitutes, and "retards" anyway. Or, maybe, they were killed by their own parents: "Tragedies, after all, happened in castles, not in low-income homes."

Wayne Williams will not be arrested till almost five hundred pages into *Those Bones Are Not My Child*, and even then on the flimsiest of fiber evidence, and even so, for the murder of an adult. Knowing what we now know from Bambara's Malleus Maleficarum, we won't for a minute believe him guilty of the murder of all these children, from Angela Bacon and Yosuf Bell to Terry Pue and the Walker boy. But his conviction was certainly convenient. The Task Force closed up shop. You aren't, after all, officially "Missing and Murdered" if nobody puts your name on the List. As the guide on an Atlanta tour bus helpfully explains:

> We got steel-and-glass towers. Got Georgia red-clay straw bricks, and the famed Georgia pine. We got long-burning fuses, short memories, and coolant systems that are state-of-the-art. Got false fronts in place and flax at our backs. Got covens and klaverns and twitchy commandos. Got fu-

neral wreaths fading on doors in our neighborhoods. Black armbands and
green ribbons discoloring in the back of dresser drawers. Got Twinkies set
on saucers and chocolate milk for curfew-free children bounding in from
play at 3:30 or 9:00 or even 10:45. We got names, dates, events, boxed,
locked, and buried. Got walls erected against question and challenge. And
roofs bolted against all types of storms.

Or, as Etta James sings, on the car radio in a Buick: "I'd rather be
a blind girl than see you turn your back on me, babe."

I've mentioned Doctorow. You may recall that the children who
disappeared from the city streets in *The Waterworks* ended up in a
lab, where their blood, bone marrow, and spinal fluid were harvested to render the Very Rich and Very Old "biomotive," after
which these Living Dead were seen to waltz, with deaf-mute care-
taker women, under the shameless stars. This is the ante Bambara
ups. She seems also to have written a sorrow-song prequel to *The Salt
Eaters,* her own 1980 black-magical-realist novel of carnival time in
the postapocalyptic future, with its Boymen, Mud Mothers, and
"unrecognizable children" who run in packs through the wasted
city, "taking over abandoned social service agencies and subways
and concert halls and armories."

No wonder we last see Zala at target practice, with a brand-new
sound-suppressing .22 caliber Walther automatic. What has happened between Bambaras is that all the missing black children have
been disappeared into prison.

# DON DeLILLO MINIMALIZES

## 1.

After a Divine Comedy, why not haiku? So *The Body Artist* is seven hundred pages shorter than *Underworld*. Don DeLillo deserves a breather. Since *Underworld*, the best English-language novel of the nineties, somehow failed to win either a Pulitzer Prize or a National Book Award, he may even deserve a free pass. When I suggested to one of the NBA fiction jurors that maybe her panel had been blitzed on dopamine, she insisted that all five of them felt *Underworld* could have been cut by at least two hundred pages, somehow.

"Somehow," thinks Lauren Hartke in *The Body Artist*: "The weakest word in the language. And more or less. And maybe. Always maybe. She was always maybeing." (Doesn't this sound like Joan Didion? It often seems that DeLillo and Didion are crouched on the same fault line, alert to the same tectonic tremor, full of the same nameless, blue-eyed willies.)

But *which* two hundred pages? A writer goes on for as long as it takes to finish what needs saying, more or less. All DeLillo did was to dream the whole repressed history of American Cold War culture, from J. Edgar Hoover to AIDS. If you are too lazy for nomadic wandering in such a brilliant maze, stick to stock quotations. And now he is likely to be punished for this starvation diet. Where are the politics? Where are the conspiracies? Still, some breathers are also a gasp. We have been wonderstruck often enough by the minimal—a Mondrian or Sung scroll.

Anyway, DeLillo's back. Each of his eleven previous novels has been a far-flung language system, where the gravity is variable.

Each includes the prose equivalent of an action painting, a Godard film, a jazz chorale, and an explosive charge like Semtex. They have been witty in turn about motels and supermarkets, movies and television, football and rock-and-roll, baseball and atom bombs, advertising and organized crime, science fiction and the stock exchange, intelligence agencies and terrorist sects. But they are also full of dense light, black bees, deserts, caves, and cults; of prophets and pilgrims. And these pilgrims, as hungry for meaning as Greek goats, are forever chewing through slick packaging, surface chatter, coded circuits, layered film, and static cling, past numbers, letters, and ideas, to "the fallen wonder of the world." Since he is smarter than we are, better informed, and a lot more sensitive to beauty and dread, trust him.

Rey Robles is a sixty-four-year-old film director with cult status but dim prospects. His third wife, Lauren Hartke, is a thirty-six-year-old performance artist alert to birds and weather. They have rented a house in the blueberry barrens on the lobsterboat coast of New England. We meet them one morning in the kitchen, talking through each other's smoke. Rey accuses Lauren: "You like everything. You love everything. You're my happy home." Lauren is trying to see the two of them, "still a little puddled in dream melt," from the point of view of the blue jay at the outside feeder. Rey drives off. But instead of returning with a can of Ajax, he goes all the way to New York to shoot himself in the apartment of his first wife, a furious fashion consultant.

About Rey, we learn that he was born in Barcelona, grew up in the Soviet Union after his father was killed in the Spanish Civil War, came of age in Paris as a street juggler and bit-part player, moved to Los Angeles for a spaghetti Western, and became what his obituary calls a "poet of lonely places," of "people in landscapes of estrangement." None of this matters. Although any other DeLillo novel would have explored a character like Rey at length and *in situ*— Madrid! Moscow! postwar Left Bank! postmodern LA!—this one is mysteriously incurious about how he lived and why he died. It insists on knowing as little about him as, apparently, his third wife does. Mostly, it wants to watch a bereft Lauren decide whether to blame herself, to unzip and spill her beings: "She heard herself say, 'I am Lauren,' like a character in black spandex in a science-fiction film." And later on: "I am Lauren. But less and less."

About Lauren, we are told that her father is a classical scholar on an archaeological dig in the Aegean, her mother was a symphony-orchestra harpist who died when she was nine, her brother is a State Department specialist on China, and she majored in philosophy at college before dropping out to join a troupe of Seattle street performers. This would seem to matter a lot, especially the dead mother: "It wasn't her fault. It had nothing to do with her." Did Lauren's mother also commit suicide? Maybe. But, once again, what Lauren doesn't know, DeLillo won't tell.

What happens next is that Lauren returns to the blueberry barrens, finds a stranger in her rented house, and undergoes a series of spiritual calisthenics unique in our literature, a kind of emergency yoga. It's as if Henry James, after *The Turn of the Screw,* had teamed up with his brother William, after *The Varieties of Religious Experience,* to write a ghost story in which—somehow!—Rumi's whirling dervish met Conrad's Secret Sharer.

2.

There are at least three DeLillos. There is, first of all, the poster boy for postmodernism—the wised-up child of randomness and incongruity; the Geronimo of vandalism, bricolage, and mediascape pastiche; the conspiracy theorist of corporate power, government secrecy, malign systems, and the "whole enormous rot and glut and glare" of pop culture and consumer violence; the hang-glider on waves of paranoia. In *Libra,* Lee Harvey Oswald is told: "This is what history consists of. It's the sum total of all the things they aren't telling us." In *Underworld,* Matt Shay senses "some deeper meaning that existed solely to keep him from knowing what it was."

This first DeLillo, cryptic and reclusive, has issued bulletins from zones of dread on "the claustrophobia of vast spaces" and "the curse of unbelonging"; on miniature golf, serial killers, "abandoned meanings," and "crisis sociology"; on the incantatory power of nostalgia and cliché. In *White Noise*, a whole town is so afraid of invisible death that the local college and local supermarket sell it like a product and sing it like a jingle: pain relievers and cough suppressants; Tegrin, Denorex, Selsun Blue; Random Access Memory, Acquired Immune Deficiency Syndrome, and Mutual Assured Destruction. In his play *The Day Room*, where straitjackets are called camisoles and you can't tell the doctors from the actors from the maniacs, we are equally menaced by heavy water, alkaline rain, thermal inversions, lackluster industrials, and saturated fats. *Ratner's Star* instructs us, like a curse: "BREATHE! GLEAM! VERBALIZE! DIE!"

Having diagnosed "an epidemic of seeing," Poster Boy disperses his cunning among the multimedia like so many angel-headed pixels, and speaks in all their tongues. Movies, for instance: According to *Great Jones Street*, "The whole concept of movies is so fundamentally Egyptian. Movies are dreams. Pyramids. Great rivers of sleep." The impossible mission in *Running Dog* is to find a porn film shot in Hitler's bunker. Volterra in *The Names* seeks to catch on camera the alphabet killer cult, Ta Onomata, in the very act of snuff: "Film is more than the twentieth-century art. It's another part of the twentieth-century mind. It's the world seen from inside." Murray in *White Noise* is asked to teach a course in the cinema of car crashes. In *Underworld*, when they aren't watching Eisenstein or the Zapruder assassination snippet, they look at surveillance tape of the Texas Highway Serial Killer.

There is more about television: *Ratner's Star* imagines a game show, "Abort That Fetus!" *Players* ends with "serial grief" on a motel TV screen. *Libra* begins with Oswald and his mother watching "blue heads" in the Bronx, either *Racket Squad* or *Dragnet*. Karen, the ex-Moonie in *Mao II*, can't get enough of the nightly news, "the terror that came blowing through the fog": "She took it all in, she believed it all, pain, ecstasy, dog food, all the seraphic matter, the baby bliss that falls from the air." Murray in *White Noise* tells students that TV offers "incredible amounts of psychic data," "opens

ancient memories of world birth," "welcomes us into the grid, the
network of little buzzing dots that make up the picture pattern," and
"practically overflows with sacred formulas."

And this brief canvas doesn't do justice to his anthropologizing of
such superstitions as advertising, which shows up in almost every
novel from *Americana* (commercials for death on hate radio) to *Underworld* (the outdoor billboard with the angel Esmeralda and the
orange juice ad). Or spectator sports: football in *End Zone*, baseball
in *Underworld*, and ice hockey in *Amazons* (published in 1980 under
the nom de plume of "Cleo Birdwell"). Or automatic sliding doors,
brand-name T-shirts, Pop Art, and UFOs. While the Internet won't
show up until the end of *Underworld*, it is a principal player in *The
Body Artist*. So is the telephone answering machine, although not
even DeLillo can improve on his earlier riff in *Mao II*:

> The machine makes everything a message, which narrows the range of
> discourse and destroys the poetry of nobody home. Home is a failed idea.
> People are no longer home or not home. They're either picking up or not
> picking up.

No wonder they love him on the Foggy Bottoms of Academe, all
those professors paddling their guitars like kayaks upstream on pop
culture's pissy waters. His rock lyrics and graffiti, his Elvis and Hitler, his mimicry and brain fade, would seem to confirm them in their
suspicion that everything in the data drizzle and the magnetic flash
is equally weightless or trivial; that all books, films, ads, TV shows,
baseball cards, and music videos are socially constructed compost
heaps of previous texts, at best unwilling stooges and at worst bad-
faith purveyors of the usual dominant discourse; and that all of us,
Chicken Littles and Tiny Tims, are likewise each the helpless vector
of forces we can't even locate, much less modify.

But there is a second DeLillo—call him the Bombhead—for
whom dread is more than a pomo lollipop, for whom the Holocaust
and Hiroshima are the sinister figures in the twentieth-century carpet, for whom not just consumer culture but also politics and history
drift deathward, like the falling of all matter in the universe. Who

hit the road in *Americana*? "Sons of the chemistry sets in the five-walled city," running away from the Pentagon's war on Vietnam, ending up in Dealey Plaza in dreadful Dallas. In *End Zone*, Major Staley was a crew member on the Nagasaki bombing mission. In *Great Jones Street*, before they get him with a trope-killing hypodermic syringe, Bucky the rock musician will lay tracks like "VC Sweetheart" and "Cold War Lover." What scientists discover in *Ratner's Star* is that the signal they thought they had picked up from outer space is in fact the boomerang echo of a chain reaction from our own distant past, when we blew ourselves up and had to start civilization all over again in a postatomic cave. Why are so many Americans abroad in *The Names*? "Bank loans, arms credits, goods, technology. Technicians are the infiltrators of ancient societies. They speak a secret language. They bring new kinds of death." JFK actually dies in *Libra*, no matter what the black-op agents thought they were up to with their masquerade. In the bottom circle of *Underworld*'s hell—deeper down than the bomb shelters, commodity pits, and radioactive waste; than denial, repression, and the fossil fuels of memory—there is a village of deformed children not on any map of Kazakhstan.

Besides this career-long leitmotif of death-dealing technology and Bombhead jitters, this morbid fascination with "the language of the mathematics of war, nuclear game theory, that bone country of tech data and little clicking words," there is his obsession with the blood-intimate relationship between intelligence agencies and terrorists; his sympathy as both a writer and a PEN activist for poet-hostages and jailbird intellectuals; and the scorching pages he has written on our urban homeless—the soot-faced pushers of shopping carts, the sleepers in tents and subway tunnels, the missing children on milk cartons, the women who live in garbage bags, "like some Bombay cartoon." Not for them a fireproof *Libra* cubicle full of "theories that gleam like jade idols."

Finally, there is DeLillo the secret sadhu, a holy man in search of God. The "christblood colors" that Sister Edgar finds on the World Wide Web in *Underworld* in the rumble and pulse of a fireball, in the skirted stem and smoking platinum cap of a mushroom cloud, when she taps out *www.dd.com/miraculum* and gets a 58-megaton bomb, have their symbolic equivalents in the other novels, too, from Dymphna, *Americana*'s Nervous Breakdown Saint, to St. Vincent who won't even answer the telephone at his own hospital in *Great Jones Street*, to the *White Noise* nun who only pretends to believe in heaven because *somebody* has to. In *Americana, End Zone, Ratner's Star, Running Dog,* and *Mao II*, there are Calvinists with bagpipes, revivalists who speak in tongues and play with snakes, armored icons and silent Luthers looking down from two-tiered Gothic windows, and a Fordham lad who strangles a German shepherd with his rosary beads. About the lapses of the Catholic Church, a character in *Americana* will explain: "It's like the lying and cheating General Motors does. You still need cars."

Nor is all of this just because DeLillo himself was trained by Jesuits at Fordham. His is a hounding after something sacred so ecumenical, it's almost promiscuous. In these pages we also inhale passing spores of animism, Taoism, Vedanta, Zen; the stray obelisk, the surprise mosaic, and the Buddhist swastika; the sperm demons of Kabbala, Hindu cosmology, and hermaphroditic doll-gods; even such "hyperatavistic" blood-cults as the Happy Valley Renegade Faction in *Great Jones Street* and the serial-killing Ta Onomata in *The Names*. Owen in *The Names* will note that "if Greek or Latin characters are paving stones, then Arabic is rain"; next wonder, "Was religion the point of language?"; and finally get the message, in Aramaic: "The river of language is God." *Mao II* informs us, "When the Old God goes, they pray to flies and bottletops." And none of this is any less peculiar than the Aztec custom of pouring the blood of slaughtered victims into the mouths of idols, or how a Mandingo priest will "hold a newborn child in his arms, whisper in its ear and spit three times in its face."

It seems to me to have been the Secret Sadhu's enterprise from the beginning, inside the Wurlitzer and glitterdome, to listen for deeper chords than disco, to seek a saving grace in more complex structures like number theory or linguistics. In *Ratner's Star* for instance, he

explores mathematics as an "avant-garde"; whole-numbered harmonies and "the strangeness, beauty and freedom of repeated se-
quences"; "ancient and naive astronomies of bone and stone" and
the modern argument between particles and waves about the substance and nature of light; the splendid examples of Archimedes,
"killed by dreamless Romans," and Descartes, buried without his
right hand. He ends up, alas, with "recursive undecidability" and a
"noncognate celestial anomaly." Endor, the mathematician turned
Kabbalist, may marvel aloud: "Einstein and Kafka! They knew each
other! They stood in the same room and talked! Einstein and
Kafka!" But we don't know what they said.

In *The Names*, that amazing thriller, he turns from the language
of science to utterance itself—secret syllables of blood recollection,
alphabets that spell the name of God, signs wrested from the "terrible holy gibberish." He looks for the "transparent word" in the
palace of Knossos, in Sanskrit pavilions, on Ashoka's rocks. But always it's beyond reach. "Don't go too far," he cautions us about vol-
canic Crete. "There's the Minotaur, the labyrinth. Darker things.
Beneath the lilies and antelopes and blue monkeys." Until a computer translates Linear A, we can't even guess what the Minoans
might have been secretly up to. DeLillo, who has seen the sign of a
double axe on a pillar crypt in a tomb-cave, like a sinister graffito,
seems to be hinting at human sacrifice. Only after his "risk analyst"
antihero is mortified to learn that, all along, he has been working for
the CIA, will he be ready to read the meaning of the Acropolis:

> This is what I found, deeper than the art and mathematics embodied in
> the structure, the optical exactitudes. I found a cry for pity. This is what
> remains to the mauled stones in their blue surround, this open cry, this
> voice we know as our own. . . . I move past the scaffolding and walk
> down the steps, hearing one language after another, rich, harsh, mysteri-
> ous, strong. This is what we bring to the temple, not prayer or chant or
> slaughtered rams. Our offering is language.

No wonder that Bill Gray, the Salingerlike blocked novelist in
*Mao II*, can no longer see himself in his own sentences. No wonder
that Bronzini, the music teacher in *Underworld*, wants to stop a little

girl in mid-hopscotch, to "stop everything for half a second, atomic clocks, body clocks, the microworld in which physicists search for time—and then run it backwards, unjump the girl, rewind the life, give us all a chance to do it over." In his very first novel, DeLillo complained: "Saints talk to birds but only lunatics get an answer."

## 3.

Which brings us back to Lauren in her rented house, because the Secret Sadhu wrote *The Body Artist*. She has sentenced herself to solitude and discipline: "There were too many things to understand and finally just one." Still, almost immediately, not even counting her erotic reveries or the Tippi Hedren birds, she has company. An upstairs noise, a "calculated stealth," proves to be a middle-aged man in his underwear who can't tell her who he is or where he came from. Instead of calling around, she feeds his face and bathes his body. "He had a foundling quality—lost and found—and she was, she guessed, the finder." So the stranger she names "Mr. Tuttle" is incorporated into her discipline, her tripartite strip-search.

First—

At odd hours, she logs on to her computer to look at "a live-streaming video feed from the edge of a two-lane road in a city in Finland." This is Kotka, where it's always the middle of the night and a webcam is always watching empty asphalt. "She didn't know the meaning of this feed but took it as an act of floating poetry." Besides: "It emptied her mind and made her feel the deep silence of other places, the mystery of seeing over the world to a place stripped of everything but a road that approaches and recedes, both realities occuring at once."

Meanwhile—

When she isn't feeding the birds or not answering the phone, she punishes her body: cat stretch, headstand, neckroll; snake shapes, flower bends, "prayerful spans of systematic breathing"; all-fours, rump up, head cranks, wheeling; emery board, pumice stone, "clippers and creams that activated the verbs of abridgement and excision"; wax strip, cold sizzle, oatmeal scrub, and bleach: "This was her work, to disappear from her former venues of aspect and bearing and to become a blankness, a body slate erased of every past resemblance." In the mirror, she wants to see someone "classically unseen, the person you are trained to look through, bled of familiar effect, a spook in the night static of every public toilet."

Simultaneously—

She reads aloud to Mr. Tuttle from a textbook on human anatomy, coaches him at nursery rhymes in French, and asks questions and records his enigmatic answers on the tape machine to which Rey had once confided his film ideas. This is what Mr. Tuttle says: "It is not able." "The trees are some of them." "Talk to me. I am talking." "I know how much this house. Alone by the sea." "Say some words to say some words." "I said this what I said." "I am doing. This yet that." "I know him where he was." "A thing of the most. Days yes years." And: "What is somehow?"

It is as if Lauren were, at once, Jane Goodall and Noam Chomsky, grilling Doris Lessing's Ben. Maybe he's from Kotka, Finland. Unless: "Am I the first human to abduct an alien?" But as these chats meander on so weirdly, like verbal Rorschachs, verging at one extreme on the aphasic and at another on the glossolalic, Mr. Tuttle seems to shift shapes, from graveyard ghost to spirit guide to dybbuk; from Jung's anima to Conrad's Secret Sharer to Toni Morrison's Beloved. Considering all those birds at the feeder, he could even be the lapwing in the Sufi parable of soul migration, flying away from the ego toward the Absolute.

In sequence, Lauren suspects: That words for him have phases, like the moon. That he has placed her in "a set of counter-surroundings, of simultaneous insides and outsides." That he mimics phrases he's heard in hiding, including her voice and Rey's. That he lives "in a kind of time that has no narrative quality." That he doesn't know how "to measure himself to what we call the Now." That he is "a piece of found art" whose future is unnamed. That he is "alone and unable to improvise, make himself up," "drifts from one reality to another," and "laps and seeps, somehow, into other reaches of being," in "bewilderment and pain," because "he is in another structure, another culture," where time, rather than a narrative, is something "sheer and bare, empty of shelter."

"Why," she wonders, "do I think I'm standing closer to you than you are to me?" But then what pops out of his mouth is this:

> Coming and going I am leaving. I will go and come. Leaving has come to me. We all, shall all, will all be left. Because I am here and where. And I will go or not or never. And I have seen what I will see. If I am where I will be. Because nothing comes between me.

Beyond eerie, this is profoundly Delphic and sort of *Godot*. Lauren cracks:

> It came out of him nonstop and it wasn't schizophrenic speech or the whoop of rippling bodies shocked by God. He sat pale and still. She watched him. It was pure chant, transparent, or was he saying something to her? She felt an elation that made it hard for her to listen carefully. Was he telling her what it was like to be him, to live in his body and mind? She tried to hear this but could not. The words ran on, sensuous and empty, and she wanted him to laugh with her, to follow her out of herself. This is the point, yes, this is the stir of true amazement. And some terror at the edge, or fear of believing, some displacement of the self, but this is the point, this is the wedge into ecstasy, the old deep meaning of the word, your eyes rolling upward in your skull.

Whoever he is, he is "here in the howl of the world. This was the howling face, the stark, the not-as-if of things," "a man who remembers the future." And it is from this howling face, and the mortification of her own flesh, and the video stream from Finland, and the voice on the answering machine, and the maddened birds on the blueberry barrens, that Lauren will later fashion her lacerating performance in a "dungeon space" at the Boston Center for the Arts, her one-woman Body Time—"a still life that's living, not painted."

Well, you are probably thinking of "The Hunger Artist." And so was DeLillo, at least last May at the New York Public Library, when he put together Kafka's story with the imprisonment of Wei Jingsheng in China and the performance art of a Russian émigré in a Soho cage, pretending to be a dog with a rubber lamb chop. I am also reminded of the strange in Camus and the nauseous in Sartre, of novels in German by Peter Handke and Christa Wolf, and of novels in Japanese by Kobo Abe and Junichiro Tanizaki, who would have loved Lauren's foot fetishism. For that matter, Paul Valéry suggests himself: *frémissements d'une feuille effacée* (shiverings of an effaced leaf).

But the bird talks back to the saint. If fairy tales and epic quests hang together according to time-tested recipes, so do most mystic journeys toward Enlightenment, from Heraclitus and Siddhartha to St. John of the Cross and William Blake; from Gnostics, Kabbalists, and the Indian ecstatics, to the flight of the Persian plover across the Seven Valleys to Self-Annihilation. The pilgrim is a soul, the bad weather is symbolic, and so is the migration. In this geography of the invisible, there are voices and visions, detachments and amazements, ravens and hounds, dark nights and rivers of light, awe and apparition, abandonment and madness, ecstasy and trance.

So it is for Lauren, scourging self, embracing mystery, reinscripting her own body for her stricken art, deciding who she will be next. And so it is for DeLillo, too, who had to abandon politics, history, personality, small talk, lyrical exhilaration, literature, and other minds, even irony, even velocity, to follow her into her howling chastisements. Not a cry for pity this time in the mauled stones. But of her grief, the two of them have made something indelible—a piercingly pure blue note.

# THE NOVELS
# OF RICHARD POWERS

1.

Blindfolded, mummified, ankle-chained to a radiator in a white room in the bare ruined choirs of bloody Beirut, Taimur Martin in *Plowing the Dark* is about as political as a mattress or a prayer mat. He is a sadsack phantom in his own life, a teacher of English who ran away from love gone wrong in Chicago to civil war in Lebanon, and now finds himself less a hostage than a "collateral pawn," held by Shiite guerrillas "for imaginary leverage in a game where no one can say just what constitutes winning."

In five years of captivity, during which he misses the velvet revolutions, the disintegration of the Soviet Union, even the Gulf War, Martin will beseech his kidnappers for explanations (not forthcoming), conversation (instead of beatings), or at least books (preferably Dickens): "I can learn from them how not to be me. . . . Somebody else, somewhere else." All he gets is an English translation of the Holy Qur'an. And try as he might to feed on the Cow, the Bee, and the Table, to feel his way through ten-verse mazes, to nest in the cave of the Prophet, a belief in God is "not the shape that my . . . astonishment takes."

Thus abandoned to empty space in a white room on a latitude of terror, Martin must try to imagine his own missing density, as if Beckett's Malone had been asked to furnish Matteo Ricci's memory palace: "Surely," he thinks, "some core must exist inside you, some essence that you haven't simply sponged from a world of others.

Some green oasis of wherewithal that won't return to desert, now that its feeder springs are sealed off." He recalls poems by Robert Frost, pages of *Great Expectations,* and bedtime stories his Persian mother used to read to him in Farsi:

> There was and there was not a great nature painter who painted a landscape so perfect it destroyed him. Each person who looked at the scene saw something different. But all saw envy, and all wanted what they saw. And those who wanted the painting most decided to kill the maker and steal the thing he made.

Finally, with broken teeth in mouth and mind, wandering a psychic street map of his lost Chicago, entering a dream museum full of banned images, forbidden fruit, and stolen fire, Martin will discover "the look of thought"—perhaps the closest Western equivalent of that Zen garden of raked gravel—in a famous painting: soap, water, and a towel; straw-colored grass, the Provençal sun, and Vincent Van Gogh in Arles. After which, an "angel terror beyond decoding" falls down on him out of the sky, and the walls of his cell dissolve.

Meanwhile, in the other half of this remarkable novel—the seventh astonishment in fifteen years by Richard Powers—on the Pacific Northwest campus of the TeraSys conglomerate, microsofties are acting up and acting out. Theirs is a latitude of play. In another sort of white room called the Cavern, a research team of engineers, mathematicians, and graphic designers, a freelance fellowship of computer-program coders and hackers as weird and fuzzy as the "orcs and elves" in a fairy tale by Tolkien, have been licensed by their corporate masters to model the mysteries of the world. "Tranced over their keyboards, their carpal tunnels hollowed out for maximum brainfinger throughput," they dream in 3-D pixels. They are creating virtual realities and "total immersion environments" that counterfeit everything from weather climates, ecosystems, and global economies to such wonders of Western art as Henri Rousseau's psychedelic *Jungle* and Egon Schiele's knotted *Embrace.* Their most whimsical project, and the least likely to make serious money for TeraSys, is the grand embodiment in banked data of a virtual reality Hagia Sophia, which is what they imagine the "Byz-antium" in the poems of Yeats to look like.

We are introduced to the orcs and elves through the skeptical eyes of Adie Klarpol, an art-market dropout who is persuaded to sign on at TeraSys by her old college chum, the renegade poet Stevie Spie-gel. To Stevie, "Code is everything I thought poetry was back when we were in school. Clean, expressive, urgent, all-encompassing." For Adie, who abandoned her "ghosted high realism" after galleries in SoHo voted down the very idea of beauty, the Cavern comes as a revelation: "This was the way the angels in heaven painted: less with their hands than with their mind." One of the orcs will actually analogize their programmed VR dreaming to the "Ur-tech" of the wall painters at Altamira and Lascaux: "Art explodes at exactly the same moment as tool-based culture." Those prehistoric magic ar-rows and red handprints "were simulations to begin with. Con-sciousness holding itself up to its own light, for a look. An initiation ceremony for the new universe of symbolic thought."

Of course, TeraSys has other plans for its new technology, from theme parks to grief-seeking missiles. Adie, Stevie, and their cohort of misfit boys like Jackdaw and Spider—"remote avatars in a wiz-ard's romp of their own devising," who grew up playing "smart" games on a computer screen as if it were "the wishing lamp that all children's stories described . . . the storybook that once expelled us and now offered to take us back in"—were naive ever to think oth-erwise; they are as innocent of corporate science and the real world as Taimur Martin in Beirut. They appreciate their mistake when the Gulf War shows up on their television monitors:

> Babylon became a bitmap. Pilots took its sand grains apart, pixel by pixel, their soldier bodies tied to weapons systems by electronic umbilical, their every joystick twitch duplicating moves over-learned in years of now-consummated simulation. Nightscopes revealed minute movements, at impossible distances, in pitch-dark. Robot stalkers chased living targets. Formal edge-detecting algorithms told heat from cold, friend from en-emy, camouflaged caches from empty countryside. Human intelligence migrated wholesale into its artifacts.

So much for the new universe of symbolic thinking. As in the Persian children's story, the perfect painting will be stolen, and the artists who painted it disposed of. But if you have ever read a Richard Powers novel—each contrapuntal, each a double helix—you already know that Adie Klarpol is likely to meet Taïmur Martin in Van Gogh's bedroom.

2.

On the road, on the raft, on the lam—ours is a culture of Shane-like vanishing acts, an agitated itchiness from Huck Finn to the Weather Underground, with intermediate stops at the Last of the Mohicans, the Lost Generation, Dean Moriarty, Billy Pilgrim, Rabbit Angstrom, and Henderson the Rain King. It's no big surprise to find lonesome rangers on every page of Powers—teachers who leave hospitals to wander in the atomic desert; scientists who desert their labs for nightshift scutwork, secretly composing music; librarians who quit their decimal systems to look for the human genome; doctors running away from war crimes and nightmare third-world childhoods; novelists hiding out in a neuroscience research project; single-mother real-estate agents marooned in metastatic randomness; Adie who has lost her art.

What does startle is the urgent longing of these pilgrims to go home again, if they can figure out where home is. In one of his novels, *Galatea 2.2*, Powers describes another, *The Gold Bug Variations*, as "a songbook of homesickness." But so are they all. And history keeps getting in the way. In each novel, he seems to hope that by striking out in two directions at once, then rigging a convergence, he can circle back to sanctuary. But to the east in *Plowing the Dark* is terror, and to the west is make-believe, so where are we? Stranded on both latitudes at the same time, in two different genres.

Simulations of 3-D space are a hoary science-fiction staple. Aldous Huxley had "feelies," Robert Heinlein a "waldo," Philip K. Dick an "empathy box," James Morrow "dream beans," John Varley "memory cubes," and Ray Bradbury interactive soaps and an illusory Africa called "The Veldt." Even William Gibson, the dean of "cyberpunk" sci-fi novelists, did drugged time in holographic "sim-stims" before shooting the digital rapids in *Neuromancer* (1984), *Count Zero* (1986), and *Mona Lisa Overdrive* (1988). But Gibson, by dreaming up a parallel universe on the reverse side of the glowing screen, a sort of circuit city he was the first to call "cyberspace," upped the ante. Whether we were novel-readers, moviegoers, e-mailers, or even Silicon Valley hackers ourselves, if we tried to picture computer "space" at all, we saw it on Gibson's terms, as a "consensual hallucination," a digitized Xanadu. Slugabed in our romper rooms, tethered to a war porn website, flatlined by an adman/music video consumer grid, crouched at our software console as though it were a harpsichord, we imagined pyramids and shopping malls of data: green crypts of offshore banking secrets, periwinkle esplanades of corporate security, the logarithmic spiral arms of military intelligence, and that "fluid neon origami trick" of levitation by which the new age mutant ninja hacker navigates this dreadful deep of meat/machine interface.

Briefly, cyberpunk was a sci-fi genre. (My personal favorites include Neal Stephenson's *Snow Crash*, with its VR "Metaverse" where you go in goggles to play with avatars of Gilgamesh. And Pat Cadigan's *Synners*, with its account of the on-line manipulation of our parietal lobes via sockets drilled directly into the limbic system, and its rock-and-roll mantra: "If you can't fuck it and it doesn't dance, eat it or throw it away." *The Star Fraction*, by Ken MacLeod, is also nifty: Lucy in the Sky with class contradictions, starring Leon Trotsky as the Big Pixel.) Cyberpunk was also an outlaw culture. (Against late capitalism and its marketing of commodified emotions, the Grace of Hip: industrial noise, gangster chic, film noir, crystal meth, performance art, Max Headroom.) And cyberpunk was a fashion statement. (Black leather, mirror shades, nose studs, nipple rings, the photoscan sequence in *Blade Runner*, and the vector graphics in Disney's *Tron*.)

Now that we are one big World Wide Web of IPOs, all this posturing seems as old as disco. In one sense, by reminding us of what computer programming was like in 1989 for those who really did it (and why they did it, and what it did to them), rather than those who used it (either for obscene profit or as baroque filigree in dystopian fables), *Plowing the Dark* is an allegory of a fall from grace, from the joyful innocence of geeks in flannel who write and crack magic code to the blithe arrogance of venture capitalists headed on Harley hogs for a Nasdaq systems crash. We go from a smiley face on an Apple icon to the Microsoft antitrust trial. But in another sense, equally important, *Plowing the Dark* is about how angels paint.

Because Powers is not a punk. He writes fiction that includes science, not science fiction. He has told an interviewer that what absorbs him is "a perpetual, precarious, negotiated trade-off" between "the life of the private self and the life of the public hive." He had first intended to become a physicist or paleontologist. As early as 1978, while studying for an MA in English, he taught himself to program computers. Appalled by the "shrill solipsism" of literary theory, he left grad school to earn a living writing the very code that Stevie in *Plowing the Dark* substitutes for poems. While science in his fiction is sacked for sensuous metaphor, it is never disrespected. It seeks system, symmetry, and coherence in the picturing of deployed matter; order in nature, essence in number, beauty in reason, and proof in the abstract pudding. Not only is *Galatea 2.2* the best novel anybody has so far written about artificial intelligence, and *Plowing the Dark* the best about virtual reality, but after a careful reading of *The Gold Bug Variations,* I am inclined to think that I could crack the genetic code myself.

Terror and its Siamese twin, state violence, have a longer literary pedigree. Picking up where Dostoyevsky, Conrad, and Malraux left off, heavyweights like Arthur Koestler, Heinrich Böll, Mary McCarthy, Alberto Moravia, Doris Lessing, Paul Theroux, Nadine Gordimer, John Le Carré, and Don DeLillo have also tried to read the mind of the ultra — "the lunatic of one idea," Victor Serge called Konstantinov in a Wallace Stevens poem — as it shape-shifts from Belfast to Beirut to Jakarta; from skyjacking a jumbo jet to bombing

an abortion clinic; from land mines, thumbscrews, death squads, and
ethnic cleansers to Pol Pot and Shining Path. Terrorists and tortur-
ers tend, in fact, to be more interesting in novels, where they have
complicated rationales, than they are in person, mouthing thuggish
bumperstickers. In order to think about horrific behavior, novelists
need to imagine minds as nuanced as their own. And so they pile
organic culture, aesthetic patterning, and gaudy mythomanias on
top of abstract grievance. They gussy up these kamikazes of Kingdom Come with Oedipus, Freud, Marx, Fanon, Dante, and Blue-
beard, as if seeking a subjective correlative for the fabulous
derangements of Gonzalo Thought.

In DeLillo's *Mao II*, a go-between in a hostage situation chal-
lenges the novelist Bill Gray: "Through history it's the novelist who
has felt affinity for the violent man who lives in the dark. Where are
your sympathies? With the colonial police, the occupier, the rich
landlord, the corrupt government, the militaristic state? Or with the
terrorist?" To which, as if anticipating Richard Powers, Gray replies:
"When you fill rooms with innocent victims, you begin to empty the
world of meaning and erect a separate mental state, the mind con-
suming what's outside itself, replacing real things with plots and
fictions. . . . This poet you've snatched. His detention drains the
world of one more thimble of meaning."

But horrific behavior doesn't need a novelist. It is perfectly capable of spinning its own excuses for abduction, torture, rape, and
murder, out of a spidery bowel and a smoked brain. Its cold, invari-
able, contemptuous purpose is to dominate and humiliate; to create,
as in the nightmares of Kafka and Foucault, a lab-rat labyrinth, a
"total immersion" maze, where our private histories, personal be-
liefs, and multiple motives are beside the brutal point. Which is why
we should be grateful to Richard Powers, all of whose sympathies
are with the snatched poets and the Taimur Martins; who feels no
affinity whatsoever for the violent man who lives in the dark; who
worries instead about "the outside's killing abundance and the inside's incapacity to know"; who insists on "the siege of concealed

meaning" in science, music, art, politics, literature, and the "dialects of desire"; who reminds us that we are ends, not means.

3.

Boy, is he smart. See him in Boston in the early eighties, a freelance programmer with a Dutch girlfriend, who just happens to be reading Walter Benjamin's "The Work of Art in the Age of Mechanical Reproduction" when he wanders one Saturday morning into a Museum of Fine Arts retrospective on German photography and sees a picture called "Young Westerwald Farmers on Their Way to a Dance, 1914." He returns home immediately and starts writing his first novel, *Three Farmers on Their Way to a Dance* (1985). Of course, the dance to which Adolphe, Hubert, and Peter are headed, with detours through the history of photography and Flanders, is the *danse macabre* of World War I. And then Powers moves to Holland, where love, as usual, goes wrong.

But not before he's written a second novel, *Prisoner's Dilemma* (1988). On the surface, it's a more conventional Freudian-fifties family romance in the Salinger/Brodkey misery mode, about a father who keeps getting fired from his high-school history-teaching jobs, a mother who worries about her husband's periodic seizures and the model utopia he's building in the attic, and four children who hate always having to move to another, drearier town. And yet it is also a gloss on game theory, a reminder of the internment camps for Japanese-Americans in World War II, an inquiry into the controlled environments of Walt Disney, a flashback to scapegoating in the witchhunt years ("another case of Hiss and Tell"), and a visit to the New Mexican desert where the physicists broke light like a yellow pencil and then quoted the Bhagavad Gita at us. Eddie Hobson could be dying of history, loneliness, or radiation poisoning. His children won't find out which until they've gone through T. S. Eliot and Alan Turing.

After which *The Gold Bug Variations* (1991), perhaps the most daunting American novel since *Moby-Dick*, a Grand Canyon of a detective story deep enough to swallow Pynchon's *Rainbow*, Nabokov's *Pale Fire*, and DeLillo's *Underworld*, with lots of room left over for Joseph McElroy's *Women and Men*. In 1957, Stuart Ressler, a lonely midwestern molecular biologist, seems on the verge of cracking the genetic code, but falls suddenly in love with a married member of his research team and disappears forever from science and recorded history. In 1982, two young lovers—a librarian who can look up anything and an art-history doctoral candidate who's lapsed into software hack-work—determine to find out what became of the biologist. Before they discover Stuart Ressler's secret, Jan O'Deigh and Todd Franklin will tour not only self-replicating molecules, differential engines, polypeptides, and Pythagoras, but also Pascal, polyphony, and the Unicorn tapestries at Cluny. Rainer Maria Rilke shows up, and so does a singing ATM machine. And I haven't even mentioned Brueghel and Vermeer. Or Paul Robeson, who climbs "Jacob's Ladder" like a protein chain. Or the teaming up of the "Gold Bug" of Edgar Allan Poe and the "Goldberg" of Johann Sebastian Bach to read "the tetragrammatonic golem recipe" of DNA. By awesome metaphor, Powers suggests that in Bach's polyphony, as in the double helix, as in kabbala, variations on just four notes, four nucleotides, and the four letters in the name of God spell out everything we need to know about "that string of base-pairs coding for all inheritance, desire, ambition, the naming need itself—first love, forgiveness, frailty."

Thus the human program is debugged.

Now although I ran away from organic chemistry in college as if it were conscription, my brother was a math major, my son is the technology editor of the on-line magazine Salon.com. and my son's mother is a neuroanatomist who once explained the synaptic cleft to me. So I'm a little less freaked by hard science than many of my peers. For pleasure as well as instruction, I read Peter Medawar and Stephen Gould. Like the character who calls himself "Richard Powers" in *Galatea 2.2*, I try for the gist and take the rest on faith. Still, *Gold Bug* hurt my head. The question is, why shouldn't a novel hurt a head that needs it? We've spent too much time worrying about the social construction of science and not enough worrying about the scientific construction of society, its rewrite of the social text. Powers, who turns intellectual activity into imaginative literature, is under no illusion that scientists are a better class of bivalve than artists, teachers, librarians, composers, or poets. But neither are they worse. Science itself "is about reverence, not mastery." Its purpose, according to *Gold Bug* biomole Ressler,

> was not the accumulation of gnostic power, fixing of formulas for the names of God, stockpiling brutal efficiency, accomplishing the sadistic myth of progress. The purpose of science was to revive and cultivate a perpetual state of wonder. For nothing deserved wonder so much as our capacity to feel it.

Such a science thrills every bit as much as art and a lot more than politics—unless the politics are those of Powers, whose next, grimmest, least theoretical, and most neglected novel was *Operation Wandering Soul* (1993). Three books in one, it is first of all a harrowing account of medical malpractice, or "Kiddie Karpentry," in the children's ward of a public hospital in the Watts section of Los Angeles. A child dies of poverty every two and a half seconds. If pediatric therapist Linda Espera and surgical resident Richard Kraft can't save these children—orphans of the projects; stick figures from the Southern nations; two-pound preemies, three-year-olds "like a fish on a barb," the little girl who refuses to talk except by pulling the string on a Chatty Cathy doll and the little boy who sticks cafeteria silverware into his prosthetic limb—then the children will have to save themselves.

The second book of the three in *Operation Wandering Soul* is an anthology of all the violence the world has ever done to children, and the dreams they dream to escape that violence. For every Secret Garden, Wonderland, Neverland or Oz, every Hansel, Gretel, Lost Boy or Peter Pan, there is a Pied Piper and an Anne Frank, a Ghost Dance and Taiping Rebellion, a Children's Crusade in France, a child prostitute in Thailand, a slum kid in London's Blitz and "a fly-fanged, glazed-eyed, successionist, baby Ibo exoskeleton" twisting its stick limbs "to reach a mother's teat no larger or moister than a shriveled mole." Against so much school-age death on the revolutionary calendars of so many maddened nation-states, against such a folklore background of child abuse, of what consolation are the stories of deliverance, the promise and curve of the fairy-tale fables that Linda Espera reads aloud in the pediatric ward? "You are going somewhere. *You are going somewhere.*"

*Wandering Soul*'s third book is the third world inside the head of the surgeon Kraft. It rushes back, this repressed memory. Kraft grew up in transit terminals, at customs checks, blowing a French horn in Lahore, Teheran, Buenos Aires, Jakarta, and Beirut, speaking a street jabber "of Farsi, Korean, Urdu, and bastard lingua franca Carib," capable of counting to one hundred in three different Chinese dialects and of praying "without comprehension in Arabic." Ever since Bangkok, he has wanted to be a bodhisattva, to make guilty amends for his Air America father, a diplomat and war criminal. Can it really be that all those atrocities, all those napalmed children, have followed him to Los Angeles, have found him in the middle of his reading of Musil's *The Man Without Qualities*? How else to explain "tiny, terrified" Joy, the twelve-year-old "refugee princess" from Laos, with the bone disease he can't fix?

Joy has read everything. Joy knows she's not going anywhere. Joy is among the wounded children who just vanish one night from Angel City. You don't want to know what happens next.

With *Galatea 2.2* (1995), his most popular novel, Powers reverted to hard science and lofty abstraction. He seems also to be questioning his own vocation. "Richard Powers," the thirty-five-year-old novelist trying to finish a fourth book ("a bleak, baroque fairy tale about wandering and disappearing children") returns as the "token humanist" and "resident alien" to the Center for the Study of Advanced Sciences at the Midwestern university where "I first saw how paint might encode politics, first heard how a sonata layered itself like a living hierarchy, first felt sentences cadence into engagement," and first betrayed his "beloved physics" by shacking up with literature. Now, contemplating "the emergent digital oversoul" on his office link to the Internet, he has begun to wonder "who in their right mind would want to read an ornate, suffocating allegory about dying pedes at the end of history"?

Besides, love has gone very wrong indeed.

But before he can whistle the middle movement of a Mozart clarinet concerto, he will be coaxed and bullied by the Center's neuroscientists into an experiment to create a network of software programs capable of a passing an oral exam for a degree in English literature. He will ghost a machine! Never mind the usual dazzling Powers footwork with "cluster analysis," "back propagation," and "isomorphic contour mapping." The real questions needing answers are: What is memory? Where, if anywhere, does it reside? Does the memory of memory constitute consciousness? How does an idea look? What if meaning is an interval, not a pitch? Can machines dream? Are you who I think you are? Am I who you think I am?

And who, especially, does "Helen" think she is? For "Helen," an artificial intelligence, a sentient machine, is the ghost these Frankensteins catch in their neural net. Well fed on Curious George and Mother Goose, La Fontaine and the *Ramayana*, the Brothers Grimm and the Admirable Bede, Helen wants to know: When is now? "Where did I come from?" "What races do I hate?" She has trouble with metaphor and similes, like "A pretty girl is like a melody." Or, "A people without history is like the wind on the buffalo grass. How?" She has been reading William Blake: "The rose is sick because the worm eated it." She will see "how the mind makes forever, in order to store the things it has already lost." In a remark so wonderfully gnomic Wittgenstein might have made it, she decides that "the life we lead is our only maybe. The tale we tell is the must that we make by living it." And not only will Helen burst into song, but after learning more than she wanted to know, she will also go away and come back: "I'm sorry. I lost heart." And when they finally ask her to explain Shakespeare's Caliban, she will shut herself off forever, after this last message:

You are the ones who can hear airs. Who can be frightened or encouraged.
You can hold things and break them and fix them. I never felt at home
here. This is an awful place to be dropped down halfway.

Clare International, the "limited-liability" corporation in *Gain*
(1998), is another kind of artificial intelligence, almost a divine being with its symbolic logo and its hymnlike theme song and its
priestly caste of lawyers in their bulletproof class-action suits. Although incorporeal, it has nonetheless evolved, like Procter &
Gamble, Colgate-Palmolive, Lever Brothers, Dow Chemical, and
Monsanto, from a family-owned soap and candle company in the
early 1800s with a commercial interest in chemistry and botany, to a
multinational research-development-and-marketing conglomerate
in the megabusiness of fertilizers, cosmetics, shampoo, grout, low-fat
chips, fresh breath, and slow death. It might even be said to have its
own eschatology, according to which profit is a whole lot more than
merely how the culture keeps score. Profit rationalizes nature, spiri-
tualizes surplus value, and is its own purpose, like consciousness.
Soap is a metaphor. Metacapitalism is all about longing.

The least demanding and most accessible of Powers's novels,
*Gain* also tends to trudge, as if on a forced march across our optic
tract, through a couple of centuries of potted company history—
protectionism, civil war, labor strife, and major-market advertising;
junk bonds, leveraged debt, shotgun merger, hostile buyout, poison
pill; detergents, deodorants, mouthwash, antacids, weather strip-
ping, and a product line so brightly branded that it's "as easy to flesh
out as any phantom, as real as the Shadow, Jack Armstrong, Jack
Benny, Ma Perkins, or Kate Smith." But the air and the water in
Clare International's company town of Lacewood, Illinois, turn out
to be chock-full of formaldehyde, benzene, dichlorodifluromethane,
and epichlorohydrin, and a surprisingly large number of people
have something seriously wrong with them.

One of them is Laura Bodey, a single mother, a real estate agent,
and a cancer patient so ingenuous as to resist joining a suit against
Clare because "cancer's not something that I really want to profit

from." Imagine that. Laura wants to take responsibility for her own life. *And* death. Whereas a limited liability corporation is responsible only to its shareholders. As if by Greek choral ode, the novel proceeds from strophe to antistrophe. Thus, for Laura: dual-agent therapy, Taxol plus cisplatin; dexamethasone, an anti-inflammatory and a steroid; Zantac, an anti-ulcerative; Zofran, to keep the nausea at bay; mannitol and gel tablets that "stink like rotting squirrel meat"; Neupogen, a registered trademark of filgrastim, a granulocyte-colony-stimulating recombinant DNA drug; calibration, after peritoneal phosphorus and concentrated chemo washes are no longer options; chalk milkshakes, swill of barium, and yet more CAT scans—until at last the IV morphine drip.

Whereas, for Clare: Snowdrop, Gristo, Tar Baby, FlapperJack Pancake Mix, and Mentine Gargle and Breath Repairer; Clarity Pore Purifier, Blue Spruce Vapogard, No-fume Enamel, Lok-Toppers, Gastrel Caps, and Partifest Non-dari Treats; not to mention Germ-Guard for your floors, Cleer-Thru for your windows, Slickote Surface, Leather Lifts, Heat 'n' Eat, Multi-pli Maxiwipes, and, of course, deniability. The odd impression is that, somehow, Erin Brockovich had gone to bed with Henry Adams.

There will be a surprise twist at the end of *Gain*. There is almost always a surprise twist at the end of a Powers novel, as if irony were a noose for lynching. Meanwhile, Laura marvels at an instant camera: "A disposable miracle, no less than the least of us."

### 4.

So consider the account so far an isomorphic contour map of the Powers-That-Be. It omits dozens of characters, all of them with something to think. And a surprising amount of sex, for people whose heads must usually be hurting. And a personal ghost or two, like his alcoholic father and his trauma-surgeon brother. As well as his scattershot humor, like a twitchy reflex. (In the middle of Los Alamos, for instance, we are asked: "Which came first, the Chicken

McNugget or the Egg McMuffin?") But homesickness is the horizon of his world.

In *Prisoner's Dilemma*, Eddie Hobson tells his children: "What we can't bring about in no way releases us from what we must" and "Do what you can while you can before you cannot." But what those children really need to know is: "What are we running from? How do we get back? Why are you leaving us?"

In *The Gold Bug Variations*, Stuart Ressler believes that "all longing converges on this mystery: revelation, unraveling secret spaces, the suggestion that the world's valence lies just behind a scrambled facade, where only the limits of ingenuity stand between him and sunken gardens."

In *Operation Wandering Soul*, Richard Kraft suspects that "home too is a way of leaving. It is *about* leaving, a departure as certain as any urge, longer even than the sense of having come from there." And he's absolutely positive that

> what *happens* is not a thing but a place. . . . *No one* this side of childhood exile, not a single memoir or condescending picture book, has ever gotten it right. But no one has ever lost it either: that first house, where want and terror, the toy soldiers of self itself, have not yet split off and solidified on contact with air.

And while the therapist Linda Espera can do nothing to fix "the parts irrevocably lost" in her children, she does have "something to leave in the dark reaches, the space in each one where the earliest, inviolable fable of self still stands intact, ready to respond to a little food, workout, heat, and play. She can plant a start in that place waiting to be proven wrong, a plot that will still heal at the first touch of fresh, outrageously naive narrative."

In *Galatea 2.2*, we are told that "love is the feedback cycle of longing, belonging, loss." And that "books were about a place we could not get back to." After Helen decides that "I don't want to play anymore," the novelist who programmed her wants to believe that "we could love more than once," but first we must know "what once means." And then there are Helen's famous last words: "I never felt at home here."

What if Adie is right in *Plowing the Dark:* "Even the myth of elemental loss somehow misses the point. It may not be in you, ever, to believe in a home of your own devising." What if her make-believe Byzantium, her Hagia Sophia, is just another empty shell?

> The room of holy wisdom is a ruin. The world's largest, as large as the ruinous world. And propped against the striped arcades, amnesiac, illiterate in the unreadable wreck, you pitch your home.

Now just listen to what Joy, the heartbreaking refugee princess, has to say to her fifth-grade class before going to the hospital, in a "Brief and True Report of the New-Found Land":

> There are no natives here. Even the resident ambers and ochers descended from lost tribes, crossed over on some destroyed land bridge, destined to be recovered from the four corners of the earth where they had wandered. She tells how a shipwreck survivor named Christbearer Colonizer washed up on the rocks of the Famous Navigators' School with a head full of scripture and childhood fantasies. And she shows how these elaborate plans for regaining the metropolis of God on Earth led step by devastating step to their own Angel *barrio.*
>
> Everything she relates she has already lived through: how that first crew survives on promises of revelation. How the Christbearer mistakes Cuba for Japan. How he makes his men swear that they are on the tip of Kublai Khan's empire. How, in the mouth of the Orinoco, he tastes the fourth river of Paradise flowing from the top of the tearshaped globe. How he sets the earth on permanent displacement.
>
> Her American history is a travelogue of mass migration's ten anxious ages: the world's disinherited, out wandering in search of colonies, falling across this convenient and violently arising land mass that overnight doubles the size of the known world. They slip into the mainland on riverboat and Conestoga, sow apple trees from burlap sacks, lay rail, blast through rock, decimate forests with the assistance of a giant blue ox. They survive on hints of the Seven Cities, the City on the Hill, the New Jerusalem, scale architectural models of urban renewal, migration's end. At each hesitant and course-corrected step, they leave behind hurriedly scrawled notes: *Am joining up with new outfit, just past the next meridian.*

It has been a while, but perhaps you are wondering about Taimur Martin, in *Plowing the Dark*. One day, for no better reason than the one he was snatched for at the start, he is abruptly released by those who seized him, a paramilitary unit of God's Partisans called the Soldiers of the Sacred Conflict. Something happened in his dream museum; he's not sure what. Never having met Adie Klarpol, who has meanwhile vanished from TeraSys, he can't explain the "angel terror" that fell down on him in the "measureless room." He only knows he has no choice "but to live long enough to learn what it needed" from him. Abduction and captivity have taught him a cheerless lesson: "There is a truth only solitude reveals. An insight that action destroys, one scattered by the slightest worldly affair: the fact of our abandonment here, in a far corner of sketched space."

How to get from this abandonment, these abductions and displacements, the atomic desert, the cancer ward, the internment camp, the children's hospital, corporate greed, and machine dreams, to Arles and Eden, base harmonies and pentimento, sanctuary and the meaning of the code—this is the brilliant project of Richard Powers. Everybody else just talks about alienation, estrangement, and the unbearable lightness of being. He actually does something about them. And what he does isn't to take a hike or a powder or a rain check or a pharmaceutical, not even a God pill. He will use everything we know from our higher brain functions about mind and body and art and longing, to find patterns and close distances. That we are around in the first place to contemplate our abandonment is pure luck and odd chance, no thanks to divine madness, and all the more reason to cherish every minute, mote, and note of it— the banned image, the forbidden fruit, the stolen fire, the random neuron. In an interview in the literary journal *Conjunctions*, Powers spelled out his own tetragrammaton:

> Art is a way of saying what it means to be alive, and the most salient
> feature of existence is the unthinkable odds against it. For every way that
> there is of being here, there are an infinity of ways of not being here.
> Historical accident snuffs out whole universes with every clock tick. Sta-

tistics declare us ridiculous. Thermodynamics prohibits us. Life, by any reasonable measure, is impossible, and *my* life—this, here, now— infinitely more so. Art is a way of saying, in the face of all that impossibility, just how worth celebrating it is to be able to say anything at all.

This antifaith has its own awe and book of wonders, opacity and dark side, ambiguities and transfigurations. His novels express all these, plus a palpable yearning for the healing light of beauty and intellect. In *The Gold Bug Variations*, Stuart Ressler is as fearful as he is heroic:

> I review the record of care we've given a spark we once thought was lit for our express warming. I feel sick beyond debilitation to think of what will come, how much more desperate the ethic of tending is, now that we know that the whole exploding catalog rests on inanimate, chance self-ignition. The three-billion-year project of the purposeful molecule has just now succeeded in confirming its own worst fear: this outside event need not have happened, and perhaps never should have. We've all but destroyed what once seemed carefully designed for our dominion. Left with a diminished, far more miraculous place—banyans, bivalves, blue whales, all from base pairs—what hope is there that heart can evolve, beat to it, keep it beating?

To which, by way of reply—not an answer but a promise—there is the perception of Jan O'Deigh, the feisty librarian, who loves the old man and the younger, and who daydreams:

> There is only one way for day to pass into dark; today has done so along a predictable sliding scale since the Precambrian. There are only a few barometric pressures, a narrow band of allowable temperatures. But however reducible to parts—degrees, pound per square inch, lumen, hour by the clock, latitude, inclination and season—however simple and limited the rules for varying these, something in the particular combination of elements is, like twelve notes and ten durations compounded into a complex cortex-storm, unique, unrepeatable, infinitely unlikely. Today in History: Bach knocks out another cantata.

And so has Richard Powers. He paints with his mind, like Adie's angels.

# BARBARA KINGSOLVER:
## OUT OF AFRICA

OUT OF A CHILD'S GAME of "Mother May I," looked down on by a green snake in an alligator-pear tree, Barbara Kingsolver has dreamed a magnificent fiction and a ferocious bill of indictment. The mothers so solicited are white American and black Congolese and matriarchal Africa herself. In their turn, on their knees, keening like birds in a rain of blood, these mothers beseech some principle of naming and knowing, some macrohistorical scale of justice and some mechanism of metamorphosis, to console them for their lost children. As in the keyed chords of a Baroque sonata, movements of the personal, the political, the historical, and even the biological contrast and correspond. As in a Bach cantata, the choral stanza, the recitatives and the da capo arias harmonize. And a whole forest sings itself.

To be less lofty about it, Kingsolver, whose own public-health-worker parents took her to the Congo when she was a child, who has been thinking about that season for thirty years while she wrote other, quieter, less ambitious books like *Animal Dreams* and *The Bean Tree*, has gone back to Africa and somehow transfigured it. *The Poisonwood Bible* is not a Safari Novel. Her village, her river, her forest, and her snake aren't symbol dumps or Rorschach tests or manhood rites or local-color souvenirs—nor a pilgrim's gasbag progress past Pygmies to afflatus. An intelligence in transit is exacerbated by particulars of place; the North American is unmoored, unmasked, astigmatic, and complicitous; the woman is decoupled, unchosen, rewound; a shadow world of the geopolitical and the clandestine rolls over domestic scruple. Not Conrad's heart-of-darkness angiogram, Graham Greene's crucifix lapel pin, Hemingway's penis fetish or Evelyn Waugh's slice of Hamlet on wry toast is powerful enough to protect these tourists from the mamba eye of Kingsolver up an alligator-pear tree, all-seeing, all-knowing . . .

From the peanut plains of Bethlehem, Georgia, in the peach-blossom summer of 1959, on a twelve-month mission to baptize and civilize the animistic heathen, the Rev. Nathan Price, his wife Orleanna and their four daughters arrive in a Congo still Belgian (though not for long)—to be greeted by bare breasts and goat stew. Before they can extricate themselves from Kitanga they will have endured a year and a half of hunger and disease, ants and snakes, wars and witchcraft, Lumumba and Mobutu, Ike and the CIA. For their incomprehension a Price will be paid: a portion of their sanity, all their arrogance, and one of their girls. On the day the child dies, so does Patrice Lumumba.

The Price women, all of them remarkable, take contrapuntal turns telling the story:

Orleanna, whose dreams are full of eyes in the trees, of rivers of wishes, of animal teeth, blames herself for failing to protect her children from Africa and their father: "No wonder they hardly seemed to love me half the time—I couldn't step in front of my husband to shelter them from his scorching light. They were expected to look straight at him and go blind." And: "I wonder what you'll name my sin. Complicity? Loyalty? Stupefaction? . . . Is my sin a failure of virtue, or of competence?" And: "Poor Congo, barefoot bride of men who took her jewels and promised the Kingdom." And: "Maybe I'll even confess the truth, that I rode in with the horsemen and beheld the apocalypse, but still I'll insist I was only a captive witness. What is the conqueror's wife, if not a conquest herself?" Finally: "And now I am one more soul walking free in a white skin, wearing some thread of stolen goods: cotton or diamonds, freedom at the very least, prosperity. Some of us know how we came by our fortune, and some of us don't, but we wear it all the same. There's only one question worth asking now: How do we aim to live with it?"

Rachel, the oldest daughter at sweet sixteen, "the most extreme blonde imaginable," a Queen of Sheba in a green linen Easter suit, batting white-rabbit eyelashes, painting her fingernails bubblegum pink to match her headband, is shocked to be anywhere with "no new record album by the Platters," but able to entertain her sisters with imitation radio commercials: "Medically tested Odo-ro-no, stops underarm odor and moisture at the source!" She's also the mistress of the delicious malaprop: "feminine wilds"; "sheer tapestry of justice," and "Who is the real Rachel Price? . . . I prefer to remain anomalous." Tata Ndu, the village chief, asks for her hand in marriage, and Eeben Axelroot, the Afrikaner bush pilot, diamond smuggler, and CIA mercenary, bargains for the rest of her. If Rachel never imagined the Congo to be more than a story she would someday tell "when Africa was far away and make-believe like the people in history books," she still knows how to bounce: "Honestly there is no sense spending too much time alone in the dark." And so she won't.

Ruth May, the youngest— "my little beast, my eyes, my favorite stolen egg," her mother calls her—populates the village with the "Lone Ranger, Cinderella, Briar Rose, and the Tribes of Ham"; teaches Tumba, Bangwa, and Nsimba to play "Mother May I"; refuses to take her quinine tablets; is so thin-skinned that she suffers Africa like a bruise; and carries around a magic matchbox with a picture of a lion on it and a chicken bone inside and a tiny hole with a tiny peg, in order to disappear herself. One of her sisters, pushing Ruth May in a swing, thinks this:

> She flew forward and back and I watched her shadow in the white dust under the swing. Each time she reached the top of her arc beneath the sun, her shadow legs were transformed into the thin, curved legs of an antelope, with small round hooves at the bottom instead of feet. I was transfixed and horrified by the image of my sister, with antelope legs. I knew it was only shadow and the angle of the sun, but still it's frightening when things you love appear suddenly changed from what you have always known.

Leah, "the tonier twin," the tomboy Goddess of the Hunt, only ceases to be desperate for the approval of her father when she decides that he's insane. And keeps a pet owl even though owls are known at night to devour souls. And is called "Leba" by the villagers, which means "fig tree" in Kikongo, instead of "Léa," which means "nothing much." And is called "béene-béene" by the schoolteacher/ revolutionary Anatole, which means "as true as true can be." And will be taught by Anatole to shoot arrows from the bow he carves for her from greenheart wood. And has read enough *Jane Eyre* and *Brenda Starr* to realize she's fallen in love with this Anatole, who "moves through the dappled shade at the edge of my vision, wearing the silky pelt of a panther." This is how Leah will end up:

> I rock back and forth on my chair like a baby, craving so many impossible things: justice, forgiveness, redemption. I crave to stop bearing all the wounds of this place on my own narrow body. But I also want to be a person who stays, who goes on feeling anguish where anguish is due. I want to belong somewhere, damn it. To scrub the hundred years' war off this white skin till there's nothing left and I can walk out among my neighbors wearing raw sinew and bone, like they do.
>
> Most of all, my white skin craves to be touched and held by the one man on earth I know has forgiven me for it.

And finally Adah, the damaged Quasimodo twin: speechless and limping, she is always left behind, even by her mother in the plague of ants: "I have long relied on the comforts of martyrdom." She was born with half her brain "dried up like a prune, deprived of blood by an unfortunate fetal mishap. My twin sister, Leah, and I are identical in theory, just as in theory we are all made in God's image. . . . But I am a lame gallimaufry and she remains perfect." In the Congo, though, nobody stares at her misshapenness; most of *them* have something missing, too. In Kitanga, she is called "white little crooked girl." And in her crooked mind, from phrases she has found in Edgar Allan Poe, Emily Dickinson, William Carlos Williams, and *Dr. Jekyll and Mr. Hyde*, she will make wicked palindromes: "Amen enema," "eros eyesore," and "Evil, all its sin is still alive!"

There is nothing Adah doesn't notice, bringing up the rear: the bodies of dead children wrapped in layers of cloth "like a large goat cheese," under a funeral arch of palm fronds, with the howling

sweet scent of frangipani; her father's First Evangelical Church of
the Lost of Cause, full of lepers and outcasts, who try Jesus on for size
because nothing else has fit; the fact that "bangala" pronounced one
way means "precious," but pronounced as her father does ("Jesus is
*bangala!*") means "poisonwood": The Lord will make you itch. It is
Adah who learns in Africa that "the transition from spirit to body
and back to spirit again" is a "ride on the power of *nommo*, the force
of a name to call oneself." *Nommo* rains from a cloud, or rises in the
vapor from a human mouth: "a song, a scream, a prayer." And it's
Adah who echoes her mother: "All human odes are essentially one.
'My life: what I stole from history, and how to live with it.'"

The history they steal from belongs to their family (an abusive
and cowardly father, gone mad for the second time in a third-world
jungle: the missionary position as a form of rape); the village (which
refuses baptism because the river is full of crocodiles, although
"Mother May I" is another matter); the Congo of the Belgians
(where the white occupiers cut off the hands of black workers who
failed to meet their rubber-plantation quota); a Congo briefly free to
elect its own future (independent for just fifty-one days in 1960, before Eisenhower authorized the murder of Lumumba for the greater
glory of rubber, copper, Kitanga's diamonds, and the cold war); all of
Africa; and all of empire. As Orleanna understands in retrospect:

> We aimed for no more than to have dominion over every creature that
> moved upon the earth. And so it came to pass that we stepped down there
> on a place we believed unformed, where only darkness moved on the face
> of the waters. Now you laugh, day and night, while you gnaw on my
> bones. But what else could we have thought? Only that it began and ended
> with us. What do we know, even now? Ask the children. Look what they
> grew up to be. We can only speak of the things we carried with us, and the
> things we took away.

How they live with what they stole involves frogs, monkeys,
thatch, mud, a parrot named Methuselah and a chameleon named
Leon. It includes mosquito netting and malaria pills, breadfruit and
manioc, bushbuck and gecko, elephant grass and bougainvillea, ta-
rantulas in the bananas and hookworms in the shoes. It engages a

six-toed *nanga*, Tata Kuvudundu, who leaves bones in a calabash bowl in a puddle of rain and his guilty footprints in the white dust around the chicken house, where "a basket of death" waits in ambush. It will take us up a colonial watchtower, into a ring of fire, as far away as Angola, Jo'burg, and the Great Rift Valley, all the way back to Atlanta, for graduate work in viruses and whiteness. It will seek some sort of balance—"between loss and salvation," damage and transgression—and settle for . . . what, precisely? A forgiving song instead of a punishing Verse? Some "miracle of dread or reverence"? An okapi like a unicorn? As once upon a time there had been the four American daughters of Nathan and Orleanna Price, "pale, doomed blossoms . . . bodies as tight as bowstrings," so in the future there will be the four African sons of Leah and Anatole, "the colors of silt, loam, dust, and clay, an infinite palette for children of their own"—suggestng to their mother "that time erases whiteness altogether."

In case I haven't made myself clear, what we have here—with this new, mature, angry, heartbroken, expansive out-of-Africa Kingsolver—is at last our very own Doris Lessing and Nadine Gordimer, and she is (as one of her characters observed of another in an earlier novel) "beautiful beyond the speed of light."

# ROBERT STONE
# IN JERUSALEM

S INCE I AM WRITING THESE WORDS for *Tikkun*,
readers will be happy to know that early on in Robert Stone's
new novel, *Damascus Gate*, a junkie and a lunatic discuss at
length "the meaning of *tikkun*." Of course, in the same greedy conversation, they will also discuss tantric Buddhism and the Book of
the Dead; kundalini yoga and Meister Eckhart; Saint Teresa of Avila
and Pico della Mirandola; Philo, Kali, Adam Kadmon, and Abulafia;
Zen, Theravada, and the Holy Ghost; bodhisattvas, *sefirot* and the
Trinity; the *Zohar*, the Shekhinah, the sentience of diamonds, and
Matronit under the dread designation of the moon.

This is a lot to cover in one night, even in a Jerusalem "of impos-
sibly delicate balances" and lurid hallucinations, where time is the
space in which we flow; where western walls, fairy-tale mosques and
bloody sepulchres—prophetic stones, hermetic cults, and siege
mentalities—catacombs, citadels, donkeys, and the desert—all
dream, in salt and chalk, of Second Comings and Third Temples and
"letters of fire"; and where everybody who is anybody wants to blow
up the Muslim shrines on Temple Mount. Nevertheless, as the half-
Jewish, half-Catholic American journalist Lucas remembers from
his major at Columbia in religion,

> *tikkun* referred to a primal accident at the beginning of time. According to
> the doctrines of the mystic Isaac Luria, the Almighty had absented him-
> self in the first and greatest of mysteries, bequeathing to his exiled, or-
> phaned creations emanations of himself. The force of these emanations
> was beyond the capacity of existence to contain them. Since the begin-

ning, the goal of the universe had been to restore the divine balance, to restore the *tikkun*, a cosmic harmony and justice, and the task had somehow fallen to mankind to set right. And each person, some Kabbalists believed, labored under his own *tikkun*, a microcosm, a succession of souls, through a process of reincarnation called *partsufim*.

Restoring this *tikkun*, in the middle of the intifada, is the secret business of most of the characters in the vivid cast of *Damascus Gate*—Lucas, who has written one book on what really happened during the invasion of Grenada and thinks he is writing another on "religious mania." Sonia, the half-black child of American Communists (and Sufi jazz singer). Raziel, the clarinet-playing, heroin-addicted son of a U.S. Congressman (and former yeshiva student, Zen monk, and Jew for Jesus). Nuala, the radical Irish "hardcase" refugee worker who has done time in Beirut, Somalia, and the Sudan (and who runs guns to Palestinian guerrillas). De Kuff, a well-born New Orleans Jewish art historian who has converted to Catholicism (and is led to believe that he is a Messiah). Linda, the American missionary's wife who volunteers at the Israeli Human Rights Coalition (and sleeps her way into the heart of the conspiracy). Zimmer, the Polish "bird of ill omen" who has informants everywhere (and intends to do something drastic and dramatic about "the mediocrity" of Israel). And Dr. Pinchas Obermann, a psychiatrist who specializes in "the Jerusalem Syndrome" that seems to afflict everyone else ("Which is coming here and God gives you a mission").

Somehow, as we have come to expect both from thrillers and the nightly Mideast news, all their feverish activity will coalesce in yet another bomb-planting plot and yet another Levantine betrayal. And the conspirators themselves will prove to be unwitting puppets, attached to strings jerked around by clandestine organs of the state. We might have hoped, like Amos Oz, for something less thrilling: "Not 'the land of the hart' and not 'the divine city reunited,' as the clichés would have it, but simply the State of Israel. Not the 'Maccabeans reborn' that Herzl talked of, but a warm-hearted, hot-tempered Mediterranean people that is gradually learning, through great suffering and in a tumult of sound and fury, to find release

both from the bloodcurdling nightmares of the past and from delu-
sions of grandeur, both ancient and modern." But we may as well be
reading David Grossman, who confessed in *The Yellow Wind* (1983):
"The impresarios of history are beyond my comprehension. They
amuse themselves with overly large toys, and the game may come
down on all our heads. For instance the game called 'Blow Up the
Dome of the Rock and Wait One Turn for the Arab World's
Reaction' . . . These are historical people, and historical people
become—at certain moments—hollow and allow history to stuff
them, and then they are dangerous and deadly."

Except that in *Damascus Gate* almost none of the principals is
Arab or Israeli, as in André Malraux's novels of the Chinese revolution almost nobody was really Chinese.

*The universe is such that it bears witness everywhere to a lost God, in man
and outside him, and to a fallen nature.* (Pascal)

That Stone finally landed in Jerusalem should come as no surprise.
The amazement is that it took so long. If you're a novelist of pilgrim-
ages who believes like Pascal that God has been lost or abducted (or
has absconded), why not start looking for him at the site where he
was last seen, igniting three combustible religions? Why not go crazy
in the original, sun-stunned desert? After New Orleans, Hollywood,
Mexico, Central America, Vietnam, and Antarctica, after radical
politics, liberation theology, race riots, blacklists, the CIA, and
Mickey Mouse, Stone is long past overdue in the capital city of transcendence, on the occasion of Israel's fiftieth birthday and his own
sixtieth, wearing Original Sin like a safari jacket—with Melville
and Conrad in one flap pocket, Marx and Freud in another, zippered
sleeves for Simon Magus, Hermes Trismegistus and lysergic acid, a
knapsack containing the whole Nag Hammadi "library in a jar," and
a glow-in-the-dark campaign button for Sophia, the whore of Gnostic wisdom.

He looks exactly like a tourist, and for whole chapters of *Damascus Gate* writes like one as well, descriptive in lavish ways that

would never have occurred to Aron in Grossman or to Fima in Oz, escorting us in shameless detail to every four-star attraction of the Old City and the New and afield, from Ottoman towers to Crusader revetments to the Eurotrash at Fink's; from the Stone of Unction, the Hill of Evil Counsel, and the Valley of Hinnom unto Yad Vashem, Masada, the Golan Heights, and the Gaza camps—except that his guidebooks include, besides Fodor's, the Dead Sea Scrolls and the Kabbala: "He could imagine the letters of the Torah as fire in the night sky. It was what the music was about. Some kind of inspired nightmare fallen from another world."

This is Lucas talking to us, but also Stone, pretending to be the Lucas who can be counted on to identify more with Peace Now than with Gush Emunim; the lonely American journalist who might be willing to "trade sanity for faith," but only in Jerusalem. And even in Jerusalem,

> sometimes the entire field of folk seemed alien and hostile, driven by rages he could not comprehend, drunk on hopes he could not imagine. So he could make his way only through questioning, forever inquiring of wild-eyed obsessives the nature of their dreams . . . listening agreeably while they poured scorn on his ignorance and explained the all too obvious.

You are reminded of Holliwell, the lonely American anthropologist in *A Flag for Sunrise*, who was "forever inquiring of helpful strangers the nature of their bonds with one another." But Stone is always dressing up—as a lonely American journalist, or anthropologist, or government intelligence agent, or documentary filmmaker. This allows him to be lurking at the scene of somebody else's catastrophic accidents of innocence or passion, to feel bad on our behalf at the brute way of the world, and to pretend that he is writing a thriller.

Lonely Lucas would like to believe what Raziel tells him: "You're one of those people who hear the sun come up." ("How flattering," he thinks: "And in spite of himself, what fun! To be special. To be part of a process that was beautiful and mysterious. To be chosen.")

In turn, he chooses to fall in love with Sonia—Sonia, the dupe of Raziel, Zimmer, and Nuala; Sonia who cries in "God's most ancient wilderness" because Fats Waller so loved Bach; Sonia who requires "the proximity of faith." This gentle Sonia will tell the perfidious Zimmer: "My country's here, sure, but my country's in the heart, too. I don't believe in a perfect world, but I believe in a better one." To which Zimmer replies: "My poor baby. You've become a liberal."

But everything and everyone, even Sonia, even Jerusalem, eventually disappoints Lucas, this "apostate wayward Christian, wandering Jew," for whom (but what did he expect?) the city is "lousy with prayers, in the mosques, in the reconstructed Temple to come, in the flickering crackhouse light of the church—all of them, behind their talk of mercy, nursing bloody vindicating covenants. Dominion of the blood and the sepulchre. The first shall be last, the crooked straight, universal revenge." Locked up overnight in the Church of the Holy Sepulchre, he emerges on a blasted heath:

> How could anyone believe that there was a covenant and a redemption to come, that this parched crescent of fundamental desire and loss, this most uneasy bargain of a place, could be called The Holy? Its monster of a God had effortlessly, fondly formed the fleet carnivorous lizard, the eyelids of morning, the submersible, red-eyed rage of Behemoth. His symbol was the crocodile. He was the crocodile.

But there is another Stone who isn't world-weary, bystanding Lucas. This other Stone, who has told us on radio that he has been arguing with God ever since he left Archbishop Malloy High School in Manhattan, gave up years ago playing the thankless role of "Christian humanist witness in a vicious world." He hounds God now in person, blaming Him for history. He has brought the Syndrome with him to Jerusalem—as we all do, a great greediness for political and religious absolutes, a kind of drug lust; we go *expecting* to be changed—and there's no reason to think he won't take it away with him again. It's part and parcel of the buried sparks and "seeds of light" Stone has found everywhere he's gone: in the almond trees, voodoo dolls, and Dante's Inferno of *A Hall of Mirrors;* the serpent rattles, crucified lambs, and martyrs carrying their heads in their hands in *Dog Soldiers*; the hanged Christ that turns into a cat nailed to a beam and burned black around its fanged teeth in *Children of Light*; the "mislaid" God, "errant Sophia," Gnostic Demiurge, Toltec stelae, and glass-box coffin in which Jesus Christ looks just like Che Guevara in *A Flag for Sunrise*; the Darwin, Melville, whale bones, "algorithmic Sun Dance," and Passion of St. Matthew in *Outerbridge Reach*. This Stone plays for keeps, not the library.

Never mind love gone wrong, the English fascist, secret agent Zimmer's "purity of purpose," the haredim demonstrating against the archaeologists, the archaeologists busy digging in Al-Aksa's bowels, the Christian fundamentalist millenarians inking blueprints for a New Jerusalem, the blood bonding on Masada's mesa, the plotters planting bombs in a labyrinth to change the world, the riot inspired by rumors of Rushdie, the counterconspiracies of Shabak or Mossad or Shin Bet hit squads, the cabinet shuffle, and the dead bodies. This is the predictable stuff of the sort of thriller Stone had to write to get us to buy *Damascus Gate*, like the exotica of tourism. It is absorbing enough, but beside the point. The point is that, once again, Stone is trying to put it all together—syncretize the mysticisms like some Serapis.

Thus poor deluded De Kuff will actually see the lions guarding the Name, the "myriads of the *Zohar*," and "the Uncreated Light among the wilderness of empty shells." And prophesy the End of Days. And die the Death of the Kiss. Raziel will actually believe, before the needle finds him again, that "Everything is Torah . . . The Sufi, the Kabbalist, the saddhu, Francis of Assisi—it's all one. They all worshipped Ein-Sof." Trinity will derive from *bereshit*, the opening word in Genesis; and the terrors and the raptures will be real, as real as the pelican of the wilderness and the owl of the desert, with a "light in their eyes . . . not their own." It is not at all an accident that the bombs will be planted in the cult chamber of Theos Hypostasis—aka Sabazios Sabaoth, the syncretic Lord of Hosts, wearing a Phyrigian cap under constellations of the Zodiac with Hebrew names, attended by the *tekuphot* and Dioscuri.

In other words—if I were Jerusalem, I wouldn't take *Damascus Gate* personally. Of T. S. Eliot, Randall Jarrell once observed that he would have written "The Waste Land" about the Garden of Eden. So it goes in Robert Stone's long argument with his Lost Father. Everybody who actually lives in the Holy City may safely resume hating everybody else. It would be much nicer, of course, if Arabs and Jews could sit down to mundane breakfast without reading the Dead Sea Scrolls as though they were a property deed or a morning paper reporting on the identity politics of the Bronze Age. If they could bring back from the market bread and olives and autumn sonatas instead of baskets of skulls and bombs with timers. If the bone-picking archaeologists could find traces of a rock-strewn tenderness instead of intuiting, from fallen columns, charred beams, headless statues, smashed pottery, shattered frescoes, Roman tunics and some Aramaic scribbled on papyrus, further evidence of a bloody covenant of charioteers, catapult stones, battering rams, and human sacrifice. If crazy beauty dreamed of peace. But, alas, Joshua is their kind of guy.

# SALMAN RUSHDIE
## GOES UNDERGROUND

---

ROM THE SATANIC VERSIFIER, more love and more death, with a song in his heart. Abundant, exuberant, cunning, hilarious and what-the-hell-go-for-broke, *The Ground Beneath Her Feet* is Salman Rushdie's Goodbye to Bombay Novel, in which India ("fount of my imagination, source of my savagery, breaker of my heart") is abandoned forever. And his "Hello, New York" Novel, in which American literature is reversible, like an error or a raincoat. And his Rock-and-Roll Novel, "a great wild bird calling out to the bird of the same species that lies hidden in his own throat, in the egg of his Adam's apple hatching, nearing its time." And his Earthquake Novel, disclosing cracks in the composure of the landmass, fissures in the body politic, faultlines in the human character and "holes in the real." And his Martian Chronicles or his Dune, intuiting an Otherworld of dead twins, horny ghosts, and snakebird gods—"spells and usurpations." Plus a splendidly inverted variation on the mythic theme of Orpheus/Eurydice, like Joseph Campbell's refried beans. And a bulging carpetbag of arsons, rape, suicide, and assassinations; a viaticum of transit zones and tempests; a glossalalia of such polyglots as Bombay's "Hug-me" (Hindi Urdu Gujarati Marathi English); and a private zoo of bees, lizards, serpents, and goats. Especially goats—scape- or sacrificial, Pan-piped and Capricorned; an excess, in fact, of goatish behaviors and Angora mohair. Goat-songs, of course, are tragedies.

This is a lot. And for more than forty years it happens all over the place, from the mutton shops, burning ghats, umbrella hospitals, and doongerwadis of Bombay to a rustbucket pirate radio ship off the North Sea coast of England; from a cactus plantation for tequila in the Mexican desert to a music producer's mini-Versailles in Maine; from African drums to Polish polkas to Italian weddings to Greek zithers to salsa and a saxophone, with time out for sitar ragas and maybe a ghazal, even unto those joyless precincts of the world "where you can be murdered for carrying a tune." And all of it is deployed with dazzle on two separate psychic fronts, neither of them popular. Consider, first, what three different characters call "outside-ness."

Kicking off is Sir Darius Xerxes Cama, a Bombay barrister, Parsi Freemason and dabbler in Indo-European mythology. (Note that, after the trouble he got himself into with Muslims and Hindus, Rushdie settled in *The Moor's Last Sigh* for making fun of Vasco da Gama's Catholics, and is reduced here to satirizing those Zoroastrian Parsis who, while feeding their dead to vultures, bet on the British and lost. There are also several Sikh jokes, with names like Will Singh, Kant Singh, Gota Singh, and Kitchen Singh.) From the scholarly likes of Max Müller and Georges Dumézil, Sir Darius is persuaded of a relationship between Indian and Homeric traditions— Sita of Ayodhya and Helen of Troy, wily Hanuman and devious Odysseus, Varuna and Ouranos—and is willing to concede that "all Aryan cultures rested on the triple concept of religious sovereignty, physical force and fertility." Still, as you'd expect of a guy who forged his credentials to gain a knighthood and who struck one of his own sons dumb with an errant cricket ball, Sir Darius is troubled by omissions: "What about *outsideness*? What about all that which is beyond the pale, above the fray, beneath notice? What about out-castes, lepers, pariahs, exiles, enemies, spooks, paradoxes? What about those who are remote?" It will occur to him at his window on the Arabian Sea: "The only people who see the whole picture are those who step out of the frame."

None of which saves the humbug from being smothered with a pillowcase by another of his weird sons, a serial-killer with a fan club.

Then there's Ormus Cama, yet a third of Sir Darius's sons: the one who isn't dumb, isn't dead, and didn't kill him. The rock composer who fell in love with his rock diva, Vina Apsara, the minute he saw her in a Bombay record shop, "even as the twenty-year-old German poet Novalis . . . took a single look at twelve-year-old Sophie von Kühn and was doomed, in that instant, to an absurd love, followed by tuberculosis and Romanticism." Who can hear the music of the future in his head exactly One Thousand and One Nights before it shows up on the Western charts. Who with his blind eye and blue guitar sees "variations, moving like shadows behind the stories we know. . . . It could be I found the outsideness of what we're inside," a "secret turnstile" out of the carnival grounds and through the looking glass, "the technique for jumping the points." There is even a Russian word for this "outsideness": *vnenakhodimost.*

None of which helps Ormus bring back Vina from the underworld that "opens and eats her like a mouth" in an earthquake on Valentine's Day 1989. You may recall that Rushdie, too, went underground on St. Valentine's Day in 1989, when the Ayatollah slapped a fatwa on him. Nor was 1989 a good year for the structural stability of the Berlin Wall.

Finally, there's our unreliable narrator, Umeed Merchant—called "Rai," which means prince, desire or will, as Umeed means hope. Who grew up in Bombay with Ormus and Vina. Whose archaeologist father dug holes in the memory of the city even as his architect mother and a "cartel of futurist vandals" threw up obliterating skyscrapers. Who will begin his career as a voyeur with photographs of "Exits" and ends it as a violence-junkie in third-world combat zones ("I come trudging home with a lifetime supply of nightmares to the sweet-dream needlework merchants and powdered happiness pashas on the stoops of the brownstones of St. Mark's"). Whose only religion is Vina worship, but who nonetheless believes in his own version of "a fourth function of *outsideness*": that "in every generation there are a few souls, call them lucky or cursed, who are simply *born not belonging*, who come into the world semi-detached, if you like, without strong affiliation to family or location

or nation or race." Because those who fear transience and uncer-
tainty "have erected a powerful system of stigmas and taboos
against rootlessness," these nonbelongers pretend to "loyalties and
solidarities we do not really feel," but their secret identities leak out
at night in dreams in which "we soar, we fly, we flee." In waking
dreams too—between the secret covers of a book, at the theater or
movies, in songs and myths—we celebrate "the tramp, the assassin,
the rebel, the thief, the mutant, the outcast, the delinquent, the
devil, the sinner, the traveller, the gangster, the runner, the mask."

But Rai can't bring back Vina, either. Nor the mother who died of
a brain tumor. Nor the father who hanged himself. Not even smelly
Bombay. "Disorientation," he explains: "loss of the East." And, of
himself, Ormus, and Vina: "We three kings of Disorient were. And
I'm the only one who lived to tell the tale."

Which, outside looking in, leads us to the second front—and a
series of Orphic questions: "Death is more than love or is it. Art is
more than love or is it. Love is more than death and art, or not. This
is the subject. This is the subject. This is it."

Who better to answer these questions than the man who poses
them, our Flying Dutchman and our Sinbad, our rogue astronaut
and communications satellite, orbiting the earthquake with a price
on his head, beaming down an occasional message to a literary
magazine or an Op-Ed Page, appearing like some ghostly avatar of
Vishnu at book parties and awards banquets despite bounty hunters
from nutcracker Alamut, and Pat Buchanans who wouldn't mind a
bit if the author of *The Jaguar Smile* were gunned down like a doggy
Sandinista, and *Esquire* Pecksniffs who'd rather he were Thomas
More, or Jan Hus, or Socrates. Rushdie, imperialism's pup, "history's
bastard," "a mongrel self." The actor, with Germaine Greer and
David Hare at Cambridge. The advertising copywriter with Fay
Weldon at Ogilvy & Mather. The book reviewer who paid dearly for
his pans of Naipaul and John Le Carré. The Salmanizer of *Midnight's Children*, in which communal pickle factory the Baby Sal-
eem was born partitioned, already cracking up. (Never mind the
Communist magicians.) Or *Shame*, in which bestiary Omar

Khayyam Shakil's three mothers and his fear of flying would cost him his head. (Never mind Pakistan.) Or *The Satanic Verses*, as if Bulgakov had written the *Ramayana*, in which vertigo "two brown men," having "climbed too high, got above themselves"—having dared "halfway between Allahgod and homo sap . . . to ask forbidden things: anti-questions"—would fall hard, into false consciousness, bad faith, and self-parody instead of metamorphosis. (Never mind "the untime of the Imam," or the brothel resembling the Kaaba, or the Prophet's favorite wife, Ayesha, who wore nothing but a cloud of butterflies while leading her village to death by drowning.) Or, after the fatwa, besides the stories collected in *East, West* and the essays collected in *Imaginary Homelands*, his lovely children's book *Haroun and the Sea of Stories*, in which Arabian Night a young boy whose mother has abandoned him will come to learn, among water genies, shadow warriors and manticores, that by Naming we create Being, that the world is full of things we haven't seen but still believe in, like Africa, submarines, a North Pole and kangaroos, not to mention the past ("did it happen?") and the future ("will it come?"), and return to his equally bereft storyteller-father the gift of gab. (Never mind Marianne Wiggins.) Or *The Moor's Last Sigh*, in which Spanish operetta we'll meet the Hindu hydrogen bomb before they actually had it; and if the mother of our fast-forward hero is India herself, his father goes all the way back five hundred years, to the fall of Granada and a spicy sexual tryst between Arab and Jew. (Never mind that a real-life Lord Ram politician named Thackeray is cleverly disguised as a fundamentalist demagogue named Fielding.)

Who else but this postcolonial Mad Hatter has gone down so many "holes in reality," and found so many hybrids and mutants? Who is more qualified to caution us that real metamorphosis is "*a form beyond*," a "new fixed thing"—not a "whimsy," but a "revelation"? "It's like when coal becomes diamond. It doesn't afterwards retain the possibility of change. Squeeze it as hard as you like, it won't turn into a rubber ball, or a Quattro Stagione pizza, or a self-portrait by Rembrandt." Who else has tried harder to compensate for, or somehow redeem us from, this chilly news, this "world of grief made real by song, by art," than Rushdie, whistling past the modern with a bull's-eye on his back?

> *It is getting harder by the moment to say boo to a goose, lest the goose in question belong to the paranoid majority (goosism under threat), the thin-skinned minority (victims of gooso-phobia), the militant fringe (Goose Sena), the separatists (Goosistan Liberation Front), the increasingly well organized cohorts of society's historical outcasts (the ungoosables, or Sched-uled Geese), or the devout followers of that ultimate guruduck, the sainted Mother Goose.*

You'll recall that Orpheus, the son of a Muse (Calliope) and a River God (Oeagrus, though Apollo may have fiddled there before him), and quite a celebrity for having luted-down the Sirens at an Argo-naut concert, was so besotted by the wood nymph Eurydice that, when she perished of a snakebite, he followed her to Hades, where his music charmed the Underworld Lords into letting him cart her back, as long as he didn't look over his shoulder. Which, of course, he did. He spent so much of the thereafter feeling sorry for himself that the women of Thrace, or maybe Bacchic maenads, tore him to shreds and bowled his prophetic head all the way to Lesbos.

Plato had no use for Orpheus, causing Phaedrus to say in one of his bullying "dialogues": "The gods honour zeal and heroic excel-lence towards love. But Orpheus . . . they sent back unfilled from Hades, showing him a phantom of the woman . . . because he seemed to them a coward . . . [who] didn't venture to die for the sake of love, as did Alcestis, but rather devised a means of entering Hades while still alive." Whereas Rushdie hasn't much use for Plato, "who preferred martyrdom to mourning, Plato the ayatollah of love."

Aeschylus, in his *Bassarae*, was more kindly disposed. So was Eu-ripides in his *Alcestis*, Virgil in his *Georgics*, and Ovid in his *Meta-morphoses*, not to mention generally favorable notices in the poetry press from Shakespeare and Milton to Walter Savage Landor and, at length, Rainer Maria Rilke—with whom Rushdie shoots some breeze since Rilke seems to feel that death turned Eurydice into a different person. ("Who?" she asks, when Hermes brings up Orpheus.) Calderon was sympathetic to the Big O in a seventeenth-century play, and so was Cocteau in his 1949 film, starring Maria Casares as Death with a motorcycle escort of Nazi leatherboy bikers. Composers, of course, haven't been able to leave him alone, from Monteverdi to Gluck.

I will not dwell on all things Orphic in the late Hellenistic period—ritual hymns, mystery cults, the Derveni papyrus, and so many theogonies and anthropogonies—because Rushdie ignores them. But I love this stuff. Did you know that there were itinerant "Orpheotelests" wandering all over the Neoplatonist world, exorcising demons, harming by magic, lecturing the luckless on the secret qualities of stones, as if they were rock musicians like Metallica?

Anyway, since variants of this high-concept story about music, love, and death show up in Norse and Celtic myths of Odin and Lug, as well as Native American lore, it's no surprise that Rushdie's found an Indian equivalent. What happened to Kama, the love god, when he tried to shoot Shiva with a dart, was that Shiva fried him with a thunderbolt. After which Kama's widow, the goddess Rati, pleaded so piteously that Shiva softened—and let love come back from the dead. Knowing this, you also now know why Ormus, in *The Ground Beneath Her Feet*, is a Cama. While Vina Apsara, born in America to an Indian father and a Greek mother, actually names herself: "vina," conveniently, is an Indian lyre, and "apsara" a swanlike water nymph. On the other hand, in profile, Vina looks like the female pharaoh Queen Hatsheput, "the first woman in recorded history," whom Vina, upon becoming her own god-queen, will call "Hat Cheap Suit." To complicate the picture, Rai, whose problem from the beginning is that he's as tone-deaf as a Nabokov or Freud, who can't even whistle, calls her "a sort of Cinderella of Troy."

So the stage is set. Never mind how Vina got to Bombay, from a past of murderous mothers and slaughtered goats. Nor why, after waiting so long to grow up to embrace her erotic fate, she'd fly away immediately after a one-night stand with Ormus, to spend another decade inventing several more selves, singing in American coffee bars, "neatnik folk dives," Slaughterhouse 22 and the Wrong End Café, wearing, among the Middle Earth and UFO psychedelics, an Afro on her head, an Om symbol on her cheek, a single Black American radical glove and maybe a wisp of "Indianized occult-chic couture." Or how come it took Ormus—the very incarnation of "the singer and songwriter as shaman and spokesman"—so long before he followed her, with his visions, "shadow selves" and "lamentation-cosmos," his Doubles and Others and Secret Sharers, through the "membrane" to the West, where he almost died until she kissed him out of his coma, after which the *Peace Ballads*, the *Quakershaker* album and . . . but read the novel.

Meanwhile, "an honorary member of the earth's dispossessed," in Indochina or Iran, in "sickening Timor," or "blasted Beirut," or some "revolution-speckled bananarama of Central America," Rai seethes:

> In the beginning was the tribe, clustering around the fire, a single multi-bodied collective entity standing back-to-back against the enemy, which was the rest of everything-that-was. Then for a little while we broke away, we got names and individuality and privacy and big ideas, and that started a wider fracturing, because if we could do it—us, the planet kings, the gobblers with the lock on the food chain, the guys in the catbird seat—if we could cut ourselves loose, then so could everything else, so could event and space and time and description and fact, so could reality itself. Well, we weren't expecting to be followed, we didn't realize we were starting anything, and it looks like it's scared us so profoundly, this fracturing, this tumbling of walls, this for-god-sake freedom, that at top speed we're rushing back into our skins and war paint, postmodern into premodern, back to the future. That's what I see when I'm a camera: the battle lines, the corrals, the stockades, the pales, the secret handshakes, the insignia, the uniforms, the lingo, the closing in, the fifty-year-old ten-year-olds, the blood-dimm'd tide, the slouching towards Bethlehem, the suspicion, the loathing, the closed shutters, the prejudgments, the scorn, the hunger, the thirst, the cheap lives, the cheap shots, the anathemas, the minefields, the demons, the demonized, the führers, the warriors, the veils, the mutilations, the no-man's-land, the paranoias, the dead, the dead.

*They believe in the Divine Mother Goddess-Ma, in her concrete high-rise in Düsseldorf. They believe in the name of God written in the seeds of a watermelon. They believe in the wise ones flying towards them in a comet's tail. They believe in rock 'n' roll.*

What Ormus hears a Thousand and One Nights before it shows up on VH-1—and his coma, coincidentally, lasts approximately two years, eight months and twenty-eight days—is whatever tune the future will dance to, like Bo Diddley or Bob Dylan or the Beatles. It's just that, till he starts writing them himself, he gets the lyrics wrong. He's channeling his dead dizygotic twin brother, Gayomart, from some otherworld Las Vegas, and there seems to be static on the woo-woo line. But what a wicked Rushdie does with these parallel and psychopompous universes is *play*.

Thus, an Elvis called Jesse Parker, whose manager's name is "Colonel" Tom Presley; a Placido Lanza and The Great Pretender, Uncle Meat and the Plastic Ono Band, Carly Simon and Guinevere Garfunkel, and Jack Haley's Meteors. Lou Reed is female, and Laurie Anderson's her man. John Lennon sings "Satisfaction" and Andy Warhol is called Amos Voight, seen often in the company of the porno actresses Angel Dust and Nutcracker Sweet. Instead of "Punk," we get "Runt, the new rejectionism." For all I'd know, groups like Icon and The Clouds, or Trex and the Glam, or Sigue Spangell and Karamadogma could be real. For a long time, I actually thought I'd heard the music of Red China and the Single Girl (Peter DeVries), Septic Tank and Fascist Toejam (Thomas Pynchon) and Pus Casserole and the Child Abusers (Tom Wolfe). But I don't get out much, and when I do, reality always seems to be raining on me. Already, U2 is singing some of the lyrics Rushdie wrote for Ormus and Vina.

Between glimpses of Vina-as-Tina-as-Janis-as-Madonna-as-Evita, and Ormus as snug in his glass coffin on stage as he was in his preemie incubator, Rushdie gives us the usual rock mise-en-scène—ridiculously young blues rockers, hard-edged raunchy women, hallucinatory troubadours, screaming feedbacklash; "slashed fabrics,

bondage thongs, body piercing, the maquillage and attitude of an-
droid replicants on the run from exterminating blade runners"; the
fan-club cultists and the deep-think CD reviewers "at whose extreme fringes lurk hairy charismatics with much the same psychiatric profiles as the self-impalers at the heart of Shiite Muharram
processions: denizens of the psychotropics of Capricorn, the lands of
the sacrificed goat"—like, for instance, his rock-critic caricatures
Rémy Auxerre and Marco Sangria. But it is this slip-sliding from
affectionate putdown to witty sendup that most persuasively suggests rock's genuine chameleonic powers, its shape-shifting trick-
sterism. See how the songwriter-singer turns into a music video,
which turns into a movie tie-in, which turns into a car commercial
or *Miami Vice*. How like the ancient absent gods! As protean as Pro-
teus, in fact—morphing as the debased equivalent of metamorphosis in a publicity age in which we sacrifice our sense of shame rather
than our kids (or goats).

American literature is likewise morphed. Besides the echoes and
taglines from Vonnegut, Didion, Pynchon, Sontag, Kosinski, and
Robert Frost, we are asked to spend time in an imaginary library
where Sal Paradise has written Beat "odes to wanderlust" and
Nathan Zuckerman is the author of *Carnovsky*, where John Shade
writes poetry and Charlie Citrine writes plays and John Yossarian
writes novels and Kilgore Trout writes science fiction, where Alfred
Fiedler Malcolm is a lisping old warhorse of a literary critic whose
Achilles heels are nipped at by young Turks like Nick Carraway and
Jay Gatsby. For that matter, Rushdie's "otherworld" bears a strong
likeness to Nabokov's Antiterra, where we might also have found
European metanovelists like Dedalus and Matzerath, and where
Pierre Menard probably did write *Don Quixote*.

And so is world history squigglevisioned and computer-
graphicked. A number of smaller countries in Western Europe—
Illyria, Arcadia, Midgard, Gramarye—vote down membership in
the Common Market. A frazzled Rai shoots combat photographs in
"the new post-Soviet hot spots of Aktynai-Asimurratova and far-

flung Nadezhda-Mandelstan." Britain under a Labour government can't seem to extricate itself from Vietnam. Lee Harvey Oswald's rifle jams, Sanjay Gandhi makes an emergency landing, Sukarno survives an attempted Communist coup, and Indira Gandhi wins a war with Pakistan. The amazing thing is, because of similar surprises later on in this dream-along docudrama, everything will turn out just the way it would have if Ormus Cama hadn't been gunned down, like John Lennon, by a crazed assassin with an .09 millimeter Giuliani & Koch automatic.

But you get the subversive idea. And I haven't even mentioned how Rushdie settles some old sorehead scores with Cat Stevens and Anatole Broyard.

> *Imagine, if you will, the elaborately ritualized (yes, and marriage-obsessed) formal society of Jane Austen, grafted on to the stenchy, pullulating London beloved of Dickens, as full of chaos and surprises as a rotting fish is full of writhing worms; swash & rollick the whole into a shandy-and-arrack cocktail, color it magenta, vermilion, scarlet, lime; sprinkle with crooks & bawds, and you have something like my fabulous home town. I gave it up, true enough; but don't ask me to say it wasn't one hell of a place.*

"Wombay," Rushdie calls it. I went there once, and looked for him, and I'm not so sure I didn't find him on Chowpatty Beach, with the contortionists; in the lobby of the Taj Hotel, among Russians and Sikhs; at low tide on the causeway to the Tomb of Haji Ali, with its barbershop quartet of the maimed, a boxed set of missing limbs singing for their supper; at the cricket club, where the editor of the English-language daily told us that he felt guilty every time he ate ice cream; by boat to Elephanta Island, where you hack your way through thickets of monkeys to get to the great cave-temple of the three-headed Shiva; at midnight on Carmichael Road, where the Indian intellectuals rose and converged and danced on the ceiling, like Sufis or Chagalls.

The point is, I knew my way around. His books were a map in my head.

But, of course, Rushdie had been banned. I even met one of the critics who'd conspired at that banning. While he claimed to admire *The Satanic Verses*, I suspect that he had only read the pages on Mahound; he seemed unaware how much of the book, like so much of *Midnight's Children* and *The Moor's Last Sigh*, was about his own Bombay. He said that I had to understand the horrific communal tensions in his country. I said they seemed to know, as well as we did, how to kill each other without the help of a novelist. Our wrangling carried us all the way up to my room, with a balcony where we watched a kite fight and then an enormous crowd, surging toward the sea with representations of Ganesh, the elephant-headed son of Shiva, the boy-god of auspicious beginnings. After which, well, like intellectuals in Jerusalem or Moscow or Mexico City, Indian intellectuals will stay up all night confiding every imaginable intimacy of their politics or culture. I gave him a book of mine. He gave me Kautilya's *Arthasastra*. Kautilya was a fourth-century B.C. Machiavelli. The *Arthasastra* is his pithy *Prince*: "Princes, like crabs, are father-eaters."

With Kautilya's help, I was able to leap conceptually from the Bronze Age slave societies of the Indus valley to the Mauryan empire, part Persian and part Seleucid—the Asiatic Mode of Production and Buddha's Wheel of Law. I was a round abacus on a bell-shaped lotus, nibbled on by elephants, horses, lions, and bulls. I liked India so much that I went to a Bollywood movie, but you really have to be into snake theology.

Rushdie likes it too, and there's a lot more Bombay in *The Ground Beneath Her Feet*, from the Hanging Gardens to Scandal Point, from the caged whores on Falkland Road to the Governors of Mahalaxmi Racecourse, from snake-buckled schoolchildren and Gold Flake cigarettes to dried bummelo and chambeli flowers—bicycle bells, warships, bootleg stills, tamarind, jasmine, coco-palms, and camels!—until suddenly, his passion unrequited, he calls it quits forever on page 249. "Optimism," says Ormus, "is the fuel of art, and ecstasy, and elation, and the supply of these is not endless." No more than I can imagine living without New York, my very own Book of Kells, can I imagine a storyteller without a home, or even a subcontinent, writing on the run, a Shadow Warrior and all-points fugitive. All the more amazing then, in a way that's awfully godlike, that as Prometheus gave us fire and Quetzalcoatl gave us music, Salman Rushdie should give us laughter, and bring back love from the dead.

# JÁCHYM TOPOL'S
# LONELY HEARTS CLUB BAND

Y OU MAY HAVE MISSED a headline the other day, in one of the sections of the *New York Times* that wasn't about nesting or e-mail: STREET CRIME HITS PRAGUE DAILY LIFE, it told us. Nothing really surprising there. But the subhead to the same story was indeed remarkable: "Czech Capital Discovers One Drawback of Democracy."

Democracy! Not, mind you, rampant inflation, staggering unemployment, runaway greed, corrupt politicians, or anything else to do with their new free-market Tinkertoy economy. It was because Czechs could now *vote* that Japanese tourists and Vietnamese "guestworkers" were no longer safe on the baroque streets of the capital of Kafka, and neo-Nazi skinheads were suddenly bashing gypsies. It was because their speech at last was free that they cried for "lustration"—a purge of anyone who ever had a cup of coffee or a Pilsner with a Party apparatchik in the bad old days before Frank Zappa. It was because of self-determination that Slovaks were licensed to hate Czechs, while Václav Havel, the reluctant politician, had to run for another term as president of his very own Republic of Dreams—roughly the size, with roughly the same population, as the state of Pennsylvania—on a platform of "Not So Fast."

We went to Prague for the first time, in the first place, because of Havel, having discovered in ourselves in the summer of 1990, after years of knowing better, a surprising capacity and an unseemly *need* to hero-worship. If not a Beckett, he was at least an Ionesco. It had been possible in New York to see *Largo Desolato* before the Velvet

Revolution, and *Audience* almost immediately afterwards, and even allowing for the rose-colored glasses we wore to these performances (the kaleidoscope eyes!), they were thrilling. An intellectual suspicious of his own intellections was at work, while all around him the world wrote another, more surprising narrative.

*Largo Desolato*, his first play out of prison in 1984, imagines Leopold Nettles, a not-so-heroic professor of philosophy, drinking rum, popping pills, listening to Beethoven, and waiting to be arrested because his essay on "Love & Nothingness" has somehow offended the State. He is besieged by people who want him to be someone else— braver, exemplary, and symbolic. A more committed dissident worries Leopold will crack. A female student, a highbrow groupie, is in love with his words, which add up to more than the man who wrote them. A couple of papermill workers promise to bring him an endless supply of pages to cover with more of these words that they don't understand. A pair of security cops want him to sign a statement saying that he hasn't written what he wrote because he is actually some other Leopold, and perhaps he is. Leopold not only believes what everybody says about him; he repeats what they say as if he had just thought of it himself. No wonder he goes crazy. Rendered into English by the Czech-born playwright Tom Stoppard, with F. Murray Abraham as Leopold in a New York production that also made its way to public television, *Largo Desolato* didn't hit us over the head with a hammer and sickle. This was the intellectual as a chameleon, a crybaby, an opportunist, a seducer, and a voyeur. And we liked him anyway. It wasn't his fault that he couldn't stand living in a permanent parenthesis, waiting for permission to resume normal life, unworthy of his momentous times.

And if it wasn't his fault, it isn't our fault, either.

No sooner had the Berlin Wall come down than Actors Studio in New York promptly mounted a production of *Audience*, a play Havel wrote in 1975, *before* he went to prison. It's also about an intellectual, forced by the State to labor in a brewery, where he finds that he doesn't understand the working class at all. In the bad old Czechoslovakia, *Audience* had never even been performed in public, although there were clandestine audio recordings (basement tapes: a sort of samizdat for the ears). Actors Studio took its production to Prague in January 1990, where it shared the stage with the first Czech production. This occasion was filmed by Jirí Menzel, the director of *Closely Watched Trains*, resulting in a user-friendly documentary called *Havel's Audience with History*, with snippets from both productions, interviews with Milos Forman, the émigré filmmaker, and Shirley Temple Black, the American ambassador, recollections by the brewmaster for whom Havel himself had toiled, and a special world-premiere appearance by the president, in a parka instead of a tux, joking with the audience and actors. Somehow, even with subtitles, the Czech version was funnier. There is obviously a Czech style, ironic, self-deprecating, and sometimes vulgar, that shows up in Hašek, Čapek, Hrabal, and Vaculik, as well as Tom Stoppard's plays and even Milan Kundera's pre-Parisian novels. The wonderful thing about Havel was that he had proved to be braver than his own alter egos, that he'd shrugged off ambivalence like a smoking jacket, pointed himself towards a magnetic pole of decencies, *and look what happened.*

And when we weren't going to see Havel at a theater, we were reading him in magazines and books—in *Letters to Olga* (from prison), *Disturbing the Peace* (a long interview that would be much revised by events) and the *New York Review* (his correspondence to the world, later published in the volume *Open Letters*). After writing plays about the breakdown of continuity and identity in the modern world; after starting a human-rights watchdog committee, Charter 77, in Prague; after seeing the magazine he edited censored into silence; after thinking subversive thoughts in front of an observation post, a sort of grandstand on stilts, that the security police built directly across the street from his apartment; after a pair of dress-rehearsal arrests . . . he was finally sent away for four years of hard labor. His weekly letters to his wife were all he was allowed to write. They began, as you'd expect, asking for cigarettes and socks. They ended as difficult essays on freedom, responsibility, and community.

"Whether all is really lost or not," he said, "depends on whether or not I am lost." His nation found him.

All right, maybe he wasn't perfect. From *Disturbing the Peace* and *Open Letters*, we gather that he had problems with feminists, though they made him feel guilty. And he misconstrued the peace movements in the West, which had a livelier sense of the possibility of change in Eastern Europe than did many dissidents. But compared to any other successful pol in the modern era, not counting Nelson Mandela of course, he was downright heroic, an intellectual Ferdinand the Bull. As far back as 1965, he had seceded from what he calls the "post-totalitarian panorama" of "pseudo-history" and "automatism," the spiderweb of secret police, anonymous informers, and faceless flunkies. Even when his plays were banned, he chose to behave as if he were free, whether in a brewery or in jail. He never contemplated leaving his country, although, typically, he wouldn't hold it against anybody who did choose to emigrate: "What kind of human rights activists would we be if we were to deny people the right that every swallow has!"

His letters, to colleagues in movements like Solidarity and readers of Western magazines, were themselves public examples of "living within the truth," vivid evidence of the existence of what he called a "second culture" of "free thought" and "alternative values," a "parallel structure" of underground theaters, shadow universities, and samizdat publishing, that would eventually undermine the police-state "world of appearances," of "ritual, facades and excuses." (If the State won't wither away, Michael Walzer once suggested, we have to "hollow it out.") By behaving as if we are free—at student protests, on strike, by refusing to vote in the farcical elections, or even by going to a rock concert—we rehabilitate "values like trust, openness, responsibility, solidarity, love." We renew relations with a vanished world where "categories like justice, honor, treason, friendship, fidelity, courage or empathy have a wholly tangible content." We reconstitute "the natural world as the true terrain of politics," "personal experience [as] the initial measure of things," and "human community as the focus of all social action, the autonomous, integral, and dignified human 'I.'"

*Open Letters* includes Havel's eighty-page essay on "The Power of the Powerless." While there isn't much in it shockingly new to any reader of Hannah Arendt, there wasn't much so shockingly new in Martin Luther King's "Letter from a Birmingham Jail," at least to readers of Thoreau on civil disobedience. But imagine, if you dare, either Thoreau or Dr. King suddenly in charge of a country, even a small one. Although in Asia intellectuals have been a part of government since at least Confucius, the record of the West is spottier. While many Greek philosophers wanted to be kings, none of them made it. In ancient Rome, Marcus Aurelius was an emperor as well as a Stoic. Does anyone remember Dinis, the Poet-King of Portugal? Aimé Césaire and Léopold Senghor, the poets of Négritude, came to power in black Africa. Mao was a part-time poet, Trotsky a culture critic with a choo-choo train, and another playwright, Herzl, more or less invented Israel. In Poland, Paderewski was a prime minister; do concert pianists count? Latin America has always mixed up literature and politics. Mexico sent its best-known novelist, Carlos Fuentes, to France as an ambassador—where Pablo Neruda was also doing diplomatic time for Chile—and its best-known poet and critic, Octavio Paz, to India. The novelist Mario Vargas Llosa ran for president of Peru and was voted down. So, too, in our own country, were William F. Buckley Jr. and Norman Mailer voted down for mayor of New York, and Upton Sinclair for governor of California, and Gore Vidal for Congress. Gary Hart wrote a novel, and a lot of good it did him.

No wonder the last thing Sam Beckett did before dying was autograph a book for Václav. All writers ought to feel better when one of them makes it really big. In his first speech to the new Republic as its new president, in December 1989, Havel struck a characteristic note: "I assume you did not propose me for this office so that I, too, would lie to you."

Now just look at us in July 1990, on the brilliant cloudless morning of our first full day in Prague, footloose on the Charles Bridge over the swan-strewn Ultava, in the shadow of a gothic tower, swarmed upon by baroque saints, lapped at by Dixieland jazz, levitating to the Castle. Maybe I was full, like Kundera, of too much lightness of being. "Levitating" is a odd word to use when history is so heavy, from the Holy Roman Empire to Stalin's squat, with time out for Jan Hus to be the first Protestant, for which they burned him at the stake. And it was an uphill hike, as if you had to earn the right to be there, from the Inn of the Three Ostriches and the Leningrad paintpots of the Malá Strana to the ramparts of Hradčany and the spires of the Jesuit Cathedral of St. Vitus. But Prague exalted. It felt like Mozart.

There was also a fragility I feared for, as Ray Bradbury feared for the fairy towers in *The Martian Chronicles*, as if the facades were sculpted of smoke. We were traveling through Eastern Europe in a kind of caravan—French journalists with four children, a Washington, D.C. science editor, a delegation of noisy New York opinionizers—that fiddled at each new site with our logarithmic scales, like slide rules. Not all of us loved Praha as haplessly as I did. There was too little to eat—no bread after nine at night, no ice cream after ten, no open cafés past midnight—and too much silence, except in our hotel, the Forum, where the Japanese tourists fought it out with the Spaniards for the occasional slice of rare roast beef. But Kafka was everywhere, like Kilroy or McDonald's. And it seemed to me that in that silence, everyone was *thinking*, and what I feared for was the dreamscape delicacy of that thought.

"Praha" means "threshold." Of what exactly? Timothy Garton Ash, who had reported on the decolonization of Eastern Europe in 1989 for the *New York Review*, and whose gee-whiz witness is now available in book form as *The Magic Lantern*, spoke of a "refolution," a combination of "reform" and "revolution" conducted as much in the media as it was on the streets, a mixture of "popular interest and elite negotiation" in which "prisoners became prime ministers and prime ministers became prisoners." He cited 1789 in France, and 1917 in Russia, and 1848 all over Europe—"the springtime of nations." He knew that there was hard work and deep trouble ahead: smashed economies, polluted environments, ethnic tensions between Czech and Slovak, German and Pole, Magyar and Romanian, Muslim, gypsy, and Jew. It was as if Stalinism—the ideology, the architecture, and the ministries of fear—had sat for forty-four years on these countries like a glacier. After the thaw, the old reptilian grudges were just itching to resume.

But this was Ash the Oxford historian, trying hard to be scholarly and objective. Much more fun was Ash the fan, who found himself in 1989 on the barricades: at the bottom of a Silesian coal mine, delivering a pro-Solidarity speech in *Polish*. Or standing by in Heroes Square in Budapest for a funeral that turned into a resurrection. Or chancing to be in Berlin on exactly that Sunday in November when the Wall came tumbling down. And, most memorably, in a theater in Prague, on a pass stamped personally by Havel, where, without any dress rehearsals, students, workers, actors, and playwrights performed the deliverance of Czechoslovakia. "There are moments," said Ash, "when you feel that somewhere an angel has opened his wings."

Our maps didn't work. They'd changed the names of subway stops to get rid of "Gottwoldova" and "Cosmonauti." You probably think the "Defenestration of Prague" was a massacre. What happened was that they tossed a couple of Roman Catholics out of a Castle window onto a dung heap. In one engraving, we saw a pair of feet making their exit, a sideways Assumption. The playwright/president himself has spoken of "the fatal frivolity with which history is made here."

The night before our levitation to the Castle, we'd gone for a stroll down Wenceslas Square, where 300,000 people had taken the keys out of their pockets and rattled them like wind chimes, "like massed Chinese bells," past the good king's statue and candles burning for the martyred students, to Staroměstské náměsti (Old Town Square), just in time for the changing of the apostles on the famous clock with the bell-ringing skeleton. If Wenceslas Square was a depressing mall of thumping discos and listless moneychangers, Old Town Square was the loveliest urban prospect I have seen in decades of goatlike globe-trudge. We had a front-row seat on the Jan Hus statue to listen to some mopheaded Beatle mimics sing "She Loves Me (Yeah Yeah Yeah)."

More than Mozart, the Beatles were what counted in 1990. We met them again on the Castle ramparts, singing "Penny Lane." On radios in taxis, in elevators at the Forum, in courtyards, wine bars, beer halls, and on the Royal Procession from Tyn Church to the Ultava, we heard "Eleanor Rigby" and "Help! (I Need Somebody)." We chased the shadow of a young artist who was building a Yellow Submarine to sail under the Charles Bridge that September. At Vyšehrad, where Princess Libuse took unto her a hardy yeoman, and so spawned the kings of Bohemia, we also listened to Led Zeppelin and the Fine Young Cannibals.

What did this mean? Havel, that leprechaun, wrote in *Disturbing the Peace* of his feelings in prison on hearing of the murder of John Lennon. He seemed to care more about Lennon than he did about Kundera, although, typically, he was kinder to Milan than he needed to be. (Kundera has had nothing to say about the Velvet Revolution. Isn't this strange? Maybe he is too busy thinking about Stockholm. But if V. S. Naipaul was silent on the subject of Salman Rushdie, and John Le Carré craven, maybe writers aren't any better than the rest of us, after all.) Havel first became a dissident while defending a censored Czech rock group. Not only had Frank Zappa beaten us to Prague, but, on the eve of our departure, Havel made it a point to show up in Spartakiadni Stadion for a Rolling Stones concert. And opening for the Stones was a Czech rock musician who had been elected to the new parliament. So: the world's first rock-and-roll president. After which, Sgt. Pepper's Lonely Hearts Club Band.

We did what tourists in Prague were expected to do—sleep in a luxury hotel, eat duck for breakfast, visit the Castle, look at graveyards. At Vyšehrad, the well-born were nicely planted (Dvořák, for example). In Josefov, it was a different story. Though our guidebook described the Old Jewish Cemetery as "picturesque," these tombstones cried out of the earth, like teeth around a scream. (And the next-door art of the death-camp children was what they must have seen.) Or we cooled our feet in the Wallenstein Gardens (a labyrinth, a grotto, peacocks). Visited the Smetana (a chambered nautilus of Art Nouveau). Went to movies on the Revolution (student heroism). Ate ice cream at the Slavia (where Sorrow-steeped young Werthers killed themselves isometrically). Snuffled cappuccino at the Europa, next door to a restaurant that was a replica of the diningroom on the *Titanic* (more Czech humor). Bought a ticket to the Magic Lantern (I *had* to go to the theater where they wrote this script) for a performance of *The Kouzeny Cirkus,* with horses, clowns, and ballerinas, as if Monty Python's *Story of Brian* had met Ingmar Bergman's *Seventh Seal.* (I'm afraid it's typical that we should have gone to the Magic Lantern for a circus, late as usual, while Timothy Garton Ash, always on time, had been there for a revolution: "swift, almost entirely nonviolent, joyful and funny.") And looked for Agnes of Bohemia . . .

Only to find instead a ten-foot sculpture of a Trabi, the East German People's Car, on four huge naked human legs, with a license plate that said: "QUO VADIS?" This whimsical cyborg, symbolizing the artist's ambivalent feelings about German reunification, had shown up mysteriously in Old Town Square two months before we did. It was allowed to remain during the "cucumber season" only because the mayor of Prague, Jaroslav Koran, was a friend of Kurt Vonnegut's, a translator of his fiction, and could be counted on to sympathize with hijinks.

I knew of the artist who sculpted the cyborg, David Cerny, though I'd never met him. He was a friend of my stepdaughter's, from before the Fall. And also the pilot of the Yellow Submarine scheduled to ship out at the end of cucumber season. He'd created, as well, a Student Slot Machine: You drop in a coin, and the Student, shooting up an arm, shouts: "Freedom! Freedom!" And, since statues in Czechoslovakia are always going up and then toppling down again because of various revolting developments, David had also invented an all-purpose Headless Dignitary, a windmill with mugshots of various Important People stuck on each of its blades, so that, no matter which way the ideological wind was blowing in whatever political weather, there was always someone to salute. Barely born in 1968, entirely innocent of Prague Spring, David and his tribe had lived by their outlaw wits in ironic opposition, in transit underground on discarded Metro tickets to sly conceptual jokes. They didn't know whether to believe that Havel was real. Nor would they even meet with *us*, their plutocratic elders, credit-card utopiaheads. Like Peter Pan, they ran away. Like the Mystery Cat in T. S. Eliot, *Macavity's not there*.

But David did show up in the world news before our next visit to Prague. Perhaps you recall the pinking of the Prague tank in 1991. Some artists who weren't named in the first small story in the *Los Angeles Times* were arrested for having painted, a shocking pink, the Soviet tank that sat as a monument to the Red Army's liberation of Prague in 1945. One of the artists claimed to have a permit for painting the tank pink, but it proved to be a forgery. This sounded to some of us, in New York, a lot like one of David Cerny's subversive jokes. But the story disappeared, and so did David, who was supposed to visit the United States that month.

There followed a couple of unsigned postcards from places like Switzerland and then a copy of the English-language expat journal *Prognosis*, from which we gathered that the pinking of the tank, on April 28, 1991, took 46 minutes and 40 litres of paint, and it looked "like a child's toy or a newborn child." Czech soldiers took twice as long to repaint the tank its primary color, on April 30, so that it looked again like James Joyce's "snotgreen scrotum-tightening sea." On May 15, twenty members of the Czech Parliament slipped out at night to paint it pink again. And Václav Havel, that Captain Kangaroo, lost his temper. David Cerny and his friends were suddenly on trial. With the surprising connivance of the mayor of Prague, Vonnegut's buddy Jaroslav Koran, they were accused of "criminal hooliganism" under Paragraph 202 of the Czech penal code—the same notorious statute that had been invoked to arrest Václav Havel in the Evil Empire days. If convicted, they faced two years in prison.

You should understand that while David's trial was going on, the Czech parliament was on television, live, in a smarmy burlesque of the old Stalinist show trials, listening to trumped-up charges against any mook who had ever blipped the sonar screen of the rabbit-eared security cops during the snotgreen years of Husak. On hearsay, reputations of such heroes of dissidence as Jan Kavan were in ruins. (Kavan's innocence was the first thing the *New Republic* and the *Nation* had agreed on in years. Christa Wolf, in the erstwhile East Germany, should have been so lucky.) But disgusting as such "lustration"— "purifying sacrifice"—might have been, none of its victims would go to jail. They hadn't pinked a tank.

After the second pinking of the tank, Havel wasn't the only dignitary to stamp his foot. "A vile act!" raged Soviet Foreign Minister Vitaly Churkin. Poor Alexander Dubcek, whose personal experience of Red Army tanks went back to 1968, was dragged out of retirement and hustled off to Moscow to apologize, on television, to the Russians. "Where will it end?" asked the president of Brigadoon, missing the point. "Will we have the St. Wenceslas statue painted red, St. Vitus Cathedral in blue, all the paintings in the galleries spray-painted?" He seemed to forget his own defense, in 1976, of the Plastic People of the Universe, at whose trial he demanded to know—I quote from *Open Letters*—why "no one present could do the one thing that was appropriate in this situation: stand up and shout: 'Enough of this comedy! Case dismissed!'"

A pro-Cerny "Pink Coalition" of artists, students, and members of KAN—the Club of Non-Aligned Party Members—then clashed with right-wing shock troops from the Movement for Civic Freedom and the Communist Party of Bohemia and Moravia. A dozen rock bands gathered on June 1 in Wenceslas Square for a designated Pink Day. Two separate bank accounts were established in Prague to pay Cerny's fines. And by signing a petition that was Pro-Pinking, some sixty deputies to the Federal Assembly and another one thousand assorted luminaries violated yet another statute, Law 165, which prohibits "the approval of a proven crime." Meanwhile, the Soviet tank itself had disappeared from its Smichov pedestal, and was said to be hidden away behind armed guards in an unnamed Prague mu-

seum. Perhaps the *New York Times* would blame this, too, on democracy.

Or maybe Walt Disney. *Prognosis* would subsequently publish
what purported to be secret correspondence between the Disney
Corporation and the Czech-Slovak Federation, proposing to sell off
Prague for a spiffy new "Prahaland" theme park, with Czech natives to be removed from Old Town Square unless they were Disney
employees wearing Mozart-era costumes; a renaming of Wenceslas
Square as "Velvet Revolution Way"; a gala re-creation every afternoon at 2 P.M. of the November 1989 demonstrations, during which,
at the horse statue, Disney Freedom Dancers would perform "We
Shall Overcome"; the re-enacting every night at 6 P.M. of the execution of Jan Hus, by the Disney Peace Dancers with a laser-light
show; the changing of the figures on the Astronomical Clock to
Dopey and Sneezy; the attaching of Mouse ears to the twin spires of
Tyn Church; and so on, unto "Kafkaesqueville" (a "black-light
mime performance about a grumpy but lovable giant insect who
awakens one morning to find out he is now a handsome prince"),
"The Party's Over" (a "lighthearted musical revue about the former
Communist regime") and "Some of Our Best Friends Are Jewish" (a
"Catskills-style dinner theater featuring famous Jewish characters
from Praha's history, held in the Olde Synagogue"). And while Walt
had never permitted the consumption of booze in any of his theme
parks, beer "is such an integral part of the rich history of Praha" that
the sale of alcohol-free lager would be permitted in designated
"Biergarten Villages."

On the other hand, while Harvard professors of overproduction
and forced consumption were busy turning Poland into another Bo-
livia, what was so funny about a Mickey Mouse Prague?

By the time we got there for the second time, in the summer of
1993, after stopping off in South Africa to meet Nelson Mandela and
switch our hero-worship, the American kids who wrote and edited
*Prognosis* were all looking for jobs at papers in the States; the Germans had opened so many outdoor cafés in Old Town Square that
you couldn't see Jan Hus; Jaroslav Koran, no longer the mayor and

no longer translating Vonnegut, was the new Czech editor of the European *Playboy*; Ivan Klima didn't even want to talk to us because, while the bleak novels he used to write for the privacy of his drawer could now be published in his homeland, nobody read or reviewed them; and "Pink Tank" T-shirts were on sale in the courtyard of the Castle.

Yes, I know, other cities and other countries have more important things to worry about than the melancholia of middle-aged American tourists with dead batteries looking for a jump-start. But I was nevertheless reminded of the *Not-Not Manifesto*, proclaimed by dissidents in the People's Republic of China on May 4, 1986, three years before blood all over Tiananmen Square:

> Not-Not: a blanket term covering the object, form, contents, methodology, process, way and result of the principles of Pre-cultural Thought. It is also the description of the primordial mien of the universe. Not-Not is not "no." After deconstructing the relationship between man and objects to their pre-cultural state, there is nothing in this universe that is not Not-Not. Not-Not is not the negation of anything. It is only an expression of itself. Not-Not is aware that liberation exists in the indefinite.

It seemed to me that "Not-Not," like "Think-Pink," was a subversive (and maybe even a rainbow) metaphysics. But rather than address this defiantly secular metaphysic, Havel was publishing essays in the *New York Review* about God and manners. Clearly, the Republic of Dreams needed another writer. I'm only sorry I had to wait seven more years to read him.

Finally: Jáchym Topol and *City Sister Silver*:

In a black forest in a Slavic state of mind, next door to a margarine warehouse that used to be a synagogue, Hansel and Gretel meet Andy Warhol. This is after Hansel, aka Potok, has quit his career as an actor, dancer, and racketeer, but before he seeks refuge from his many enemies among the People of the Dump in Blue Velvet Prague. It is after Gretel, aka Cerna, has stopped singing lugubrious songs in seedy dives, but before she sells her body to the circus. It is after a dream of gray Carpathian wolves, but before a nightmare passage on a turbo-charged shinkansen full of Red Army officers, German shepherds, mamluks, and demons. It is after horrific visions of Auschwitz, and a descent by bathysphere into the bottom-feeding depths of Bohemian folklore, and lots of creepy behavior by tribes, spooks, hitlers and stalingos—but before the medallion of the Black Madonna is melted down to make a silver bullet to kill the Devil.

"Did it ever occur to you," wonders Gretel to Hansel, "that maybe we're under a spell an what happened didn't happen?" On the other hand, there really is a Warhol Museum in eastern Slovakia, where Andy's family came from. On the third hand, just six pages later: "Mordy tvoyay keerpicha hochetsia! somebody screamed."

I am sneaking sideways into a labyrinth. Jáchym Topol, the author of *City Sister Silver,* is the son of a dissident playwright who translated Shakespeare into Czech; the grandson of a Renaissance scholar who died during the Nazi occupation before he could finish his trilogy on Michelangelo; a samizdat poet, a rock balladeer, a literary editor, and a documentary filmmaker. At age fifteen, Topol was the youngest signer of the Charter 77 petition asking his non-profit police state to honor the human rights provisions of the Helsinki accords. At age twenty-seven, he was in the Magic Lantern Theatre when Vaclav Havel wrote a brand-new social contract. *City Sister Silver* is a first novel the way that *The Tin Drum* and *Midnight's Children* were first novels—a prodigal astonishment; an emancipation proclamation.

Like Rushdie, Topol has written an opera about changelings, magic carpetbaggers, born to a world-historical crisis—except that they are Havel's children instead of Gandhi's. Like Grass, he wants to wash the taste of shame out of the mouth of his Mother Tongue. This means ransacking European literature in general, from Homer to Dostoyevsky to "Bowdlair," and Czech literature in particular, from fourteenth-century belles lettres to the Hussite reformation to the Hapsburgs to Hašek's good soldier Švejk and Čapek's automatons, plus anything else that comes in handy, from infernal Dante, prophetic Blake and the Brothers Grimm to, say, Mikhail Bulgakov.

(Black snow, fatal eggs, time machines, Satan.) Or Anthony Burgess. (Hansel/Potok reads *Clokwork Pomegranate*.) Or the Beats. (Topol has translated Kerouac.) Not to mention Raymond Chandler, Thomas Pynchon, Mad Max, and cyberpunk. (Long goodbyes, paranoid quests, junkyard futures, machine dreams.) And, surprisingly, Karl Marx. ("All that is solid melts into air, all that is holy is profaned . . .")

Looking down on everyone, of course, is the Prague-born Jew who wrote in German and whose sacred name, like the name of the G-d of the Israelites, can't be spelled out: K---a.

Wow. It's a heavy burden of symbolic weight for any thriller to carry around. And *City Sister Silver* is a thriller—rife with real-estate and drug deals, weapons sales and snuff flicks, child porn and terrorism. After the Velvet Revolution of 1989, which Topol calls an "explosion of time," children of the "Monster" emerge from their tribal underground into sudden free-fall. Hungry for meaning, instead they make money. Money multiplies by division, like cells. Coins are "the eyes of a wide-ranging organism, their gaze as cool as the distant stars, the cold wind blows over them too." But Potok and his buddies—however swift, clever, and wised-up from time done in prisons and in psycho wards—are no match for the grown-up mafias, the new gangs from as far away as Southeast Asia, and the old spooks who have merely switched sides. One by one, in turf wars, race riots, cop vendettas and geopolitical conspiracies involving everybody from the Black Horsemen to the Pioneers for a Red Future to the Flying Fish Under Water, they are gunned down, drowned, or disappeared into wells. And Potok is on the run.

With Cerna, his sexy "sister," his Platonic other, the song to his dance, an incest victim and a floozy. Which is when *City Sister Silver* becomes a semitriumphant love story, heartbreaking, hilarious, and a lot raunchier than anything we've seen in translations from the Czech of Kundera, Havel, Skvorecký, Klima, Vaculik, Hrabal or, certainly, Jiří Weil. It is, morever, a love story that survives on the far consoling side of pain:

I could only gently point out how extremely fortunate it is when all the cruelty that's been, is, an always will be isn't so visible cause you're with someone you hold, an your palm's just right to cover their heart, worn paper-thin with anxieties . . . to shield it from the barb of solitude that drives you mad, pounding, an you hold that someone so tight that you also cover yourself.

But when Potok and Cerna flee Prague, the "Little Mother," they drop off the cliff of our world. They enter fairytale and myth. They fall into a Neolithic swoon that goes past Logos and Lupus all the way back to the Venus of Dolní Vestonice, the Great Mother of Moravia. They are under the hammer and the wheel again of Svantovit, Slavic Lord of Lightning, the four-faced god of Elbe dwellers, Who Drinks Blood from the Heart of Darkness and Renders His Children's Enemies Lame and Fearful. To be sure, the slaves Hansel and Gretel stumble on in an underground iron-melting factory wear zebra stripes, so it must be a gulag or a death camp. But it also belongs to a book of Kazakh legends, and the drones could just as well be mankurts—young men captured in battle, whose shaved heads were capped with camel-skin patches that shrank as they dried in the sun, squeezing mind out of memory unto madness. If postrevolutionary Prague is all primitive accumulation, straight out of Marx, these Bohemian woods are full of Freud's primal hordes.

Something else is going on. For Topol, the explosion of time is also an explosion of language. Czech itself—debased by empire and occupation; stupefied by ideology; a "slave tongue" of "blather, babel, and babylon"—is decolonized, mutating, and up for grabs. "All through the Hitleriad an the bolshevik era, every Czech ate the same crap." But now, to admix with the old rhetorics of Lord Vladan Dragac, there are "heavy, serious words" like "penance"; brand-new vocabularies of Spanish and Laotian; "borders of poetry . . . as flexible as the borders of the Chinese state"; secret meanings in pop tunes played on grunge guitars; lingos of advert, fax-speak, and broken English; sign language in a convent garden.

I'm innocent of Czech except as overheard while climbing to the Castle or down below in Old Town's music-box Baroque and Art

Deco. But clearly Topol compounds high mandarin with street slang, while satirizing his own gleeful fractures, to achieve an amphetamine rush. Just as clearly, Alex Zucker's translation is a labor of love and an act of heroism. A hum comes off each page. And from these shape-shifts, these church bells and stigmata, these "husks of corn like scalps," this "sacred delirium of dream dance," we end up with not only a scandalous satyricon of the Post-Revolution, in which Prague is the capital of greed instead of Kafka, and a freshly minted twenty-first-century myth, in which it is briefly possible to believe that a newborn baby may be a Messiah, but also an entirely original novel, in which one of those old-fashioned go-for-broke Author Gods, like an aborigine on outback walkabout, sings the worldscape into being.

*Part Three*

LOST CAUSES

# DANCING TO A TUNE
# BY EUGENE V. DEBS

I N   O F F H A N D , birdsong passing, Marguerite Young observes: "As for the nineteenth century, it may be said that it was probably the leakiest century there ever was and so would remain." By leaky perhaps she means wounded. Still, why the nineteenth and not, say, the fifteenth century? Weren't there also lots of holes in the twelfth? Or maybe she means wordy, rhetorical, inflated, gaseous— like grand opera, Romantic poetry, psychoanalysis, and such blimps of ink as *Das Kapital, Les Misérables, Moby-Dick,* and Darwin.

But Young won't pause to parse. She's as flighty as her "long-limbed seraphim." She has been describing Mark Twain's sojourn on the Great Salt Lake with Brigham Young. (Yes, Marguerite and Brigham were distantly related; Moroni is one of her angels.) She is about to visit the Mormon mikado's thick-walled compound, Lion House, with its schoolroom, weaving chamber, soap shed, buttery, 29 wives and 110 children. She will presently explain the Golden Bee Hive and then, having digressed to tell us how Karl Marx felt about the Manchester Mormons who used to blow their noisy trumpets through the bedroom window of his buddy Engels, lightfoot on to note that in 1844, the same year Joseph Smith was lynched, Marx and Engels published *Dialectical Materialism,* which would have been at least coincidental, if not interesting, had they ever written any such thing, which they didn't.

*Harp Song for a Radical: The Life and Times of Eugene Victor Debs*—reverie, breviary, apostrophe, incantation, dirge—may be the leakiest book I've ever reviewed. Like an Old Norse burial mound, it is full of the bones of bygone utopians (Robert Owen, Etienne Cabet, Henry George and Father Rapp). Like a Buddhist stupa, it honors left-wing secular saints (John Brown, Susan B. Anthony, Mother Jones, Haymarket martyrs and Molly Maguires). Like a Toltec stele, it speaks of savage gods (oil, steel, Gould and Pullman). Like a Dos Passos addendum, it snapshoots oddballs and wildcards (Pinkerton and his spies, Gatling and his gun, Emma Lazarus, Jesse James and Whistler's mother). If a surprising number of pages are devoted to contemplating Heinrich Heine, the German poet with "cataracts like snowflakes blotting out the vision in his eyes," many more are lavished on James Whitcomb Riley, the Hoosier versifier Young had intended to write a biography of until she got sidetracked for twenty-eight years.

What it *isn't*, really, is a biography of Debs, whom she calls "the Garrison and Wendell Phillips of the day's abolitionists, the Charles Martel of wage slavery, the St. John crying in the wilderness, the preacher of the gospel of labor . . . a Wilberforce and a Kossuth and a Mazzini and a Chrysostom compounded." And not only because *Harp Song* stops short before the 1894 Pullman strike that almost destroyed his union, after which Debs would live another thirty-two years, found the American Socialist Party, run five times for president, and lose the soul of organized labor to Samuel Gompers. (Young apparently intended three volumes, eight hundred pages each, and by the time of her death in 1995 had completed twice as much manuscript as Knopf chooses to publish.) It also scants his serial suspicion of, and opposition to, boycotts, strikes, industrial unionism, and insurrectionary violence. And it is disdainful of the ideology and party politics of anything that smacks of "scientific socialism." It comes out instead for moonbeams. As in her *Angel in the Forest: A Fairy Tale of Two Utopias* (1945), the heart of the poet (*Prismatic Ground*) and of the novelist (*Miss MacIntosh, My Darling*) belongs to those dreamers for whom the New World was the "millennial continent." More, or less, than history, *Harp Song* is theology and romance.

A sermon, then—on Wealth and Want, on toads and firebirds— in passionate paratactic "dragnet" sentences that swoon on, some- times, almost, forever, as in (hold your breath)—

> In the time of the mystical pre-Marxist utopias springing up with the help of angel apple pickers in the case of the Shakers, for whom the golden apples of paradise were shaken from the trees and the angels even pinned notes upon the apple boughs—the tutelary visit of the Angel Gabriel to Father Rapp upon the banks of the Wabash and the repetition of that visit in Economy near Pittsburgh—even the attribution to the secular Robert Owen of the characteristics of an angelic guide who would pilot all man- kind from the old immoral world to a new moral world—the presump- tion of Swedenborgian transcendentalists as to the sacredness of mankind in a state of socialism, whether Owenite or Fourierite or a duke's mixture of both—the many-branching legend of the discovery of the lost Cana- dian bible which showed the transformation of an angel into a postman carrying in his bag along a New York country road Joseph Smith's *Book of Mormon* or the angel in Illinois who, twenty feet high, a prehistoric In- dian mound builder, had come up like smoke from a hole in the ground to give to Joseph Smith his tutelary advice—this continent had been swept over by so many wild waves of cooperative communal spiritualism that for a time it had almost become a communal nation and, although the passion for spiritual regeneration by brotherhood had undergone some degenera- tive influences during the Civil War, still might have reacted favorably to Marx's most mystifying dialectical materialism if only it had been called dialectical spiritualism and thus had not alienated so many people by its suggestion that unrefined, coarse worldly goods like corn and coal and oil were its chief concern.

On the one hand, it's nice to see someone standing up for utopian communities, which have taken their lumps in American literature, from Nathaniel Hawthorne making fun of Brook Farm in *The Blithesdale Romance* to Mary McCarthy making fun of Dwight Macdonald and Philip Rahv in *The Oasis*. On the other, since we obviously very much need it, there is a superb biography of Debs to consult instead, Nick Salvatore's 1983 Bancroft Prize–winning *Eu- gene V. Debs: Citizen and Socialist* (University of Illinois Press), which never even mentions Owen, Rapp, Fourier, Joseph Smith, James Whitcomb Riley, or the Angel Gabriel.

*A banker's Olympic became more and more despotic over Aesop's frog em-*
*pire. One might no longer croak except to vote for King Log or—failing*
*storks—for Grover Cleveland, and even then could not be sure where King*
*Banker lurked behind.* (Henry Adams)

*High finance ain't burglary, an' it ain't obtaining money by false pretenses,*
*an' it ain't manslaughter. It's what ye might call a judicious selection fr'm th'*
*best features ov them ar-rts.* (Finley Peter Dunne)

*He wants stagnation, degradation, slavery. He demands that his word shall*
*be supreme—that when he takes snuff, his serfs shall sneeze.* (Eugene V.
Debs)

Although an amazing number of footloose utopians ended up in
Young's Midwest, they came from all over elsewhere—refugee
radicals from the failed revolutions of 1848 in France, Italy, Germany, and the Austro-Hungarian Empire; Chartists from England;
famine-fleeing Irish; gold rushers, communards, and religious dissidents; Mormons and Icarians, Perfectionists and Saint-Simonians,
Millerites and Brisbaneites. And while they'd move on to experiment in alternative modalities in such dreamscapes as Carthage,
Oneida, Nauvoo, New Helvetia, Harmony, Nashoba, and Zoar, at
least half seem to have stopped at one time or other at the Shakespeare Hotel in New York, where anarchist-utopians dined on a roast
pig with red flags. And then to have moseyed over to Clinton Hall to
talk reform theory with Robert Owen, where a young journalist
named Walt Whitman found them to laugh at—even if Walt also
saw "a vision, however far off, of the relation existing between all
men as members of one great family; the duty and pleasure of loving
and helping one the other; the dwelling together of the nations in
peace, as being of the same flesh and blood and bone and bound
together by the ties of common brotherhood."

You may experience Walt's mixed feelings yourself, a smile and a
tear, on reading about the "opium-drenched nineteenth-century
psychology of madness and death and dreams, dreams of awakening
again, dying again but to live"; bird tongues, worker bees, and swan
brotherhoods; angel-infested Swedenborg and Ludwig Börne, the

revolutionary with a butterfly net; sacred scrolls, flying capes, and Egyptian mummies; a Sun Woman, a red dragon, a Book of Revelations, and the sacrifice of little red shoes to the god of snow. But if we believe Young, the same people also brought us, if not women's suffrage and the abolition of slavery, then at least a League of the Just, an International Workingmen's Association, singing societies, health and death insurance (and building and loan funds) for wage laborers, the Knights of Labor, and maybe even Wobblies.

And it's wonderful, however casually, to meet these people—like Father Rapp, who may have inadvertently killed his own son by gelding him "for the crime of having placed his seed in woman's body." Or Frances Wright, a ward of Jeremy Bentham's, a friend to Shelley and Lafayette, who looked like Minerva with her raggedy chestnut curls, her icicle-cold blue eyes, "and her sharp features stained almost black by the burning light of the sun"; who started her own Greek city-state, on a plantation on the Fox River in Tennessee, to educate slaves into "the hardships of freedom"; and who would then remove herself and her fortune to the West Indies and a second commune she ruled like an empress "before whom they wafted their purple plumes like fans with which to shoo away the sand flies from her ever-watching face where the waves of the sea swept in and the waves of the sea swept out."

Certainly they are better company than such villains of hers as Allan Pinkerton, the son of a Glasgow blacksmith, who grew up to become a Chartist agitator until an informer ratted on his cause in the great strike of 1839, after which he shipped off and sold out to the New World, becoming the boss of a whole army of *professional* informers (and thus his own class enemy). Or Dr. Richard Jordan Gatling, whose crank-operated grim reaper, Young tells us, would be used by federal troops at Homestead, and by mercenary hirelings of the owners against coal miners on strike at Coeur d'Alene, Cripple Creek, and Goldfield. (In fact, there were neither Gatling guns nor federal troops at Homestead; the Pinkertons and the Pennsylvania state militia used repeating rifles on the workers.) Or General George Armstrong Custer, to whom Young assigns the slaughter of

Chief Black Kettle's Cheyennes at Sand Creek in 1864, prefiguring
the massacre of more "reds" on strike in the tent city of Ludlow. (In
fact, Custer spent the Civil War killing Confederates instead of Indians, although he'd make up for this omission after Appomattox.)
And this is not to neglect Hayes and Harrison, Gould and Harriman,
Fisk and Frick. Or Woodrow Wilson, who let Gene Debs rot in prison
for opposing the war Wilson had promised not to get us into.

Best of all is Wilhelm Weitling, about whom we hear at length:
the wandering tailor from the cathedral town of Magdeburg. The
red-capped Roman Catholic "worker-Christ" who did hard time in
prison in 1843 for mocking God and Switzerland. The visionary who
believed that coins should be stamped with the emblems of labor
(hammer, anvil, chisel, saw) instead of the heads of kings. The "future revolutionary anarchic socialistic communitarian," whose first
book, *Wounds and Balsam*, was all poems. The player, in exile in
Belgium, of card games with Marx and Engels, neither of which
"Brussels sprouts" had ever dug a ditch, plowed a field, or sewn a
suit. The Johnny Appleseed of social gospels in New York, Pitts-
burgh, Cincinnati, St. Louis, and New Orleans, seeking with a bag of
foolscap pamphlets to bring the nation "from woe to weal." The
inventor of a universal language, a perfect lathe, and a gizmo for
automatically punching button holes whose patent was filched by
Singer Sewing Machine. And the godfather, at the confluence of the
Volga and Turkey Rivers in territorial Iowa, of the failed utopia of
Kolonie Kommunia.

Weitling, a one-man band of Accordion Crimes, is clearly meant
by Young to stand for all the idealism and disappointment of the
entire tribe of splendid nomadic cranks—their stubborn selflessness
and equally obstinate self-delusion, their gypsy flair and magpie
looniness. (Today they'd have a website, if not a militia.) Weitling
for instance once had a run-in with Heine, who wrote Marx a letter
about him, which small-craft warning Karl had to take seriously
because, after all, Heinrich had saved his daughter Jenny from choking on a fish bone by slapping her upside-down, although whether
this happened before Heine's proposal to bring God to trial at the bar

of the Society for the Prevention of Cruelty to Animals, or after the poet began to identify with Harriet Beecher Stowe's Uncle Tom, isn't clear from Young's text, which has already taken flight again to inform us that Engels, when a young poet in Germany, had translated Shelley's "Queen Mab" from English "into the language of grunting, groaning hogs."

To all these Appleseeds, America seemed a tabula rasa on which to scribble their new and improved social contracts. That they were doomed from the get-go Young will blame oddly on our Civil War. Through a prism of draft riots she sees that war as entirely economic—vampire capitalism fang deep at the throat of the working class; Darwinian industrialism, red in tooth and beastly claw, ravishing American Innocence; and a terrible victory for "the great plutocrats" of rails, iron, steel, lead, coal, and oil "who were like the toad dreaming of being the largest toad in the world, larger than all the other toads combined." Young is therefore obliged to picture Reconstruction as a carpetbagging shuck, and to abuse radical Republicans (who borrowed more than she credits from the same European ideologies as her utopians) as "Lords of Grab and Graft"—"the vindictives, the Jacobeans." It's the same bumptious reading of our history that we got in the triumphalist textbooks of the fifties. Can you imagine? The mint juleps of the Old South couldn't vote, but their butler *could!* Someone one day is bound to rewrite Reconstruction in light of what's recently happened in South Africa—a redistribution of power without a redistribution of wealth. (And by "Jacobean" does she really mean seventeenth-century England and the revenge plays of Webster and Middleton? Or is she thinking instead of Jacobins and the French Terror? Help! )

On this crucial score, *Harp Song* is downright reactionary.

> *While there is a lower class I am in it, while there is a criminal element I am of it, and while there is a soul in prison I am not free.* (Eugene V. Debs)

But how do the Appleseeds connect to Debs? As near as I can tell, his father Daniel "Dandy Lion" Debs may have stopped at the Shakespeare Hotel on his way from Alsace-Lorraine, where he had been disinherited for marrying a girl who worked in his father's factory, to Terre Haute, Indiana, where he laid tracks for the Vandalia railroad until he and Daisy could open their own grocery store, in whose backroom Eugene Victor (for the author of *The Wandering Jew*, Eugène Sue, and the author of *Les Misérables*, Victor Hugo) was born on November 5, 1855. Otherwise, the only connection is the dead baby daughter Daniel and Daisy left behind in Brooklyn, "with the white rose under her chin and white hood and white shroud in her little white coffin" in the very same Green-Wood cemetery "where one day the socialist tailor Weitling would be buried."

This is a mighty stretch. Certainly Daniel didn't bring up his first son on Swedenborg, Joseph Smith, El Dorado or lost Atlantis. He read to him instead from the French poets and quoted a lot of Rousseau and Voltaire. Nor would the heroes of Eugene's boyhood be Icarians or Brisbaneites. They included rather Tom Paine and Thomas Jefferson, John Brown and Dred Scott. His own reading, after the little redbacked McGuffeys on which Young does a terrific riff, ranged from Goethe, Hugo, Racine and La Fontaine, to Dante, Shakespeare, Shelley and Burns, plus Balzac, Dumas and Dickens, plus Gogol and Cervantes, at least till his first sabbatical in prison, where he became notorious for reading Marx. And we should not omit his mother's influence, perhaps decisive: "When [he] heard the whistle of the night express, the train became a living thing to him. Daisy told the little boy that the sparks of the fire flying upward out of the engineer's caboose were the golden bees flying out of a beehive."

What follows, among dilations and digressions on Lew Wallace, John Wilkes Booth, John Peter Altgeld and Ralph Ingersoll, is mythic Debs, full of birdsong: The inspector of ties, bolts and nuts "walking the rails with his eyes downward and often kneeling, crawling to repair a broken rail or lift a dead or wooden dog." The high-school dropout paintshop apprentice graduating to locomotive fireman, a "stoker of coal, a lightning slinger." The night-school student in telegraphy and bookkeeping, the schmoozer in St. Louis pigs'-feet bars, the orator at rallies of the Brotherhood of Locomotive Firemen, the editor of *The Locomotive Fireman's Magazine*, the city clerk who refused to fine "street girls," the state legislator who introduced hopeless bills on behalf of workmen's compensation and women's suffrage, and the relentless labor organizer who crisscrossed the continent to rouse his indentured rabble against the toads and Pinkertons.

About the pseudonymous correspondence from the field to his *Locomotive Fireman's Magazine*, on crimes and atrocities in the class war, on lost limbs and lost lives, there was a peculiar modernist/futurist poetry that Young revels in—horror stories posted from Total Wreck, Link Block, Eccentric Scoop, Plug and Foam, Gravity, Third Rail, Smoke Stack, and Headlight. Or from Tired Tool, Loose Bolt, Arctic Blast, Loose Screw, Broken Wheel, and Screech Owl. And a poetry as well about the names of the union lodges Debs helped organize, like Orphan's Hope, Arbitration, Stone Ballast, White Breast, Deep Water, Tried and True, Friendship, and Covenant. For that matter, Haymarket and Homestead sound pretty, too.

When, in 1885, he married Katherine "Ducky" Metzel—described by his loyal younger brother Theodore as "a self-adorning clotheshorse"—the railroad brotherhoods would send them as wedding presents a very long bed, a Turkish ruby upholstered divan, Oriental rugs, a Persian jar for preserving rose petals, a mother-of-pearl hanging lamp with pale-violet glass prisms, a leather rocking chair, and a French rococo clock. None of this made up for the fact that Kate's "tipped womb" meant there would never be children. Instead, looking down from the mantle at the desk, glowered busts of Rousseau and Voltaire, of Hugo and Keats, of Ingersoll and Dickens.

Have I mentioned the digression on *Martin Chuzzlewit*? There's another on George Eliot. And a third, using up *Harp Song*'s last thirty pages, on Fyodor Dostoyevsky, Vissarion Belinsky, and Whistler's Bible-toting mother in Czarist Russia.

By stopping short of the Pullman strike, Young manages not to mention that Debs would love a woman other than his wife for the last quarter of his life, and to avoid all that tiresomely difficult nitty-gritty involving Morris Hillquit, Victor Berger, Daniel DeLeon, and the factional fighting that bled the Left of its energy to stave off Gompers and the cannibalizing "partnership" by which Big Business succeeded in merging with, gobbling up, and downsizing Big Labor, unto a modern era where a union leader is as easily and cheaply bought as a public intellectual. We are left with lurid images of the mock-execution of a Russian novelist and the very real lynching of the Molly Maguires, at which girls looked on in their summer dresses.

This, maybe, is where I ought to talk about the footnotes. (There aren't any.) Or where I ought to complain about a woozy impressionism that leaves us uncertain throughout what really happened and what just makes a good story. (But it seems to me that we have been *Dutch*ed for years by biographies in which Freud is a character telling us what to think, or Joseph Campbell, or Jesus Christ, or Karl Marx, and sometimes even malice and envy.) Or where I ought to tote up the discrepancies between Young's Gene and Nick Salvatore's. (From Salvatore, for example, one gathers that Debs was a lot more ambivalent about his father than Young would have us believe.)

But neither Young nor Salvatore ever really explains why Debs—such a close chum of all the Babbitts in Terre Haute, those merchant princelings who found him jobs and gave him loans and helped elect him to any office he sought—chose to be radical instead of rich. And isn't that the cautionary point? Once upon a leaky time, a young man rejected the fluid logic of upward mobility to money-grubbing career goals, stretch-limo perks, and a golden handshake unto golf and coronaries. Once upon the nineteenth century, even *before* French existential humanism, a self-taught white male intellectual *thought against his own privilege*—which, after all, is what reading should encourage anyone to do, deep down in library worlds that imagine the strangely other and heretofore inarticulate—and decided to enlist on the side of the serfs. Why, back then, was that? Instead of now, when the equally privileged are rather to be found, in their media pillboxes, Beltway blisterpacks, and academic bunkers, in a rush to enlist as Pinkertons, and the whole idea of justice, either social or economic, is a smutty chortle?

# WHY SOCIALISM NEVER HAPPENED HERE

A T A FREE CONCERT in Battery Park in New York City in the first spring of the twenty-first century, the British folksinger Billy Bragg observed between Woody Guthrie riffs that the only signs of socialism he had seen anywhere in these United States were the public library and the car-pool lane.

If I were socialism, I'd have skipped this country entirely. Imagine an eye in the sky—a phoenix, a dove, a stormy petrel or a Sputnik—on a scouting mission from the failed revolutions of 1848, or maybe the Paris Commune. Looking down, canting counterclockwise on its powerful left wing, what would it see? From sea to shining sea: long-distance loneliness . . . Deerslayers, cow punchers, whaling captains and raft river rats . . . Greedheads, gun nuts and religious crazies . . . Carpetbaggers, claims jumpers, con men, dead redskins, despised coolies, fugitive slaves and No Irish Need Apply . . . Land grabs, lynching bees and Love Canals . . . Lone Rangers, private eyes, serial killers and cyberpunks . . . Silicon Valley and the Big Casino . . . IPOs and Regis.

Not exactly the ideal social space for a radical Johnny Appleseed to plant his dream beans. Early on in *It Didn't Happen Here: Why Socialism Failed in the United States*, Seymour Martin Lipset and Gary Marks quote the historian Richard Hofstadter: "It has been our fate as a nation not to have ideologies but to be one." And late in the game the authors speak for themselves: "A culture can be conceived as a series of loaded dice," in which "past throws" constrain the present. By then they have comparison-shopped on the Labor-Left all over the world, consulted everybody from Trotsky and Gramsci to Irving Howe and Ira Katznelson, and outlined, rehearsed, staged, critiqued, summarized, reiterated, rewound, rerun, and Mobius-looped every conceivable scenario. The odds, they conclude, were so steeply stacked against socialism in America that its defeat was "overdetermined."

Lipset professes public policy at George Mason University, and is a fellow at the Hoover Institution. Marks professes political science at the University of North Carolina, and directs its Center for European Studies. They are fair-minded, openhanded, flat-footed, and lily-livered (that is, value-neutral). They aren't saying that socialism *deserved* to flunk our litmus test because there's something *wrong* with it. Nor are they saying there's anything *right* about it, either, unless its washout would help explain why we happen to be the only Western democracy without a comprehensive health-care system, the only one that doesn't provide child support to all of its families, and the worst offender on economic inequality—with a greater gap between rich and poor than any other industrialized nation, double the differential of the next worst down the list; the richest nation in the world, where, nevertheless, one child out of every five is born beneath the subsistence line. What they *do* say is that almost everything exceptional and distinctive about America made socialism a harder sell here than it was in, for instance, Australia. And that the pigheaded behavior of American Socialists only compounded the problem.

Be warned that Lipset and Marks say these things over and over again, after which they repeat them, in the approved reverse-gear style of academic monographs whose feet, like those of the legendary Mikea Pygmies of Madagascar, point backwards to confuse their enemy trackers. And yet I can't think of any crime scene Lipset and Marks haven't dusted, nor any suspect they haven't cuffed.

The big picture is that, from the get-go, our "core values" glowed in the dark like Three Mile Island: an ethos of individualism, a *Weltanschauung* of antistatism, and a blank check from God. We sprang full-blown from John Locke's higher brow, a natural-born hegemony of bourgeois money-grubbers—unscathed by medieval feudalism (with its fixed classes of aristocracy and forelock-tugging peasants); exempt from nineteenth-century Europe's ideological power-grabbing fratricides (by virtue of early white male suffrage, lots of land, waves of immigrants to assume the lousiest jobs while the native-born upwardly mobilized themselves, and a ragtag diversity that undermined nascent class consciousness while permitting the merchant princelings to play workers of different racial and ethnic backgrounds against each other in a status scramble); and insulated from revolting developments—insurgencies, mutinies, Jacqueries, even mugwumps and goo-goos—by a political system so partial to the status quo that it's almost arteriosclerotic (a winner-take-all-Presidency, a fragmenting federalism, a bought judiciary, and a two-party Incumbent Protection Society).

So everybody is measured by his or her ability to produce wealth, those who die with the most toys win, anyone who fails to prosper is morally condemned, and a vote for Ralph Nader, Ross Perot, John Anderson, George Wallace, Henry Wallace, or Robert La Follette—not even to mention Norman Thomas and Eugene V. Debs—is considered to be a waste of franchise.

To be sure, we have had more than our fair share of labor violence. Otherwise, we would never have needed Pinkertons. One recalls, at random, the Haymarket riot, the Homestead strike, and the Ludlow massacre; Harlan County and Coeur d'Alene; steel workers in Chicago and Detroit, textile workers in Lawrence and Paterson, dock workers in San Francisco, rubber workers in Akron, and grave diggers in New Jersey; Joe Hill, Big Bill Haywood, Tom Mooney, Mother Jones, Molly Maguires and Wobblies. But the most depressing chapters in *It Didn't Happen Here* are devoted to a labor movement that had already internalized the all-American ethos of antistatist individualism before the first left-wing agitator explicated the first contradiction—a working class needing to lose a lot more than its chains. "I'm all right, Jack" and "Less Filling! Tastes Great!" don't add up to "From each according to his abilities, to each according to his needs."

Thus the whole idea of a labor party here, anything like those that developed in European nations or Canada and Australia, seems chimerical when we read how such radicals as the Knights of Labor and the Industrial Workers of the World—more anarcho-syndicalist than socialist or Marxist—disdained reform politics every bit as much as conservative craft unionists in the American Federation of Labor. The AFL, in its turn, worked just as hard to protect the skilled jobs of its white native-born membership from a lumpenproletariat of African Americans and immigrants as it did to wring concessions from rapacious employers. (The AFL, until the Great Depression, actually opposed minimum-wage legislation, state provision of old-age pensions, compulsory health insurance, and limitations on the manly work week. Nor should we ever forget a 1902 pamphlet that Samuel Gompers wrote himself: "Meat vs. Rice: American Manhood vs. Asiatic Coolieism: Which Shall Survive?")

Or when we read how the Socialist Party, as fetishistic about doctrine as any Protestant sect, refused to join in coalitions with allies like the North Dakota Non-Partisan League, the Minneosta Farmer-Labor Party, the Commonwealth Federations of Washington and Oregon, the Working Class Union in Oklahoma, or Upton Sinclair's Campaign to End Poverty in California—and in many localities went so far as to expel, for "opportunism," members who joined a union or, even worse, ran for office on a coalition ticket and *won* a municipal election. (Inconstant Debs, a five-time candidate for president on the Socialist line, was quoted famously: "There was a time in my life, before I became a Socialist, when I permitted myself to be elected to a state legislature, and I have been trying to live it down ever since. I am as much ashamed of that as I am of having gone to jail.")

Or when we read how the Depression-born alternative to the AFL, the more-inclusive Congress of Industrial Organizations, alert to the possibilities of prolabor legislation, nevertheless rushed into the co-opting embrace of F. D. R. so quickly and uncritically as to compromise its subsequent leverage on the Democratic Party, even after it was obedient enough to purge its own left wing in the late

1940s. (How prescient the old Socialist Norman Thomas seems now, having warned back then that the New Deal was "an elaborate scheme for stabilizing capitalism through associations of industries that could regulate production in order to maintain profits.")

So much for solidarity. In fact, only once in this century did organized labor desert the Democratic Party, after its nomination of the antilabor John W. Davis in 1924. Which was also the only national election year when the Socialists made common cause with another party, the Progressives. And so La Follette got 16.6 percent of the vote. And so the Democrats, learning their lesson, made sure to nominate a prolabor Al Smith the next time around. And yet how soon the Left forgot about the practical payoffs that can sometimes accrue from rejecting the "lesser evil" thesis. And so now organized labor and disorganized labor, too, are both on the wrong side of the candystore window, looking in from the dumpster as megamerging downsizers, flyboy bond traders, and multinational vulture capitalists eat the truffles and sodomize the sales clerks. The typical chief executive of a big company earns 170 times as much as the typical worker. One-third of the labor force earns less than $15,000 a year. The average hourly wage adjusted for inflation is lower today than it was in 1973. The very definition of inflation has been helpfully "adjusted" to exclude food and energy. And politicians of both bought parties are in thrall to a Clairvoyant Master of the Temple of Karnak, a High Priest of the Hermetic Secrets of the Sacred Science of the Pharaohs, the Gnome of Fed: Alan (Chuckles) Greenspan.

But socialism had other difficulties. For one, while we tend to think of immigration as a tide that brought us the socialist Germans of Milwaukee, the socialist Finns of Minneapolis, and the socialist Jews of New York, never mind the socialist Dutch of Reading, Pennsylvania—and how one cheers their radical initiatives of rural cooperatives and credit banks; of state-owned terminal elevators, flour mills, packinghouses and cold-storage plants; of city-owned coalyards, ice plants, stone quarries, and electric utilities; of cooperative housing, hot-lunch programs in the elementary schools, and direct election of school board members; of civil service standards for the police and fire departments, public works for the unemployed, and free medical care—that same tide brought in the far more numerous potato-famine Irish and southern Italians, most of them Roman Catholics inclined to obey the priests of a Church whose anathematizing of godless socialism had been codified in two different Papal encyclicals. And the Militia of Christ had more money to spend than was ever discovered in a Wobbly strike fund.

For another, while Lipset and Marks call our electoral system a wash, neither inhibiting nor encouraging socialism or any other third-party alternative, they arrive at this judgment by apples-and-oranges analogy. The logic of a primary-and-party-convention process, they inform us, "is fundamentally similar to the two-ballot system" in many European countries: "Party factions, which in a two-ballot system would be separate parties, can contest primaries and then coalesce with other factions in the general election, or run independently as third candidates."

This is so much static, obscuring the fact that what our primaries do is aggrandize the two-party system at the expense of outgunned, outmanned, out-soft-monied Greens, Trots, Flat Earthers, and Right-to-Lifers. To vote at all in a primary I must be registered in one or another party, and choose only among its competing candidates. Whereas in France, for example, any registered voter can vote for any party in the first round. All those parties receiving one-eighth of the vote advance to the second round, with time off between to form coalitions with likeminded partners. Even the smallest of parties has a chance to advance during both rounds. In France besides, on a local level, half of all elected officials must now be women. More wondrous still, the passionate particularities of a party vote for the European Parliament will be reflected in their exact proportion to the total count, whether that proportion constitutes a majority, a plurality, a handful, or merely a single deputy. It's a mosaic instead of a duochrome; the grand theory accommodates and approximates its noisy fractals.

For a third, the American Socialist Party opposed the First World War. Many socialists, after all, had voted for Woodrow Wilson when he promised to keep us out of it. But he lied. And while socialists all over Europe rallied to the slaughter under their respective flags, the American party stuck to its principles, for which it was repressed— and not only by the usual firings of teachers, shutting down of news- papers, breaking up of meetings and arrestings on suspicion, but by the infamous Palmer Raids, the refusal to seat duly elected repre- sentatives in Congress and state legislatures, and the jailing of Eu- gene Debs. Never mind that the American party was right (a point that seems not to have occurred to Lipset and Marks). So severely were they punished for opposing a criminally stupid bloodbath that the party never recovered. The authors insist that only the native- born white component of the movement suffered unto extinction, mostly out West; that the big-city ethnic enclaves hunkered down and kept on trucking. But American socialism lost its shock troops, its assembly-line and Deep South labor organizers, its youth bri- gades, and whatever élan it might have mustered for the long struggle against not only metastasizing capitalism, but also serial- killing Stalinism.

Because of course it was the Stalinists who took over left-wing organizing in the Popular Front period, even as they lied about their ultimate loyalties. And when they, too, succumbed to Cold War paranoia and McCarthyite repression, there was nobody left to pick up the sticks and do any stitching. "We were, most of us, fleeing the reality that man is alone upon this earth," wrote Murray Kempton in his elegy for thirties radicalism. "We ran from a fact of solitude to a myth of community. That myth failed us because the moments of test come most often when we are alone and far from home and even the illusion of community is not there to sustain us."

I would like to feel the way Nadine Gordimer felt when Susan Sontag asked her, on public television in the late eighties, whether she didn't agree that the old categories of Left and Right had become outmoded. Gordimer smiled sweetly: "Well, Susan, I still believe with Jean-Paul Sartre—that socialism is the horizon of the world." But I am reluctantly persuaded otherwise. Obviously, the utopia- nism I concocted for myself in high school in the fifties—equal parts of John Dos Passos, the One Big Rock Candy Union in the fitful memory of an old Wobbly I met on the Pike in Long Beach, California, and the bad dreams of the United Auto Workers area rep who let me follow him around to local union halls while he popped Antabuse to keep from drinking himself to death because he felt guilty for surviving the CIO's left-wing purge—was all a bagpipe dream. How lonely the literature seems where I've made my makeshift home. How full of hopelessness are Melville in *Benito Cereno*, Twain in *Pudd'nhead Wilson*, and Richard Wright in *Native Son*. How problematic our romance with money in the gangster novels of Saul Bellow, E. L. Doctorow, and William Kennedy. How improbably often the characters in our canonical fiction are on the run, like Ahab and Huck, or Neal Cassady and Rabbit Angstrom. How deeply weird and perverse is our fascination with the iconology of the filthy-rich: the famous Steichen portrait of J. P. Morgan with a paring knife and an endangered apple; the Spruce Goose of Howard Hughes; the Rosebud sled of Citizen Kane; the death-in-the-saddle of Nelson A. (for Attica) Rockefeller; the severed ear of the kidnapped Getty; John Jacob Astor, who slaughtered all the otters in Hawaii before building us a library; Daniel Guggenheim, who cut a silver deal with Porfirio Díaz in Mexico and helped out King Leopold II of Belgium with his Congo before endowing us a museum; Andrew Carnegie who, before he gave us a music hall, also gave us the Homestead strike . . .

We have seen the future and it's selfish. Lottery! Globocop! It seems to me that Lipset and Marks should be a lot sadder than they sound—but then they, too, are all right Jack.

# AMERICA,
# THE SOLITARY VICE

1.

Briefly, the sound you hear on your MP3Lit audio clip is the flushing of "social capital" down the drain, the glub-glub of expiring citizenship, the death gurgle of American fraternity, sorority, reciprocity, solidarity, and volunteer-fire-brigade togetherness.

In *Bowling Alone: The Collapse and Revival of American Community*, Harvard political scientist Robert D. Putnam crunches numbers to indicate that by just about every conceivable measure— from voter turnout and Sunday school attendance to the habits we report, the opinions we express, and the fears we confide to pollsters, social scientists, people meters, time diaries, and the DDB Needham Life Style Archive—we are less inclined than we used to be to leave the house for any reason except work. Nor do we invite folks over as often for games of bridge, hands of poker, kinky sex, or plotting coups. Since 1968, "civic engagements" of every sort have plunged by 20 to 40 percent across the American board. Irrespective of race, creed, class, income, marital status, and erogenous zone, fewer of us trust our neighbors or our institutions, volunteer our time or energy, pitch in or help out. Whether for meetings of the school board, the union local, the Odd Fellows, the Boy Scouts, or Hadassah, we are failing to show up. We even write fewer letters to editors and congressmen.

Everywhere that Putnam looks, he sees a rising tide of apathy and a downward trajectory to "malaise." In this unbrave new Malaisia, it's not just that we are a third less likely to attend town meetings and donate blood than Americans were in the sixties, and give a smaller percentage of our income to charity—that we are less Masonic, less Jaycee, and less in League with Women Voters. If formal religious worship has fallen only 10 percent, participation in the social life of the church and synagogue, from Bible studies to potluck picnics, has dropped by a third since the sixties and a half since the fifties. The figures are likewise down, by 10 to 20 percent in the last two decades, for fishing, hunting, camping, skiing, jogging, swimming, tennis, softball, football, and volleyball. All the women playing sports (after Title IX) and all the children playing soccer (now that there are college scholarships), all the Twelve Steppers and all the New Age encounter groupies, don't make up for huge defections elsewhere in the culture. More than twice as many adults have dropped out of league bowling in the last twenty years than have ever been in all the self-help programs combined, including Weight Watchers and Alcoholics Anonymous.

While the gross numbers may be up for memberships in professional societies, the proportions are down, considering how many more professionals there are now. (For instance, the ratio of lawyers to the rest of us has doubled since 1970, maybe because the rest of us no longer trust anybody unless we have a legal contract plus our personal pit bull. But the American Bar Association's "market share" of this excess fell a third in the same three decades.) The picture's even bleaker if we look for members who do more than merely pay their dues. Don't tell me you are a card-carrying member of the ACLU, the Children's Defense Fund, Greenpeace, and Amnesty. So am I. And neither of us has gone to a single meeting of any of these organizations. Instead, we have written a check for a lobbying group with a professional staff in Washington or New York. We could be living right next door to each other and not know that we are "members" of the same interest group. We are, instead, "consumers" of a direct-mail cause.

In other words, like a bunch of hippies, we are dropping out. Unless, that is, we happen to have been born between 1910 and

1940—in which case, we belong to Putnam's "long civic generation" and can be counted on to do a lot more good than those narcissistic babyboomers who, when they aren't pushing money
through their modems, are probably watching soft porn on cable
television. When handing out blame for our antisocial funk, Putnam assigns the biggest chunk to self-involved boomers, the next
biggest to time-stealing television, and smaller percentiles to mobility and urban sprawl (relocation, the lonely commute), financial
anxiety (fear of falling, downsized syndrome), workplace blues
(which we used to call the alienation of labor), working mothers
(there goes the PTA), and a general agnosticism or paranoia about
reality itself. He sees little evidence that the behavior of government, the decline of traditional families, or the advent of rap music
and the Internet has much to do with it. He doesn't even mention
the designated hitter in American League baseball.

Of course, he is guessing. And so will I. But it's always fun to beat
up on boomers with a stick. And they will certainly be sorry. They'll
be sorry, first of all, because joining a group is good for everybody.
"Civic virtues," Putnam notes, tend to "cluster." If you belong to a
service club, you are more likely to volunteer in a meals-on-wheels
or reading program, contribute to a library building fund, and vote
for a school or sewer bond. Thus, as if by shrewd investment, a single
act of wandering into a "domain of sociability" multiplies to help
create the social capital that trickles down to benefit education,
health, seniors, children, the lonely, the needy, and the strange. (My
favorite odd datum in this fact-filled book suggests that people who
listen to lots of classical music are more likely to attend Cubs games
than people who don't.) They'll be even sorrier because joining is
better for body and soul. Medical studies indicate it's *healthier* to get
out of the house: "As a rough rule of thumb," Putnam tells us, "if
you belong to no groups but decide to join one, you cut your risk of
dying over the next year in *half*. If you smoke and belong to no
groups, it's a toss-up statistically whether you should stop smoking
or start joining."

Otherwise, move to North Dakota—for reasons I won't go into, although Putnam does at length, North Dakota is a social-capital exception to the sullen rule of Malaisia—and wait for a revival of something like the Progressive movement that saved us from the social Darwinism of the Gilded Age almost exactly a century ago. E-mail and webhead bulletin boards might help, too, if they encouraged us to meet face to face with like-minded strangers and raise some political heck. Touchingly, Putnam hopes such a revival would include campaign finance reform, and citizens who voted as if they were fans; reduction of the criminal discrepancy between rich and poor; a more family-friendly and community-congenial workplace; fewer automobiles and more pedestrians in our neighborhoods and public spaces; less television in our wired caves and more sing-alongs, theater festivals, and break-dancing in our streets. While he's at it, I would like my Volkswagen bug back, the one with the peace-symbol daisies on it.

Thus ends the synopsis. Now begins the rant.

2.

Let me say this about crybaby boomers. The reason they weep is that all that they wanted in the idealistic sixties was social justice, racial harmony, peaceable kingdoms, multiple orgasms, and Joan Baez. What they got, besides assassinations and a tantrum of the cadres, was Nixon and AIDS.

Let me say this about television. Yes, the same people who own it also own everything else. And they commune with their mystical parts through the medium of advertising agencies whose hypno-therapeutic practice is, as Barbara Ehrenreich has explained, to sell us cars by promising adventure and to sell us beer by promising friendship. And it is clearly not in the best commercial interests of such ownership to devote a lot of time to bad-news programs about declining cities, corporate predation, race war, foreign-policy adventurism, indeterminate sexuality, or anything else that readers of Putnam and gazers at Salon.com can be counted on to care about.

But the surprise is, if you actually *watch* television, it's not as bad as it ought to be, and certainly not as bad as people like Putnam say it is. And I'm not just talking about the remedial seriousness of PBS series like "Frontline" and "P.O.V.," Bill Moyers on Iran/contra, Frederick Wiseman on public housing, Ofra Bickel on the satanic-ritual abuse hysteria, "Tongues Untied," and "Eyes on the Prize." Nor C-Span's pair of citizen bands, its lizardly eye on Congress, and its bookchat programs. Nor Discovery's remarkable miniseries on the CIA, David Halberstam's History Channel account of the 1950s, Neal Gabler's A & E meditation on Jews, movies, and the American Dream, John Frankenheimer's films for HBO and TNT on Attica and George Wallace, the development on premium-cable of documentary units like HBO's "America Uncovered" (capital punishment and homophobia) and Cinemax's "Reel Life" (war crimes against Muslim women in Bosnia and the rape of Ecuador's rain forest by American oil companies), and not even our very good fortune that distributorless movies like Anjelica Houston's *Bastard Out of Carolina* and Adrian Lyne's *Lolita* show up on Showtime.

Never mind any of this, and the Lifetime Women's Film Festival, and Bravo's exposés of journalists on junkets, and cable movies that take the risky sort of chances from which networks and public TV flinch. The fact remains that, in spite of Jerry Springer, *commercial* television, in its movies, dramatic series, and even its sitcoms, has more to tell us about common decency, civil discourse, and social justice than big-screen Hollywood, big-time magazine journalism, and most book publishers. Seeking to please or distract as many people as possible, to assemble and divert multitudes, it is famously inclusive, with a huge stake in consensus. Of course, brokering social and political gridlock, it softens lines and edges to make a prettier picture. But it is also weirdly democratic, multicultural, utopian, quixotic, and rather more welcoming of difference and diversity than the audience watching it. It has been overwhelmingly pro-gun control and anti-death penalty; sympathetic to the homeless and the ecosystem; alert to alcoholism, child abuse, spouse-battering, sexual discrimination and harassment, date rape, and medical malpractice. It was worried about AIDS as early as 1983, in an episode of *St. Else-*

*where*, ten years before Tom Hanks appeared in *Philadelphia*. And television—where the ad cult meets the melting pot to stipulate a colorblind consumer—may be the only American institution outside of public school to still believe in and celebrate integration of the races.

Until Harvard can explain why the nation got so mean while TV was telling us to be nicer to women, children, minorities, immigrants, poor people, sick people, old people, odd people, and strangers, one of its professors shouldn't say that "prevailing television coverage of problems such as poverty leads viewers to attribute those problems to individual rather than societal failings and thus to shirk our own responsibility for helping to solve them"—because it isn't true.

And let me say this about bowling. In fact, even now, hardly anybody bowls alone. Bowling as we know it derives from an ancient Polynesian ritual called Ula Maika, in which stones were hurled at standing objects from a distance of sixty feet. Nobody knows why, but sixty feet it remains today. And since bowling got gentrified, with "boys" replaced by automatic pinsetters, alleys renamed "lanes," slim-line plastic contour chairs in multiple pastel hues, and compressed-air blowers to cool the warriors' sweaty palms, it has become, as Putnam tells us, "the most popular competitive sport in America." Bowlers outnumber joggers and golfers two to one, soccer players three to one, and tennis players four to one. Ninety-one million of us bowled in 1996, 25 percent more of us than voted in the 1998 Congressional elections. What pains Putnam is that fewer of us bowl as members of a team, in a league, in a "domain of sociability" where "cohorts" develop cooperative habits and skills. While the total number of bowlers in America increased 10 percent between 1980 and 1993, league bowling fell by more than 40 percent.

What he neglects to mention is that many of us who used to go bowling with our families, or on dates, were driven out of the game in the 1970s by the very leagues he celebrates (who monopolized most of the lanes) and by the very teams whose dismemberment he mourns (who sneered at civilians). About these teams you should know that their principal business, in green Shantung jackets with Aztec serpent totems and bulging purple stretch pants, was to topple themselves with as many beers as soon as possible. As the composer Frank Zappa once observed:

> Consumption of beer leads to military behavior. One day you're going to read about some scientist discovering that hops, in conjunction with certain strains of "yeast creatures," has a mysterious effect on some newly discovered region of the brain, making people *want to kill*—but only in groups. With whisky, you might want to murder your girlfriend—but beer makes you want to do it with your buddies watching.

I am inclined to think that such groups have about as much civic virtue as, say, gangbangers, the Ku Klux Klan, and the Michigan and Montana militias, all equally blotto on bottled bile. Putnam himself observes that religious fundamentalists in general, and Operation Rescue activists in particular, are exceptions to the general trend toward Malaisian noninvolvement. Some of us are actually relieved that the annual membership renewal rate of the NRA is only 25 percent, that the Promise Keepers can no longer fill a football stadium, and that the Christian Coalition and the Moral Majority are every bit as much mail-order consumer causes as the National Audubon Society and the L. L. Bean Catalog. Some of us moved to big cities in the first place to escape small-town book burners.

Anyway, with the ebbing of the leagues, those of us who have tried once more to bowl find to our astonishment that we are required to relinquish one of our own street shoes before we will be allowed to borrow, for a price, a pair of ratty rentals. They don't *trust* us. Imagine that.

## 3.

And so I come to my last big qualm about this fascinating and meticulous scorecard on "bonding" and "bridging," machers and schmoozers, the rise of rap and decline of newspapers; these twenty-four chapters, three appendices, a hundred charts, a thousand foot-

notes; this encyclopedia of industrial averages in a market for
meaning so bearish that the suicide rate for our youngsters has almost tripled. I wonder if some of our suspicion—of institutions, of
groups, of strangers—hasn't been thrust upon us like a lousy credit
rating.

There is the insurance agency finding a reason to refuse our claim,
the HMO deciding we have the wrong disease, the bank-owned
credit card company compounding its own interest, and the employer who listens in on our phone calls and voice-mail, reads our
e-mail and computer files, videotapes our workstation, and sucks our
blood to test for drugs. There is the corporate branding of our commons, the spin-doctor scripting of our public life, and the malign
neglect of our public schools. There is soft money, hate radio, the
gated communities that instruct us what flowers to plant and which
colors to paint our gingerbread houses, the malls that abolish our
First Amendment right to free speech and assembly, and, wherever
we look, urban spaces increasingly militarized—what Mike Davis
in *City of Quartz* called "the architectural policing of social bound-
aries" and "the totalitarian semiotics of ramparts and battlements."

So determined was Los Angeles, you'll remember, to make sure
that its upscale downtown merchants would be forever safe from
another Watts riot that, starting in the 1970s, it turned itself into a
fortress, with corporate citadels and surveillance towers, elevated
"pedways" and subterranean concourses, "tourist bubble" parks and
panopticonic shopping strips, residential enclaves like hardened
missile silos, and libraries like dry-docked dreadnoughts. Add to this
a pacification of the human-landfill poor in strategic-hamlet housing projects, urban Bantustans, and Bedouin encampments, on bar-
ricaded streets in inner-city neighborhoods bereft of public toilets
("crime scenes") and zoned against cell phones and whistling, with
barrel-shaped bus benches to make sure you can't sleep on them,
caged cash registers in the convenience stores, bulletproof acrylic
turnstiles in the fast-food joints, metal detectors in the hospitals,
lockdowns in the elementary schools, and curfews that outlawed

groups of more than two juveniles from "associating in public view" in their own front yards.

And, as Davis reports in his sequel to *City of Quartz, Ecology of Fear*, it worked. No sooner had Simi Valley acquitted the cops who rioted all over Rodney King than "sentient" buildings with mainframe brains went into prevent mode. Steel gates rolled down over entrances to the great bank towers, escalators froze, electronic locks sealed off pedestrian passages, and a financial district prophylacticked against sans-culottes went on happily recycling Japan's trade surplus into Southland turf-and-surf. Too bad about the Koreans. Too late for all of us.

Of course, it's almost as much fun badmouthing LA as it is beating up on the crybaby boomers with one of the Von Trapp children. So let me just briefly mention San Francisco—where 35 percent of the venture capital in this country makes itself at grabby home, where rents went up 37 percent from 1996 to 1997, and where the Silicon Valley nouveau riche are driving all the bohemian artists out of the Mission District from which those artists had earlier evicted the working poor, for the greater glory of condos, boutiques, and yupscale restaurants and bars—before deploring my own hometown, where our mayor has a built-in balcony, from which he barks our marching orders; where the last eight years have been less about government than they have been about obedience training; where lawful assembly and such free-speechifying as may attend its occasion, on the part of minorities, students, artists, journalists, drivers of taxicabs, and advocates for the homeless, are subject to feudal dispensation; where a gentrifying holy war has been declared on squeegee men ("drug-addicted psychopaths"), licensed street vendors (banned during daylight hours from midtown and from the financial district), bicycle messengers and delivery boys (mostly immigrants), hookers and sex clubs, underaged drinkers, aggressive panhandlers, Fourth of July Mafia fireworks, Chinese New Year's celebrations, salsa music on Amsterdam Avenue, and boom boxes everywhere; where the budget has been slashed for parks, recreation, hospital workers, afterschool sports, enrichment programs, and every social service for the poor from medical assistance to foster care to food stamps to heating for the elderly, while zoning variances, tax abatements, and customized incentives are eagerly offered to First Boston, Depository Trust, Viacom, and the Stock Exchange. But crime is down, unless you count police brutality.

I am reminded of the late Donald Barthelme, who wrote that "We have rots, blights and rusts capable of attacking the enemy's alphabet," plus "real-time online computer-controlled wish evaporations." Barthelme went on: "There are flowers all over the city because the mayor doesn't know where his mother is buried."

So I ask Putnam: "Community" for whom? Shoppers? There is an old English proverb: "They agree like bells; they want nothing but hanging."

# PUFF,
# THE MAGIC CYBERDRAGON

WAVE GOODBYE to the social contract. Say howdy to the hypercapitalists. See these bright new angels taking a flyer over the rainbow. They do not sow, neither do they reap, and heavy lifting is against their religion. Instead, they rent, lease, franchise, outsource, interconnect, parallel process, multitask, and dot com.

Call them accessories—after the fact, to the crime—of the "weightless" New Economy. Or players, hopscotching imaginary grids in simulated worlds in giddy digitopias. Or feedback loops, for whom marketing is a value additive. Or "proteans" (shifting shapes) and "thespian personas" (acting out) on a pomo stage of self as spectacle. Or "cool hunters," "amenity migrants," and "leisure colonists"—lonesome rangers in the global theme park, scarfing up local cultures and exotic experiences like alien sperm-suckers, and then selling our own stolen subjectivity back to us in disposable packages: logoed, branded, prefab.

According to futurist Jeremy Rifkin, who in previous books has viewed with alarm everything from the decline of cattle culture (*Beyond Beef*) to robotic factories (*The End of Work*) to genetic engineering (*The Biotech Century*), those of us who aren't angels or accessories in the New Economy are "nodes embedded . . . in a wired world of pure process and sheer temporality," a "surrogate social sphere tucked inside a commercial wrap"—where consumerism supersedes citizenship; where access is more important than ownership; where services and memories are sold instead of products and things; where corporate capitalism has dematerialized into webs of mutual interests and networks of strategic alliances; where the usual greedheads have an option to buy our airwaves, waterways, mineral veins, and gene pools; where megalo-media monopolies socialize and spin-cycle virtual Americans; and where life itself is available by subscription only, a paid-for Gibsonian sim-stim zap to the synaptic cleft.

And that's the good news. The bad news in *The Age of Access: The New Culture of Hypercapitalism Where All of Life Is a Paid-For Experience* is that most of this is at the expense of the other four-fifths of the non–North American, non-European world. Rifkin may be a futurist but he's not an idiot. He's heard of the digital divide. He's aware of the underworld of the propertyless outside this "new and totalizing social space." He knows that while Nike, with revenues of more than $4 billion in 1998, owns no factories, machines, or real estate to speak of, and may even be said to lease Michael Jordan on behalf of Swoosh, the 450,000 Asian sweatshop workers who produce Nike shoe lines don't make enough of a daily wage to buy their daily bread. That 65 percent of the human population has never made a telephone call, and 40 percent doesn't have electricity. That Americans spend more money every year on cosmetics ($8 billion), and Europeans on ice cream ($11 billion), than it would cost to provide basic education, clean water, and rudimentary sanitation for the two billion people—most of them South of us—who currently go without schools or toilets.

But these people don't buy books that view with alarm. Neither, in fact, do the rest of us unless the alarmism is hyperbolic. Thus, it's not enough that Rifkin should tell us what we have already been told by Neal Gabler, Robert McChesney, and Naomi Klein about the long-term shift from industrial to cultural production; the outsourcing of jobs to anywhere safe from collective bargaining; the trillion-dollar-a-year marketing of movies, music, television, tourism, theme parks, "destination entertainment centers," wellness, fashion, cuisine, and the virtual worlds of cyberspace; the commodification of every kind of play (sports, arts, gambling, fraternal activity, social movements, and civic rituals) into "customized cultural experiences" (like Club Med) and "mass commercial spectacles" (like the Steroid Bowl); the franchising of everything from fast food to managed healthcare to retirement communities to prisons; the leasing of everything from the cars we drive to time-shares in our condos to the Microsoftware in our stained-glass Windows; and the licensing of everything from the seeds we've planted to the germ plasms of our livestock to our personal DNA.

None of this is enough. He must also insist on a paradigm shift, without which futurology is mere journalism. Thus, everything he has just told us means not only the end of the class war and a "right-left" political dynamic (though Rifkin does admit "the nagging question of who should control the means of production"), but of property itself ("mine and thine"). "A world structured around access relationships," we are told, "is likely to produce a very different kind of human being." To wit: "Our codes of conduct, our civic values, indeed our deepest sense of who we are" are "cast adrift in a new, less material, less boundaried, more intangible world of commodified services" where we must "rethink the social contract from beginning to end" and come up with a brand new "archetype." It's not merely that "everything we know is suddenly passé"; more grimly, we are plunged into a "change so vast in scale that we are barely able to fathom its ultimate impact," which change "could spell a death sentence for civilization as we know it."

Happily or not, none of this is true. Leasing deals—as innocent as Hertz and Avis, or as invidious as tenant farming—have been around since ancient Mesopotamia. (See Wittfogel on hydraulic civilizations and "the Asiatic mode of production.") Service relationships that differ not a jot from those we have long suffered with our stockbroker and our insurance agent do not require the rethinking of a social contract that nobody ever thought about the first time, except six eighteenth-century philosophers who immediately reached an adjournment of minds. (Even if an anthropological inquiry into the stock exchange as a form of superstitious magic *is* greatly overdue, with Alan Greenspan as the Wizard of Oz.) Property hasn't gone away just because some people rent more and different kinds of it to others. Property has just expanded its vampire definition of itself, to make proprietary claims on speech, thought, the visual field, and the double helix, to stake out ideas as if they were beach-front views, to buy up patents, copyrights, trademarks, and trade secrets as if they were shares in the Great Chain of Being. (In fact, fewer and fewer deregulated fat cats sit on more and more property every year. Don't you hate it when a left-wing grinch reminds you that the richest 10 percent of American families own more than two-thirds of this country's wealth? That Bill Gates, as Rifkin himself observes, is now richer than half of the American people combined?) Nor is there any discernible rush on anyone's part to divest themselves of anything at all, not when home ownership is the highest it has ever been, not when the goodies include cell phones, laptops, and jet-propelled sneakers. (Just because corporations are selling us their brand doesn't mean they aren't also selling us their products. It only means they're selling more products, updated, with a shorter and shorter shelf-life.)

Which isn't to say that Rifkin is as off-base here as he was in *The End of Work*. (Boy, didn't work make a comeback between bestsellers?) His heart is in the right place, and so are his worrywarts. When he gets up a full head of steam—as he does, for instance, in going after gated communities, third-world sweatshops, and biotech giants like DuPont; when he's explaining how Monsanto tried to rip off Indian farmers with self-sterilizing seeds; when he's down with the blood proteins, the spleen tissues, and the stem cells—he raises blisters. And when he suggests that the very model of a service relationship is the HMO, he's downright scary.

He doesn't need the futurist apocalyptics. He needn't have tried to explain postmodernism and communications theory (such potted précis!). Or felt he had to quote so many Freds (Hegel, Schiller, Jameson) to make up for the market babble of the business school professors. Or have talked himself into a corner by going on far too long about the profound importance of "kinship, ethnicity, geography, and shared spiritual visions," till an editor must have reminded him that all this sounds a bit too much like the blood and soil of the fascists and he had better cover his tracks. Nor should he have risked such goofy generalizations as this, brought on like the noisy elephants in *Aida* very early in the book, and then repeated in paraphrase much later:

> From the beginning of human civilization to now, culture has always preceded markets. People create shared meaning and values and build social trust in the form of social capital. Only when social trust and social exchange are well developed do communities engage in commerce and trade. The point is, the commercial sphere always has been derivative of and dependent on the cultural sphere.

This isn't true, of Hong Kong, for one example, or Los Angeles, for another, or New York City, for a third. Speaking only for New York, I will say that we have from the beginning been all about money; culture was an afterthought that only occurred to us when it seemed likely to grub a buck, too. All this vaporing just gets in the way of where Rifkin's straightforward reporting ought to take us, which is to a genuine politics of resistance requiring a coalition even bigger than the one that made Seattle sleepless.

Finally, I'm agnostic about whether the theme-parking of the known globe differs all that radically from the ideological proselytizing of the great religions. (Suppose we were to think of cathedrals as Christianity's home office, the parish church as a franchise, the soul as property, the Passion Play as a TV commercial, and hell as a Fall into Debt? In which case, the revealed Word is a program and downloading eucharistic.) Nor am I persuaded that the modern feeling of weightlessness, the unbearable lightness of American being, owes any more to the New Economy than it does to a larger confusion of psychic realms in which buying, selling, leasing, and renting are merely a component. We are insecure and negligent in our parenting and citizenship, caught between a public sphere (corporations, officialdom) that feels hollow, and a private circle (family) that feels besieged. We are no longer safe on the tribal streets; equally weightless, in orbit and cyberspace; balloonlike in exile or migration; tiddlywinks on a credit grid; fled abroad like jobs and capital; missing, like runaway children; bugged, tapped, videotaped, downsized, hijacked, organ-donored, gene-spliced, lite-beered, vacuum-sealed, overdrawn, nonrefundable, void where prohibited, and *stealthed*. Not even to mention those problematic dislocations caused by sleep paralysis, temporal lobe lesions, overmedication, bad-trip designer drugs, frequent flying, seasonal affective disorders, bad workplace ergonomics, anorexia, and liposuction.

As Karl Marx explained in his infamous *Manifesto*:

> All fixed, fast-frozen relations, with their train of ancient and venerable prejudices and opinions, are swept away, all new-formed ones become antiquated before they can ossify. All that is solid melts into air, all that is holy is profaned, and men at last are forced to face . . . the real conditions of their lives and their relations with their fellow men.

He was talking, of course, about hypercapitalism in the nineteenth century, which would cause, in the twentieth, two world wars, at least as many revolutions, overproduction, forced consumption, and the blues.

# RHAPSODY IN RED, WHITE, BLUE, AND GLITZ

Before we turn to Joe Eszterhas, a Hollywood screenwriter, and Bill Clinton, a Hollywood president, let's think for a minute about the culture of celebrity.

In a cool ode between hot epistles in the first century B.C., the poet Horace told us: "Many brave men lived before Agamemnon; but all are overwhelmed in eternal night, unwept, unknown, because they lack a sacred poet." Horace knew what he was oding about. For years, along with Virgil and Livy, he had written the ancient Roman equivalent of publicity releases and liner notes for the Emperor Augustus. So pleased, in fact, was Augustus at the job his pet writers did for him in the department of *pontifex maximus* image-enhancement that he scrapped his own memoirs. It should come as no surprise that from these same writers Antony and Cleopatra got a bad press. Who knew, for instance, that Cleo before Actium had been a working queen as well as a sexpot? That she spoke nine languages, wrote some books, and cut a deal with the Nabataeans for oil rights in the Dead Sea?

But in the long history of celebrity—from Achilles sulking in his tent to Lindbergh over the Atlantic, from Alex the Great on coins to Elvis on a stamp, from Socrates to Kurt Cobain, not to mention Jesus, Napoleon, Joan of Arc, Louis Armstrong, and Mother Teresa—what goes around comes around. In later centuries, whenever they needed a bad girl or a *femme fatale* or a campy Sphinx, Cleo attracted a slew of publicists: poets like Chaucer, Shakespeare, and Pushkin; novelists like Charlotte Brontë and Edith Wharton; painters like Tiepolo, composers like Berlioz, and moviemakers like Cecil B. DeMille. What boys have done to impress girls, from Helen of Troy to Jodie Foster, will always be written up at epic length, either by sportswriters like Homer in the old Greek league or by gossip columnists like Plutarch and Liz Smith.

Honor, fame, glory, buzz: Winning a war has usually been good for a monument and maybe a marching song. Sainthood helps. So does kingship. And ever since Jack the Ripper serial killers have gotten a lot of ink. The fame game is unpredictable. Notice that, in the long run, Horace and Virgil beat out Augustus. While it's easy to see in retrospect that the first Elizabeth of England and the fourteenth Louis of France ended up emblematic of their epochs because they had Shakespeare and Racine to stage them, nobody knew at the time that these writers themselves would become even bigger names, ushering in a cult of the artist that was to endure, through the Romantic poets, at least till Hemingway. As once upon a Renaissance, hero-worshippers (the first fans) flocked to the noble feet of Erasmus or Spinoza, so in the eighteenth and nineteenth centuries the Grand Tour came to include Rousseau, Goethe, and the Bayreuth Meistersinger. Boswell, taking time off from Dr. Johnson, went so far as to sleep with Rousseau's mistress, Thérèse, hoping that greatness would somehow rub off on him. Lord Byron popularized incest, as well as dying young abroad.

It is in the protean nature of celebrity to shift shapes according to what a society in any given period has been encouraged to value—or taught to fear. Thus, on the one hand: the unique, the unprecedented, the fabulous surprise, the terrible waste, the incredibly lucky, the superbly athletic; wise men, gurus, the self-sacrificing, and the Cinderella; the first or last; pirates and cowboys. While, on the other: the monstrous, power mad, genocidal, filthy rich, and kinky; the satanic prince and the black witch; traitors and infanticides; Attila and Rasputin. But such shapes also shift according to the technology available. Until 1839, in order to celebrate our leaders and our heroes, we had to get along with theaters and cathedrals, sculptures and paintings, ballads and folk tales, slowly moving type and the loose change of the realm's coin. (And tombs, too: Tutankhamen may have been a third-rate king, but he got himself buried in a style so grand as to stick forever in the mind's eye.) After 1839, all of a sudden, there were photographs, to be followed in bewildering rapidity by radio, motion pictures, television, a World Wide Web, and branding: Michael Jordan for the Sweatshops of Swoosh.

Matthew Brady met P. T. Barnum. A democratic society and a popular culture changed the fame game utterly. Instead of royal fiat, aristocratic privilege, artistic license, or plutocratic clout—the self-made man! "It occurs to me," wrote the English poet Philip Larkin, "that the apparatus for the creation and maintenance of celebrities is vastly in excess of material fit to be celebrated." This missed the point. In America, beginning with the mass-circulation magazines of the late-nineteenth century; on to the Jazz Age conjunction of vaudeville and Broadway theater, ad agencies and tabloid newspapers, bestseller lists and Billboard charts, Tin Pan Alley and Harlem nightclubs, Madison Square Garden and radio variety shows; up through Hollywood, Ed Sullivan, and the first television networks; all the way to Microsoft and Matt Drudge, we were inventing brand-new categories of the glamorous and delirious, the envied and the pilloried; Rambos and dreamboats, Times Square and Graceland.

Recall that end run around Protestant respectability in the 1920s, in a backstage idiom of peekaboo, know-it-all, and "what's-it-to-you?", a saloon-society pastiche of racetrack and underworld lingos, a pastrami slanguage of fan speak, jive talk, promoter hype, punk attitude, and populist nose-thumbing—when the legs of the chorus girls went on forever, the gangsters were as cute as Gatsby, and motormouth Walter Winchell, under his signature snapbrim fedora, with a cigarette hanging out of his mouth like a fuse, got up from his table at the Stork Club after collecting confidential tips from lickspittle press agents (Babe Ruth, Charles Lindbergh, and J. Edgar Hoover *all* had press agents) for his Hearst column and his radio broadcast to "Mr. and Mrs. America and all the ships at sea," to tool the predawn New York streets listening to a police band and packing a snub-nosed .38.

Or when Ed Sullivan, whose "rilly big show" lasted twenty-three years on CBS, brought on animals and acrobats, ventriloquists and marching bands, David Ben-Gurion, Brigitte Bardot, and the Singing Nun. For Ed, who went to newspapers instead of college, all that mattered was the talent, the uniqueness. Anybody, by being better at what they did than everybody else who did it, could achieve his show, the odder the better. What we saw on his screen was the peculiar sanction of the democratic culture—from Willie Mays, Phyllis Diller, Tiny Tim, and Tanya the Elephant, to Wernher von Braun, the Nazi rocketeer, and Risë Stevens, singing "Cement Mixer Putty-Putty." Ed's role was to confirm, validate, and legitimize singularity. Had he been around in fin de siècle Vienna, he would have put on Freud, Herzl, Schnitzler, and a twelve-toned Schönberg. History *mit Schlag*! Or, in Weimar Germany, Kurt Weill, Lotte Lenya, Rosa Luxemburg, and Bertolt Brecht, not to mention Adolf and his laughing gas.

After Ed, this role was assumed by Johnny Carson on the *Tonight* show, telling us when it was all right to laugh at Richard Nixon or Tammy Faye Bakker. But after Carson, there seems to have been an absence of sanctioning authority, a hole in the wall into which Letterman and Leno rush; MTV, E!, *Talk Soup*, and the Comedy Channel; *Saturday Night Live* with jokes about Monica, O.J., Michael Jackson, and Lorena Bobbitt; Oprah, Geraldo, and Montel; *People* and *Entertainment Weekly*; Jim Romenesko's media gossip and *Vanity Fair*'s Oscar party; starlets who babble on about their substance abuse and their molestations, rock musicians addled on cobra venom, war criminals whose mothers never loved them, and survivors of abduction by horny aliens. Hostages are celebrities, and assassins, and fertility-pill quintuplets. They all arrive at rehab with a PR agent, an entourage, a ghostwriter for their nonbook, bodyguards, and paparazzi. Because of wire taps and surveillance cameras, nothing they ever do will go unnoticed, and none of it will ever be forgotten either, because the great omnivorous media maw, in the frantic business of telling stories about the celebrities it has manufactured by the gross, then gobbling up everything that moves, finds itself still hungry for more, and thus regurgitates what it has already devoured, in Nick at Nite reruns, or on classic movie channels, or with rental video cassettes—an endless recycling of faces that ought decently to have been allowed to fade and of sins that should long ago have been forgiven. There is hardly anyone left who hasn't already been and will forever be a soft-boiled fifteen-minute Warhol egg.

Then again, as Henry Kissinger has pointed out: "The nice thing about being a celebrity is that when you bore people, they think it's their fault."

Clearly, the more we do it, the less there is to celebrate. So long as you agree that this is deplorable, we are ready to proceed.

2.

Bill Clinton doubtless deserves *American Rhapsody*. The rest of us may feel the need for something else—a sedative, a gene-splice, or a lobotomy. Four-hundred pages of helium and heartburn go up in a hot-air stink-bomb balloon, as if Joe Eszterhas had set fire to his own farts.

Eszterhas is the Hollywood screenwriter who gave us *Basic Instinct*, *Showgirls*, *Sliver*, and *Jade*, although he blames these toads in the erotic garden on a "twisted little man inside me," a "back-alley homunculus" who hacks into his PC and splatterpixels wet dreams. He prefers to think of the authentic Joe as the nobler noodle who gave us *F.I.S.T.* (on Jimmy Hoffa), *Betrayed* (on American neo-Nazis), *Music Box* (on the Holocaust), and *Telling Lies in America* (on growing up in Cleveland with a Hungarian father, apparently his own). He once reported for *Rolling Stone*, where everybody snorkeled sex and drugs. He aspires to be a Hunter Thompson, doctoring journalism unto Gothic gonzo. He uses "we" a lot, as though he spoke for crybaby boomers everywhere. Count at least one of us out.

The noble noodle has read the footnotes in the Starr Report, the memoirs of Gennifer Flowers, the Lewinsky-Tripp telephone transcripts, the supermarket tabloids, Michael Isikoff in *Newsweek*, Matt Drudge in cyberspace, and Lucianne Goldberg's mind, from which he decants a racy sort of pulp nonfiction featuring the first rock-and-roll president of the United States—a "horndog" with Arkansas "pussy lips," "a sixties kid, waging the good fight against the forces of racism and intolerance, against Nixon and the Marlboro Man and the right-wing pentecostal nutbags possessed and held in thrall by the unborn fetus and the Confederate flag and the Protocols of the Elders of Zion"—whose "mad priapic obsession" with his own wayward "Willard" turned him into "the wet spot on America's bed." Not only that, but Joe thinks he probably raped Juanita Broaddrick.

Whereas the Twisted Little Man, who seems to want to be Lenny Bruce more than Hunter Thompson, imagines himself into the equally twisted secret beings of Ken Starr, Bob Dole, George Dubya, "Al Gorf," "John Wayne McCain," Hillary Rodham and—the crotch shot, as it were—"Willard" himself in detumescent funk. Each receives an interior monologue so tone-deaf to the speech patterns of the supposed originals as to suggest that Eszterhas has Marlon Brando's tampons stuck in his ears. (Although I hate to admit it, Anonymous Klein in *Primary Colors* at least knew how to listen.) But each monologue is also printed in boldface type, so we always know when Joe's just kidding.

There is, besides, a third Joe—call him Esztrogen or Esztosterone—who dishes the Hollywood dirt. He's a Walter Winchell wannabe, a pre-Drudge dot-dot commie. Thus, for no particular reason except that Esztosterone thinks Hollywood somehow signifies America, he gives us the deep skinny on studio blow jobs after lunch at the Brown Derby, plus Ryan O'Neal and Farrah Fawcett, Sharon Stone and Alec Baldwin, David Geffen and Keanu Reeves, and Clara Bow and the USC football team. I would otherwise have never known that the aforementioned Marlon "decorated walls with his old girlfriends' Tampax and collected stool samples from his visitors while living on his private Fijian island."

Some of this dirt-dishing aggrandizes self. Esztrogen actually seems to believe that Bill Clinton built his fantasy life, that pathetic phallacy, around the Twisted Little Man's screenplay for *Basic Instinct*, and that O. J. got the idea for a dead Nicole — on June 12, just like the movie! — from his screenplay for *Jagged Edge*. But more of it reeks of flopsweat and payback. If, after *Showgirls*, nobody in Hollywood would give Joe a job, then he'd do a job on Hollywood. Sharon Stone, with the most to complain about of all the people pilloried in these pages, has said of *American Rhapsody*: "I thought it was hilarious. I knew he was very funny, but I didn't know he could write comedy." Joe liked this comment so much he quoted it in a Salon.com interview, adding that "some of us around Knopf were so happy about her statement that there was some talk about putting it as a blurb on the paperback." Irony is wasted on punks.

Nor should I neglect one last Joe, the born bully who has listened to so much rock-and-roll that he thinks he's a Street Fightin' Sex Pistol. This is the swaggart who threatens kickboxer Jean-Claude Van Damme's double-dealing agent:

> I'll tell you what I'm going to do, Jack. I'm going to come down there with a baseball bat and bust your knees so you can't walk. Then I'm going to bust your ribs so you can't breathe. Then I'm going to bust your ears so you can't hear. I'd bust your head, but you can't think anyway. So I'm going to bust your balls so you can't fuck.

Charm City, from which all these contentious Joes voortrek by covered Porsche into the bewilderedness, hunker down with their Thai hash pipes in a Native American sweat lodge for a Vision Quest and an Esalen rub, and beseech themselves: How did it happen that Bill Clinton, one of "us," a Fleetwood Mick, the first president ever photographed wearing a *Rolling Stone* T-shirt and the first to know all the words to "Louie Louie," the sax-blowing "pop-gutted Jumpin' Jack Flash" who "was supposed to put our kick-ass primal inner beat into the Oval Office" . . . how could such a slick Willie have ended up not only disgracing his entire generation but also making Joe Ezsterhas rethink his own macho-rubbishy career and spaghetti-Western manhood? Because Joe and Bill had both bought into the same sixties! Wearing funky bell-bottoms and no underwear, carrying around *Siddhartha* and Chairman Mao's *Little Red Book*, firing up doobies with a Smile lighter, listening to Hendrix and the Plaster Casters, treating women as if they were "holes" — Joe, too, had wanted to be a rock star *for the groupies*! "Rock-and-roll was about sex, not about love," he says. "It was about excess, not about romance." And: "We swore by our genitals, the way Nixon swore by his 'old Quaker mother.' We were our own vast Bay of Pigs — roiled up and flooding the Berlin walls of Puritan resistance." And then, after a couple of paragraphs of porn fantasy about "getting it on" with Bernardine Dohrn ("our pinup girl, our real babe in bandoliers," with her hair dyed the color of Ho Chi Minh's flag), this clotted cream:

> We were a counterculture, an America within Amerika, arrogant, self-righteous, even jingoistic about our values, heroes, and music. "I Can't Get No Satisfaction" was our "Battle Hymn of the Republic"; "Sympathy for the Devil" our "Star-Spangled Banner"; Woodstock our D day; Altamont our Pearl Harbor; Dylan our Elvis; Tim Leary our Einstein; Che Guevara our Patrick Henry.

What do you mean, *we*, white man? Not, presumably, including Martin Luther King and all those gentlefolkies who sang "We Shall Overcome" instead. Nor, of course, the women, who had already begun to deconstruct themselves and hummed another tune. But back to "our" story.

In the sweat lodge, chewing on the Culture Wars, Eszterhas elaborates an eschatology part Wagnerian Nipple Ring, part Gilbert & Sullivan and part Who, whose doctrinal key is hate — *by* Richard Nixon (of the sixties) and also *for* Richard Nixon (by the sixties). For the flower children, Nixon embodied evil: "His smile was the frozen, gleeful smile of the KGB or Gestapo torturer, about to turn up the current. His eyes were the black holes in a mossy Transylvanian graveyard where bats with furry wings cavorted among gorgons . . ." Anything "Night Creature" Nixon was *against*, "we" had to be *for*, including hedonism (also known as fucking around).

Without Dick, there couldn't have been a Lucianne Goldberg, who got her start as the "Bag Lady of Sleaze" by spying on McGovern for Nixon's campaign in 1972; who went on to write soft-porn novels like *People Will Talk, Madam Cleo's Girls,* and *Purr, Baby, Purr;* and who, as a literary agent, was already handling Dolly Kyle's tell-all about sex with young Bill when who should ring but Linda Tripp, "the Ratwoman," who got *her* start as "a creep and a spook" black-bagging for the Pentagon's supersecret antiterrorist Delta Force, but who has just been fired from Clinton's White House because Kathleen Willey is better looking. And without the Ratwoman and the Bag Lady there would have been no tape recordings of the intimate chitchat between Tripp and the Valley Girl with Baby Fat, poor Monica Lewinsky— "Why don't you just fuck your father and get it over with?" Ratwoman told her—not to mention the dimes dropped on the Special Prosecutor to set up an FBI ambush at a wired lunch, the inside tips to Isikoff at *Newsweek*, or the leaks all over Matt Drudge, "The Scavenger of Cyberspace," after which, waving the semen-stained blue dress like a caution flag at a stockcar race, they called off blow jobs at 1600 Pennsylvania Avenue, though everybody's lips are zipped about oral-anal rimming.

That's as *Showgirls* sleazy as I'm prepared to go. With apologies to Kurt Cobain, it smells like teen spirit. I have also decided not to get into what Dominick Dunne didn't know and when he didn't know it, to omit more than this one reference to Bob Packwood ("Reptile Tongue, the Man with the Horny Hands"), and to refuse to think at all about Arianna Stassinopoulos ("The Sorceress from Hell"), except to recall that when she married Michael Huffington, after dating Mort Zuckerman and Jerry Brown, the wedding guests included Henry Kissinger, Barbara Walters, Norman Mailer, and Helen Gurley Brown. Whereas you will be relieved to learn that while Hillary, with Jean Houston's help, may have communed with Eleanor Roosevelt and Gandhi, she drew the line at Jesus Christ.

Any array of satanic forces requires, in cosmic compensation, avenging angels. According to Joe, Elvis remained President because James Carville ("Serpent Head") kicked some ass, and Vernon Jordan ("The Ace of Spades") dodged a smoking bullet, and Larry Flynt (the speedfreak pornographer with a pump in his pants) blackmailed Congress with what his private dicks dug up on Republican hanky-panky. Much is made of the peculiar fact that Jordan and Flynt were both shot by the same assassin. More should have been made of the obscene fact that Vernon Jordan's law firm numbers among its clients the People's Republic of China, the Korean Trade Association, the government of Colombia, and sundry Japanese multinationals; that Jordan and his wife sit on the board of directors of the Permanent Government of American Express, Dow Jones, Sara Lee, Xerox, Revlon, RJR Nabisco, J. C. Penney, Bankers Trust, and Union Carbide. But who's counting? I am about to jump off this Mystery Train.

Any nitwit knows that Bill Clinton held onto office, in spite of the Spiteful Prosecutor, because of his high approval ratings in the polls in the middle of All-Monica-All-the-Time on cable TV. And the ratings were high because of the economy, stupid. And it ought to be obvious to anyone except a Hollywood screenwriter that the public didn't care if the Alto Sax of the Free World was a randy creep so long as the creep put money in our wallets. Rape might be a different story, but having raised the subject of Juanita Broaddrick, Joe fails to pursue it, not even when "Willard" takes over the book to rhapsodize himself as Bill's search engine, Minuteman missile, ruby slippers, Hope Diamond, eternal flame, Rosebud, banana peel, and Dodi al-Fayed. And who better to pursue such a story than the screenwriter who ordained the wholly gratuitous rape of the only likable character in all of *Showgirls*?

From Watergate to Profligate: Speaking as someone who voted for Nader in the last farce, I wish Bill had quit after a single term. (For a truly refreshing change of pace, why not become a nun?) Not, however, because he can't keep his hands off X-chromosomes with Big Hair in the Oval Orifice. (So what? About *her* husband, Marilyn

Quayle once explained: "Dan would rather play golf than have sex any day.") Rather because, half Peter Pan and half spineless Slinky, he had a habit of selling out every liberal principle he'd previously, orally sexed—from healthcare to food stamps; from gay rights to affirmative action to RU-486; from Zoe Baird and Kimba Wood to Lani Guinier and Jocelyn Elders. Because of his born-again enthusiasm for Wall Street and the bond market and his smart-bombing of dumb Sudanese (wag that dog!). And because of his craven coddling of the monopolistic broadcast industry, his budget-pandering to the Pentagon, and his abandonment of public schools. Not to mention his mindless continuation of Nixon's War on Drugs and the Bill of Rights, which sent another 630,000 people to state and federal prisons, upping our behind-bars population to ten million, mostly minority males. In fact, Our Bill's hounding by a Specious Prosecutor with the same lofty contempt for due process as Nixon is the only thing attractive about the man. And that hounding got a shrewder treatment in a two-part episode of *Law & Order* on NBC than it does in *American Rhapsody*.

We might also ask, which Eszterhas doesn't, what good this abandonment of principle has done for a Democratic Party which, in the first six years of Clinton, lost eight seats overall in the Senate, forty-eight seats in the House of Representatives, eleven governorships, nine state legislatures, and 1,254 legislative seats, heading into the year when those legislatures would draw up new congressional districts. For his Party and my politics, the guy has been a disaster.

3.

Am I deluding myself? No, I am not. It didn't used to be this bad.

In the spring of the revolutionary year of 1968, on the Hudson River side of Manhattan, at a party fizzed and finger-fed by *Esquire* know-it-alls, in front of one of those high-rise blue aquarium windows that look down on Grant's Tomb, the white liberals were disdaining black folks for liking Bobby Kennedy too much and Eugene McCarthy not at all. It was no more than the usual condescending twitter until suddenly a big cat, an African panther, scattered these pouter pigeons and the room was thick with ruffled feathers. She was our worst fear—black, beautiful, laughing at us in our very own Shakespeare, but with a lilting lash. She had seen some streets, as well as the library. In fact, before coming to New York to edit textbooks for Random House, she had taught the likes of Stokely Carmichael and Claude Brown in the nation's capital. There, she had seen a car stop on a SW sidestreet, and the attorney general of the United States leave his jacket on the back seat, loosen his tie, roll up his sleeves, and shoot some baskets on a cement court with black schoolchildren, who liked him quite a lot. In her own opinion, maybe black folks, having had so much practice with the problem, knew who their friends were better than white liberals full of theory. My, but she could scourge.

This was my first glimpse of Toni Morrison, like your first glimpse of the cloud chamber of a cyclotron. Who knew she'd later write some novels? She gave me permission to be partisan, entirely subjective, perhaps ferocious. Later that summer at the Democratic convention in Chicago, two months after Bobby Kennedy had been shot dead, after the chartered bus behind a squad-car escort, past the checkpoints into the barbed-wire ring around the slaughterhouse, wearing an embossed "PRESS" ID tag like a scarlet letter, surrendering my briefcase for inspection against bombs and guns, permitted into a gallery already preempted by municipal serfs from Mayor Daley's Department of Sanitation and Counterterrorism, watching Hubert's whips trash the peace plank, fleeing the scene on foot in the middle of a transportation strike, finding myself safer on the very black South Side than I'd later be in front of the Hilton, where I saw everybody I'd ever known in the antiwar movement, and many I wish I hadn't, get the crap kicked out of them, it seemed to me the system and empirical reality were both rotten.

Twenty years later, William Kennedy would write a novel, *Quinn's Book*, that imagined a young Irish American newspaper reporter come back from the Civil War to a *class* war: To labor riots and a forced relocation of lullaby-singing poor white Irish from Dutch-

Nativist Albany in box cars, like the Indians before them and the Jews after. To the lynching of an underground railroad conductor. To fire, flood, demented pigs, and a fantasy of revolutionary alliance between the have-not Irish and the have-not blacks, an army of "paddyniggers." And to a treasure buried in the bottom of a bird cage—a bloody coin, a divine riddle, an ancient magic Celtic disk—that would turn this journalist into a warrior dreaming "a savage dream of a new order: faces as old as the dead Celts, forces in the shape of a severed head and a severed tongue." So be warned.

Like El Cid, who was said to have been so indispensable in driving the Moors out of Spain and back to Africa—for the greater glory of a whiter God in the eleventh century—that his own men propped up his Charlton Heston corpse in a silver saddle on a black horse to send him holy-warrior trotting off to battle yet again, so the old soldiers, epic poets, and court historians of our sorrier century peddle Kennedys just as dead. I've not yet recovered from the 1998 celebration of the thirtieth anniversary of Bobby's assassination, a similar body-snatching—the abduction by polliwogs of the second son of Camelot, the nation's younger brother.

Michael Knox Beran—who was two years old when Sirhan Sirhan killed Bobby in a hotel kitchen moments after he won the California Democratic primary—told us in *The Last Patrician* that this "revolutionary priest" was really a closet conservative. That tragedy had taught him to suspect the "foggy platitudes" and "feudal sentimentality" of an "effete" elite and the siren song of the Enlightenment. That he was on his existential way to rejecting not only big government and the paternalism of the old-money Ivy League mandarinate that had bossed the rest of us ever since it got a monkey-gland transplant from Teddy Roosevelt, but to rejecting as well the whole idea of the welfare and national security states. That instead of Adlai Stevenson or Henry Stimson he was Ralph Waldo Emerson or Natty Bumppo. Beran wrote so gracefully, with apposite citations here of Evelyn Waugh and there of T. S. Eliot, it took a while to realize he was making it up as he skinny dipped along, out of muddled vehemence, class animus, and maybe even an itchy resentment of some of the aristocratic spas where he himself had done hard time (Groton, Columbia, Yale). I'm in favor of class animus. I think the trouble with this country is that peasants have money. I'd like to see the homeless slash the tires and strangle the chauffeurs of every stretch limo daring to pause at a traffic light. But it's odd that someone as alert as Beran to striations of status, to the tree rings, peat bogs, and fossil beds of buried class distinction in the great American massif, should have scanted the Irishness and clannishness of the Kennedys, so much that was blood-feud tribal about them—especially when he seemed to want to Pat Buchananize poor dead Bobby.

Jeff Shesol—who wasn't born till two years after the hotel kitchen—told us in *Mutual Contempt* that the hatred of Bobby and L. B. J. for each other shadowed and shaped every aspect of our swamp-fever politics in the sixties, from Vietnam to civil rights to the Great Society. While the obvious reasons for their hard feelings were specified at prurient length, with a slight tilt in Bobby's favor, not quite so obvious and mostly unspecified were the ways in which this personal antipathy did any such shaping. Had they *liked* each other, would we have been spared Nixon in a whirlybird, fleeing Watergate for San Clemente? Would Bobby have stayed in the Cabinet, rather than run for the Senate? Would L. B. J. not have escalated the war, nor pushed through the 1964 civil-rights bill, nor dreamed up and then abandoned, his War on Poverty—which faltered, incidentally, not because money ran out in the open wound of Southeast Asia but because will ran out in Congress; not because "maximum feasible participation" by the poor *didn't* work, but because it *might* have, and the ripple effects of Head Start among sharecroppers in Mississippi, Vista among coal miners in Appalachia, rural legal assistance for farmworkers in California, and community corporations in inner-city Newark terrified the local pols.

Neither Shesol, though he had access to oral histories that flesh out what had before been merely adumbrated, nor Beran, though he bristled with the internal contradictions of a work-in-progress that ended at age forty-two, told us much we didn't know from the first generation of Bobby books—the valentines by Ed Guthman, David

Halberstam, Penn Kimball, Jack Newfield, Arthur Schlesinger Jr., and Jules Witcover, or the poison pills by Ralph de Toledano and Victor Lasky—and considerably less about Bobby as attorney general than we learned from Victor Navasky in *Kennedy Justice*. Nor did either of them credit the rest of the Republic—the freedom-riders, the war-resisters, the flower children; the teachers, the clergy, and the angel-headed hipsters; the gospel, folksongs, anthems, rock, and blues; the rainbow shape of moral passion made coherent—for ending the long Ike snooze, for opening windows as if they were veins. Once more, tediously, history was confined to what white men did in the daytime, for which they got famous.

For the same thirtieth anniversary, Maxwell Taylor Kennedy—three years old when his father died in Los Angeles—edited Bobby's private journal, his day thoughts, his night-shrieks, and those snippets of Great Writers and tragic poets he chose to copy down for meditation, into a handsome commemorative volume with an affecting mix of candid snapshots and speech-writer aperçus, entitled *Make Gentle the Life of This World: The Vision of Robert F. Kennedy*. Quoted most often by far was Albert Camus, twenty times by my count. There was a clear sense in *Make Gentle* of R. F. K.'s growth through pain to an appreciation of the reality of lives less gilded; of the distance he traveled, against his will, from Camelot, that swashbuckling James Bond wet dream of witty violence, insolent cool, dry Martinis, brand-name snobbery, killer gadgets, musical beds, gang-bang counterinsurgency scenarios, and contempt for women and for other cultures; of why he came to be believed in both Watts and Jo'burg. We were even reminded of his startling statement, on emerging from a mine shaft on the floor of the ocean off the coast of Chile, where the miners were all Communists: "If I worked in this mine, I'd be a Communist too." And there was this resonant passage from Hemingway:

> If people bring so much courage to this world the world has to kill them or break them, so of course it kills them. The world breaks everyone, and afterward many are strong at the broken places. But those that will not break, it kills. It kills the very good and the very gentle and the very brave

impartially. If you are none of these you can be sure it will kill you too, but there will be no special hurry.

Such was also the mood of *Robert F. Kennedy: A Memoir*, a three-hour wallow in feeling lousy, on the Discovery channel in June 1998. The first hour was narrated by Glenn Close, the second by Mario Cuomo, the third by Ving Rhames—a not untypical smorgasbord of enthusiasts. Throughout, Jack Newfield of the New York *Daily News* interviewed the children, the colleagues, the surprising Shirley MacLaine (a Bobby-pledged delegate to the 1968 Chicago convention), the inevitable Doris Kearns Goodwin, and those journalists (Pete Hamill, Jimmy Breslin, Peter Maas, Murray Kempton) who could be counted on to feel that more than a Kennedy died thirty years ago. Maas told the story of a devastated attorney general showing up at a 1963 Christmas party for orphans, just because he'd promised to. And of his being greeted by a small child who shouted "They killed your brother! They killed your brother!", before bursting into tears. And of his picking her up, and stroking her head, and assuring her: "That's all right—I've got another."

So I felt lousy right along with them. He was the last American politician I cared about or cried for, the only one since Lincoln as novelistically interesting as, say, a Havel or a Mandela. Clinton, who should wear a V-chip on his jogging shorts, tells us that he feels our pain. Bobby embodied it. "Unacceptable," was his mantra, as "Intolerable" was Wittgenstein's. Then he'd do something radical to fix it, which never seemed to him enough. Has there ever been a sadder pair of eyes, so much brokenness that mended badly, such a sense of swimming up from the bends of despair toward an empathic grasp of all who are dispossessed, all that's bereft? "Sirhan Sirhan is a Yippie!" said Jerry Rubin, that poisoned Twinkie. But Robert Lowell wrote another epitaph, full of loneliness like "a thin smoke thread of vital air": "For them, like a prince, you daily left your tower / to walk through dirt in your best cloth. Here now, / alone, in my Plutarchan bubble, I miss / you, you out of Plutarch, made by hand— / Forever approaching our maturity." Actually, Bobby said his favor-

ite poet was Aeschylus, for the tragedy. And, from Aeschylus, his
favorite lines: "In our sleep, pain which cannot forget falls drop by
drop upon the heart until, in our own despair, against our will, comes
wisdom through the awful grace of God."

Forget El Cid. Like the Camus he quoted so often, or the Orwell
who shows up on rare occasions, we invoke him to look better to
ourselves. We wear his skin, as if from a brave bear we've slain. Or as
Kurt Vonnegut recommended we read great books: "the way a
young animal might eat the hearts of brave old enemies." Or as
Denver warned her ghostly sister about their difficult mother, in
Toni Morrison's *Beloved*: "Watch out for her; she can give you
dreams."

Does Bill Clinton give us dreams? Not any that we'd be quick to
admit.

4.

And if it didn't used to be this bad, what happened? I'm more inclined to believe a Susan Faludi than I am a Joe Eszterhas, because
she does her homework. Faludi's *Stiffed: The Betrayal of the American Man* took a beating from most of the critics a year ago. But most
of those critics were of course men, in well-paying jobs at nicely
upholstered media factories, in such a hurry to esteem themselves
that they were not about to admit to anything askew about the image they want their bosses and girlfriends to see and what they actually feel when they read Bret Easton Ellis or watch pro wrestling.
And the critics who were female just couldn't stand it that Susan
Faludi, of all people, was suddenly soft on men, that she was *worried*
about us.

Well, Faludi is still a feminist, and proud of it. She began thinking
her way into her remarkable new book eight years ago, while sitting
in on meetings of a Southern California domestic-violence group, to
which men who had battered the women in their lives went for
therapeutic counseling instead of jail—the same group, in fact, that
O. J. Simpson was supposed to attend before he begged off by prom-

ising to telephone his shrink. The author of *Backlash* sought some insight into a male rage that seemed to hate the very idea of female free agency. Maybe patriarchy was a hormone. Maybe the violence, and the need to control and dominate, were hard-wired: a warrior program; a Samson complex.

But if feminism is her lens and compass, even her furnace and fuel, journalism is her splendid trade. Throughout *Stiffed*, Faludi listens like a tuning fork, and picks up vibrations. What she heard at the therapy sessions, rather than frustrated fantasies of a will-to-power, was out-of-control and at-a-loss. These men were losers—of their jobs, their homes, their wives, their cars, and their identities. What if American manhood is every bit as much a culturally constructed set of expectations and presumptions as American womanhood, a pulpy fiction of imaginary Alamos and Iwo Jimas, a classic-comics *Iliad* of High Noon and Super Bowl, a mixed-media confabulation of raccoon hats, Green Berets, and Dirty Harry/Rambo role-play? Wouldn't men, then—downsized, frontierless, benched—be just as much victims of social myth-making as the women they angrily blame for their impotence?

And so, leaving behind preconception, Faludi packed her bags and traveled to the poles and tropics—to Lakewood, California, the first planned community of nuclear families in housing strips (and the first shopping mall), with its tens of thousands of laid-off McDonnell Douglas aerospace engineers and its Pop Warner team of Spur Posse punks competing to score the biggest number of high-school girls. To Charleston, South Carolina, where all the drag queens at the local gay bar date Citadel cadets. To Cleveland, Ohio, where misfit fans put on dog masks and bay at their football team. To Denver, Colorado, headquarters of the Promise Keepers, where Jesus Christ will save, if not your job, at least your marriage. To South Central LA, where gangbangers strut and fret. To Waco, Texas, where the Branch Davidians may or may not have been firebombed, but the militia men of the Republic of Texas stand ready to avenge them. To downtown New York City, where slick fashion magazines like *Details* celebrate a bonfire-of-the-vanities "ornamental culture" in which men, like women before them, are evaluated strictly according to style and celebrity, as packaged sex objects. To the moon, where astronauts like Buzz Aldrin discovered they were window-dressing in a staged-for-TV PR spectacle. To the not-so-distant past of the Great Depression, the Second World War, and the My Lai massacre. And to Hollywood.

There are two Hollywoods in *Stiffed*. The first is the one we think we know, the LA of Joe Eszterhas, where Sylvester Stallone turned an antiwar novel into gung-ho *Rambo* because he hated his father. The other, deep in the San Fernando Valley, specializes in the production of upmarket porn. If Faludi could venture with members of the Spur Posse to a fast-food shop for a chatty lunch, and with a Hillary-hating insurance salesman to a Larimer County firing range to try out his shotgun, and to jail for follow-up interviews with a publicity-hungry gangbanger and an alcoholic aerospace engineeer, she could surely go to the Valley. And there, on a Trac Tech sound stage, she found one of the symbolic meanings implicit in her title. Nowadays, women not only star in porn movies, but are the money-makers and power brokers. Men are paid peanuts for the exceedingly brief "money shot"—an ejaculating penis. Not surprisingly, these men are liable to, ah, performance anxiety.

But the other meaning of *Stiffed* also implies performance anxiety. Faludi has talked to hundreds of men. They either don't know or don't care that she's a famous feminist. They *need* to talk to a woman, and are right to do so. This particular woman wants to change their world. They have been cheated—of heroic roles, meaningful work, job security, wifely adoration, mastery of the universe, self-respect, and the big score. Somehow, somewhere, a promise had been made to them, and then betrayed. By whom? The search for a Hillary to blame is increasingly frantic. According to Faludi:

> What began in the 1950s as an intemperate pursuit of Communists in the government, in the defense industries, in labor unions, the schools, the media, and Hollywood, would eventually become a hunt for a shape-shifting enemy who could take the form of women at the office, or gays

in the military, or young black men on the street, or illegal aliens on the border, and from there become a surreal "combat" with nonexistent black helicopters, one-world government, and goose-stepping U.N.-peacekeeping thugs massing on imaginary horizons.

Faludi faults instead (1) a postwar national security state that gave these men corporate cubicles and beanies until their cost-plus contracts got canceled, after which the dumpster. (2) A celebrity/media culture that honors actors, athletes, rock stars, even skinheads and serial killers, more than it does skilled labor, company loyalty, civic duty, or steadfast parenting. And (3) most of all, their own fathers, about whom they all speak obsessively, those men who came back silent from World War II with no history or craft, no secret tips to pass on to their sitcom-watching baby boomer sons, who would in their turn duly beget Posses of Spurs. Faludi herself mourns the passing of older ideas of traditional masculinity that included home-steading, care-taking, community-building, and mentoring (besides the more celebrated arts of points scored and Indians killed).

There isn't a subject she touches on—from the space program to Tailhook to Rodney King to Si Newhouse—that she doesn't illuminate in prose as graceful as a gazelle, with statistics that startle us into sentience. There isn't an Angry White Male she encounters who won't be heard out respectfully, almost groomed, for nuance and clues. And there's not a jot of jargon in the whole book, not a single overdetermined site or the slightest trace of pomosexuality. If I miss any mention of, say, the nonviolence of Dr. Martin Luther King and how come this model of masculine forbearance flinched in the face and the fist of Black Power, well, any book must stop short somewhere. And if I am more inclined to blame vampire capitalism than absent fathers, well, it happens I grew up in the Lakewood, California, she talks so much about, next door to McDonnell Douglas, where the churches looked like airports and the high schools looked like filling stations, and it often seemed that I was the only boy in the housing tract or at the mall without a father to betray me, and maybe I ought to be grateful.

5.

But I'm just one of many peepsqueaks in the infotainment shuck,
like Joe Eszterhas. And *American Rhapsody* would be just one more
heat-seeking piffle in the long-distance Culture Wars, certainly not
worth all these words, were it not for the fact that it's symptomatic of
the mush we've made of critical analysis in this country, the abandonment not only of principle but of actual reporting like Susan
Faludi's and of actual politics, like Robert Kennedy's; another sign of
the noisy triumph of the infantile notion that everything with a paid
publicist or a heat trace—manners and morals, scruples and kinks,
Hollywood and Washington, pop culture and poets in prison, frantic
buzz and profound belief, sex, drugs, hair, music, pure math, deep
structure, affirmative action, hate radio, soft money, Montana militias, Space Cowboys, Cheez Doodles, the *Zeitgeist* and the blues—
*all* of them, the good, the bad, the ugly, the virtual, the backstory,
liner notes and war crimes, are one big blob of mediated Silly Putty
(call him Morph), rolling over the citizen, flattening difference, distinction, and nuance. In this Total Immersion Environment, everything from acid trips and coke busts to conversion experiences and
downsizing, from class animus to satanic child abuse, means *something*, but nothing means more than anything else, or matters more,
or even *weighs* more, and all of them are interchangeable. It's as if,
after so much fancy criticism based on spectacle and simulacra,
we've decided that not only are we unreliable narrators of our own
lives but that it's something to be proud of.

If Joe Eszterhas is moved to rethink the hair on his palms, let him
do it for his own reasons on his own airtime, not mine. No mystical
umbilicus ties the very different high crimes and misdemeanors of a
screenwriter and a president to some cultural determinism. The
fault, dear Brutus, is not always in our rock stars. Or in our generation (that famously branded Gap). Hardly any of us behaved as
badly as Bill *or* Joe. Maybe it's time we stopped reviewing our lives
for style points, as if they were *performances*, because we're dying

from it. Culture isn't always politics, celebrity seldom anymore implies significance, and life is *never* rock-and-roll.

Real people have problems too, like race hatred, corporate greed, economic inequality, lousy schools, exploding prisons, Asian sweatshops, African famine, even ecocide. So Dennis Miller on *Monday Night Football* is not as important as what Rupert Murdoch has done to Fox News, and Amadou Diallo signifies more than Tiger Woods. Instead of thinking about focus groups, Razor scooters, or Ally McBeal, why don't we ban land mines? I don't know why our superheroes like to cross-dress in their underwear, and I don't need to. In the long run, whether or not Courtney Love has sold out doesn't matter as much as the fact that Bill Clinton did.

Look, real citizenship is hard, and almost as much of a drag as real thinking. I nod out on my own nostalgia, too, in front of VH1. But after a hit of caffeine, I'm reasonably sure that Sid Vicious didn't die for *my* sins. Nor is it likely that Bruce Springsteen, plus all the assistant professors of cultural studies in the liminal world, will add up to a barricade big enough to slow down the tanks, the bombs, and the tiddlywinks on the World Bank credit grid. It is even less likely that an outlaw culture of computer hackers can win the war against late capitalism and its marketing of commodified emotions with nothing more than nose studs, nipple rings, vector graphics, industrial noise, and the grace of hip. I can run away in the approved American manner, like Bonnie and Clyde, Thelma and Louise, Jack Kerouac and Rabbit Angstrom, in a tin lizzie, an SUV, an Eszterhas Porsche, a Max Apple ice-cream truck, or a Ken Kesey DayGlo Merry Prankster bus, over the dead bodies of James Dean, Jayne Mansfield, Nathanael West, Grace Kelly, and Albert Camus. But when I come back, it will still be to a city whose giddiest activity is "trading in futures," to a country where a third of the population is equipped with 230 million firearms and the mortality rate for black infants is twice that of whites, and to a world in which the richest 20 percent of humanity has seventy times as much wealth as the poorest 20 percent, while a child dies from poverty *every two and a half seconds*.

And, yes, I get paid for style points and irony, too. But if I must

read a Hollywood screenwriter's take on the decline of political culture, let it be Joan Didion, in one of her subversive novels. Better yet,
the Joan Didion who gave up style points entirely in her nonfiction
*Salvador*. Looking one day for Halazone tablets to put into her
drinking water, she ventured into "Central America's Largest Shopping Mall." On the other side of the weapons check, where paté de
foie gras was on sale to matrons in tight Sergio Leone jeans, along
with Bloomingdale's beach towels and bottles of Stolichnaya vodka,
the Muzak was playing "I Left My Heart in San Francisco" and
"American Pie." And in the public square outside, soldiers with guns
forced young civilians into unmarked vans. And Joan Didion decided not to be ironic.

In the sixties, that too-much-drooled-upon decade, there were
tambourines and there were tantrums, and they killed some of our
best people. But Bill Clinton is his own fault.

# BLOWING HIS NOSE
# IN THE WIND

---

1.

Bob Dylan wrote "A Hard Rain's a-Gonna Fall" in the summer of 1962, in a matter of minutes, on Wavy Gravy's typewriter, after reading William Blake. "That song kind of roared right out of the typewriter," Wavy Gravy remembers. "It roared through him the way paint roared through van Gogh."

Wavy Gravy, in case you are wondering how to become a Ben & Jerry's ice-cream flavor, was the Merry Prankster who introduced young Dylan to everybody hip in Greenwich Village in the early sixties, from Allen Ginsberg to Lenny Bruce to Theolonius Monk. He was also heard to whisper, during Martin Luther King's "I Have a Dream" speech on the steps of the Lincoln Memorial in 1963, "I hope he's over quick, Mahalia Jackson's on next." And he later served as master of ceremonies at the 1969 Woodstock music festival. Bob Dylan actually happened to be living in Woodstock at the time of this pep rally, but chose to perform instead on the Isle of Wight, off the south coast of England, for $50,000 plus expenses—although he would manage to make it to Woodstock the Sequel, in 1994, for $600,000.

Anyway, Wavy Gravy's 1962 intuition of afflatus accords with Dylan's own. "The songs are there," the boy genius told *Sing Out!* "They exist all by themselves just waiting for someone to write them down." If "Hard Rain" painted itself, "Like a Rolling Stone" would come to him in 1965 like "a long piece of vomit." To Robert Shelton he explained in 1966 that "anytime I'm singing about people and if the songs are dreamed, it's like my voice is coming out of their dream." Much, much later, after being baptized in the Pacific Ocean, a born-again Bob would credit God. And then vandals stole the handle.

One thinks not only of Saint Theresa ravished unto Transverbation by a Spear of Gold, and of Yeats seized by automatic writing, but also of Ormus Cama in Salman Rushdie's novel *The Ground Beneath Her Feet*. Ormus, a modern day Orpheus—the son of the muse Calliope and the river god Oeagrus, the incarnation of "the singer and songwriter as shaman and spokesman"—hears the music of the future A Thousand and One Nights before it shows up in everybody else's ears. Tunes the rest of us are doomed to dance to somehow get channeled to him in advance, from an otherworldly jukebox, through the stillborn body of his dead zygotic twin (probably an Elvis reference). If he sometimes messes up the words, it's because he lives on the wrong end of a popular music wormhole "at whose extreme fringes lurk hairy charismatics with much the same psychiatric profiles as the self-impalers at the heart of Shiite Muharram processions: denizens of the psychotropics of Capricorn, the lands of the sacrificed goat."

> *But I see through your eyes*
> *And I see through your brain*
> *Like I see through the water*
> *That runs down my drain.*

Ormus, one of Rushdie's trademark metamorphs, seems to me a closer analogue to Dylan in his lonely bus on his Never-Ending Tour, picking up coded transmissions through the fillings in his teeth from hobo minstrels, protest troubadours, tambourine existentialists, Mystic Bards and Brother Bobs, than, say, the "American Brecht" that John Clellon Holmes once called him, or the "Hebrew Boddhisatva" of Allen Ginsberg, or "an Elvis of the mind" (David Hajdu), or a "rock-and-roll Zarathustra" (Jim Miller), or a "rock-and-roll Rimbaud" (Miller again, but the French poet is also mentioned by many other English majors).

Rimbaud? Only if you've never read either the *Illuminations* or *Tarantula*. Only then can you pretend that when Dylan gave up "finger-pointing" protest music for a Fender Stratocaster at the 1965 Newport Folk Festival, it was the same as Rimbaud giving up revolutionary politics after the slaughter of the Paris Communards in 1871. To be sure, Arthur and Bob were equally scornful and equally opportunistic. ("To whom shall I hire myself?" asked Arthur. "What beast should I worship? What holy image are we attacking? Which hearts shall I break? What lie must I keep?—In what blood shall I walk?") But when Rimbaud no longer had anything fresh to say, he stopped making albums.

Given that I'm about to contribute to the literature of hyperventilation on the overwrought occasion of Dylan's sixtieth birthday, you ought to know where I stand. Because Joan Baez loved him a lot, I have to assume that he is not as much of a creep as he so often seems. But I'm entitled to doubts about anybody whose favorite Beatle was George. And don't tell me it's all about the music. The whole Dylan package has been marketed as attitude; wrapped in masks. Music is about music. Biographies are about behavior. Caring about the music is what makes our interest in the behavior more than merely prurient. If you'd really rather not have known that Pythagoras hated beans, Spinoza loved rainbows, and Ingmar Bergman was a lousy father, you're a better person than I am, although we both have a long way to go before we're as good as Joan Baez.

2.

*I wish that for just one time*
*you could stand inside my shoes*
*You'd know what a drag it is*
*to see you*

Think of David Hajdu's *Positively 4th Street: The Life and Times of Joan Baez, Bob Dylan, Mimi Baez Fariña, and Richard Fariña* as *A Little Night Music* scored for dulcimer and motorcycle. Or a pas de quatre, with wind chimes, love beads, and a guest-appearance entre-chat by Thomas Pynchon. As David Hajdu, whose biography of Billy Strayhorn, *Lush Life*, is an ornament of jazz lit, rotates among his principals until at last they settle down to play house in Carmel and Woodstock, he is such an ironist among blue notes, so knowledgeable about their performing selves on stage, in bed, and in our mezzotinted memories, that he seems almost to be whistling scherzos. So we follow Bobby Zimmerman, aka Shabtai Zisel ben Avraham, a Russian-Jewish college dropout who left Minnesota to look for Woody Guthrie, and Richard Fariña, an Irish-Cuban altar boy from Flushing, Queens, who majored in literary ambition at Nabokov's Cornell, as they advance their careers by sleeping with Joan Baez and her sister Mimi, the singing daughters of a Mexican-American physics professor who trained Cold War military engineers. And Hajdu also knows precisely where to stop the music, just this side of lapidary, in 1966, when a matched pair of motorcycle accidents—a zygotic twinship—killed off Fariña two days after the publication of his only novel, *Been Down So Long It Looks Like Up to Me*, and sent the substance-abusing Dylan into the first of his many gnomic seclusions.

This countercultural *Les Liaisons Dangereuses* began on a Greenwich Village street corner in 1961, when an unknown Fariña said to a little-known Dylan, "Man, what you need to do, man, is hook up with Joan Baez. She is so square, she isn't in this century. She needs you to bring her into the twentieth century, and you need somebody like her to do your songs. She's your ticket, man. All you need to do, man, is start screwing Joan Baez." To which an insouciant Dylan replied: "That's a good idea—I think I'll do that. But I don't want her singing none of my songs." It would end twenty-five years later—after Richard had dumped his first wife, Carolyn Hester, to get as close as he could to Joan by courting and marrying her teen-aged sister Mimi; after Bob used Joan to get famous and then did everything he could think of to ridicule and degrade her, to which she responded with a love song, "Diamonds and Rust," that would have shamed any other cad this side of Dr. Kissinger's princely narcissism; after Vietnam, Watergate, and Ronald Reagan—when Brother Bob saw the Widow Mimi for the first time since Richard's death, and sought to comfort her with these apples: "Hey, that was a drag about Dick. It happened right around my thing, you know. Made me think."

And love is just a four-letter word.

Post-docs in Dylanology will most appreciate Hajdu's revisionist account of Newport in 1965. He blames the boos on a lousy sound system in worse weather. How could anyone have been surprised at Dylan's plugging himself in, when his new album, *Bringing It All Back Home*, with its hit single, "Subterranean Homesick Blues," had been on the charts for four months, and you couldn't turn on the radio without hearing "Like a Rolling Stone"? Assistant professors of *Gravity's Rainbow* will be delighted to hear from Tom Pynchon, who was a buddy of Richard's at Cornell, and best man at his wedding to Mimi in Carmel, to which he hitchhiked from Mexico because he didn't have a driver's license, and agreed to be interviewed for Hajdu's book by fax, and is quoted not only in a blurb for *Been Down So Long* ("This book comes on like the Hallelujah Chorus done by two hundred kazoo players with perfect pitch"), but also in a personal note to the needy author:

> But to you, wild colonial maniac, about all I can say is holy shit. . . . This thing man picked me up, sucked me in, cycled, spun and centrifuged my ass to where it was a major effort of will to go get up and take a leak even, and by the time it was over with I know where I had been.
>
> If you want comparisons, which you don't, I think most of Rilke.

For those of us who are amateurs—that is, those of us who still enjoy the great songs but are inclined to believe that there are whole decades of Dylan more interesting to read about in Greil Marcus ("What is this shit?") than to listen to on our speaker systems— *Postively 4th Street* is a cohort story. I like cohort stories: about Partisan Reviewers, Abstract Expressionists or the Beats; the New York Brat Pack and the Chinese Misties. I think it's terrific that young singers and songwriters, like young writers and artists, fester together in seedy nests or move in herds like thick-skinned ungulates across the inky savannahs of the culture, dodging potshots from the great white hunters at Establishment media. So what if they hurt one another while the rest of us are waiting to see which one turns into a unicorn? My favorite *Positively* scene is when Bob, Joan, Richard, and Mimi visit Henry Miller, the Tropic of Cancer himself rusticating in Pacific Palisades, whom only Richard has read. Henry, of course, wants either Baez (or both), but has to settle for playing Ping-Pong with Mr. Tambourine Man.

I also love their cover stories: Dylan, who grew up in Hibbing, Minnesota, with fine china, crystal glass, sterling silver cutlery, a spinet piano, and a chandelier, whose father bought him a pink Ford convertible and a Harley, whose only real job ever in the real world was as a busboy one summer at the Red Apple Cafe in Fargo, North Dakota, told everybody in Manhattan that he had been raised in foster homes, had Sioux Indian blood, sang for his supper in carnivals from age fourteen, played piano on early Elvis records, picked up guitar licks from a New Mexico blues musician named Wigglefoot, wrote songs for Carl Perkins in Nashville, and earned walking-around money as a Times Square hustler. Fariña, whose father was a toolmaker and whose first job out of college was at the J. Walter Thompson advertising agency, working on the Shell Oil account, advised the credulous that his father was a Cuban inventor and his mother an Irish mystic, that he had been born at sea, and had run guns for Castro, and had sunk a British sub for the IRA, and had been expelled from Cornell for leading a riot, and slept with a loaded .45 under his pillow in case of assassins.

Haven't we all fudged our résumés? But who knew that organized folksinging, like organized labor, organized religion, and organized crime, could be a medium of upward mobility?

### 3.

*They'll stone you when you're riding in your car*
*They'll stone you when you're playing your guitar*
*But I would not feel so all alone*
*Everybody must get stoned*

Think of Howard Sounes's *Down the Highway*, on the other hand, as a surveillance tape. Or maybe a transcript of the black-box audio recovered from the crash site of the never-ending tour bus. Either lumbering way, it wants to be exhaustive, like a commission report or a Dreiser. (*An American Tragedy* comes to mind.) British journalist Sounes, who has also written a biography of Charles Bukowski, tracks Dylan from the four-year-old who used to entertain his family with a rousing rendition of "Accentuate the Positive" to the sixty-year-old who has authorized himself to sing "Forever Young" in a television commercial for iMac Apple computers. And besides mentioning every book, record, gesture, arrangement, or idea that Dylan ever stole in his lordly passage from Hard Rain to Sweet Jesus, Sounes will also name the names of every girlfriend, fraternity brother, business associate, disordered groupie, and discarded mentor or buddy; every musician at every gig or recording session; and every influence from Buddy Holly, Hank Williams, Little Richard, Muddy Waters and Jimmy Reed, to James Dean and Marlon Brando, to Woody Guthrie, Pete Seeger and Odetta, to *Gunsmoke*'s Matt Dillon and Graceland's Elvis and the Beatles and Saint Augustine.

Most of this you probably already knew from previous biographies by Anthony Scaduto, Robert Shelton, Bob Spitz, and Clinton Heylin, whose ferociously opinionated *Bob Dylan: Behind the Shades* has just been "revisited" and updated for the birthday party and is lots more fun than Sounes. But some of it you didn't—such as his second marriage to one of his African-American backup singers, Carolyn Dennis, to legitimize his sixth child, Desiree Gabrielle Dennis-Dylan. Moreover, after interviewing everybody in the vicinity at the time, Sounes suggests that Dylan's famous 1966 motorcycle accident might not have been as medically serious as previously supposed, but more of an excuse to drop out, sober up, and recharge, after *Highway 61*, *Blonde on Blonde*, and all that hash and all those amphetamines in Australia.

In fact, while heavy drinking seems to have been Dylan's biggest problem most of his career—he finally quit in the mid-nineties—1966 is associated in both books with everything from pot to speed to LSD and maybe even heroin, leaving Dylan "skeletal and green." (There is even a theory that "I Want You" in *Blonde on Blonde* was "about heroin" rather than a woman.) While we burned Dylan for fuel, he seems to have been running on fumes. The 1975 Rolling Thunder Revue, to which Baez, Allen Ginsberg, Sam Shepard, Joni Mitchell, and Stevie Wonder signed on, though they can't be blamed for *Renaldo & Clara*, sounds in Sounes like a coke bust waiting to happen to a tabloid. And by Thanksgiving 1976, when the Band let Martin Scorsese film *The Last Waltz*, they even had a backstage snorting room, painted white and decorated by noses cut out of Groucho Marx masks, with a tape of sniffing noises. Hajdu tells us that in 1964 and 1965, while Dylan was typing those "prose-poems" that eventually added up to *Tarantula*, he got by on black coffee and red wine. But to compose what Baez thought of as his increasingly nihilistic songs, he chain-smoked marijuana. It's an odd division of labor enticements—sort of like Jean-Paul Sartre's staying sober to write his novels and *Les Mots*, whereas, for philosophy, he was usually doped up on a compound of aspirin and amphetamines called corydrane, stoning himself to kill God.

So now ask yourself if Dylan's notorious indifference to the niceties of cutting a record, to the relative merits of a mulitude of sessions musicians, to the desires and opinions of his fans and audience, to whether he had any business on a stage, taking their money, when he was wired out of his skull, or in a recording studio, martyrizing thugs like Joey Gallo; combined with his disdain for former colleagues, ex-friends, and previous incarnations, contempt for other artists like Harry Belafonte and Theodore Bikel who cared about causes he could no longer use, like civil rights, and surliness unto Road Rage; even his unintelligible weirdness on such public occasions as his accepting the Tom Paine award from the Emergency Civil Liberties Union in November 1963 with a monologue that empathized with Lee Harvey Oswald—"But I got to stand up and say I saw things that he felt in me," which must be what inspired Jerry Rubin, five years later, to proclaim that "Sirhan Sirhan is a Yippie!"—well, ask yourself if some of this might have owed as much to chemicals as it did to authenticity. Elvis envy! Don't think twice.

Still, for those of us who aren't Dylanologists, there is much in *Down the Highway* that is wonderfully surprising. Did you know that Dylan's first song was about Brigitte Bardot? That his favorite film is *Shoot the Piano Player*, with Charles Aznavour? That his favorite artist is Marc Chagall? That his first wife had been a Playboy bunny? That Sid Vicious of the Sex Pistols seems not to have liked him? That Tiny Tim was a member of his Woodstock entourage? That after Jesus he took up sailing and boxing. That, with Bob's help and some high-grade pot, Paul McCartney not only discovered the meaning of life but also wrote it down? "There are seven levels."

It takes a lot to laugh; it takes a train to cry.

4.

*The geometry of innocence flesh on the bone*
*Causes Galileo's math book to get thrown*
*At Delilah . . .*

Joan Baez, or so Hajdu quotes her mother, "always thought she was ugly." Even on Mt. Auburn Street in Cambridge in 1958, in her own mind "I was still the girl the kids used to taunt and call a dirty Mexican," so "pathologically insecure about her appearance" that she mugged at cameras in self-defense, and so self-conscious about what she imagined to be the small size of her breasts that she always wore a light floral jumper over her bikini. Joan Baez? I saw her with my own eyes in Cambridge in 1958, after I'd heard her with my own ears one warm spring night when "All My Trials" came through the window into the basement of the college newspaper on Plympton Street. It was the purest voice I'd ever heard, like listening to the wild blue yonder. And when I rushed out to see what such a voice looked like, she was, of course, beautiful beyond the speed of light. And still is, like her fellow pacifist Aung San Suu Kyi.

This is the woman that Dylan and his coke-addled cohort chose to humiliate on camera in D. A. Pennebaker's documentary, *Don't Look Back*, on their 1965 concert tour of England. She is also made to symbolize, in both these books, a phony folkie subculture which Dylan, of course, would rile and rock and raunch and roll. "The virgin enchantress," Hajdu calls her, as well as "Glinda, the Good Witch of the North." How precious her flock, those middle-class flower children of a Harvard-educated twelve-string banjo like Pete Seeger. What poseurs, like a bunch of Bambis at some hootenanny salt lick, or a seminar on creative nonviolence at a Quaker meeting of vegetarian carpenters. Over such a quilting bee, the hermit-monk Dylan would ride roughshod, not side-saddle, on his Golden Calf—the Biggest of Boppers.

According to Hajdu the Newport Folk Festival in 1959 was "a popular summer attraction for the suburban leisure class of the post-war boom economy." And "the nascent discontent on college campuses" in 1962 was "a mobilization in the name of political and moral principle that was also a fashion trend and a business opportunity." And, by 1965 at Newport, if Baez and Dylan weren't around, "no one poolside seemed to know which way to point his lounge chair." Actually, I remember sleeping on the beach because we couldn't afford a motel.

Sounes, who is English and may not know any better, arches his eyebow at 1963 Newport because the setting itself "underscored the gulf between the proletarian roots of the music and the privileged

lives of most of the performers and the majority of the audience." I
guess he missed Dylan, later on, at Royal Albert Hall in London.
And it's this same summer he's talking about when he speaks of
"antiwar sentiments then in vogue." Would that they had been in
vogue, months before the assassination of John Kennedy, when the
only Americans yet in Vietnam were still called "advisers."

But more schematic than the books have been the reviews of
them, everywhere from the *Washington Post* to the online magazine
Salon.com, buying into an antithesis between folkies and rockers
and plunking down in belligerent favor of the snarl and the stomp,
as if we couldn't listen to both; as if in fact we hadn't been listening,
not only to Seeger and Odetta and Baez, but also to Motown and
James Brown and the Drifters, even before Bob Dylan, while nursing his hurt feelings that Carl Sandburg had never heard of him, was
so stunned to pick up the Beatles on his car radio singing "I Want to
Hold Your Hand" that he was moved to the Bob equivalent of a
Gettysburg Address: "Fuck! Man, that was fuckin' great! Oh, man—
fuck!"

Never mind the failure of anybody to take Joan Baez's Quaker
pacifism seriously, from Joan Didion in 1966 to Jonathan Yardley in
2001. Never mind whose career looks more honorable and who's really posturing at the end of an awful century—those acoustic guitar
players who went south for civil rights and tried to stop troop trains
with their middle-class bodies, or the Macho Rubbish Rehab Ram-
blers with their amplified electric chairs and enough *attitude* to trash
a hotel room and gang-bang a groupie. Never even mind that a
whole lot of things are also always going on besides popular music;
that there is news, too, on the wounded radio.

> *Mama's in the fact'ry*
> *She ain't got no shoes*
> *Daddy's in the alley*
> *He's lookin' for the fuse*

Besides telling us that "folk music is a bunch of fat people," these
are the thoughts of Citizen Bob after the Kennedy assassination:

All I can say is politics is not my thing at all. I can't see myself on a platform talking about how to help people. Because I would get myself killed
if I really tried to help anybody. I mean, if somebody really had something
to say to help anybody out, just bluntly say the truth, well obviously
they're gonna be done away with. They're gonna be killed.

To which he added:

You can't go around criticizing something you're not part of and hope to
make it better. It ain't gonna work. I'm just not gonna be a part of it. I'm
not gonna make a dent or anything, so why be a part of it by even trying
to criticize it? That's a waste of time. The kids know that. The kids today,
by the time they're twenty-one, they realize it's all bullshit. I know it's all
bullshit.

I'm not surprised he found God in 1979. It was a very seventies
thing to do, like Rolfing, Arica, acupuncture, and biofeedback. Like
tantric yoga and the hot tubs of Esalen. Or Jonestown and est. Like
pet rocks, WIN buttons, smiley faces, and swine-flu vaccine booster
shots. It led directly to power ballads and Ronald Reagan and the
Last Tango on Mr. Sammler's Planet. Meanwhile, some of the rest of
us were required to think about the women's movement, and read
Toni Morrison, and poke at the meaning of a James Baldwin sentence: "If I am not who you say I am, then you are not who you think
you are."

Baez has recorded this exchange with Dylan, in March 1965: "I
asked him what made us different, and he said it was simple, that I
thought I could change things, and he knew that no one could." It
was a puerile thing to say, a species of adolescent fatalism, a waste of
our precious time. No wonder he's back on the bus. If we really have
to choose between, on the one hand, sex, drugs, rock-and-roll, and
the world exactly as it is and ever shall be, or, on the other hand, such
sixties folkie fantasies as fishes and loaves, community and solidarity, peaceable kingdoms and rainbow coalitions, sanctuary, and, of
course, Joan Baez—well, where do I sign?

Just like a woman.

*Part Four*

# EPILOGUE (AM I BLUE?)

# HOW THE CAGED BIRD
# LEARNS TO SING

L IKE A TRIBAL WARRIOR in the *Ramayana*, throwing dice, juiced on soma, I want to tell some stories and brood out loud. But it's tricky. My favorite stories are all about what *they* did to me. What I've done to myself, I am inclined to repress, sublimate, or rationalize. Once upon a time, I was a *Wunderkind*. Now I'm an old fart. In between, I've done time at *National Review*, Pacifica Radio, and the *Nation*; the *New York Times* and Condé Nast; *New York* magazine during and after Rupert Murdoch; National Public Radio and the Columbia Broadcasting System. I was a columnist for *Esquire*, whenever Dwight Macdonald failed to turn in his "Politics" essay; at the old weekly *Life* before it died for *People*'s sins; at *Newsweek* before the *Times* made me stop contributing to a wholly-owned subsidiary of its principal competitor; at *Ms.* during its Australian walkabout interim; and at *New York Newsday* before it was so rudely "disappeared" by a Los Angeles *Times Mirror* CEO fresh to journalism from the Hobbesian underworlds of microwave popcorn and breakfast cereal sugar-bombs. And I've written for almost anyone who ever asked me at newspapers like the *Washington Post*, the *LA Times*, and the *Boston Globe*, at magazines like *Harper's*, the *Atlantic*, *Vogue*, and *Playboy*, and at dot-coms like *Salon*. I like to think of myself as having published in the *New York Review of Books*, the *New Statesman*, the *Yale Review*, and *Tikkun*. But there was also *TV Guide*.

This sounds less careerist than sluttish. It is, however, a sluttishness probably to be expected of someone who had to make a living after he discovered that the novels he *reviewed* were a lot better than the novels he *wrote*. We may belong to what the poet Paul Valéry called "the delirious professions"—by which Valéry meant "all those trades whose main tool is one's opinion of one's self, and whose raw material is the opinion others have of you"—but reporters, critics, and "cultural journalists," no less than publicists, are tweety birds in a corporate canary-cage. Looking back, I see that what I required of my employers was that they cherish my every word, and leave me alone. If I understand what Warren Beatty was trying to tell us in the movie *Reds*, it is that John Reed only soured on the Russian Revolution after they fucked with his copy.

On the other hand, as Walter Benjamin once explained:

> The great majority of intellectuals—particularly in the arts—are in a desperate plight. The fault lies, however, not with their character, pride, or inaccessibility. Journalists, novelists, and literati are for the most part ready for every compromise. It's just that they do not realize it. And this is the reason for their failures. Because they do not know, or want to know, that they are venal, they do not understand that they should separate out those aspects of their opinions, experiences, and modes of behavior that might be of interest to the market. Instead, they make it a point of honor to be wholly themselves on every issue. Because they want to be sold, so to speak, only "in one piece," they are as unsalable as a calf that the butcher will sell to the housewife only as an undivided whole.

I throw in Walter Benjamin, who killed himself a step ahead of Hitler, to muss the hair of the academics among you. Having been to too many conferences where working reporters and media theorists are at each other's throats before the first coffee break, I seek to ingratiate myself. If it will help to wear a Heidegger safari jacket, Foucault platform heels, Lacan epaulets, and a Walter Benjamin boutonniere, I'll also bring the Frankfurtives and the Frenchifieds. Indeed, the production process of every major news-gathering organization can be thought of—in Foucault's terms—as an allegory of endless domination, like hangmen torturing murderers or doctors locking up deviants. And whether they know it consciously or not, these organizations are in the "corrective technologies" business of beating down individuals to "neutralize" their "dangerous states," to create "docile bodies and obedient souls." How we escape their "numbing codes of discipline," if we ever do, is more problematic. Somehow, art, dreams, drugs, madness, "erotic transgression," "secret self-ravishment," and "going postal" seldom add up to an "insurrection of unsubjugated knowledges." I like to think of myself as Patsy Cline. I sang the same sad country songs before I ever got to the Grand Ole Opry. After the Grand Ole Opry, I can always go back to the honkytonks.

Another paradigm is sociobiological. Everything is hardwired, from the behavior of ants, beetles, Egyptian fruit bats, and adhesive-padded geckos to the role of women, the caste system in India, the IQ test scores of black schoolchildren, and the hierarchy of the newsroom. If the people on top of this Chain of Being are mostly male and mostly pale, in the missionary position, talk to Darwin about it. They have been Naturally Selected. Moreover, inside such a white-noise system, there is a positive feedback loop between nature and nurture, thousands of teensy units of obedience training called "culturgens," dictating what societies can and can't do, obsessing in favor of patriarchy and "objectivity," deploring socialism and "bad taste." Having ceded ultimate authority, on the one hand, to the credentialed nitwits of the minisciences, and, on the other, to the chirpy gauchos of the media pampas, we may thus find it difficult, ever again, to think through dilemmas of personal conscience, which look a lot like bad career moves.

Molly Ivins, who was fired from the *New York Times* for saying "chickenplucker" in its pages, has admitted that if she ever dies, what it will say on her tombstone is SHE FINALLY MADE A SHREWD CAREER MOVE. Molly also claims that she's actually played, on a juke box somewhere, a country and western song called "I'm Going Back to Dallas to See If There Could Be Anything Worse Than Losing You."

A third paradigm is novelistic. It's amazing to me how much the controlled environments of both CBS and the *New York Times* resemble Tsau, the utopian community on a Botswana sand dune in

Norman Rush's *Mating,* with windmills, boomslangs, dung carts, abacus lessons, militant nostalgia, ceramic death masks, "Anti-Imperialist Lamentations," a Mother Committee, and an ostrich farm. And how similar the plantations of Murdoch and Newhouse are to Orwell's *Animal Farm* and Kafka's Penal Colony. Whereas Pacifica Radio and the *Nation* bring to mind Voltaire's *Candide.* On these margins, where everybody is paid so poorly that office politics are ideologized into matters of first principle, a little more self-censorship might actually be a good idea. I am reminded of what Amos Oz said in *The Slopes of Lebanon* about the Israeli Left:

> The term Phalaganist is derived from the Greek word 'phalanx.' The phalanx, in the Greek and Roman armies, was a unique battle formation. The soldiers were arranged in a closed-square formation, their backs to one another and their faces turned toward an enemy who could neither outflank nor surprise them, because in this formation the men gave full cover to one another in every direction. The lances and spears pointed outward, of course, in all four directions.
>
> The moderate, dovish Israel left sometimes resembles a reverse phalanx: a square of brave fighters, their backs to the whole world and their faces and their sharpened, unsheathed pens turned on one another.

But, wherever, they *always* fuck with your copy.

So much for the Big Pixel. Now for the prurient details. Stuck as I am on my periphery of books, movies, and television programs, I can't tell you for sure whether Tom Friedman, when he covered the State Department for the *Times,* should have played tennis with the Secretary of State. Or if Brit Hume, when he covered the White House for ABC, should have played tennis with George the First. Or if Rita Beamish of the Associated Press should have jogged with George. Or if it was appropriate for George and Barbara to stop by and be videotaped at a media dinner party in the home of Al Hunt, the Washington bureau chief of the *Wall Street Journal,* and his wife, Judy Woodruff, then of the *MacNeil/Lehrer Newshour,* now an anchor on CNN. Or if one reason Andrea Mitchell, who covered Congress for NBC, seemed to show up so often in the presidential box at the Kennedy Center was that she just happened to be living with Alan Greenspan, the chairman of the Federal Reserve. Nor can I be absolutely positive that there is something deeply compromised about George Will's still ghostwriting speeches for Jesse Helms during his trial period as a columnist for the *Washington Post*, and prepping Ronald Reagan for one of his debates with Jimmy Carter, and then reviewing Reagan's performance the next day in his column, and later on writing a speech Reagan delivered to the House of Commons. Or Morton Kondracke and Robert Novak collecting thousands of dollars from the Republican Party for advice to a gathering of their governors. Or John McLaughlin's settling one sexual harassment suit out of court, facing the prospect of at least two more—and nevertheless permitting himself to savage Anita Hill on his own *McLaughlin Report*. Or, perhaps most egregiously, Henry Kissinger, on ABC TV and in *his* syndicated newspaper column, defending Deng Xiaoping's behavior during the Tiananmen Square massacre—without telling us that Henry and his private consultancy firm had a substantial financial stake in the Chinese status quo.

For that matter, who knows deep down in our heart of hearts whether the nuclear-power industry will ever get the critical coverage it deserves from NBC, which happens to be owned by General Electric, which happens to manufacture nuclear-reactor turbines? Or if *TV Guide*, while it was owned by Rupert Murdoch, was ever likely to savage a series on the Fox network, also owned by Rupert Murdoch, who was meanwhile busy canceling any HarperCollins books that might annoy the Chinese with whom he was dickering for a satellite-television deal? Or whether ABC, owned by Walt Disney, will ever report anything embarrassing to Michael Eisner, the Mikado of Mousedom? It wasn't the fault of journalists at ABC's *20/20* that Cap Cities settled the Philip Morris suit before selling out to Disney. But nobody quit, did they? Nor was it the fault of journalists at *60 Minutes* that CBS killed another antismoking segment, to be immortalized later in Michael Mann's movie *The Insider*; it was the fault instead of the CBS legal department, on behalf of a Larry Tisch who actually owned a tobacco company of his own, on

the eve of a big-bucks sale of his network to Westinghouse. But nobody quit there either, did they, not even the aggrieved producer,
Lowell Bergman, until two years later? Nor have any of the bubble-
headed Beltways on the all-Monica-all-the-time cable yakshows
quit in embarrassment and humiliation, renouncing their lucrative
lecture fees, after being totally wrong in public about almost everything important since the 1989 collapse of the nonprofit police states
of Eastern Europe.

Stop me before I go on about the petroleum industry and public
television's shamefully inadequate coverage of the Exxon Valdez oil
spill, not to mention Shell Oil's ravening of Nigeria. Or say something I'll regret about the $7 million a year that the *MacNeil/Lehrer
Newshour* gets from Archer Daniels Midland, the agribiz octopus
whose fixing of prices and bribing of pols got so much attention in
1995 everywhere except on *Newshour*. How suspicious is it that so
many Random House books were excerpted in the *New Yorker* back
when Harry Evans ran the publishing house, his wife Tina Brown
ran the magazine, and all of them were wholly owned subsidiaries of
Si Newhouse? Is anybody keeping tabs on what *Time*, *People*, and
*Entertainment Weekly* have to say about Warner Brothers movies?
What else should we expect in a brand-named, theme-parked country where the whole visual culture is a stick in the eye, one big sell of
booze, gizmos, insouciance, "life styles," and combustible emotions?
Where the big-screen rerelease of George Lucas's *Star Wars* trilogy
is brought to you by Doritos and the associated sale of stuffed Yodas,
Muppet minotaurs, trading cards, video games, and a six-foot-tall
Fiberglas Storm Trooper for $5,000? Where the newest James Bond
is less a movie than a music-video marketing campaign for luxury
cars, imported beers, mobile phones, and gold credit cards? Where
Coke and Pepsi duke it out in grammar schools, and Burger King
shows up on the sides of the yellow buses that cart our kids to those
schools, in whose classrooms they'll be handed curriculum kits
sprinkled with the names of sneaker companies and breakfast cere-
als. Where there is a logo, a patent, a copyright, or a trademark on
everything from our pro athletes and childhood fairy tales to the

human genome, and Oprah is sued for $12 million by a Texas beef lobby for "disparaging" blood on a bun during a talkshow segment on spongiform encephalopathy and Creutzfeldt-Jakob disease.

And where, I might add, all of us "delirious professionals" sign away, in perpetuity, our intellectual property rights and our first-born children to synergizing media monopolies that will downsize our ass before the pension plan kicks in. Karl Marx made a mini-comeback on the 150th birthday of his *Communist Manifesto*. But years before he wrote the *Manifesto*, he was overheard to say: "Since money, as the existing and active concept of value, confounds and exchanges everything, it is the universal *confusion and transposition* of all things, the inverted world, the confusion and transposition of all natural and human qualities." In other words, if money's the only way we keep score, every other human relation is corrupted.

There is a great line in one of Grace Paley's books: "Then, as often happens in stories, it was several years later." Let me now get up close and personal.

Not long after I took charge of the *Times Book Review*, in the early 1970s, I had a surprise visitor. Lester Markel, the editor who had invented the Sunday *Times* with all its many sections, the eighth-floor Charlemagne who was rumored like Idi Amin to have stocked his fridge with the severed heads of his many enemies, liked to stop in and sit a while, like a bound galley or an urgent memo. This was because, after his forced retirement, he wasn't welcome in anyone else's office. Alone among the editors of the various Sunday sections, I had never worked for nor been wounded by him. I was, besides, a fresh ear. It was rather like chewing the early-morning fat with the corpse of Prester John.

It turned out that Markel was writing his memoirs. And he was having trouble finding a publisher. I made some suggestions and some calls. Never mind the propriety of the editor of the *Times Book Review* lobbying a publisher on behalf of an author with a manu-script for sale. We achieved a contract. And I didn't see Markel for months. Until, of course, galleys of his book came in. And so did he, with suggestions for reviewers. I had to acquaint him with the etiquette of disinterested criticism. After which, he fixed me with the basilisk's blood-freezing eye. And I still had the problem of finding a reviewer who would pay Markel his due as a giant of yore, while not at the same time neglecting to mention his memoir's tendency towards stupefaction—a reviewer who would not only be fair, but who would be *perceived* as fair by everybody else. I'd already been burned by my predecessor, who left me for my very first issue a review of the memoirs of another retired *Times* executive, Turner Catledge, by one of his best friends at the University of Mississippi.

Let me digress for a moment to observe that a *Times* executive who wrote a book could always count on generous review attention so long as he was retired. As Wilfrid Sheed reminded us in *Max Jamison,* his novel about criticism: "They were soft, affable people who wouldn't hurt you because they couldn't bear to be hurt themselves. Paternal organizations were built on great piles of spiritual blubber." But the same has not until recently been true lower down the totem pole, for the serfs. And these serfs write a lot of books. When Christopher Lehmann-Haupt and I alternated as daily critics we looked at these books the same as we'd look at any other. If we liked it or it seemed at least symptomatic of something compelling in the larger culture that we wanted to sermonize about, we'd review it. If not, we didn't. Pretty simple. You will have noticed that in recent years books by *Times* employees are farmed out to freelancers. They are never reviewed by in-house critics. This, we are told, is to avoid the appearance of conflict of interest. Sounds good. Never mind just how often these outside reviews are actually negative. But have you also noticed that this new policy means that *all* books by *Times* writers are *always* reviewed in the daily paper? Minus Saturdays and Sundays, there are 261 book reviews published in the daily *New York Times* every year. There are 65,000 new books published in the United States every year. Some of these books are more equal than others in the paper of record.

Back to Lester Markel, and the paragon I needed to review him. That paragon, clearly, was Ben Bagdikian—a hugely respected, eminently fair-minded, award-winning reporter, and also a gent, who had gone to academe. And he agreed to do the review. And then just when the days before publication of Markel's memoir dwindled down to a precious few, Bagdikian called in a pickle. He had been hired by the *Washington Post*. And the *Washington Post* had a policy that prohibited any of its employees from writing for the *New York Times*. (The *Times*, in fact, had the same policy in reverse, which is why they'd told me to stop writing a TV column for *Newsweek*, which was owned by the *Washington Post*.) Anyway Ben was stuck. Well, I needed to know, was he still willing to do the review if I could somehow get the *Post* to make an exception in this one instance, to which of course we had entered into an agreement before he sold his soul to the company store? Yes, he said; he'd already done the work.

So I called Bill McPherson, the editor of the *Washington Post Book World*, whom I knew from literary cocktail parties, explaining my Markel problem, and beseeching him to intercede on my behalf with *Post* pooh-bah Ben Bradlee, whom I had met once at a Harvard *Crimson* alumni softball game and another time, I'm sorry to say, in the Hamptons. A long week passed. Finally McPherson called. Bradlee would relent on Bagdikian, on one condition. And what was that condition? It was that I, personally, agree to review a book of Bradlee's choice for the *Washington Post*. Done, I said, figuring I'd square it somehow with the *Times*. Which book? Well, Bradlee hadn't made up his mind. Okay, so I got my Bagdikian review, which was as scrupulous as I had hoped, and published it, which stung Markel to furious rebuttal in a letter-to-the-editor, which received from Bagdikian a mildly puzzled response, which correspondence dragged on intolerably until I called it off, after which I never saw Lester Markel in my office again.

But that's not the point of this story. A year later the phone rang, and it was McPherson, and he said: "Bradlee's calling in his chit." Which book, I asked? Well—and McPherson was embarrassed— Sally Quinn is about to publish a book on her year at CBS. That's the one. Many of you are too young to remember that there was a Ben Bradlee before Jason Robards played him in the film version of *All the President's Men*, and that this Ben Bradlee left his wife for Sally Quinn, a reporter for the *Washington Post* Style section, and that this Sally Quinn then left the *Post*, briefly, for a CBS morning show about which most TV critics had been savage, although at least one of us, me, had been lukewarm in *Life* magazine.

Nor is the point of this story that I refused to write that book review. The point is that Lester Markel had no business in my office, that I had no business trying to find him a publisher or arranging for a judicious review—and that Bradlee's way is how the big boys play the game. While making sure your girlfriend gets a talked-about review, at the same time stick it to your principal competitor. Only Bagdikian emerges with honor. Which, some years later, is exactly what I told a class Bagdikian taught in "The Ethics of Journalism" at Berkeley. These students, including my own son, were amused at an anecdote starring their professor, but didn't get the ethics of it. It seemed sort of locker-room to them, as it seemed to graduate students from the Columbia journalism school in a seminar I taught myself. They were all children of the triumph of a glossier idea of journalism in which production values were more important than legwork—journalism as performance art, all tease and no scruple, alpha slick and extreme tabloid, and not usefully to be distinguished from the cool ads for anorexia and heroin.

I am aware that my own regard for books is overly worshipful— one part Hegel, one part Tinkerbell, with garnishes of Sacred Text, Pure Thought, and Counter-Geography—at a time when most of the dead trees in the chain stores have titles like *How I Lost Weight, Got Rich, Found God, and Changed My Sexual Preference in the Bermuda Triangle*. But I also know it is just as hard to write a bad book as a good one, and a lot easier to review one than achieve one, and if book critics in mainstream newspapers and magazines seem to have appointed themselves the hall monitors of an unruly schoolboy culture—this one gets a pass to go to the lavatory; that one must sit in the corner wearing a dunce cap—then it's a condescension and contempt passed down and internalized from bosses like Bradlee for whom the whole thing is a whimsical scam. I've yet to meet a media boss who didn't think all of the books of all of his friends deserved a sympathetic review. Nor have I met a media boss who thought I should ever use as a reviewer anybody who has ever criticized him or his friends. Max Frankel, who accuses me in his autobiography of trying to turn the *Times Book Review* into a combination of the *Village Voice* and the *New York Review of Books*, once called me on the carpet for using Timothy Crouse as a reviewer because Crouse had made fun of his Washington press corps friends in *The Boys on the Bus*. Abe Rosenthal not only called me on the carpet for saying nice things on the daily book page about I. F. Stone and Nat Hentoff, but suspended me from the job entirely after I panned a book, *The Second Stage*, by his friend Betty Friedan. The next thing I knew, they had killed a *sports* column I wrote, during the pro football strike, pointing out that the head of the Players Union, Ed Garvey, used to spook for the CIA. This, of course, goes beyond the butthole politics of the buddy-bond. It's over in another office, where foreign editor Jimmy Greenfield killed a "Private Lives" column I wrote after a visit to the Philippines, back when the Frog Prince Ferdinand and his Dragon Lady were still in charge, and playwrights like Ben Cervantes were still in prison, and Greenfield in New York knew more about it than I did in Manila, where a goon in a blue jumpsuit followed me out of the Palace of Culture, all over the landfill in the Bay, unto a lurid jeepney.

This sounds like whining. It *is* whining. A primary characteristic of any news organization is the subculture of the gripe, populated entirely by crybabies. (As if we ever had it harder than a school teacher, a factory worker, a farmer, or a cop; as if we'd ever been threatened with redundancy, much less a firing squad; as if our slippery slide weren't down into a wad of cotton candy.) And so I could go on about what happened to Richard Eder as the theater critic, and to Ray Bonner at El Mozote, and the class-action suit filed by the women of the *Times*, for which I was deposed, and Roger Wilkins, who quit the paper to write his own book (which I so incautiously reviewed), and Jerzy Kosinksi, and Neil Sheehan, and Attica, and AIDS. I could even tell you about having to write my review of the first volume of Henry Kissinger's memoirs two days early, so that it could go all the way to the top to be vetted, after which I *was* permitted to suggest that some of us, on hearing from Henry that his only sleepless night in public service had been on the eve of his first mixer with the Red Chinese debutantes—well, some of us thought that maybe he should have tossed and turned more often. And I still don't know who cut the last two paragraphs of a review I wrote about a couple of JFK assassination books in 1970; those paragraphs, asking questions about the sloppiness of the Warren Commission Report, simply vanished between the first edition and the last, an incriminating fact on microfilm that is periodically rediscovered by assistant professors of conspiracy theory, who promptly write me paranoid letters, which I dutifully forwarded to Abe until he defected to a crosstown paper.

No wonder that when Ed Diamond, while researching his book on the *Times*, mentioned my name to John Rothman, the Keeper of the Archives, Rothman sniffed: "Some people just aren't good *Times*men." And then just as quickly edited himself: "Some people aren't good *organizational* men." I could live happily with that, had I quit on any one of a dozen fraught occasions. But I allowed myself to be promoted instead, and stuck around for sixteen years. And when I finally did leave, it wasn't over an issue of principle. Those of us who go over the wall—who leave the Catholic Church or the Communist Party or the *New York Times*—usually decide at last to jump because of something small. You have swallowed a whole history of whoppers, but there is a fatigue about your faith. Without any warning, the elastic snaps, and you are hurled out of the closed system into empty space, and your renunciation, arrived at by so many increments, looks almost capricious. In my case, I decided to believe that the brand-new *Vanity Fair* would be a serious magazine, as did many of my friends, for at least three months. Three months was all it took to teach most of us that Condé Nast was half Fuddlecumjig, the township in Oz where jigsaw people fall apart every time they hear an unexpected noise, and half Ouidah, the viceroyal seat of the African slave trade. Actually, I was in Jerusalem writing a story on Peace Now when they called the Sling Shot Bar at the King David Hotel to tell me to come back, that they had fired the editor who hired me, and it wasn't going to be a Peace Now kind of magazine anymore. But when we leap over a wall, we always imagine that *they*, whoever *they* are, will love us more in the outside world. They will love us just as much, or as little, as we serve their interest.

But to finish with the *Times*: When I told them I was quitting, first they said that I had promised I never would. Well, never say never. Then they explained, "The *Times* is a centrist institution, and *you* are not a centrist." Fair enough, although the center sure had moved since they hired me directly out of the antiwar movement. Finally, they screamed at me: "We made you! You'd be nothing without the *Times!*" This surprised. It had never before occurred to me that they'd published what I wrote, two or three times a week, out of the kindness of their hearts—that we hadn't somehow been *even* every day. For years after, I thought of this departing as Freudian-dysfunctional. Maybe they wanted to be our fathers. Maybe *we* wanted them to be our fathers. Oedipus! Peter Pan! Then I began to wonder whether there wasn't about our servitude some elements of an abusive marriage—tantrums, fists, and fear; excuses, apologies, and denials; dependency and self-loathing—battered wives and battered writers. Now, contemplating all the ghosts in this smog machine, I'm inclined to remember the theater tickets, and the stock options, and all the cocktail parties I got invited to as if I were important.

Paul Krassner, the Yippie editor of the *Realist*, once explained to a conference on "Media and the Environment" how to tell the difference between "news" and "dreaming." When you see something you don't believe, you should flap your arms like wings. If you seem then to be flying, it's a dream. In this dreamtime, I am overdue at CBS, where I've spent the last twelve years.

Before I was hired at *Sunday Morning*, I asked for a free hand in choosing which television programs I reviewed, regardless of network. My own credibility was at stake. I was assured of a hands-off policy. That was three presidents of CBS News ago.

In fact, for the first seven or so years, I was, if not ignored, then rather negligently embraced as a sort of punctuation mark, a change of rhythm or a passionate parenthesis, in one of the vanishingly few network news programs to embody and cherish old-fashioned journalistic standards. When *Sunday Morning* wasn't thinking about culture, its splendid idea of news was to notice that, hey, here's a social problem, here are some people trying to do something about it, and why don't we spend eight whole minutes seeing if what they're doing actually works? Those of you who can only recall Charles Kuralt as a kind of Will Rogers with a lariat of homespun anecdotes and decencies need reminding that he'd been a fine reporter in Southeast Asia and Latin America; that he went to China at the time of Tiananmen, where his take was very different from Dr. Kissinger's; that he expressed his doubts, over the air, about the Gulf War. It's not just that he listened better than most people talk; he was an exacerbated conscience of his profession. He even refused to appear on the *Murphy Brown* sitcom: "I don't know where the line is," he told me, "but that's crossing it." With his passing, we are diminished in heart and scruple.

But the world of television journalism has been changing, not since O. J. or Monica or the Internet, but ever since they discovered that news can be a "profit center." I should have got an inkling my first year on air, when I reviewed a public-TV documentary on Edward R. Murrow, whose valor and grace made him our very own tragic hero. Emerging on CBS television from the radio and the war, he grasped the new medium's power to modify the way a nation thought about itself, then watched helplessly as that medium pawned that power to the ad agencies, and smoked himself to death. He even *looked* like Albert Camus, the Shadow Man of the French Resistance—Bogart with a microphone. We were reminded in the documentary that he had been stunned when they opened the gates of Buchenwald. That he cared so much about words, he often forgot to look at the camera. That he made up *See It Now* as he went along, forever over budget. That after his famous demolition job on Joe McCarthy, Alcoa dropped its sponsorship of *See It Now* and William Paley, the Big Eye in the Black Rock Sky, turned against his best-known reporter, bumping the program from prime time. That in his last few years at CBS before he resigned in 1961, there were many more *Person to Person* chats with the likes of Marilyn Monroe than there had ever been exposés like "Harvest of Shame" on the plight of the migrant farmworkers. What I should have noticed at the time was the allegorical nature of the Murrow story. In every institution of our society, but especially the media, there have always been brilliant young men—and men almost all of them have always been— who find surrogate fathers as Murrow found Paley. For a while in this relationshop of privilege, patronage, and protection, these young men imagine that they can go on being brilliant, on their own terms, forever, immune to the bottom-line logic of a corporate culture which for its own reasons has surrounded and preserved them in bubblewrap. But we are not at all fathers and sons; we are landlords and tenants; owners and pets. It shouldn't surprise the brilliant young men, and yet it always surprises the brilliant young men, when the party's over and the pets are put to sleep.

I am once again peripheral to the larger story. But when CBS lost pro football, and then a bunch of affiliate stations, to Rupert Murdoch's Fox, everybody freaked. One Thursday, I went in as usual to submit a script for TelePrompTing, record the voiceover for my tape package, and go home again to watch more television. Later that afternoon, the executive producer called. The then president of CBS News—he's gone now, Eric Ober, or how likely is it that I'd be telling you this?—had seen that I was reviewing a TV movie forthcoming on Fox, a feature-length reprise of the old *Alien Nation* sci-fi series, and he'd hit the roof. He had to go to an affiliates' meeting next Monday morning. They would chew his ears off, after hearing their own network promote a program on the evil empire's competing schedule. I said that I'd been specifically promised this would never happen; that, anyway—and never mind my poor powers to cloud anybody's mind, including A. C. Nielsen's—it couldn't really be my problem if the corporation's stock went up or down, or if the president of CBS News had to go to an affiliates' meeting or a therapist. I was told they'd get back to me, and late that night they did. Ober was adamant. Then, I said, I guess I'll have to quit. Don't be silly and overreactive, I was told. And then the executive producer *handled* me. A month before, I had proposed a piece about Doris Lessing, on the occasion of her seventy-fifth birthday and the first volume of her autobiography. Nobody, then, had been interested. But now, if I wanted to sit down immediately and write it up, they'd run it on Sunday in place of *Alien Nation*. Quid pro quo, Q.E.D., ad nauseam and beat vigorously.

It occurs to me that thirty years ago *Life* magazine rejected a "Cyclops" column of mine all about Richard Nixon as a jack-in-the-box television president: Surprise! Look what Daddy brought home from the Cold War! A secret bombing of Cambodia! Then, too, I vented at length to a sympathetic but helpless editor. The next day, *Life* magazine sent me a brand-new color TV set—my very first. All night long, with my children, I shopped for friendship in the gorgeous beer commercials. So Doris Lessing is a sort of color television set.

What followed Doris Lessing—since, if I couldn't review the network competition, I refused to review CBS, although cable and public television were still fair game—was some strong encouragement for me to branch out more, into movies and books. This made rationalizing easy. More books is always better. Free movies spice it up, even though you quickly realize that TV is more various and interesting. They still, amazingly, let me say exactly what I want to about abortion and capital punishment, racism and homophobia, misogyny and war. (We are hired for for our stylistic bag of tricks, our jetstream vapor trails, not our politics. Had my politics been right-wing rather than left, somebody else would have overpaid for this vapor.) And there's a new president of CBS News. If I combine network shows in a thematic clump, one from column A, two from column B, I am back in the consumer-guide business (except during "sweeps" months, when the affiliates have sworn the network to a blood oath not ever to mention a program not on CBS, or even to interview an actor on a program on any another channel). What's more, this wandering in the wilderness has led me belatedly to realize that we end up, in the cultural-journalism business, reviewing the buzz more often than the artifact itself. That the more money spent on promotion, the more attention we have to pay, no matter what our opinion or the object of it. If it's heavily hyped, it automatically becomes newsworthy. So long as we are safely talking about what everybody else is talking about, we will sound *smart*. Never mind the little foreign movie with the distracting subtitles; nobody else will review it, either.

So I'm smarter now. Flap your arms if you think you're dreaming.

The sad thing is that, since now at last I am old enough to be too old, almost, for network television—a demographic undesirable to the ad agencies—my very senior citizenship means that my children are out of college, I own the roof over my head, and I ought to be immune to the terrors of authenticity. I need not be beholden to those who choose to leak on me, nor belong to any hard-wired paradigm that imagines itself a fourth branch of the government, even a separate country, with its own pomp, protocols, dress codes, foreign policy, and official secrets, lacking only its own anthem and maybe a helicopter beanie. And yet the *Times* paid for that house, CBS bought me a new kitchen, and in the last decade I have vacationed in China, Egypt, India, and Zimbabwe. I've actually stayed in hotels like the Danieli in Venice, the Peninsula in Hong Kong, and the Oriental in Bangkok, despite the fact that I know I don't belong there—that you can take the boy out of his class, but not the class out of the boy.

This is the deepest censorship of the self, an upward mobility and a downward trajectory. Once upon a time way back in high school, we thought of reporters as private eyes. We thought of journalism as a craft instead of a club of professional perkies who worry about summer homes, Tuscan vacations, Jungian analysis, engraved invitations to Truman Capote parties, and private schools for our sensitive children. We scratched down an idea on a scrap of yellow paper, typed it up on an Underwood portable, took it below to the print shop, set it on a Linotype machine, read that type upside down, ran off a proof on a flatbed press, and seemed somehow to connect brain and word, muscle and idea, blood and ink, hot lead and cool thought. But that was long before we got into the information-commodities racket, where we have more in common with Henry Kravis and Henry Kissinger than we do with papermakers and deliverymen, or those ABC technicians who were so recently so alone, on strike, on Columbus Avenue. After which our real story is ourselves, at the Century Club or Elaine's or a masked ball charity scam—Oscar de la Renta, Alex Solzhenitsyn, and Leona Helmsley invite you to Feel Bad About the Boat People at the Museum of Modern Art—with plenty of downtime left, after we've crossed a picket line by phoning in our copy to the computer, to mosey over to Yankee Stadium, where Boss Steinbrenner will lift us up by our epaulets to his skybox to consort with such presbyters of the Big Fix as Roy Cohn and Donald Trump, and you can't tell the pearls from the swine.